George A. Henty

Held fast for England

A Tale of the Siege of Gibraltar (1779-83)

George A. Henty

Held fast for England
A Tale of the Siege of Gibraltar (1779-83)

ISBN/EAN: 9783337081232

Printed in Europe, USA, Canada, Australia, Japan

Cover: Foto ©Andreas Hilbeck / pixelio.de

More available books at **www.hansebooks.com**

HELD FAST FOR ENGLAND

A TALE OF THE SIEGE OF GIBRALTAR

(1779–83)

BY

G. A. HENTY

Author of " The Dash for Khartoum; " " Redskin and Cow-Boy; " " With Lee in
Virginia; " " Bonnie Prince Charlie; " " In the Reign of Terror; "
" By Right of Conquest; " &c.

ILLUSTRATED BY GORDON BROWNE

NEW YORK

CHARLES SCRIBNER'S SONS

1917

PREFACE.

My dear Lads,

The Siege of Gibraltar stands almost alone in the annals of warfare, alike in its duration and in the immense preparations made by the united powers of France and Spain for the capture of the fortress. A greater number of guns were employed than in any operation up to that time; although in number, and still more in calibre, the artillery then used have in modern times been thrown into the shade in the sieges of Sebastopol and Paris. Gibraltar differs, however, from these sieges, inasmuch as the defence was a successful one, and indeed at no period of the investment was the fortress in any danger of capture save by hunger. At that period England was not, as she afterwards became, invincible by sea; and as we were engaged at the same time in war with France, Spain, Holland, and the United States, it was only occasionally that a fleet could be spared to bring succour and provisions to the beleaguered garrison. Scurvy was the direst enemy of the defenders. The art of preserving meat in tins had not been discovered, and they were forced to subsist almost entirely upon salt meat; during the first year of the siege the supply of fresh vegetables was scanty in the extreme, and the garrison consequently suffered so severely from scurvy that at one time scarcely half of the men of the garrison were strong enough to carry a firelock and perform their duty. The providential capture of a vessel laden with oranges and lemons checked the ravages of the scourge, and the successful efforts of the garrison to raise vegetables prevented it from ever afterwards getting a firm hold upon them. In such a siege there was but little scope for deeds of individual gallantry. It was a long monotony of hardship and suffering, nobly endured, and terminating in one of the greatest triumphs ever recorded in the long roll of British victories.

Yours sincerely,

G. A. HENTY.

CONTENTS.

ILLUSTRATIONS.

HELD FAST FOR ENGLAND.

CHAPTER I.

"SOMETHING LIKE AN ADVENTURE."

HAD Mr. Tulloch, the head-master and proprietor of a large school at Putney, been asked which was the most troublesome boy in his school, he would probably have replied, without hesitation, " Bob Repton ; " but, being a just and fair-minded man, he would have hastened to qualify this remark by adding, " Most troublesome, but by no means the worst boy ; you must understand that. He is always in scrapes, always in mischief. In all my experience I have never before come across a boy who had such an aptitude for getting into trouble ; but I have nothing else to say against him. He is straight-forward and manly. I have never known him to tell a lie to screen himself. He is an example to many others in that way. I like the boy in spite of the endless trouble he gives, and yet there is scarcely a day passes that I am not obliged to cane him, and even that does him no good as far as I can see, for he seems to forget it five minutes after it is over. I wonder sometimes if he has really got hardened and doesn't feel it. He is sharp, and does his lessons well ; I have no difficulty with him on that score, but he is a perfect imp of mischief."

With such characteristics it need hardly be said that Bob Repton was one of the most popular boys at Tulloch's school.

School-life was in those days (for it was in August, 1778, that Bob was at Tulloch's) a very different thing to what it is at present. Learning was thrashed into boys. It was supposed that it could only be instilled in this manner; and although some masters were of course more tyrannical and brutal than others, the cane was everywhere in use, and that frequently. Lads then had far less liberty and fewer sports than at present; but as boys' spirits cannot be altogether suppressed even by the use of the cane, they found vent in other ways, and there was much more mischief and more breaking out of bounds than now take place. Boys were less trusted and more harshly treated; in consequence of which there was a kind of warfare between the masters and the boys, in which the masters, in spite of their canes, did not always get the best of it.

Bob Repton was nearly fifteen. He was short rather than tall for his age, but squarely built and strong. His hair could never be got to lie down, but bristled aggressively over his head. His nose was inclined to turn up, his gray eyes had a merry mischievous expression, and his lips were generally parted in a smile. A casual observer would have said that he was a happy-go-lucky, merry, impudent-looking lad; but he was more than this. He was shrewd, intelligent, and exceptionally plucky, always ready to do a good turn to others, and to take more than his fair share of blame for every scrape he got into. He had fought many battles, and that with boys older than himself, but he had never been beaten.

The opinion generally among the boys was that he did not feel pain, and, being caned so frequently, such punishment as he got in a fight was a mere trifle to him. He was a thorn in the side of Mr. Purfleet, the usher who was generally in charge of the playground, who had learned by long experience that whenever Bob Repton was quiet he was certain to be planning some special piece of mischief.

The usher was sitting now on a bench with a book in his

hand, but his attention was at present directed to a group of four boys who had drawn together in a corner of the playground.

"There is Repton again," he said to himself. "I wonder what he is plotting now. That boy will be the death of me. I am quite sure it was he who put that eel in my bed last week, though of course I could not prove it."

Mr. Purfleet prided himself on his nerve. He had been telling the boys some stories he had read of snakes in India, among them, one of an officer who, when seated at table, had felt a snake winding itself round his leg, and who sat for several minutes without moving, until some friends brought a saucer of milk and placed it near, when the snake uncurled itself and went to drink.

"It must have required a lot of nerve, Mr. Purfleet," Bob Repton had said, "to sit as quiet as that."

"Not at all, not at all," the usher replied confidently; "it was the natural thing to do. A man should always be calm in case of sudden danger, Bob. The first thought in his mind should be, 'What is this?' the second, 'What had best be done under the circumstances?' and these two things being decided, a man of courage will deal coolly with the danger. I should despise myself if I were to act otherwise."

It was two nights later that the usher, having walked down between the two rows of beds in the dormitory, and seeing that all the boys were quiet and apparently asleep, proceeded to his own bed, which was at the end of the room and partly screened off from the rest by a curtain. No sooner did he disappear behind this than half a dozen heads were raised. An oil-lamp burned at the end of the room, affording light for the usher to undress, and enabling him, as he lay in bed, to command a general if somewhat faint view of the dormitory. Five minutes after Mr. Purfleet had disappeared behind the curtain, the watching eyes saw the clothes at the end of the bed pulled down, and caught a partial view of Mr. Purfleet as he climbed in. A second later there was a yell of terror, and the usher leapt from the bed. Instantly the dormitory was in an uproar.

"What is it, Mr. Purfleet,—what is the matter, sir?" and several of the boys sprang from their beds and ran towards him, the only exceptions to the general excitement being the four or five who were in the secret. These lay shaking with suppressed laughter, with the bed-clothes or the corner of a pillow thrust into their mouths to prevent them from breaking out into screams of delight.

"What is it, sir?"

It was some time before the usher could recover himself sufficiently to explain.

"There is a snake in my bed," he said.

"A snake!" the boys repeated in astonishment, several of the more timid at once making off to their beds.

"Certainly, a snake," Mr. Purfleet panted. "I put my legs down, and they came against something cold, and it began to twist about. In a moment, if I had not leapt out, I should no doubt have received a fatal wound."

"Where did it come from? what is to be done?" and a variety of other questions burst from the boys.

"I will run down and get three or four hockey sticks, Mr. Purfleet," one of the elder boys said.

"That will be the best plan, Mason. Quick, quick! There, do you see it moving under the clothes?"

There was certainly something wriggling, so there was a general movement back from the bed.

"We had better hold the clothes down, Mr. Purfleet," Bob Repton said, pushing himself forward. "If it were to crawl out at the top and get on to the floor it might bite a dozen of us. I will hold the clothes down tight on one side if someone will hold them on the other."

One of the other boys came forward, and the clothes were stretched tightly across the bed by the pillow. In a minute or two Mason ran up with four hockey sticks.

"Now, you must be careful," Mr. Purfleet said, "because

if it should get out the consequences might be terrible. Now, then, four of you take the sticks, and all hit together as hard as you can—now."

The sticks descended together; there was a violent writhing and contortion beneath the clothes, but the blows rained down fast, and in a very short time all movement ceased.

"It must be dead now," Bob Repton said. "I think we can look at it now, sir."

"Well, draw the clothes down very gently, boys, and be ready to strike again if you see the least movement."

The clothes were drawn down till the creature was visible.

"It must be a cobra," the usher said, looking at it from a distance. "It is thick and short; it must have escaped from somewhere. Be very careful, all of you."

Mason approached cautiously to get a nearer view, and then exclaimed, "Why, sir, it is an eel!"

There was a moment's silence, and then a perfect yell of laughter from the boys. For a moment the usher was dumbfounded; then he rallied.

"You will all go to your beds at once," he said. "I shall report the matter to Mr. Tulloch in the morning."

The boys retired laughing to their beds, but above the din the usher heard the words in a muffled voice, "A man should always be calm in sudden danger." Another voice, equally disguised, said: "Yes, he should first ask himself 'What is this?' then ' What had best be done under the circumstances?'" A third voice then took it up: "It follows that a man of courage will deal coolly with the danger." Then there was a chorus of half a dozen voices, "I should despise myself if I were to act otherwise."

"Silence!" the usher shouted, rushing down the line between the beds. "I will thrash the first boy who speaks." As Mr. Purfleet had one of the hockey sticks in his hand, the threat was sufficient to ensure silence.

To the relief of the two or three boys engaged in the

affair, Mr. Purfleet made no report in the morning. Mr. Tulloch by no means spared the cane, but he always inquired before he flogged; and as the usher felt sure that the snake story would be brought forward by way of excuse for the trick played upon him, he thought it better to drop it, making a mental note, however, that he would get even with Bob Repton another time; for he made sure that he was at the bottom of the matter, especially as he had been one of those who had listened to the snake story.

Mr. Purfleet was held in but light respect by the boys. He was a pale young man, and looked as if he had been poorly fed as a boy. He took the junior classes, and the belief was that he knew nothing of Latin.

Moffat, who took the upper classes, was much more severe, and sent up many more boys to be caned than did the junior usher; but the boys did not dislike him. Caning they considered their natural portion, and felt no ill-will on that account, while they knew that Mr. Moffat was a capital scholar, and though strict was always scrupulously just. Above all, he was not a sneak. If he reported them he reported them openly, but brought no accusation against them behind their back; while Mr. Purfleet was always carrying tittle-tattle to the head-master. There was, therefore, little gratitude towards him for holding his tongue as to the eel, for the boys guessed the real reason of his silence, and put it down to dread of ridicule and not to any kindliness of feeling.

"Purfleet would give sixpence to know what we are talking about, Bob," one of the group talking in the corner of the playground said.

"It is worth more than that, Jim: still we shall have to be extra careful. He suspects it was our lot who played him the trick about the eel, and he will do his best to catch us out in something. Well, as I was saying, Johnny Gibson has got a first-rate dog for rabbits, and he says there are lots of them up on the Common. I told him that I would come, and I expected two or three more, and we would meet him at the top of the hill at four o'clock to-morrow morning. It will be getting light by that time. Of course we shall get out in the usual way, and we can be back by half-past six, and no one will be any the wiser. Old Thomas never comes down till a quarter to seven, I have heard him a dozen times; he just comes down in time to ring the bell for us to get up."

"Oh, I ain't afraid of Thomas," one of the others said; "but I am afraid of Purfleet."

"There need be no fear about him. He never wakes till the bell rings, and sleeps like a top. Why, he didn't wake the other morning when we had a scrimmage and you tumbled out of bed. Besides, we all sleep at the other end of the room, and even if he did wake up in the night he wouldn't notice that we had gone, especially if we shoved something in the bed to make a lump. My only fear is that we shan't wake. We ought to keep watch till it's time to get up, but I am sure we shouldn't keep awake. We must all make up our minds to wake at three, then one of us will be sure to do it. And mind, if one wakes he must promise not to go to sleep again before he hears the hall clock strike, and knows what time it is. If it is before three he can go off to sleep again; that way one of us is sure to be awake when it strikes three."

"I say, sha'n't we just be licked if we are found out, Bob?"

"Of course we shall; but as we get licked pretty well every day that won't make much difference, and we shall have had awful fun. Still, if any of you fellows don't like it don't you go. I am going, but I don't want to persuade any of you."

"Of course we are going if you are going, Bob. What are we going to do with the rabbits?"

"Oh, I settled Johnny Gibson should keep them. He is going to bring his dog, you know; besides, what could we do with them? We can't cook them, can we?"

As it was clear to all the party that this could not be managed, no objection was raised to this disposal of their game.

Bob Repton slept but little that night. They went to bed at eight, and he heard every hour strike after nine, dozing off occasionally, and waking up each time convinced that the clock would strike three next time. At last he heard the three welcome strokes, and at once got up and went to the beds of the other three boys. They were all sound asleep, and required some shaking before they could be convinced that it was time to get up. Then each boy put his bolster in his bed, rolled up his night shirt into a ball and laid it on the pillow, and then partly covered it up with the clothes. Then they slipped on their shirts, breeches, and stockings, and, taking their jackets and shoes in their hand, stole out of the door at their end of the room and closed it behind them. They then crept downstairs to the room where their caps were kept, put on these and their jackets, and each boy got a hockey stick out of the cupboard in the corner in which they were kept. Then they very cautiously unfastened the shutter, raised the window, and slipped out. They pulled the shutter to behind them, closed the window, and then put on their shoes.

"That is managed first-rate," Bob said, "there wasn't the least noise. I made sure Wharton would have dropped his shoes."

"Why should I drop them more than anyone else?" Wharton asked in an aggrieved voice.

"I don't know, Billy. The idea occurred to me. I didn't think anyone else would do it, but I quite made up my mind that you would."

"Well, I wish you wouldn't be so fast about making up your mind, then," Wharton grumbled. "I ain't more clumsy than other people."

"You are all right," Jim Sankey put in. "Bob's only joking."

"Well, he might as well joke with somebody else, Jim. I don't see any joke in it."

"No, that is where the joke is, Billy," Bob said. "If you did see the joke there wouldn't be any joke in it. Well, never mind, here is the walnut-tree. Now, who will get over first?"

The walnut-tree stood in the playground near the wall, and had often proved useful as a ladder to boys at Tulloch's. One of its branches extended over the wall, and from this it was easy to drop down beyond it. The return was more difficult, and was only to be accomplished by means of an old ivy which grew against the wall at some distance off. By its aid the wall could be scaled without much difficulty, and there was then the choice of dropping twelve feet into the playground, or of walking on the top of the wall until the walnut-tree was reached. Tulloch's stood some little distance along the Lower Richmond Road. There were but one or two houses standing back from the road between it and the main road up the hill, and there was little fear of anyone being abroad at that time in the morning. There was as yet but a faint gleam of daylight in the sky, and it was dark in the road up the hill, as the trees growing in the grounds of the houses on either side stretched far over it.

"I say," Jim Sankey said, "won't it be a go if Johnny Gibson isn't there after all?"

"He will be up there by four," Bob said confidently. "He said his father would be going out in his boat to fish as soon as it began to be daylight, because the tide served at that hour, and that he would start as soon as his father shoved off the boat. My eye, Jim, what is that ahead of us? It looks to me like a coach."

"It is a coach or a carriage or something of that sort."

"No, it isn't, it is a light cart. What can it be doing here at this hour? Let us walk the other side of the road."

They crossed to the left as they got abreast of the cart. A man whom they had not noticed before said sharply:

"You are about early."

"Yes, we are off to work," Bob replied, and they walked steadily on.

"He couldn't see what we were like," Jim Sankey said when they had got a hundred yards further.

"Not he," Bob said. "I could not make out his figure at all, and it is darker on this side of the road than it is on the other. I say, you fellows, I think he is up to no good."

"What do you mean, Bob?"

"Well, what should a cart be standing on the hill for at this time in the morning? That's Admiral Langton's, I know; the door is just where the cart was stopping."

"Well, what has that got to do with it, Bob? The cart won't do him any harm."

"No, but there may be some fellows with it who may be breaking into his house."

"Do you think so, Bob?"

"Well, it seems likely to me it may be his house or one of the others."

"Well, what are we to do, Bob?"

"I vote we see about it, Jim. We have pretty nearly half an hour to spare now before Johnny Gibson will come along. We have got our hockey sticks, you know."

"But suppose there shouldn't be any men there, Bob, and we should be caught in the grounds, they would think we were going to steal something."

"That would be a go," Bob said; "but there isn't likely to be anyone about at half-past three, and if there were I don't suppose he would be able to catch us. But we must risk something anyhow. It will be a bit of fun, and it will be better than waiting at the top of the hill with nothing to do till Johnny Gibson comes."

They were now past the wall in front of Admiral Langton's, and far out of sight of the man in the cart.

"There is some ivy on this wall," Bob said; "we can climb over it by that. Then we will make our way along until we can find some place where we can climb over into the admiral's garden."

"Perhaps there are some dogs about," Wharton objected.

"Well, if there are they are most likely chained up. We must risk something. Well, here goes. If you don't like it, Wharton, you can stay behind." So saying he put his hockey stick between his teeth, and then proceeded to climb up the wall by means of the ivy.

The wall was but nine feet high, and as soon as he gained the top Bob said:

"Come on, you fellows. I am going to drop down."

In two minutes he was joined by the other three.

"There is a path just beyond," Bob said; "let us go by that. Don't you fellows say a word. As Wharton says, there may be some dogs about."

Quietly they stole along the path, which ran parallel to the road, until it turned off at right angles.

"Now, the first tree that grows against the wall we will get over by," Bob whispered.

After going twenty yards he stopped. "This tree will do."

"But what are you going to do if there should be some men?" Wharton asked, in a tone that showed he objected altogether to the proceeding.

"It depends upon how many of them there are," Bob replied. "Of course the admiral has got some men in the house, and they will wake up and help us if we give the alarm. Anyhow, we ought to be able to be a match for two men with these sticks, especially if we take them by surprise. What do you say, Jim?"

"I should think so," Jim replied. "Anyhow, if you are game to go on, I am. What do you say, Fullarton?"

"Oh, I am ready," Fullarton, who was a boy of few words, replied. "Only, if there is anyone, Bob, and we get into a row with them, of course it will all come out about us, and then sha'n't we get it just!"

"I suppose we shall," Bob admitted: "but I don't see we can help that. Well, we are in for it now;" and he began to climb the tree, and, working along a limb which extended over the wall, he dropped down into the garden. The others soon joined, Wharton being more afraid of staying behind by himself than of going with the rest.

"Now, what are we to do next?"

"I should say we ought to find out whether anyone has got into the house, that is the first thing. Then, if they have, we have got to try to wake up the people, and to frighten the men inside. Have you got some string in your pockets?"

"I have got some." They all had string.

"What do you want string for, Bob?"

"String is always useful, Jim. We may want to tie their hands. But what I was thinking was, we might fasten it across the stairs or some of the passages, and then set up a sudden shout, and they would think the watchmen had come and would make a bolt, and when they got to the string over they would go, and then we would drop on them with these hockey sticks before they could get up. Well, come on. There mayn't be anyone here after all. Now we will go up to the house and creep round."

The house stood thirty or forty yards away, and, stepping as noiselessly as they could, the boys crossed the lawn and moved along the front. Suddenly Tom Fullarton caught hold of Bob's arm.

"Look, Bob, there is a light in that room! Do you see— through the slit in the shutters?"

"So there is. Well, there is no mistake now, there must be some fellows belonging to that cart inside. That must be the drawing-room or dining-room, and they would never have lights there at this time of night. Now, let us find out where they got in. This is something like fun, it beats rabbit-hunting all to nothing. Now mind, you fellows, if we do come upon them and there is a fight, you remember the best place to hit, to begin with, is the ankle. You have only just got to fancy that it is a bung, and swipe at it with all your might. Anyone you hit there is sure to go down, and if he wants it you can hit him over the head afterwards. Now, come along, I expect they got in at the back of the house."

They soon came upon a door at the side of the house. It was open.

"That looks as if they had been let in," Bob whispered. "See, there is a light in there somewhere! Come on. Now let us take our shoes off." The others were thoroughly excited now, and followed Bob without hesitation.

"Bob, is the key in the door?" Jim whispered.

"Yes, on the inside. They have been let in. I wish I dare lock it and take the key away. Let me see if it turns easy." Very gently he turned the key, and found the bolt shot noiselessly. It had doubtless been carefully oiled. He turned it again, shut the door, locked it, and put the key in his pocket.

Then they crept on tiptoe along the passage. At the end were two large chests strengthened with iron bands. A lighted lantern stood upon them. Bob peered round the corner into the hall. No one was to be seen, but he heard a noise through an open door, from which came a stream of light. Motioning the others to stand still, he crept forward noiselessly till he could look into the room. A man was occupied in packing some articles of massive plate, clocks, and other valuables into a sack. He was alone. Bob made his way back to the others.

"There's only one fellow there," he said; "if there are any more they are upstairs. Let us have this one first—his back is to the door. Now, Wharton, you hold our handkerchiefs and the string; if he don't look round, I will jump on his back and have him down. The moment he is down you two throw yourselves on him, and you shove the handkerchiefs into his mouth, Wharton. In the surprise he won't know that we are only boys, and we will tie his hands before he has time to resist. Now, come on."

They were all plucky boys, for Wharton, although less morally courageous than the others, was no coward physically. Their stockinged feet made no sound, and the man heard nothing until Bob sprang on to his back, the force sending him down on to his face. Bob's arm was tightly round his throat, and the other two threw themselves upon him, each seizing an arm, while Wharton crammed two handkerchiefs into his mouth. The man's hands were dragged behind his back as he lay on his face, and his wrists tied firmly together. He was rendered utterly helpless before he had recovered from the first shock of surprise.

"Tie his ankles together with the other two handkerchiefs," Bob said, still lying across him. "That is right. You are sure they are tight? There, he will do now; I must lock him in." This was done. "Now, then, let's go upstairs. Now fasten this last piece of string across between the banisters six or eight steps up. Make haste," he added, as a faint cry was heard above.

It did not take a second to fasten the string at each end, and then grasping their sticks the boys sprang upstairs. On gaining the landing they heard voices proceeding from a room along a corridor, and as they crept up to it they heard a man's voice say angrily: "Now we ain't going to waste any more time; if you don't tell us where your money is, we will knock you and the girl on the head. No, you can't talk, but you can point out where it is. We know that you have got it. Very well, Bill, hit that young woman over the head with the butt of your pistol; don't be afraid of hurting her. Ah! I thought you would change your mind. So it is under the bed. Look under, Dick. What is there?"

"A square box," another voice said.

"Well, haul it out."

BOB AND HIS COMPANIONS SURPRISE THE BURGLARS.

"Come on," Bob Repton whispered to the others; "the moment we are in, shout."

He stood for a moment in the doorway. A man was standing with his back to him holding a pistol in his hand; another similarly armed stood by the side of a young woman, who, in a loose dressing-gown, sat shrinking in an arm-chair, into which she had evidently been thrust; a third was in the act of crawling under the bed. An elderly man in his night-shirt was standing up. A gag had been thrust into his mouth, and he was tightly bound by a cord round his waist to one of the bed-posts. Bob sprang forward whirling his hockey stick round his head, and giving a loud shout of "Down with the villains!" the others joining at the top of their voices.

Before the man had time to turn round, Bob's stick fell with all the boy's strength upon his ankle, and he went down as if he had been shot, his pistol exploding as he fell. Bob raised his stick again, and brought it down with a swinging blow on the robber's head. The others had made a rush together towards the man standing by the lady. Taken utterly by surprise, he discharged his pistol at random and then sprang towards the door. Two blows fell on him, and Sankey and Fullarton tried to grapple with him, but he burst through them and rushed out.

Bob and Wharton sprang on the kneeling man before he could gain his feet, and rolled him over, throwing themselves upon him. He was struggling furiously, and would soon have shaken them off, when the other boys sprang to their assistance.

"You help them, Jim. I will get this cord off," Fullarton said, and running to the bed began to unknot the cord that bound the admiral. The ruffian on the ground was a very powerful man, and the three boys had the greatest difficulty in holding him down, till Fullarton slipped a noose round one of his ankles, and then jumping on the bed hauled upon it with all his strength, the admiral giving his assistance.

"Get off him, he is safe!" he shouted; but the others had the greatest difficulty in shaking themselves free from the man, who had fortunately laid his pistol on the bed before he crawled under it to get at the box. Jim Sankey was the first to shake himself free from him, and seeing what Fullarton was doing he jumped on to the bed and gave him his assistance, and in half a minute the ruffian's leg was lashed to the bed-post, at a height of five feet from the ground. Just as this was done there was a rush of feet outside, and three men, one holding a cutlass and the other two armed with pokers, ran into the room. It was fortunate they did so, for the man whom Bob had first felled was just rising to his feet; but he was at once struck down again by a heavy blow over the head with the cutlass. By this time the admiral had torn off the bandage across his mouth.

"Another of them ran downstairs, Jackson. Give chase. We can deal with these fellows."

The three men rushed off.

"Well, I don't know who you are," the admiral went on, turning to the boys, "but you turned up at the nick of time, and I am deeply indebted to you, not only for saving my money, although I should not have liked to lose that, but for having captured these pirates. That villain has not hurt you much, I hope?" for both Bob and Jim Sankey were bleeding freely from the face from the heavy blows the robber had dealt them.

"No, sir: we are not hurt to speak of," Bob said. "We belong to Tulloch's school."

"To the school!" the admiral exclaimed. "What on earth are you doing here at four o'clock in the morning? But never mind that now. What is it, Jackson, has he got away?"

"No, sir; he was lying in a heap at the bottom of the stairs. There was a lanyard fastened across."

"We tied a string across, sir, as we came up," Bob explained.

"Well done, lads! Are there any more of them, Jackson?"

"Don't see any signs of any more, admiral. There are the two plate chests in the passage, as if they had been brought out from the butler's strong room in readiness to take away."

"Where is the butler? He must have heard the pistol-shots!" the admiral exclaimed angrily.

"He is not in his room, admiral. We looked in to bring him with us. The door was open, but he isn't there."

"There is another man in the drawing-room tied up," Bob said. "He was putting a lot of things into a sack."

"The scoundrel! Perhaps that is the butler," the admiral said. "Well, Emma, you had better go back to bed again. Jackson, you stand guard over these two villains here, and split their heads open if they venture to move. Now let us go and see to this other fellow."

The admiral proceeded downstairs, followed by the boys. The other two servants were standing beside the third robber, who was still insensible. "You keep watch over him, John," the admiral said. "Williams, you come with us; there is another man in the drawing-room, but he is tied up."

"There is the key, sir," Bob said, producing it. "We thought it safest to lock him up."

"Upon my word, young gentlemen, you seem to have thought of everything. If I were in command of a ship I should like to have you all as midshipmen."

The door was open; the man was still lying on the ground, but had rolled some distance from where they had left him. He had succeeded in getting his feet loosened from the handkerchief, but the whip-cord round his wrists had resisted all his efforts to break or slacken it. He was panting heavily from the exertions he had made.

"It is Harper," the admiral said in a tone of indignation and disgust. "So, you treacherous scoundrel, it was you who let these men in, was it? Well, it is a hanging matter, my lad, and if any fellow deserves the rope, you do. You had better go and get some more cord, Williams, and tie all these four fellows up securely. Let Jackson see to the knots.

"Where did the scoundrels get in?" he asked, turning to the boys.

"At the door at the end of the passage, sir, where the plate chests are standing. We found it open; here is the key of it. We locked it after we came in, so as to prevent anyone from getting away. There is another man with a cart in the road."

"We will see to him directly we have got the others all tied up safely," the admiral said. "That is the first thing to see to."

In five minutes the four men were laid side by side in the hall, securely bound hand and foot.

"Now, Williams, you keep guard over them. Jackson, do you and John sally out. There is a cart standing outside the gate and a fellow in it, bring him in and lay him alongside the others." The boys followed the two men to see the capture. The light had broadened out over the sky, and it was almost sunrise as they sallied out. They went quietly along until they reached the gate, which stood ajar, then they flung it open and rushed out. To their disappointment the cart was standing about fifty yards lower down the hill. The man was in it, with his whip in one hand and the reins in another, and was looking back, and the moment he saw them he struck the horse and drove off at the top of his speed. The pace was such that it was hopeless for them to think of following him.

"I expect he heard the pistol shots," Jackson said, "and sheered off a bit so as to be able to cut and run if he found his consorts were in trouble. Well, we cannot help it; we have taken four prizes out of the five, and I call that pretty fair."

"I think we had better go now," Bob said. "We have got a friend waiting for us."

"Then he must wait a bit longer," Jackson said; "the admiral will want to ask you some more questions. But if your friend is anywhere near, one of you might run and tell him to back and fill a bit till you come to him."

"Tell him to do what?" Jim Sankey asked.

"Tell him to wait a bit, lad."

"I will run up," Wharton said. "Shall I tell him we sha'n't want him at all to-day, Bob?"

"I think so, Wharton. You see it is four o'clock now, and we mayn't be able to get away for half an hour, and it will be too late then. Besides, Jim and I have been knocked about too much to care for rabbit-hunting now. You tell him we will go some other day."

"You needn't tell him that, Wharton," Fullarton put in. "It will be some time before we get a chance, you may be sure."

"All right! tell him to go home then, Wharton. Tell him I will make it all right with him for losing his morning's work. Of course you will come in here when you come down the hill again."

Wharton nodded, and started at a run up the hill, while his companions accompanied the two men into the house. The admiral was down in the hall again. He had now had time to add to his former scanty costume.

"Get the shutters of the drawing-room open, Jackson," he said, after hearing the report of the man's escape, "and tell the maids—I suppose they are all up—to light a fire and get some coffee ready at once, and something to eat. Now, young gentlemen, sit down and tell me all about this business. Now, which of you will be spokesman?"

Jim nodded to Bob.

"It's his doing, sir; I mean about our coming in here. We should never have thought anything about the cart if it hadn't been for Bob, and we didn't much like coming; only he pretty well made us, and he arranged it all."

"That's all rot," Bob said. "We were just all in it together, sir, and this is how it was." And he told the whole story of what had taken place.

"Well, you couldn't have done better if you had been officers in His Majesty's service," the admiral said. "You have saved me the loss of my two plate-chests, of all the plate in this room, and that couldn't be counted in money, for they were most of the things given me at different times on service, and of £500 I had in that box upstairs—altogether at least £2000 in money value. More than that, you prevented my being captured, and it would have been a sorer blow to me than the loss of the money if those scoundrels had had their way and had got off scot free. But you haven't told me yet how you happened to be going up the hill at half-past three o'clock in the morning. What on earth were you doing there? Surely your master does not allow you to ramble about in the middle of the night."

"Well, no, sir; that is the worst of it," Bob said. "You see I had arranged with one of the fishermen's boys, who has got a first-rate dog, that we could meet him upon the Common, and do some rabbit-hunting. We slipped out from Tulloch's, and meant to have been back before anyone was up. And now I expect we shall get it nicely, because I suppose it must all come out."

The admiral laughed. "You are four nice young scamps!" he said, for Wharton had rejoined them before Bob had finished the story; "but it is not for me to blame you. It will certainly have to be told, lads, because you will have to appear as witnesses at the trial of these fellows; but I will go down myself the first thing in the morning and speak to your master."

"Thank you, sir," Bob said, "it won't make any difference about the thrashing: we are bound to get that. But we sha'n't mind that, we are pretty well accustomed to it. Still, if you speak for us, I expect we shall get off with that, otherwise I don't know what Tulloch would have done when he found out that we had been slipping out at night."

"I expect it is not the first time you have done it?"

"Well, no, it is not, sir. We have been out two or three times with one of the fishermen in his boat."

"I expect you are nice young pickles," the admiral said. "Well, what time does school begin?"

"Half-past seven, sir."

"Very well, then. I will be there at that hour, lads, and do my best for you. You see, with those faces of yours you would be sure to be noticed anyhow, and I hope you wouldn't in any case have been mean enough to screen yourselves by lying."

"That we shouldn't," Bob said. "I don't think there is a boy in the school who would tell a lie to Tulloch."

"That is right, lads. A gentleman will never tell a lie to screen himself when he has got into a scrape. I wouldn't keep the smartest young officer in the service on board a ship of mine if I caught him telling a lie, for I should know that he would not only be a blackguard but a coward. Cowardice is at the bottom of half the lying of the world. I would overlook anything except lying. Upon my word, I would rather that a boy were a thief than a liar. Well, here is breakfast. Now sit down and make yourselves at home, while I go up and see how my daughter is after the fright she has had."

Half an hour later, after eating a hearty breakfast, the four boys started for school.

CHAPTER II.

A GREAT CHANGE.

IT was just striking six when they again climbed over the wall and descended by the tree. They had had a discussion whether they should wait until the doors were opened and walk quietly in, or return as they left. They adopted the latter plan, because they thought that if the matter was reported to Mr. Tulloch he might proceed to administer punishment before the admiral arrived to give his version of the affair. The door was still ajar. As they opened it they gave an exclamation of surprise, for there, sitting on a chair in the passage, was Mr. Purfleet. He smiled unpleasantly. "So here you are. You have had a pleasant ramble, no doubt, but I don't quite know what view Mr. Tulloch may take of it."

"It was very good of you to sit up for us, Mr. Purfleet," Bob said quietly; "but you see we had left the door open, and could have got in by ourselves. I hope you will not have caught cold sitting there only in a dressing-gown."

"You are an impudent young scamp!" Mr. Purfleet said in a rage. "You will laugh with the other side of your mouth presently. You and Sankey are nice-looking figures, ain't you, with your faces all cut and swollen."

"We have been a little in the wars," Bob replied.

"I don't want to hear anything about it," the usher replied. "You will have to explain matters to Mr. Tulloch."

"So I suppose, Mr. Purfleet. Well, Jim, we'll go and have a good wash. The bell will be ringing in half an hour."

So saying, Bob went into the lavatory, followed by his companions, while the usher returned upstairs. He was certainly disappointed. Quietly as the boys had dressed, the slight noise they had made in closing the door had woke him. He thought little of it, but just as he was going off to sleep again he heard the bolts of the door below withdrawn. He at once got up and walked to the other end of the dormitory, and discovered that the four boys were missing. Chuckling to himself that he should now be able to repay the grudge he owed to Bob, he put on his dressing-gown and went downstairs, and had sat there for three hours momently expecting their return. He had certainly felt chilly, but had borne it patiently, comforted by the joyful expectation of the utter dismay that would be felt by the culprits when they saw him. The meeting had not passed off at all as he had anticipated, and he could only console himself by thinking that his turn would come when he made his report to Mr. Tulloch.

The four boys did not return to the dormitory, but after they had washed strolled about in the playground. There was quite a ferment in the dormitory when their absence was perceived, and the others noticed the four made-up figures in their place. The operation of dressing was got through with much greater alacrity than usual, and when they went downstairs and saw the four missing boys in the playground, these were at once surrounded by an excited throng. They refused, however, to answer any questions.

"You will hear it all in good time," Bob said. "We have been out, and we have been caught; that is all I am going to tell you."

At the usual hour the bell rang, and the boys assembled in the school-room. The two ushers were in their places. They waited three or four minutes for Mr. Tulloch to appear, then the door opened and the man-servant entered, and, walking up to Mr. Moffat, said a word or two. The latter nodded.

"Lessons will begin at once," he said in a loud voice. "The first class will come up to me."

The boys of this class, who occupied the senior dormitory, at once began their lessons, while Mr. Purfleet took the lower class. The second class, including Bob and his friends, remained in their places. In a quarter of an hour the door opened and Mr. Tulloch entered, accompanied by Admiral Langton. Mr. Tulloch was looking very serious, while the admiral looked hot and angry.

"We are going to catch it," Bob whispered to Jim Sankey. "I knew the admiral wouldn't be able to get us off."

"I wish all the boys to return to their places, Mr. Moffat. I have something to say," Mr. Tulloch said in a loud voice.

When the boys were all seated he went on: "Admiral Langton has been telling me that four of my boys were out and about soon after three o'clock this morning. The four boys in question will stand up. I do not say that this is the first time that such a serious infraction of the rules of the school has taken place. It has happened before. It may, for aught I know, have happened many times without my knowledge; but upon the occasions when it has come to my knowledge the offenders have been most severely punished. They must be punished now. Admiral Langton has been telling me that the boys in question have behaved with very great courage, and have been the means of saving him from the loss of a large sum of money and plate, and of capturing four burglars."

A buzz of surprise passed round the school.

"That this conduct does them great credit I am fully prepared to admit. Had they been aware that this burglary was about to be committed, and had they broken out of the house in the middle of the night for the purpose of preventing it, I allow that it might have been pleaded as an excuse for their offence; but this was not so. It was an accident that occurred to them when they were engaged in breaking the rules, and cannot be pleaded as a set-off against punishment.   Admiral Langton has pleaded with me very strongly for a pardon for them, but I regret that I am unable to comply with his request.   The admiral, as a sailor, is well aware that discipline must be maintained, and I am quite sure that when he was in command of a ship he would not have permitted his judgment to be biased by anyone.   I have put it to him in that way, and he acknowledges that to be so.   The two matters stand distinct.   The boys must be punished for this gross breach of the rules.   They may be thanked and applauded for the courage they have shown and the valuable service they have rendered to Admiral Langton.   I have, however, so far yielded to his entreaties, that while I must administer a severe caning for the gross breach of the rules, I shall abstain from taking any further steps in the matter, and from writing to the boys' parents and guardians requesting them to remove their sons from the school at once, as I certainly otherwise would have done.   At the same time, I am willing to hear anything that these boys may have to urge in explanation or defence of their conduct.   I have already been informed by Admiral Langton that their object in so breaking out was to hunt rabbits up on the Common."

"I wish to say, sir," Bob said in a steady voice, "that it was entirely my doing.   I made the arrangements and persuaded the others to go, and I think it is only right that they should not be punished as severely as I am."

"We were all in it together, sir," Jim Sankey broke in. "I was just as keen on it as Bob was."

"So was I," Fullarton and Wharton said together.

"Well, lads," Admiral Langton said, taking a step forward and addressing the boys in general, "as your master says, discipline is discipline; this is his ship, and he is on his own quarter-deck; but I wish to tell you all that in my opinion you have every reason to be proud of your schoolfellows.   They behaved with the greatest pluck and gallantry, and were I again in command of a ship I should be glad to have them serving me.   I am only sorry that I cannot persuade Mr. Tulloch to see the matter in the same light as I do. Good-bye, lads!" and he walked across and shook hands with the four boys. "I shall see you again soon;" and the admiral turned abruptly and walked out of the school-room.

Mr. Tulloch at once proceeded to carry his sentence into effect, and the four boys received as severe a caning as ever they had had in their lives; and even Bob, case-hardened as he was, had as much as he could do to prevent himself from uttering a sound while it was being inflicted. Lessons were then continued as usual until eight o'clock, when the boys went in to breakfast. After that was over they went into the playground until nine, and the four culprits gave the rest a full account of the events of the night.

"I don't mind the thrashing," Bob said, "although Tulloch did lay it on hot. It was well worth it, if it had only been to see that sneak Purfleet's face when the admiral told the story. I was watching him when Tulloch came in, and saw how delighted he was at the tale he was going to tell, and how satisfied he was that he should get no end of credit for sitting three hours in his dressing-gown in order to catch us when we came in. It was an awful sell for him when he saw that the admiral had come out with the whole story, and there was nothing whatever for him to tell."

When they went into the school again Mr. Tulloch said: "Boys, I hear that four of your number have behaved with great gallantry. They have prevented a serious robbery, and arrested the men engaged in it. I shall therefore give you a holiday for the remainder of the day. The four boys in question will proceed at once to Admiral Langton's, as they will be required to accompany him to Kingston, where the prisoners will be brought up before the magistrates."

There was a general cheer from the boys, and then Bob and his companions hurried upstairs to put on their best clothes, and ran off to the admiral's.

"Well, boys, is it all over?" he asked as they entered.

"All over, sir," they replied together.

"Well, boys, I think it was a shame, but I suppose discipline must be maintained in school as well as on board a ship; but it vexes me amazingly to think that I have been the means of bringing you into it."

"It is just the other way, sir," Bob said; "and it is very lucky for us that we came in here, sir, instead of going up to the Common as we intended. One of the ushers found out that we had gone, and sat up until we came back; and if it had not been for you we should not only have got a thrashing, but should all have been expelled; so it is the luckiest thing possible that we came in here."

"Well, I am very glad to hear that, boys. It has taken a load off my mind, for I have been thinking that if you had not come in to help me you would have got back without being noticed. Emma, these are the four lads who did us such good service last night. They caught sight of you before, but you were hardly in a state to receive them formally."

The young lady laughed as she came forward and shook hands with them.

"You need not have mentioned that, papa. Well, I am very much obliged to you all, for I have no doubt they meant to have my watch and jewels as well as papa's money."

"Now, it is time for us to be off," the admiral said. "My carriage is at the door, and a fly. You two who have been knocked about had better come with my daughter and myself. The others can either ride inside the fly, or one can go on the box of each vehicle, as you like."

Wharton and Fullarton both said that they should prefer going outside, and in a few minutes they were on their way, the three men-servants riding inside the fly. The prisoners had been sent off two hours before in a cart under the charge of the two local constables. The case lasted but an hour, the four men being all committed for trial. The party then returned to Putney, the admiral insisting upon the boys stopping to lunch with him. After the meal was over, he inquired what they were going to do on leaving school, and what profession they intended to adopt.

Bob was the first questioned.

"I am going to be a wine-merchant, sir," he said. "I have got no choice about it. I lost my father and mother years ago, and my guardian, who is an uncle of mine, is in the wine trade, and he says I have got to go in too. I think it is horrid, but there is no good talking to him. He is an awfully crusty old chap. I should like to be a soldier or a sailor, but of course it is of no use thinking of it. My guardian has been very kind to me even though he is so crusty, and it wouldn't be right not to do as he tells me; and I don't suppose the wine business is so very bad when one is accustomed to it."

"Has your uncle any sons, lad?"

"No, sir, he is an old bachelor, and he says that some day I am to have his business."

"Then you can't do better than stick to it, lad," the admiral said. "A boy who has before him the prospect of a solid, substantial living on shore is simply a fool if he goes to sea. It is a rough life and a hard one, and if you don't get shot or drowned you may get laid on the shelf with the loss of a limb, and a pension that won't find you in grog and tobacco. It is a pity, for you would have made a good officer; but you will be vastly better off in all respects at home, and I can tell you there is not one sailor out of five who would not jump at a berth on shore if he could get the chance."

Sankey's father was a country clergyman, and at present Jim had no particular prospect.

"Would you like to go to sea, boy?"

"Yes, sir; I should like it of all things."

"Very well; give me your father's name and address and I will write to him about it."

Fullarton's father was a landed proprietor in Somersetshire, and he was the eldest son. Wharton was to be a lawyer, and was to begin in his father's office in a year or two. Admiral Langton took notes of the addresses of the boys' relatives. When he had done that he said to them: "Now, lads, I know you would rather be off. I remember when I was a midshipman I was always glad enough to escape when I had to dine with the captain."

A week later a young man came down from a city watchmaker's with four handsome gold watches and chains for the boys, with an inscription stating that they had been presented to them by Admiral Langton in remembrance of their gallant conduct on the night of August 6th, 1778. They were immensely delighted with the gift, for watches were in those days far more expensive luxuries than at present, and their use was comparatively rare. With the watches were four short notes from the admiral, inviting them to come up on the following Saturday afternoon. They had by this time received letters from their friends, who had each received a communication from the admiral expressing his warm commendation of their conduct, and his thanks for the services that the boys had rendered.

Jim Sankey's father wrote saying that the admiral had offered to procure him a berth as a midshipman at once, and that he had written thankfully accepting the offer, as he knew that it was what Jim had been most earnestly wishing; though, as he had no interest whatever among naval men, he had hitherto seen no chance of his being able to obtain such an appointment. This communication put Jim into a state of the wildest delight, and rendered him an object of envy to his school-fellows. Fullarton's father wrote his son a hearty letter congratulating him on what he had done, and saying that he felt proud of the letter he had received from the admiral. Wharton's father wrote to him sharply, saying that thief-taking was a business that had better be left to constables, and that he did not approve of freaks of that kind.

Mr. Bale wrote an irascible letter to Bob. "My dear nephew," he began, "I am astonished and most seriously displeased at contents of communication I have received from a person signing himself J. Langton, admiral. I gather from it that instead of pursuing your studies you are wandering about at night engaged in pursuits akin to poaching. I say akin, because I am not aware whether the wild animals upon the common are the property of the lord of the manor or whether they are at the mercy of vagabonds. It appears to me that there can be no proper supervision exercised by your masters. I spoke to you when you were here six weeks ago as to your school reports, which, although fairly satisfactory as to your abilities, said there was a great want of steadiness in your general conduct. I am convinced that you are doing no good for yourself, and that the sooner you settle down to a desk in my office the better. I have therefore written this morning informing Mr. Tulloch that I shall remove you at Michaelmas.

"Your sister has been here with her husband to-day. I am sorry to say that they do not view your wild and lawless conduct in the same light that I do, and that they are unable to see there is anything positively disreputable in your being mixed up in midnight adventures with burglars. I am glad to gather from Admiral Langton's letter that Mr. Tulloch has seen your conduct in the proper light, and has inflicted a well-merited punishment upon you. All this is a very bad preparation for your future career as a respectable trader, and I am most annoyed to hear that you will be called on to appear as a witness against the men who have been captured. I have written to Admiral Langton acknowledging his letter, and expressing my surprise that a gentleman in his position should give any countenance whatever to a lad who has been engaged in breaking the rules of his school, and in wandering at night like a vagabond through the country."

Bob looked rather serious as he read through the letter

for the first time, but after going through it again he burst
into a shout of laughter.

"What is it, Bob?" Tom Fullarton asked.

"Read this letter, Tom. I should like to have seen the
admiral's face as he read my uncle's letter. But it is too
bad. You see I have regularly done for myself. I was to
have stopped here till a year come Christmas, and now I
have to leave at Michaelmas. I call it a beastly shame."

It was some consolation to Bob to receive next morning
a letter from his sister, saying she was delighted to hear how
he had distinguished himself in the capture of the burglars.
"Of course it was very wrong of you to get out at night;
but Gerald says that boys are always up to tricks of that
sort, and so I suppose that it wasn't so bad as it seems to
me. Uncle John pretends to be in a terrible rage about it,
but I don't think he is really as angry as he makes himself
out to be. He blew me up and said that I had always
encouraged you, which of course I haven't; and when
Gerald tried to say a good word for you, he turned upon
him and said something about fellow-feeling making men
wondrous kind.

"Gerald only laughed, and said he was glad my uncle had
such a good opinion of him, and that he should have liked to
have been there to lend a hand in the fight; and then uncle
said something disagreeable, and we came away. But I feel
almost sure that Uncle John is not really so angry as he
seems; and I believe that if Gerald and I had taken the
other side, and had said that your conduct had been very
wicked, he would have defended you. It was stupid of us
not to think of it, for you know uncle always likes to dis-
agree with other people—there is nothing he hates more
than their agreeing with him. His bark is much worse
than his bite, and you must not forget how good and kind
he has been to us all.

"You know how angry he was with my marriage, and he
said I had better have drowned myself than have married a

soldier, and I had better have hung myself than have married an Irishman—specially when he had intended all along that I should marry the son of an old friend of his, a most excellent and well-conducted young man with admirable prospects. But he came round in a month or two, and the first notice of it was a letter from his lawyer saying that, in accordance with the instruction of his client, Mr. John Bale, he had drawn up and now enclosed a post-nuptial settlement, settling on me the sum of £5000 consols, and that his client wished him to say that, had I married the person he had intended for me, that sum would have been doubled.

"The idea, when I never even saw the man! And when I wrote thanking him, he made no allusion to what he had said before, but wrote that he should be glad at all times to see my husband and myself whenever we came to town, but that, as I knew, his hours were regular and the door always locked at ten o'clock—just as if Gerald was in the habit of coming in drunk in the middle of the night! Fortunately nothing puts Gerald out, and he screamed over it; and we went and stopped a week with uncle a month afterwards, and he and Gerald got on capitally together considering. Gerald said it was like a bear and a monkey in one cage; but it was really very funny. So I have no doubt he will come round with you. Do try and not vex him more than you can help, Bob. You know how much we all owe him."

This was true. Bob's father had died when he was only three years old, he being a lawyer with a good business at Plymouth; but he had made no provision for his early death, and had left his wife and two children almost penniless. Mr. Bale had at once taken charge of them, and had made his sister an allowance that enabled her to live very comfortably. She had remained in Plymouth, as she had many friends there. Her daughter Carrie, who was six years older than Bob, had four years before married Gerald O'Halloran, who was then a lieutenant in the 58th Regiment, which was in garrison there. He had a small income derived from an estate in Ireland, besides his pay, but the young couple would have been obliged to live very economically had it not been for the addition of the money settled on her by her uncle. Her mother had died a few months after the marriage, and Mr. Bale had at once placed Bob at the school at Putney, and had announced his intention of taking him in due time into his business.

The boy always spent one-half of his holidays with his uncle, the other with his sister. The former had been a trial both to him and to Mr. Bale. They saw but little of each other; for Mr. Bale, who like most business men of the time lived over his offices, went downstairs directly he had finished his breakfast, and did not come up again until his work was over, when, at five o'clock, he dined. The meal over, he sometimes went out to the houses of friends or to the halls of one or other of the city companies to which he belonged. While Bob was with him he told off one of the foremen in his business to go about with the boy. The days, therefore, passed pleasantly, as they generally went on excursions by water up or down the river, or sometimes, when it was not otherwise required, in a light cart used in the business, to Epping or Hainault Forest.

Bob was expected to be back to dinner; and, thanks to the foreman, who knew that his employer would not tolerate the smallest unpunctuality, he always succeeded in getting back in time to wash and change his clothes for dinner. The meal was a very solemn one, Mr. Bale asking occasional questions, to which Bob returned brief answers. Once or twice the boy ventured upon some lively remark, but the surprise and displeasure expressed in his uncle's face at this breach of the respectful silence then generally enforced upon the young in the presence of their elders, deterred him from often trying the experiment.

Mr. Bale was as much bored as was Bob by these meals, and the evenings that sometimes followed them. He would have been glad to have chatted more freely with his nephew, but he was as ill at ease with him as he would have been with a young monkey. There was nothing in common between them, and the few questions he asked were the result of severe cogitation. He used to glance at the boy from under his eyebrows, wonder what he was smiling to himself about, and wish that he understood him better. It did not occur to him that if he had drawn him out and encouraged him to chatter as he liked, he should get underneath the surface, and might learn something of the nature hidden there. It was in sheer desperation at finding nothing to say that he would often seize his hat and go out when he had quite made up his mind to stay indoors for the evening. Bob put up as well as he could with his meals and the dull evenings, for the sake of the pleasant time he had during the day; but he eagerly counted the hours until the time when he was to take his place on the coach for Canterbury, where the 58th were now quartered. He looked forward with absolute dread to the time when he would have to enter his uncle's office.

"What is the use of being rich, Carrie," he would say to his sister, "if one lives as uncle does? I would rather work in the fields."

"Yes, Bob; but you see when you get to be rich you needn't live in the same way at all. You could live as some traders do, in the country at Hampstead, Dulwich, or Chelsea, and ride in to business; and you can, of course, marry and enjoy life. One needn't live like a hermit all alone because one is a trader in the city."

The one consolation Bob had was that his uncle had once said that he considered it was a great advantage to any young man going into the wine trade to go over to Spain or Portugal for two or three years, to learn the whole routine of business there, to study the different growths, and know their values, and to form a connection among the growers and shippers. Bob had replied gravely that he thought this would certainly be a great advantage, and that he hoped his uncle would send him over there.

"I shall see when the time comes, Robert. It will, of course, depend much upon the relations between this country and Spain and Portugal, and also upon yourself. I could not, of course, let you go out there until I was quite assured of your steadiness of conduct. So far, although I have nothing to complain of myself, your schoolmaster's reports are by no means hopeful on that head. Still, we must hope that you will improve."

It was terrible to Bob to learn that he was to go fifteen months sooner than he had expected to his uncle's, but he was somewhat relieved when, upon his arrival at the house at Philpot Lane, his uncle, after a very grave lecture on the enormity of his conduct at school, said:

"I have been thinking, Robert, that it would be more pleasant both for you and for me that you should not at present take up your abode here. I am not accustomed to young people. It would worry me having you here, and, after your companionship with boys of your own age, you might find it somewhat dull. I have therefore arranged with Mr. Medlin, my principal clerk, for you to board with him. He has, I believe, some boys and girls of about your own age. You will, I hope, be able to make yourself comfortable there."

"Thank you, uncle," Bob said, suppressing his impulse to give a shout of satisfaction, and looking as grave as possible. "I think that would be a very nice arrangement."

"Mr. Medlin is a very trustworthy person," Mr. Bale went on. "He has been with me for upwards of twenty years, and I have the greatest confidence in him. You had better sit down here and take a book. At five o'clock come down into the counting-house, Mr. Medlin will leave at that hour."

Bob had hitherto avoided the counting-house. He had occasionally on previous visits slipped down to his friend the foreman, and had wandered through the great cellars and watched the men at work bottling, and gazed in surprise at the long tiers of casks stacked up to the roof of the cellar, and the countless bottles stowed away in the bins. Once or twice he had gone down into the counting-house with his uncle, and waited there a few minutes until the foreman was disengaged. He had noticed Mr. Medlin at work at his high desk in one corner, keeping, as it seemed to him, his eye upon two young clerks who sat on high stools at opposite sides of the desk on the other side of the office. Mr. Medlin had a little rail round the top of his desk, and curtains on rods that could be drawn round it. He was a man of six- or seven-and-thirty, with a long face smooth shaven. He always seemed absorbed in his work, and when spoken to by Mr. Bale, answered in the fewest possible words in an even, mechanical voice. It had seemed to Bob that he had been entirely oblivious to his presence, and it did not appear to him now, as he sat with a book before him waiting for the clock on the mantel to strike five, that existence at Mr. Medlin's promised to be a lively one. Still, as there were boys and girls, it must be more amusing than it would be at his uncle's, and, at any rate, the clerk would not be so formidable a personage to deal with as Mr. Bale.

At one minute to five he went down, so as to open the counting-house door as the clock struck. As he went in through the outer door his uncle came out from the inner office.

"Ah! there you are, Robert. Mr. Medlin, this is my nephew, who, as we have arranged, will take up his residence with you. I am afraid you will find him somewhat headstrong and troublesome. I have already informed you why it has been necessary to remove him from school. However, I trust that there will be no repetition of such follies, and that he will see the necessity of abandoning school-boy pranks and settling down to business."

"Yes, sir," Mr. Medlin replied, seeing that his employer expected an answer.

Bob had noticed that although the clerk's eyes were directed upon him, there appeared to be no expression of interest or curiosity in them, but that they might as well have been fixed upon a blank wall.

"Your boxes have already been sent round in the cart to Mr. Medlin's, Robert. I don't know that there is anything else to say. Mr. Medlin will, of course, put you in the way of your duties here, but if you have anything to say to me, any questions to ask, or any remarks, connected with the business or otherwise, you wish to make, I shall always be ready to listen to you if you will come into the counting-house at half-past four."

So saying Mr. Bale retired into his private room again. Mr. Medlin placed his papers inside his desk, locked it, took off his coat and hung it on a peg, put on another coat and his hat, and then turned to Bob. "Ready?"

"Quite ready."

Mr. Medlin led the way out of the counting-house, and Bob followed. Mr. Medlin walked fast, and Bob had to step out to keep up with him. The clerk appeared scarcely conscious of his presence until they were beyond the more crowded thoroughfare, then he said:

"Two miles out Hackney way. Not too far?"

"Not at all," Bob replied. "The farther the better."

"No burglars there. Wouldn't pay." And Bob thought that the shadow of a smile passed across his face.

"We can do without them," Bob said.

"Hate coming here, I suppose?"

"That I do," Bob said cordially.

Mr. Medlin nodded. "Not so bad as it looks," he said, and then walked on again in silence. Presently there was a break in the houses. They were getting beyond the con-fines of business London.

"Do you see this little garden?" Mr. Medlin asked suddenly, in a tone so unlike that in which he had before spoken that Bob quite started. The lad looked at the little patch of ground with some stunted shrubs, but could see nothing remarkable in it.

"Yes, I see it, sir," he said.

"That, Bob," Mr. Medlin went on, "for I suppose you are called Bob, marks the end of all things."

Bob opened his eyes in astonishment, and again examined the little garden.

"It marks, Bob, the delimitation between London and country, between slavery and freedom. Here every morning I leave myself behind, here every evening I recover myself, or at least a considerable portion of myself; at a further mark half a mile on, I am completely restored. I suppose you used to find just the same thing at the door of the school-room?"

"A good deal, sir," Bob said in a much brighter tone than he had used since he said good-bye to the fellows at Tulloch's.

"I am glad you feel like that. I expect you will get like that as to the city in time; but mind, lad, you must always find yourself again. You stick to that. You make a mark somewhere, leave yourself behind in the morning, and pick yourself up again when you come back. It is a bad thing for those who forget to do that. They might as well hang themselves—better. In there," and he jerked his thumb back over his shoulder, "we are all machines, you know. It isn't us, not a bit of it. There is just the flesh, the muscle, the bones, and a frozen bit of our brains, the rest of us is left behind. If, as we come out, we forget to pick it up, we lose ourselves altogether before long, and then there we are, machines to the end of our lives. You remember that, Bob. Keep it always in mind."

"It is a pity that my uncle didn't get the same advice forty years ago, Mr. Medlin."

"It is a pity my employer did not marry. It is a pity

my employer lives in that dull house in that dull lane all by himself," Mr. Medlin said angrily. "But he has not got rid of himself altogether. He is a good deal frozen up, but he thaws out sometimes. What a man he would be if he would but live out somewhere, and pick himself up regularly as I do every day! This is my second mark, Bob, this tree growing out in the road. Now, you see, we are pretty well in the country. Can you run?"

"Yes, I can run pretty well, Mr. Medlin."

"Very well, Bob. You see that tree growing out beyond that garden wall about four hundred yards on. It is four hundred and twenty, for I have measured it. Now, then, you walk on fifty yards, and then run for your life. See if I don't catch you before you are there."

Bob, wondering as he went along at the astounding change that had come over his companion, took fifty long steps, then he heard a shout of "Now!" and went off at the top of his speed. He was still a hundred yards from the mark when he heard steps coming rapidly up behind him, and then the clerk dashed past him and came in fully twenty yards ahead.

"You don't run badly," he said as Bob stopped, panting. "My Jack generally comes to meet me, and I always give him seventy yards, and only beat him by about as much as I do you. He couldn't come this afternoon. He is busy helping his mother to get things straight. I expect we shall meet him presently. Well, what are you laughing at?"

"I was just thinking how astonished my uncle would be if he were to see us."

Mr. Medlin gave a hearty laugh. "Not so much as you would think, Bob. Five years ago my employer suddenly asked me, just as we were shutting up one afternoon, if I was fond of fishing. I said that I used to be. He said, 'I am going down for a fortnight into Hampshire. I have no one to go with, suppose you come with me.' I said, 'I will.' He said, 'Coach to-morrow morning, eight o'clock, Black

Horse Yard.' I was there. As we went over London Bridge I found myself as usual, and he found himself. I explained to him that I could not help it. He said he didn't want me to help it. We had a glorious fortnight together, and we have been out every year since. He never alludes to it between times, no more do I. He is stiffer than usual for a bit, so am I. But we both know each other. You do not suppose that he would have sent you to me if he hadn't known that I have got another side to me?"

"Well, I should not have thought," Bob said, "from the way he talked when he introduced me to you, that he ever had such an idea in his mind."

"He was obliged to talk so," Mr. Medlin said laughing. "We were just machines at the time, both of us. But he talked in quite a different way when we were down fishing together three weeks ago. He said then you were rather a pickle, and that he didn't think you would do yourself any good where you were, so that he was going to bring you up to business. 'I don't want him to turn out a dull block-head,' he said, 'and so I propose that you should take charge of him, and teach him to keep himself young. I wish I had done it myself.' And so it was settled. There is no better employer in the city than your uncle. There is not a man or boy about the place who isn't well paid and contented. I used to think myself a lucky man before we went out fishing together for the first time; but six months after that he gave me a rise that pretty well took my breath away. Ah! here come the young uns."

A couple of minutes later four young people ran up. There was a boy about Bob's age, a girl a year younger, a boy and another girl in regular steps. They greeted their father with a joyous shout of welcome.

"So you have got everything done," he said. "I thought you would meet me somewhere here. This is Bob Repton, my employer's nephew and future member of the firm. Treat him with all respect and handle him gently. He is a desperate fellow though he doesn't look it. This is the young gentleman I told you of, who made a night expedition and captured four burglars."

After this introduction Bob was heartily shaken by the hand all round, and the party proceeded on their way, the two girls holding their father's hand, the boys walking behind with Bob, who was so surprised at the unexpected turn affairs had taken, that for a time he almost lost his usual readiness of speech.

CHAPTER III.

HAWTHORNE COTTAGE, Mr. Medlin's abode, was a pretty little house standing detached in a good-sized garden surrounded by a high wall.

"Here we are, mother," the clerk said, as he led the way into a cozy room where tea was laid upon the table, while a bright fire blazed in the grate. A very pleasant-faced lady, who did not look to Bob more than thirty, although she must have been four or five years older, greeted her husband affectionately.

"My dear," he said, "in the exuberance of your feelings you forget that I have brought you home a visitor. This is Mr. Robert Repton. While he is resident in the house he may be greeted as Bob. We had a race, and he runs faster than Jack; fifty yards in four hundred and twenty is the utmost I can give him."

"What nonsense you do talk, Will," his wife said, laughing. "I am sure Master Repton must think you out of your mind."

"It is a very jolly way of being out of his mind, Mrs. Medlin. You don't know how pleased I am."

"He thought I was an ogre, my dear, and that you were an ogress. Now let the banquet be served; for I am hungry, and I expect Bob is too. As for the children, they are always hungry; at least it seems so."

It was a merry meal, and Bob thought he had never enjoyed one as much except at his sister's. After tea they had music, and he found that Mr. Medlin performed admirably on the violin, his wife played the spinet, Jack the clarionet, and Sophy, the eldest girl, the piccolo.

"She is going to learn the harp presently," Mr. Medlin explained; "but for the present, when we have no visitors, and I don't count you one after this evening, she plays the piccolo. She is a little shy about it, but shyness is the failing of my family."

"It is very jolly," Bob said. "I wish I could play an instrument."

"We will see about it in time, Bob. We want a French horn, but I don't see at present where you are to practise."

"Has uncle ever been here?" Bob asked late in the evening.

"Yes; he came here the evening we got back from our fishing expedition. He wanted to see the place before he finally settled about you coming here. My wife was a little afraid of him; but there was no occasion, and everything went off capitally, except that Sophy would not produce her piccolo. I walked back with him till he came upon a hackney coach. He said as he got in, 'I have spent a most pleasant evening, Medlin. You are a very lucky fellow.' I went back to work the next morning, and we both dropt into the old groove, and nothing more was said until yesterday, when he informed me that you would come to-day."

"Oh, dear!" Bob said, as he started with the clerk at eight o'clock on the following morning. "Now I am going to begin at that wretched counting-house."

"No, you are not, Bob. You are not coming in there at present. When your uncle and I were talking—when we were fishing, you know—he said that he saw no use in your going in there at present, and thought it would be quite time for you to learn how the books are kept in another three or four years, and that till then you could go into the cellar. You will learn bottling, and packing, and blending, and something about the quality and value of wines.

You will find it much more pleasant than being shut up in a counting-house making out bills and keeping ledgers."

"A great deal," Bob said joyfully. "I sha'n't mind that at all."

Bob observed a noticeable change in his companion's demeanour when he arrived at the tree, and on passing the last garden his face assumed a stolid expression, his brisk springy walk settled down into a business pace, his words became few, and he was again a steady and mechanical clerk.

A fortnight later Bob was summoned to the counting-house.

"Mr. Bale wishes to see you," Mr. Medlin said. Bob entered, wondering what he was wanted for.

"I received a subpœna a week ago, Robert, for you to attend as a witness at Kingston to-morrow. These interruptions to business are very annoying. I did not mention it to you before, for if I had done so, you would be thinking of nothing else. This morning I have received a letter from Admiral Langton requesting me to allow you to go down by the stage this afternoon and to sleep at his house. He will take you over in the morning, and you will sleep there again to-morrow night, and come back by the early stage. I trust that you will endeavour to curb your exuberance of spirits. This is a very grave matter, and anything like levity would be altogether out of place. The letter says that the stage leaves the Bell Tavern at four o'clock."

Bob replied gravely that he would be there in time, and went off to his work again until twelve o'clock.

When he arrived at the admiral's at a quarter to six a lad in midshipman's uniform came rushing out into the hall.

"Hulloa, Bob!"

"Why, Jim!—but no, I suppose I ought to say, Mr. James Sankey to an officer of your importance. How comes it, sir, that you are so soon attired in His Majesty's uniform?"

"I will punch your head, Bob, if you go on with that nonsense. But I say, isn't it jolly? The very afternoon after you left came down a big letter with a tremendous seal, and therein I was informed that I was appointed to His Majesty's ship *Brilliant*, and was ordered to join immediately. Of course I did not know what to do, so I came up here, and who do you think I found here?—Captain Langton, the admiral's son, who is in command of the *Brilliant*. Of course it was he who had got me the appointment. He was very kind, and told me that I could not join until after this trial, so that I could go down home and stop there till to-day; and the admiral sent me straight off to be measured for my uniform. When I started next day he gave me a letter to my father, an awfully nice letter it was, saying that he intended to present me with my first outfit. I got here about an hour ago, and have been putting on my uniform to see how it fitted."

"You mean to see how you looked in it, Jim? It looks first-rate. I wish I was in one too, and was going with you instead of sticking to Philpot Lane."

"I am awfully sorry for you, Bob. It must be beastly."

"Well, it is not so bad as I expected, Jim; and uncle is turning out much better; and I don't live there, but with the head clerk out at Hackney. He is an awfully jolly sort of fellow; you never saw such a rum chap. I will tell you all about it afterwards. I suppose I ought to go in and see the admiral."

"He is out at present, Bob. He will be back at eight o'clock to supper, so you can come up and tell me all about it. Captain Langton is here too."

Captain Langton spoke very kindly to Bob when the two boys came down to supper, and told him that if at any time he changed his mind, and there was a vacancy for a midshipman on board his ship, he would give him the berth. "I should be very glad to have you with me," he said, "after the service you rendered my father and sister."

On the following morning Fullarton and Wharton came up from the school, and two carriages conveyed the witnesses over to Kingston. The prisoners, Bob heard, were notorious and desperate criminals, whom the authorities had long been anxious to lay hands on. The butler was one of the gang, and had obtained his post by means of a forged character. The trial only occupied two hours, for, taken in the act as the men were, there was no defence whatever. All four were sentenced to be hung, and the judge warmly complimented the four boys upon their conduct in the matter. The next morning Bob returned to his work in the city.

For the next three months his existence was a regular one. On arriving in the cellar he took off his jacket and put on a large apron that completely covered him, and from that time until five o'clock he worked with the other boys bottling, packing, storing the bottles away in the bins, or taking them down as required. He learned from the foreman something of the localities from which the wine came, their value and prices, but had not begun to distinguish them by taste or bouquet. Mr. Bale, the foreman said, had given strict orders that he was not to begin tasting at present. Three days before Christmas one of the clerks brought him down word that Mr. Bale wished to see him in the office at five o'clock.

During the three months he had scarcely spoken to his uncle. The latter had nodded to him whenever he came into the cellar, and had regularly said, "Well, Robert, how are you getting on?" to which he had as regularly replied, "Very well, uncle." He supposed that the present meeting was for the purpose of inviting him to dine at Philpot Lane on Christmas-day, and although he knew that he should enjoy the festivity more at Hackney, he was prepared to accept it very willingly.

"I have sent for you, Robert," Mr. Bale said, when he entered his office, "to say that your sister has written to ask me to go down to spend Christmas with her at Portsmouth. As her husband's regiment is on the point of going abroad, I have decided on accepting her invitation, and for the same reason I shall take you down with me. You will therefore have your box packed to-night. I shall send down a cart to fetch it to-morrow. You will sleep here to-morrow night, and we start the next morning."

"Thank you very much, uncle," Bob said in delight; and then seeing that nothing further was expected of him he ran off to join Mr. Medlin, who was waiting for him outside.

"What do you think, Mr. Medlin? I am going down to spend Christmas at my sister's."

"Ah!" the clerk said in a dull unsympathetic voice. "Well, mind how you walk, Mr. Robert. It does not look well coming out from a place of business as if you were rushing out of school."

Bob knew well enough that it was no use whatever trying to get his companion to take any interest in matters unconnected with business at present, so he dropped into his regular pace, and did not open his lips again until they had passed the usual boundary.

Then Mr. Medlin said briskly, "So you are going down to your sister's, Bob?"

"Yes; that will be first-rate, won't it? Of course I went down in the summer to Canterbury and hardly expected to go again this year. As I have only been three months here, I did not even think of going. It will be the last holiday I shall have for some time. You know Carrie said when she wrote to me a month ago that the regiment expected to be ordered abroad soon, and uncle said it is on the point of going now. He is coming down with me." His voice fell a little at this part of the announcement.

"He is, eh? You think you will have to be on your best behaviour, Bob?"

"Before you told me about him, Mr. Medlin, I should have thought it would quite spoil the holiday. But I do not feel it so bad now."

"He will be all right, Bob. You have never seen him outside the city yet. Still, I shouldn't be up to any tricks with him, you know, if I were you—shouldn't put cobbler's wax on his pigtail, or anything of that sort."

"As if I should think of such a thing, Mr. Medlin!"

"Well, I don't know, Bob. You have made Jack pretty nearly as wild as you are yourself. You are quite a scandal to the neighbourhood, you two. You nearly frightened those two ladies next door into fits last week by carrying in that snow man and sticking it up in their garden when you knew they were out. I thought they were both going to have fits when they rushed in to tell me there was a ghost in their garden."

"I believe you suggested it yourself, Mr. Medlin," Bob said indignantly. "Besides, it served them right for coming in to complain that we had thrown stones and broken their window when we had done nothing of the sort."

"It was rather lucky for you that they did so, Bob; for you see we were all so indignant then that they didn't venture to accuse you of the snow-man business, though I have no doubt they were convinced in their own minds that it was you. But that is only one out of twenty pranks that you and Jack have been up to."

"Jack and I and someone else, Mr. Medlin. We carry them out, but I think someone else always suggests them."

"Not suggest, Bob; far from it. If I happen to say that it would be a most reprehensible thing if anyone were to do something, somehow or other that is the very thing that Jack and you do. It was only last week I said that it would be a very objectionable trick if anyone was to tie paper bands round the neck of the clergyman's black cat who is always stealing our chickens, and to my surprise the next morning when we started for business there was quite a crowd outside his house watching the cat calmly sitting over the porch with white bands round its neck. Now, that is an example of what I mean."

"Quite so, Mr. Medlin, that is just what I meant too; and it was much better than throwing stones at him. It is a savage beast though it does look so demure, and scratched Jack's hand and mine horribly when we were tying on the bands."

At the tree the others met them, and they laughed and chatted all the way back, the young ones expressing much regret, however, that Bob was to be away at Christmas.

At the appointed time Mr. Bale and Bob took their places on the coach. The latter felt a little oppressed, for his uncle had the evening before been putting him through a sort of examination as to the value of wines, and had been exceedingly severe when Bob had not acquitted himself to his satisfaction, but had mixed up Malaga with Madeira and had stated that a French wine was grown near Cadiz.

"I expect I shall know them better when I get to taste them," Bob had urged in excuse. "When you don't know anything about the wines it is very difficult to take an interest in them. It is like learning that a town in India is on the Ganges. You don't care anything about the town, and you don't care anything about the Ganges, and you are sure to mix it up next time with some other town on some other river."

"If those are your ideas, Robert, I think you had better go to bed," Mr. Bale had said sternly; and Bob had gone to bed, and had thought what a nuisance it was that his uncle was going down to Portsmouth just when he wanted to be jolly with Carrie and her husband for the last time.

Little had been said at breakfast, and it was not until the coach was rattling along the high-road and the last house had been left behind him that Bob's spirits began to rise. There had been a thaw a few days before, and the snow had disappeared, but it was now freezing sharply again.

"The air is brisk. Do you feel it cold, Robert?" Mr. Bale said, breaking silence for the first time.

"I feel cold about the toes and about the ears and nose, uncle," Bob said, "but I am not very likely to feel cold anywhere else."

His uncle looked down at the boy, who was wedged in between him and a stout woman. "Well, no," he agreed; "you are pretty closely packed. You had better pull that muffler over your ears more. It was rather different weather when you went down to Canterbury in the summer."

"That it was," Bob replied heartily. "It was hot and dusty just, and there were a man and woman sitting opposite who kept on drinking out of a bottle every five minutes. She had a baby with her too, who screamed almost all the way. I consider I saved that baby's life."

"How was that, Robert?"

"Well, you see, uncle, they had finished their bottle by the time we got to Sevenoaks, and we all got down for dinner there, and before we sat down the man went to the bar and got it filled up again. A pint of gin filled up with water; I heard him order it. He put it in the pocket of his coat, and hung the coat up on a peg when he sat down to dinner. I was not long over my dinner, and finished before they did, and I took the bottle out and ran out to the yard and emptied it, and filled it up with water, and put it back in the pocket again without his noticing it. You should have seen what a rage he was in when he took his first sip from the bottle after we had started. He thought the man at the inn had played him a trick, and he stood up and shouted to the coachman to turn back again; but of course he wasn't going to do that, and every one laughed except the woman. I think she had had more than was good for her already, and she cried for about an hour. The next two places where we changed horses we did it so quick that the man hadn't time to get down. The third place he did, and, though the guard said we shouldn't stop a minute, he went into the public-house. The guard shouted, but he didn't come out, and off we went without him. Then he came out running, and waving his arms, but the coachman wouldn't stop; the woman got down with the child at the next place we changed horses, and I suppose they went on next day; and

if they started sober they did perhaps get to Dover all
right."

"That was a very nasty trick," the woman who was sitting
next to Bob said sharply.

Bob had noticed that she had already opened a basket on
her lap, and had partaken of liquid refreshment.

"But, you see, I saved the baby, ma'am," Bob said
humbly. "The woman was sitting at the end, and if she
had taken her share of the second bottle the chances are she
would have dropped the baby. It was a question of saving
life, you see."

Bob felt a sudden convulsion in his uncle's figure.

"It is all very well to talk in that way," the woman said
angrily. "It was just a piece of impudence, and you ought
to have been flogged for it. I have no patience with such
imperent doings. A-wasting of good liquor too."

"I don't think, madam," Mr. Bale said, "it was as much
wasted as it would have been had they swallowed it, for at
least it did no harm. I cannot see myself why, because
people get outside a coach they should consider it necessary
to turn themselves into hogs."

"I will trouble you to keep your insinuations to yourself,"
the woman said in great indignation. "You ought to be
ashamed of yourself at your age encouraging a boy in such
ways. There is them as can stand the cold and there's
them as can't, and a little good liquor helps them wonderful. I am sich myself." And she defiantly took out her
bottle from her basket and applied it to her lips.

"I was not speaking personally, my good woman," Mr.
Bale said.

"I would have you to know," the woman snapped, "that
I ain't your good woman. I wouldn't demean myself to the
like. I will ask this company if it is right as a unprotected
female should be insulted on the outside of one of His Majesty's mails?"

The other passengers, who had been struggling with their

laughter, endeavoured to pacify her with the assurance that no insult had been meant; and as Mr. Bale made no reply, she subsided into silence, grumbling occasionally to herself.

"I am a-going down," she broke out presently, "to meet my husband, and I don't mind who knows it. He is a warrant officer, he is, on board the *Latona*, as came in last week with two prizes. There ain't nothing to be ashamed of in that. And I will thank you, boy," she said, turning sharply upon Bob, "not to be a-scrouging me so. I pay for my place, I do."

"I think you ought to pay for two places," Bob said. "I am sure you have got twice as much room as I have. And if there is any scrouging, it isn't me."

"Would you have any objection, sir," the woman said majestically to a man sitting on the other side of her, "to change places with me? I ain't a-going to bear no longer with the insults of this boy and of the person as calls himself a man a-sitting next to him."

The change was effected, to Bob's great satisfaction.

"You see, Robert, what you have brought down upon me," Mr. Bale said. "This comes of your telling stories about bottles when there is a woman with one in her basket next to you."

"I really was not thinking of her when I spoke, uncle. But I am glad now, for I really could hardly breathe before. Why, uncle, I had no idea you smoked!" he added, as Mr. Bale took a cigar-case from his pocket.

"I do not smoke when I am in the city, Robert; but I see no harm in a cigar, in fact I like one, at other times. I observed a long pipe on the mantel-piece at Mr. Medlin's, and indeed I have seen that gentleman smoke when we have been out together, but I have never observed him indulging in that habit in the city."

"Oh, yes! he smokes at home," Bob said.

"I have great confidence in Mr. Medlin, Robert. You have been comfortable with him, I hope?"

"Could not be more comfortable, sir."

"An excellent man of business, Robert, and most trustworthy. A serious-minded man." Bob was looking up, and saw a little twinkle in Mr. Bale's eye. "You don't find it dull, I hope?"

"Not at all dull, sir. Mr. Medlin and his family are very musical."

"Musical, are they, Robert?" Mr. Bale said in a tone of surprise. "As far as I have seen in the counting-house I should not have taken him to be musical."

"No; I don't think you would, uncle. Just the same way as one wouldn't think it likely that you would smoke a cigar."

"Well, no, Robert. You see one must not always go by appearances."

"No, sir; that is just what Mr. Medlin says," Bob replied smiling.

"Oh, he says that, does he? I suppose he has been telling you that we go out fishing together?"

"He did mention that, sir."

"You must not always believe what Medlin says, Robert."

"No, sir? I thought you told me he was perfectly trustworthy?"

"In some points, boy; but it is notorious that from all times the narratives of fishermen must be received with a large amount of caution. The man who can be trusted with untold gold cannot be relied upon to give with even an approach to accuracy the weights of the fish he has caught, and indeed all his statements with reference to the pursuit must be taken with a large discount. You were surprised when you heard that I went fishing, Robert?"

"Not more surprised than I was when you lit your cigar, sir."

"Well, you know what Horace said, Robert. I forget what it was in the Latin, but it meant, 'He is a poor soul who never rejoices.' The bow must be relaxed, Robert, or it loses its stiffness and spring. I myself always bear this in mind, and endeavour to forget that there is such a place as the city of London, or a place of business called Philpot Lane, directly I get away from it."

"Don't you think that you could forget, too, uncle, that the name I am known by in the city is Robert, and that my name at all other times is Bob?"

"I will try to do so, if you make a point of it," Mr. Bale said gravely; "but at the same time it appears to me that Bob is a name for a short-tailed sheep-dog rather than for a boy."

"I don't mind who else is called by it, uncle. Besides, sheep-dogs are very useful animals."

"They differ from boys in one marked respect, Bob."

"What is that, uncle?"

"They always attend strictly to business, lad. They are most conscientious workers. Now this is more than can be said for boys."

"But I don't suppose the sheep-dogs do much while they are puppies, uncle."

"Humph! I think you have me there, Bob. I suppose we must make allowances for them both. Well, we shall be at Guildford in half an hour, and will stop there for dinner. I shall not be sorry to get down to stamp my feet a bit; it is very cold here, in spite of these rugs."

It was seven o'clock in the evening when the coach drew up at the George Hotel in Portsmouth. Captain O'Halloran was at the door to meet them.

"Well, Mr. Bale, you have had a coldish drive down to-day. How are you, Bob?"

"At present I am cold," Bob said. "The last two hours have been bitter."

"I have taken bed-rooms here for you, Mr. Bale. There is no barrack accommodation at present, for everyone is back from leave. Any other time we could have put you up. Now, if you will point out your baggage my man will see it taken up to your rooms, and you can come straight on to me. Carrie has got supper ready, and a big fire blazing. It is not three minutes' walk from here."

They were soon seated at table, and after the meal was over they drew round the fire.

"So you have really become a man of business, Bob," his sister said. "I was very glad to hear from your letter that you liked it better than you expected."

"But it will be a long while yet before he is a man of business, niece. It is like having a monkey in a china shop. The other day I went down to the cellar just in time to see him put down a bottle so carelessly that it tumbled over. Unfortunately there was a row of them he had just filled, and a dozen went down like nine-pins. The corks had not been put in, and half the contents were lost before they could be righted. And the wine was worth eighty shillings a dozen."

"And what can you expect of him, Mr. Bale?" Gerald O'Halloran said. "Is it a spalpeen like that you would trust with the handling of good wine? I would as soon set a cat to bottle milk."

"He is young for it yet," Mr. Bale agreed. "But when a boy amuses himself by breaking out of school at three o'clock in the morning and fighting burglars, what are you to do with him?"

"I should give him a medal for his pluck, Mr. Bale, and let him do something where he would have a chance of showing his spirit."

"And make him as wild and harum-scarum as you are yourself, O'Halloran, and then expect him to turn out a respectable merchant afterwards? I am sure I don't wish to be troubled with him till he has got rid of what you call his spirits; but what are you to do with such a pickle as this? There have been more bottles broken since he came than there ordinarily are in the course of a year; and I suspect him of corrupting my chief clerk, and am in mortal apprehension that he will be getting into some scrape at Hackney and make the place too hot for him. I never gave you credit for much brains, Carrie, but how it was you let your brother grow up like this is more than I can tell."

Although this all sounded serious, Bob did not feel at all alarmed. Carrie, however, thought that her uncle was greatly vexed, and tried to take up the cudgels in his defence.

"I am sure Bob does not mean any harm, uncle."

"I did not say that he did, niece; but if he does harm it comes to the same thing. Well, we need not talk about that now. So I hear that you are going out to the Mediterranean?"

"Yes, uncle; to Gibraltar. It is a nice station everyone says, and I am very pleased. There are so many places where there is fighting going on now that I think we are most fortunate in going there. I was so afraid the regiment might be sent either to America or India."

"And I suppose you would rather have gone where there was fighting, O'Halloran?"

"I would," the officer said promptly. "What is the use of your going into the army if you don't fight?"

"I should say, What is the use of going into the army at all?" Mr. Bale said testily. "Still, I suppose someone must go."

"I suppose so, sir," Captain O'Halloran said, laughing. "If it were not for the army and navy, I fancy you trading gentlemen would very soon find the difference. Besides, there are some of us born to it. I should never have made a figure in the city, for instance."

"I fancy not," Mr. Bale said dryly. "You will understand, O'Halloran, that I am not objecting in the slightest to your being in the army. My objection solely lies in the fact that you, being in the army, should have married my niece, and that instead of coming to keep house for me comfortably, she is going to wander about with you to the ends of the earth."

Carrie laughed. "How do you know someone else would not have snapped me up if he hadn't, uncle?"

"That is right, Carrie. You would have found her twice as difficult to manage as Bob, Mr. Bale. You would never have kept her in Philpot Lane if I hadn't taken her. There are some people can be tamed down, and there are some who can't, and Carrie is one of the latter. I should pity you from my heart if you had her on your hands, Mr. Bale. If ever I get to be a colonel, it is she will command the regiment."

"Well, it is good that one of us should have sense, Gerald," his wife said, laughing. "And now you had better put the whisky on the table, unless uncle would prefer some mulled port wine."

"Neither one nor the other, my dear. Your brother is half asleep now, and it is as much as I can do to keep my eyes open. After the cold ride we have had, the sooner we get back to the 'George' the better. We will breakfast there, Carrie. I don't know what your hours are, but when I am away on a holiday I always give myself a little extra sleep. Besides, your husband will, I suppose, have to be on duty; and I have no doubt it will suit you as well as me, for us to breakfast at the 'George.'"

"Perhaps it will be better, uncle, if you don't mind. Gerald happens to be orderly officer for the day, and will have to get his breakfast as he can, and will be busy all the morning; but I shall be ready for you by ten."

At that hour Bob appeared alone. "Uncle won't come round till one o'clock, Carrie. He said he should take a quiet stroll round by himself and look at the ships, and that no doubt we should like to have a talk together."

"Is he very cross with you, Bob?" she asked anxiously. "You know he really is kind at heart, very kind; but I am afraid he must be very hard as a master."

"Not a bit, Carrie. I expected he was going to be so, but he isn't the least like that. He is very much liked by every one there. He doesn't say much, and he certainly looks stiff and grim enough for anything; but he isn't so really, not a bit."

"Didn't he scold you dreadfully about your upsetting those twelve bottles of wine?"

"He never said a word about it, and I did not know at the time he had seen me. John, the foreman, the one who used to take me out in the holidays, would not have said anything about it; he said of course accidents did happen sometimes with the boys, and when they did he himself blew them up, and there was no occasion to mention it to Mr. Bale when it wasn't anything very serious. But, of course, I could not have that, and said that either he must tell uncle or I should. It really happened because my fingers were so cold I could not feel the bottle. Of course the cellar is not cold, but I had been outside taking in a waggon-load of bottles that had just arrived, and counting them, and my fingers got regularly numbed. So John went to the counting-house and told him about the wine being spilt. He said I wished him to tell him, and how it had happened."

"What did uncle say, Bob?"

"He said he was glad to hear that I told John to tell him, but that he knew it already, for he had just come down to the cellar when the bottles went over, and as he didn't wish to interfere with the foreman's work, had come back to the counting-house without anyone noticing he had been there. He said of course boys could not be trusted like men, and that as he had chosen to put me there he must put up with accidents. He never spoke about it to me till last night."

"Well, he seemed very vexed about it, Bob, and made a great deal of it."

"He didn't mean it, Carrie; and he knew I knew he didn't mean it. He knows I am beginning to understand him."

That evening Mr. Bale sent Bob back to the hotel by himself.

"I thought I would get him out of the way," he said when Bob had left. "I wanted to have a chat with you about him. You see, Carrie, I acted hastily in taking him away from school; but it seemed to me that he must be getting into a very bad groove to be playing such pranks as breaking out in the middle of the night. I was sorry afterwards; partly because it had upset all my plans, partly because I was not sure that I had done the best thing by him.

"I had intended that he should have stopped for another year at school; by that time he would be between sixteen and seventeen, and I thought of taking him into the office for six months or so to begin with, for him to learn a little of the routine. Then I had intended to send him out to Oporto for two years, and then to Cadiz for two years, so that he would have learnt Portuguese and Spanish well, got up all there was to learn about the different growths, and established friendly relations with my agents.

"Now, as it happens, all these plans have been upset. My agent at Oporto died a month ago, his son succeeds him; he is a young man, and not yet married. In the first place, I don't suppose he would care about being bothered with Bob; and, in the second place, boys of Bob's age are not likely to submit very quietly to the authority of a foreigner. Then, too, your brother is full of mischief and fun, and I don't suppose foreigners would understand him in the least, and he would get into all manner of scrapes.

"My correspondent at Cadiz is an elderly man without a family, and the same objection would arise in his case; and, moreover, from what I hear from him and from other Spanish sources, there is a strong feeling against England in Spain; and now that we are at war with France and have troubles in America, I think it likely enough they will join in against us. Of course my correspondent writes cautiously, but in his last letter he strongly advises me to buy largely at once, as there is no saying about the future, and several of my friends in the trade have received similar advice. I have put the boy into the cellar, for at the moment I could see nothing else to do with him. But, really, the routine he is learning is of little importance, and there is no occasion for him to learn to do these things himself. He would pick up all he wants to know there when he came back, in a very short time."

"Then what are you thinking of doing, uncle?" Carrie asked after a pause, as she saw that Mr. Bale expected her to say something.

"It seems to me that a way has opened out of the difficulty. I don't want him to go back to school again. He knows quite as much Latin as is required in an importer of wines. I want him to learn Spanish and Portuguese, and to become a gentleman and a man of the world. I have stuck to Philpot Lane all my life, but there is no reason why he should do so after me. Things are changing in the city, and many of our merchants no longer live there, but have houses in the country, and drive or ride to them. Some people shake their heads over what they call new-fangled notions. I think it is good for a man to get right away from his business when he has done work. But this is not the point. Bob is too young to begin to learn the business abroad. Two years too young at least. But there is no reason why he should not begin to learn Spanish. Now, I thought if I could find someone I could intrust him to, where his home would be bright and pleasant, he might go there for a couple of years. Naturally I should be prepared to pay a fair sum, say £200 a year, for him: for of course no one is going to be bothered with a boy without being paid for it."

Carrie listened for something further to come. Then her husband broke in: "I see what you are driving at, Mr. Bale, and Carrie and myself would be delighted to have him. Don't you see, Carrie? Your uncle means that Bob shall stop with us and learn the language there."

"'That would be delightful!" Carrie exclaimed enthusiastically. "Do you really mean that, uncle?"

"'That is really what I do mean, niece. It seems to me that that is the very best thing we could do with the young scamp."

"It would be capital!" Carrie went on. "It is what I should like above everything."

"A nicer arrangement couldn't be, Mr. Bale; it will suit us all. Bob will learn the language, he will be a companion to Carrie when I am on duty, and we will make a man of him. But he won't be able to go out with us, I am afraid. Officers' wives and families get their passage in the transports, but I am afraid it would be no use to ask for one for Bob. Besides, we sail in four days."

"No, I will arrange about his passage, and so on. Well, I am glad that my proposal suits you both. The matter has been worrying me for the last three months, and it is a comfort that it is off my mind. I will go back to my hotel now; I will send Bob round in the morning, and you can tell him about it."

CHAPTER IV.

BOB went round to the barracks at half-past nine.

"Uncle says you have a piece of news to tell me, Carrie."

"My dear Bob," Captain O'Halloran said, "your uncle is a broth of a boy. He would do credit to Galway; and if anyone says anything to the contrary I will have him out to-morrow morning."

"What has he been doing?" Bob asked. "I told you, Carrie, yesterday, he wasn't a bit like what he seemed."

"Well, Bob, you are not going to stay at his place of business any longer."

"No! Where is he going to send me—to school again? I am not sure I should like that, Carrie. I didn't want to leave, but I don't think I should like to go back to Cæsar and Euclid and all those wretched old books again."

"Well, you are not going, Bob."

"Hurry up, Carrie!" her husband said. "Don't you see that you are keeping the boy on thorns? Tell him the news without beating about the bush."

"Well, it is just this, Bob. You are to come out for two years to live with us at Gibraltar, and learn Spanish."

Bob threw his cap up to the ceiling with a shout of delight, executed a wild dance, rushed at his sister and kissed her violently, and shook hands with her husband.

"That is glorious!" he said when he had sufficiently recovered himself for speech. "I said uncle was a brick, didn't I? but I never dreamt of such a thing as this."

"He is going to pay very handsomely while you are with us, Bob; so it will be really a great help to us, besides we will like to have you with us. But you will have to work hard at Spanish, you know."

"Oh, I will work hard," Bob said confidently.

"And be very steady," Captain O'Halloran said gravely.

"Of course," Bob replied. "But who are you going to hire to teach me that?"

"You are an impudent boy, Bob," his sister said, while Captain O'Halloran burst out laughing.

"Sure, he has us both there, Carrie. I wonder your uncle did not make a proviso that we were to get one of the padrés to look after him."

"As if I would let a Spanish priest look after me!" Bob said.

"I didn't mean a Spanish priest, Bob. I meant one of the army chaplains. We always call them padrés. That would be worth thinking about, Carrie."

"Oh, I say," Bob exclaimed in alarm, "that would spoil it altogether!"

"Well, we will see how you go on, Bob. We may not find it necessary, you know; but you will find you have to mind your P's and Q's at Gib. It is a garrison place, you know, and they won't stand nonsense there. If you played any tricks they would turn you outside the lines, or send you up to one of the caverns to live with the apes."

"Are there apes?" Bob asked eagerly. "They would be awful fun, I should think. I have seen them at Exeter 'Change."

"There are apes, Bob; but if you think you are going to get near enough to put salt on their tails you are mistaken."

"But am I going out with you?" Bob asked. "Why, to-morrow is Christmas-day, and you sail two days after, don't you? and I shouldn't have time even to go up to town and down to Putney to say good-bye to the fellows. I should like to do that, and tell them that I am going abroad."

"You are not going with us, Bob, and you will have time for all that. We could not take you in the transport, and uncle will arrange for a passage for you in some ship going out. Of course he knows all about vessels trading with Spain."

"Well, we sha'n't have to say good-bye now," Bob said. "I haven't said much about it, but I have been thinking a lot about how horrid it would be, after being so jolly here, to have to say good-bye, knowing that I shouldn't see you again for years and years. Now that is all over."

A few minutes later Mr. Bale came in. He had assumed his most business-like expression, but Bob rushed up to him.

"Oh, uncle, I am so obliged to you! It is awfully kind."

"I thought the arrangement would be a suitable one," Mr. Bale began.

"No, no, uncle," Bob broke in. "You would say that if you were in Philpot Lane. Now you know you can say that you thought it would be the very jolliest thing that was ever heard of."

"I am afraid, niece, that the sentiment of respect for his elders is not strongly developed in Bob."

"I am afraid not, uncle; but, you see, if elders set an example of being double-faced to their nephews, they must expect to forfeit their respect."

"And it is a lot better being liked than being respected, isn't it, uncle?"

"Perhaps it is, Bob; but the two things may go together."

"So they do, uncle. Only I keep my respect for Philpot Lane, and it is all liking here."

They spent two more delightful days at Portsmouth: visited some of the ships of war and the transport in which the 58th was to sail, and went over the dockyard. The next morning Mr. Bale and Bob returned by the early coach to London, as the boxes and trunks and the portable furniture had to be sent off early on board. Mr. Medlin was less surprised at hearing that Bob was going to leave than the latter had expected.

"You know, Bob, I was away one day last week. Well, I didn't tell you at the time where I was, because I was ordered not to; but your uncle said to me the evening before, 'I am going to drive down by coach to Windsor, Mr. Medlin, and shall be glad if you will accompany me.' I guessed he wanted to talk about things outside the business; and so it was. We had a capital dinner down there, and then we had a long talk about you. I told him frankly that though I was very glad to have you with me, I really did not see that it was of any use your being kept at that work. He said that he thought so too, and had an idea on which he wanted my opinion. He was thinking of accepting your sister's invitation to go down and spend Christmas with her, and intended to ask her if they would take charge of you for a couple of years, in order that you might learn Spanish. Of course I said that it was the very best thing in the world for you, and would not be any loss of time, because if you could speak Spanish well you would learn the business much more quickly when you went to Cadiz, and need not be so long abroad then."

"I shall be awfully sorry to go away from you, Mr. Medlin, and from Mrs. Medlin and the others. It has been so jolly with you, and you have all been so kind."

"Yes, it has been very comfortable all round, Bob, and we shall all be sorry that you are going; but I did not expect we should have you long with us. I felt sure your uncle would see he had made a mistake in taking you into the place so young; and when he finds out he has made a mistake he says so. Some people won't; but I have known him own up he has been wrong after blowing up one of the boys in the cellar for something he hadn't done. Now, there is not one employer in a hundred who would do that. Yes, I felt sure that he would change his mind about you, and either send you back to school again or make some other arrangement; so I wasn't a bit surprised when he spoke to me last week. Still, we shall all be sorry, Bob."

Another fortnight passed without Bob hearing more, except that he was taken by Mr. Medlin to various shops, and a large outfit was ordered.

"You will bear in mind two things, Mr. Medlin," his employer had said. "In the first place, that my nephew will grow in the next two years. Therefore order some of his things to fit him now, and some to be made larger and in more manly fashion. Give instructions that when these are finished they are to be put in tin cases and soldered down, so as to be kept distinct from the others. In the second place, you will bear in mind that clothes which would be perfectly right and suitable for him here will not be at all suitable for him there. He will be living with an officer, and associating entirely with military men, and there must therefore be a certain cut and fashion about his things. Of course I don't want him to look like a young fop; but you understand what I want. There will be no boys out there, it is therefore better that he should look a little older than he is. Besides, I think that boys, and men too, to some extent, live up to their clothes. I do not think that I have anything else to say, Mr. Medlin, except that, as he will not be able to replace any clothes he may destroy out there, and as he is sure to be climbing about and destroying them in one way or another, it is necessary that an ample supply should be laid in."

Mr. Medlin had scrupulously carried out all these instructions, and Bob was almost alarmed at the extent of the wardrobe ordered.

"I know what I am doing, Mr. Robert," for they were in the city when Bob made his protest; "I am quite sure that my employer will make no objection to my ordering largely, but he would certainly be much displeased if I did not order what he conceived to be sufficient."

At the end of the fortnight Mr. Bale informed Bob that

he had arranged for his passage to Gibraltar in the brig *Antelope*. "She is bound to Valencia for fruit. She is a fast sailer and is well armed. There will be no other passengers on board; but as I am acquainted with the captain, who has several times brought over cargoes for me from Cadiz and Oporto, he has agreed to take you. I would rather you had gone in a ship sailing with a convoy, but as there was a very strong one went at the time the transports sailed there may not be another for some time. These small vessels do not wait for convoys, but trust to their speed. You can now discontinue your work here, as you will probably wish to go down to Putney to say good-bye to your friends there. The brig will sail next Monday, but you will go down on Saturday by coach to Southampton, where she now is; I shall request Mr. Medlin to see you on board. He tells me that your outfit is completed, and your trunks, with the exception of what will be required upon the voyage, will be sent off by the carrier-waggon on Wednesday. On Thursday afternoon you will leave Mr. Medlin's and stay here till you start."

The week passed quickly. Bob enjoyed his day at Putney, where, after saying good-bye to his old school-fellows, he called upon Admiral Langton, who was very glad to hear of the change in his prospects.

"It will do you good," he said, "to go out into the world and see a little of life. It was a dull thing for a lad of your age and spirits to be couped up in a counting-house in the city; but now that you are going to Gibraltar, and afterwards to Cadiz and Oporto, and will not return to settle down to business until you are one-and-twenty or so, I think that the prospect before you is a very pleasant one, and I am glad that your uncle has proved altogether different to your anticipations of him. Well, you are sure to see my son at Gibraltar sometimes. I shall write to him and tell him that you are there, and as your friend Sankey is on board the *Brilliant*, it will be pleasant for both of you. Only don't lead him into scrapes, Bob; midshipmen are up to mischief enough on their own account."

"Everyone always seems to think I am getting into scrapes, admiral. I don't think I get into more than other fellows."

"I rather think you do, Bob. Mr. Tulloch certainly intimated to me that you had a remarkable talent that way if in no other. Besides, your face tells its own story. Pickle is marked upon it as plainly as if it were printed. Now you must have supper with us at seven o'clock and catch the eight o'clock stage. You can stay until then, I hope?"

"Yes, sir. I told Mr. Medlin that I might not come back until the last stage."

At parting the admiral placed a case in Bob's hands. "There, my lad, are a brace of pistols. You won't have any use for them for some years to come, I hope; but if you stay out in Spain and Portugal they may prove useful. Those fellows are very handy with their knives, and it is always well to be armed if you go about at night among them. I should advise you to practise shooting whenever you get an opportunity. A pistol is an excellent weapon if you really know how to use it, but is of no use at all if you don't. Another thing is, you may get involved in affairs of honour. I consider duelling to be a foolish practice, but it is no use one person standing up against a crowd. It is the fashion in our days to fight duels, and therefore it is almost a necessity for a gentleman to be able to shoot straight; besides, although you might be able to avoid fighting a duel with any of your countrymen, there is no possibility of getting out of it if you become involved in a quarrel with a foreigner. In that case an Englishman who showed the white feather would be a disgrace to his country.

"Another advantage of being a good shot, I mean a really good shot, is that if you get forced into an affair, and are desirous of giving a lesson but no more to an opponent, you have it in your power to wing him; whereas if you are only a tolerably good shot, you can't pick your spot, and may, to your lasting regret, kill him. But all this is in the future, Bob. I have fought several duels myself with those very pistols, and I am happy to say I have never killed my man, and shall be glad to believe, Bob, that they will always be used in the same spirit."

Bob's last two evenings before sailing were more pleasant than he had expected. Mr. Bale seemed to forget that he was still in Philpot Lane, and chatted with him freely and confidentially. "I hope that I am doing the best for you, Bob. I know this is an experiment, and I can only trust that it will turn out well. I believe you have plenty of sound sense somewhere in your head, and that this association with a number of young military men will not have any bad effect upon you, but that, after four or five years abroad, you will not be less but rather more inclined to settle down to business. I regard you as my son, and have indeed no relations whom I care for in any way except you and your sister. I trust that when you come back you will apply yourself to business without becoming, as I have done, a slave to it.

"I might, if I chose, make you altogether independent of it; but I am sure that would not be for your good. There is nothing more unfortunate for a young man belong ing to the middle classes than to have no fixed occupation. The heir to large estates is in a different position. He has all sorts of responsibilities, he has the pursuits of a country gentleman, and the duties of a large land-owner; but the young man of our class, who does not take to business, is almost certain to go in for reckless dissipation or gambling. I have seen numbers of young men, sons of old friends of my own, who have been absolutely ruined by being left the fortunes their fathers had made, simply because they had nothing with which to occupy their minds. It is for this reason, Bob, that I chiefly wish you to succeed me in my business. It is a very good one. I doubt whether any other merchant imports such large quantities of wines as I do.

"During the next few years I shall endeavour to give up as far as I can what I may call private business, and deal entirely with the trade. I have been doing so for some time, but it is very difficult to give up customers who have dealt with me and my father before me. However, I shall curtail the business in that direction as much as I can, and you will then find it much more easily managed. Small orders require just as much trouble in their execution as large ones, and a wholesale business is in all respects more satisfactory than one in which private customers are supplied as well as the trade. I am entering into arrangements now with several travellers for the purpose of extending my dealings with the trade in the provinces, so that when it comes into your hands you will find it more compact, and at the same time more extensive than it is now.

"I am glad that I have had you here for the past four months. I have had my eye upon you more closely than you suppose, and I am pleased to see that you have worked well and willingly; far more so than I expected from you. This has much encouraged me in the hope that you will in time settle down to business here, and not be contented to lead a purposeless and idle life. The happiest man, in my opinion, is he who has something to do, and yet not too much; who can, by being free from anxieties regarding it, view his business as an occupation and a pleasure, and who is its master and not its slave. I am thinking of giving Mr. Medlin a small interest in the business. I mean to make a real effort to break a little loose from it, and I have seen enough of him to know that he will make a very valuable junior. He is a little eccentric, perhaps, a sort of exaggeration of myself, but I shall signify to him that when he comes into the firm I consider that it will be to its advantage that he should import a little of what we may call his extra-official manner into it.

"In our business, as I am well aware, although I do not possess it myself, a certain cheerfulness of disposition and a generally pleasing manner are of advantage. Buyers are apt to give larger orders than they otherwise would do under the influence of pleasant and genial relations, and Mr. Medlin can, if he chooses, make up for my deficiencies in that way. But I am taking the step rather in your interest than in my own. It will relieve you of a considerable portion of the burden of the business, and will enable you to relax somewhat when you are disposed if you have a partner in whom you can place thorough confidence. I do not wish you to mention this matter to him, I would rather open it to him myself. We will go on another fishing expedition together, and I think we can approach it then on a more pleasant footing than we could here. He has modelled himself so thoroughly upon me, that the matter could only be approached in so intensely a business-like way here that I feel sure we should not arrive at anything like such a satisfactory arrangement as we might do elsewhere."

In the course of the week Captain Lockett of the *Antelope* had called at the office, and Bob had been introduced to him by Mr. Bale. He was a hearty and energetic-looking man of some five-and-thirty years of age.

"I shall want you to go to Cadiz for me next trip, Captain Lockett," Mr. Bale said. "I am having an unusually large cargo prepared for me; enough, I fancy, to fill up your brig."

"All the better, sir," the sailor said. "There is nothing like having only one shipper, it saves time and trouble; but I should advise you to insure it for its full value, for the channel swarms with French privateers at present, and the fellows are building them bigger, and mounting heavier guns than they used to do. I am mounting a long eighteen as a swivel-gun this voyage, in addition to those I carried before. But even with that there are some of these French craft might prove very awkward customers if they fell in with us. You see, their craft are crowded with men, and generally carry at least twice as many hands as ours. It is just the same with their fishing-boats. It takes about three Frenchmen to do the work of an Englishman."

"Well, don't get caught this time, Captain Lockett. I don't want my nephew to learn to speak French instead of Spanish, for there is very little trade to be done in that quarter at present, and what there is is all carried on by what I may call irregular channels."

"I fancy there is a great deal of French wine comes into this country still, sir, in spite of the two nations being at war. It suits both governments to wink at the trade. We want French wine, and they want English money."

"That's so, Captain Lockett; but at any rate we can't send English buyers out there, and must take what they choose to send."

On Saturday morning Bob said good-bye to his uncle, with an amount of feeling and regret he would have considered impossible four months previously. Mr. Medlin accompanied him to Southampton, and the journey was a very lively one.

"Good-bye, Bob," the clerk said, as they shook hands on the deck of the *Antelope*. "You will be a man when I see you again, that is, if you don't come home for a bit before going to the people at Cadiz and Oporto. You will be coming into the firm then, and will be Mr. Robert always."

"Not if we go out fishing expeditions together," Bob said and laughed.

"Ah! well, perhaps that will be an exception. Well, good-bye, a pleasant voyage to you, and don't get into more scrapes than you can help."

"Oh, I am growing out of that, Mr. Medlin!"

"Not you, Bob. They may be different sorts of scrapes in the future, but scrapes there will be, or I am a Dutchman."

"Well, youngster, are you a good sailor?" the captain

asked, as the *Antelope* with all sail set ran down South-ampton water.

"I hope I am, captain, but I don't know yet. I have gone out sailing in boats at Plymouth several times in rough weather, and have never felt a bit ill; but I don't know how it will be in a ship like this."

"If you can sail in rough water in a boat without feeling ill, you ought to be all right here, lad. She is an easy craft as well as a fast one, and makes good weather of it in anything short of a gale. There is eight bells striking, that means eight o'clock and breakfast. You had better lay in as good a store as you can. We shall be outside the Needles, if the wind holds, by dinner-time, and you may not feel so ready for it then."

The second-mate breakfasted in the cabin with the captain and Bob, the first-mate remaining on deck. The second-mate was a young man of three or four-and-twenty, a cousin of the captain. He was a frank, pleasant-faced young sailor, and Bob felt that he should like him.

"How many days do you expect to be in getting to Gibraltar, captain?"

"About ten, if we have luck; twenty if we haven't. There is never any saying."

"How many men do you carry?"

"Twenty-eight seamen, the cook, the steward, two mates, and myself, and there are three boys. Thirty-six all told."

"I see you have eight guns besides the pivot-gun."

"Yes. We have plenty of hands for working them if we only have to fight one side at once, but we shouldn't be very strong-handed if we had to work both broadsides. There are four sixteen-pounders, four twelves, and the pivot, so that gives three men to a gun, besides officers and idlers. Three men is enough for the twelves, but it makes rather slow work with the sixteens. However, we may hope that we sha'n't have to work both broadsides at once. We carry a letter of marque, so that in case of our having the luck to fall in with a French trader we can bring her in. But that is not our business; we are peaceful traders, and don't want to show our teeth unless we are interfered with."

To Bob's great satisfaction he found that he was able to eat his dinner with unimpaired appetite, although the *Antelope* was clear of the island, and was bowing deeply to a lively sea. The first-mate, a powerful-looking man of forty, who had lost one eye, and whose face was deeply seamed by an explosion of powder in an engagement with a French privateer, came down to the meal, while the second-mate took the duty on deck. Bob found some difficulty in keeping his dish before him, for the *Antelope* was lying well over with a northerly wind abeam.

"She is travelling well, Probert," the captain said. "We have got her in capital trim this time. Last time we were too light, and could not stand up to our sails. If this wind holds we shall make a fast run of it. We will keep her well inshore until we get down to the Scillys, and then stretch across the bay. The nearer we keep to the coast the less fear there is of running against one of those French privateers."

The wind held steady, and Bob enjoyed the voyage immensely as the brig sailed along the coast. After passing Portland Bill they lost sight of land, until, after eight hours' run, a bold headland appeared on the weather-beam.

"That is the Start," the captain said. "When I get abeam of it we shall take our bearings, and then shape our course across the bay. If this wind does but hold we shall make quick work of it."

Presently the tiller was put up, and as the brig's head paid off the yards were braced square, and she ran rapidly along towards the south-west with the wind nearly dead aft. The next morning when Bob went on deck he found that the wind had dropped, and the brig was scarcely moving through the water.

"This is a change, Mr. Probert," he said to the first-mate, who was in charge of the deck.

"Yes, and not a pleasant one," the officer replied. "I don't like the look of the sky either. I have just sent down to the captain to ask him to step on deck."

Bob looked round. The sky was no longer bright and clear. There was a dull, heavy look overhead, and a smoky haze seemed to hang over the horizon all round. Bob thought it looked dull, but wondered why the mate should send for the captain. The latter came up on deck in a minute or two.

"I don't much like the look of the sky, sir," the mate said. "The wind has died suddenly out this last half-hour, and the swell has got more kick in it than it had. I fancy the wind is going round to the south-west, and that when it does come it will come hard."

"I think you are right, Mr. Probert. I glanced at the glass as I came up, and it has fallen half an inch since I was up on deck in the middle watch. I think you had better begin to take in sail at once. Call the watch up from below. It is not coming yet, but we may as well strip her at once."

The mate gave the order to the boatswain, whose shrill whistle sounded out, followed by the shout of "All hands to take in sail!" The watch below tumbled up.

"Take the royals and topgallant sails off her, Mr. Probert; double reef the topsails, and get in the courses."

Bob watched the men as they worked aloft, and marvelled at the seeming carelessness with which they hung on, where the slip of a foot or hand would mean sudden death, and wondered whether he could ever attain such steadiness of head. Three quarters of an hour's hard work and the mast was stripped, save for the reduced topsails.

"Get in two of the jibs and brail up the spanker."

This was short work. When it was done the second-mate, who had been working forward, looked to the captain for further orders. The latter had again gone below, but was now standing on the poop talking earnestly with the first-mate.

"Yes, I think you are right," Bob heard the captain say. "The glass is still falling, and very likely it will be some time before we want these light spars again. There is nothing like being snug."

"Aloft again, lads!" the mate sung out, "and send down the yards and topgallant masts."

"Now she is ready for anything," the captain said, when the men again descended to the deck.

Bob, who had been so intently watching the men that he had not looked round at the sky since they first went aloft, now had time to do so, and was startled with the change that had come over the sea and sky. There was not a breath of wind. There was a dull, oily look on the water, as it heaved in long regular waves, unbroken by the slightest ripple. Black clouds had banked up from the south-west, and extended in a heavy arch across the sky but little ahead of the brig. From its edge ragged fragments seemed to break off suddenly and fly out ahead.

"It is going to blow and no mistake," the captain said. "It is lucky that we have had plenty of time to get her into fighting trim. You had better get hold of something, lad, and clutch it tight. It will begin with a heavy squall, and like enough lay her pretty well over on her beam ends when it strikes her."

Higher and higher the threatening arch rose, till its edge stood over the mainmast. Then the captain cried: "Here it comes, lads; hold on every one!"

Looking ahead Bob saw a white line. It approached with wonderful rapidity, and with a confused rushing sound. Then in a moment he felt himself clinging as if for life to the stanchion of which he had taken hold. The wind almost wrenched him from his feet, while at the same moment a perfect deluge of water came down upon him.

He felt the brig going further and further over, till the deck beneath his feet seemed almost perpendicular. The captain and first-mate had both grasped the spokes of the wheel, and were aiding the helmsman in jamming it down. Bob had no longer a hold for his feet, and was hanging by his arms. Looking down, the sea seemed almost beneath him, but with a desperate effort he got hold of the rail with one hand and then hauled himself up under it, clinging tight to the main-shrouds. Then he saw the second-mate loose the jib halliards, while one of the sailors threw off the fore-staysail sheet, and the spanker slowly brought the brig's head up into the wind.

As it did so she righted gradually, and Bob regained his place on deck, which was still, however, lying over at a very considerable angle. The captain raised his hand and pointed to the main-topsail, and the second-mate at once made his way aft with some of the men, and laying out on the weather rigging made his way aloft. The danger seemed to Bob so frightful that he dared not look up. He could hear through the pauses of the blast the mate shout to the men above him, and in a few minutes they again descended to the deck. Even Bob could feel how much the brig was relieved when the pressure of the topsail was taken off. The lower planks of the deck rose from the water, and although this still rushed in and out through the scupper holes, and rose at times to the level of the bulwark rail, he felt that the worst was over.

One of the men was called to assist at the helm, and the captain and mate came forward to the poop rail.

"That was touch and go, youngster!" the former shouted to Bob.

"It was," Bob said. "More go than touch, I should say, for I thought she had gone altogether."

"You had better go below and change your things. Tell the steward to bring me my oilskins out of my cabin. You had better keep below until this rain has stopped."

Bob thought the advice was good, so he went down and got into dry clothes and then lay down on the cabin sofa to leeward; he could not have kept his place on the other side. The rain was still falling so heavily on deck that it sounded like a waggon passing overhead, and mingled with this noise was the howl of the wind and the swashing of the water against the ship's side. Gradually the motion of the vessel became more violent, and she quivered from bow to stern as the waves struck her. Although it was early in the afternoon it became almost as dark as night in the cabin. The steward had brought him a glass of hot grog as soon as he had changed his clothes, and in spite of the din he presently fell off to sleep. When he woke the rain had ceased; but the uproar caused by the howling of the wind, the creaking of the spars, and the dashing of the waves was as loud as before. He soon made his way up on deck and found that a tremendous sea was running. The fore-topsail had been got off the ship, the weather sheets of the jib and fore-staysail hauled across, and the vessel was making comparatively little way through the water. She was, in fact, although Bob did not know it, lying to under these sails and the spanker. It all looked so terrible to him that he kept his place but a few minutes, and was then glad to return to the sofa below. In a short time the captain came down.

"How are you getting on, lad? All in the dark, eh? Steward, light the lamp and bring me a tumbler of hot grog. Keep the water boiling: the other officers will be down directly. Well, what do you think of it, young gentleman?"

"I don't like it at all," Bob said. "I thought I should like to see a storm, but I never want to see one again."

"I am not surprised at that," the captain said with a laugh. "It is all very well to read about storms, but it is a very different thing to be caught in one."

"Is there any danger, sir?"

"There is always more or less danger in a storm, lad: but

I hope and think the worst is over. We are in for a heavy gale, but now that the brig has got through the first burst there is not much fear of her weathering it. She is a capital sea boat, well found and in good trim, and we were fortunate enough in having sufficient warning to get her snug before the first burst came. That is always the most dangerous point. When a ship has way on her she can stand almost any gale, but when she is caught by a heavy squall when she is lying becalmed you have to look out. However, she got through that without losing anything; and she is lying to now under the smallest possible canvas, and if all goes well there is no reason whatever for anxiety."

"What do you mean by 'if all goes well,' captain?"

"I mean as long as one of her masts isn't carried away, or anything of that sort. I daresay you think it rough now, but it is nothing to what it will be by to-morrow morning. I should advise you to turn in at once. You could see nothing if you went up, and would run the risk of being washed overboard or of getting a limb broken."

Bob's recollections of his position as the ship heeled over when the storm struck her were still far too vivid for him to have any desire for a repetition of it, and he accordingly took the captain's advice and turned in at once. When he got up in the morning, and with some difficulty made his way on deck, he found that, as the captain predicted, the sea was far heavier than the night before. Great ridges of water bore down upon the ship, each seeming as if it would overwhelm her, and for the first few minutes Bob expected to see the brig go head-foremost and sink under his feet. It was not till he reflected that she had lived through it for hours that he began to view the scene with composure. Although the waves were much higher than when he had left the deck on the previous afternoon, the scene was really less terrifying.

The sky was covered with masses of gray cloud, ragged and torn, hurrying along with great velocity, apparently but a short distance above the masthead. When the vessel rose on a wave, it seemed to him that the clouds in places almost touched the water, and mingled with the masses of spray caught up by the waves. The scud, borne along by the wind, struck his face with a force that caused it to smart, and for a time he was unable to face the gale even for a minute. The decks were streaming with water. The boats had disappeared from the davits, and a clean sweep seemed to have been made of everything movable. Forward was a big gap in the bulwark, and as the brig met the great waves masses of green water poured in through this and swept along the deck waist-deep. The brig was under the same sail as before, except that she now showed a closely reefed fore-topsail. When he became a little accustomed to the sea and to the motion, he watched his time and then made a rush across from the companion to the weather bulwark, and got a firm hold of one of the shrouds. The captain and the second-mate were on the poop near the wheel. The former made his way to him.

"Good-morning, Master Repton! Managed to get some sleep?"

"Yes, I have slept all night, captain. I say, isn't this tremendous? I did not think anything could be like this. It is splendid, you know, but it takes one's breath away. I don't think it is blowing quite so hard, is it?"

"Every bit as hard, but it is more regular, and you are accustomed to it."

"But I see you have got up some more sail."

"Yes, that's to steady her. You see when she gets into the trough between these great waves the lower sails are almost becalmed, and we are obliged to show something above them to keep a little way on her. We are still lying to, you see, and meet the waves head on. If her head was to fall off a few points and one of these waves took her on the beam, she would go down like a stone. Yes, the brig is doing very handsomely. She has a fine run, more like a schooner than a brig, and she meets the waves easily and rises to them as lightly as a feather; she is a beauty! If you are going to stay here, lad, you had better lash yourself, for it is not safe standing as you are."

CHAPTER V.

AS he became more accustomed to the scene around him, and found that the waves were more terrible in appearance than reality, Bob began to enjoy it, and to take in its grandeur and wildness. The bareness of the deck had struck him at once, and he now saw that four of the cannon were gone—the two forward guns on each side; and he rightly supposed that these must have been run out and tumbled overboard to lighten the ship forward, and enable her to rise more easily to the waves. An hour later the second-mate came along.

"You had better come down and get some breakfast," he said. "I am going down first."

Bob threw off the rope and followed the mate down into the cabin. Mr. Probert had just turned out. He had been lying down for two or three hours, having gone down as daylight broke.

"The captain says you had better take something before you go on deck, Mr. Probert," the second-mate said. "He will come down afterwards and turn in for an hour or two."

"No change, I suppose?"

"No. She goes over it like a duck. The seas are more regular now, and she is making good weather of it."

Bob wondered in his own mind what she would do if she was making bad weather.

The meal was an irregular one. The steward brought in three large mugs half filled with coffee, a basket of biscuits,

and a ham.   From this he cut off some slices, which he laid
on biscuits, and each of them ate their breakfast, holding
their mugs in one hand and their biscuits and ham in the
other.   As soon as they had finished, the two officers went
on deck, and directly afterwards the captain came down.
Bob chatted with him until he had finished his breakfast,
and then went up on deck again for two or three hours.
At the end of that time he felt so completely exhausted
from the force of the wind and the constant change of the
angle at which he was standing, that he was glad to go below
and lie down again. There was no regular dinner, the officers
coming below by turns and taking a biscuit and a chunk of
cold meat standing.   But at tea-time the captain and second-
mate came down together, and Bob, who had again been
up on deck for a bit, joined them in taking a large bowl of
coffee.

"I think the wind is blowing harder than ever," he said
to the captain.

"Yes, the glass has begun to rise a little : and that is
generally a sign you are getting to the worst of it.   I expect
it is a three-days' gale, and we shall have it at its worst
to-night.   I hope by this time to-morrow we shall be beginning to shake out our reefs.   You had better not go up any
more.   It will be dark in half an hour, and your bunk is the
best place for you."

Bob was not sorry to obey the order, for he felt that the
scene would be a very terrible one after dark.   The night,
however, seemed to him to be a miserably long one, for
he was only able to doze off occasionally, the motion being
so violent that he had to jam himself in his berth to
prevent himself from being thrown out.   The blows with
which the waves struck the ship were tremendous, and so
deeply did she pitch that more than once he thought that
she would never come up again, but go down head-foremost.   Once he thought he heard a crash, and there were
orders shouted on the deck above him ; but he resisted the

desire to go up and see what it was, for he knew that he could do nothing, and that in the darkness he could see but little of what was going on.

With the first gleam of daylight, however, he got out of the bunk. He had not attempted to undress, having taken off his shoes only when he lay down. Having put these on again he went up. There was but little change since the previous morning, but looking forward he saw that the bowsprit was gone, and the fore-topmast had been carried away. The sea was as high as ever, but patches of blue sky showed overhead between the clouds, and the wind was blowing somewhat less violently.

"We have been in the wars, you see, youngster," the captain said when Bob made his way aft: "but we may thank God it was no worse. We have had a pretty close squeak of it, but the worst is over now; the wind is going down, and the gale will have blown itself out by this evening. It was touch-and-go several times during the night, and if she had had a few more tons of cargo in her she would never have risen from some of those waves; but I think now we shall see Oporto safely, which was more than I expected about midnight."

For some hours Bob himself had considerable doubts as to this, so deeply did the brig bury herself in the waves: but after twelve o'clock the wind fell rapidly, and although the waves showed no signs of decreasing in height, their surface was smoother, and they seemed to strike the vessel with less force and violence.

"Now, Mr. Probert," said the captain, "do you and Joe turn in till first watch: I will take charge of the deck. After that you can set regular watches again."

The main-topsail was already on her, and at six o'clock the captain had two of its reefs shaken out, and the other reef was also loosed when Mr. Probert came up and took charge of the first watch at eight bells. That night Bob lay on the floor, for the motion was more violent than before, the vessel rolling gunwale under; for the wind no longer pressed upon her sails and kept her steady, and he would have found it impossible to maintain his position in his berth. In the morning he went up. The sun was rising in an unclouded sky; there was scarce a breath of wind; the waves came along in high glassy rollers—smooth mounds of water which extended right and left in deep valleys and high ridges. The vessel was rolling tremendously, the lower yards sometimes touching the water. Bob had to wait some time before he could make a rush across to the bulwark, and, when he did so, found it almost impossible to keep his feet. He could see that the men forward were no longer crouching for shelter under the break of the fo'castle, but were holding on by the shrouds or stays smoking their pipes, and laughing and joking together. Until the motion abated somewhat it was clearly impossible to commence the work of getting things in order.

"Did the bowsprit and mast both go together?" Bob asked Joe Lockett, who was holding on to the bulwark near him.

"Yes, the bowsprit went with the strain when she rose, having buried herself half-way up the waist, and the topmast snapped like a carrot a moment later. That was the worst dive we made. There is no doubt that getting rid of the leverage of the bowsprit right up in her eyes eased her a good bit; and as the topmast was a pretty heavy spar too, that also helped."

"How long will it be before the sea goes down?"

"If you mean goes down enough for us to get to work—a few hours; if you mean goes down altogether, it will be five or six days before this swell has quite flattened down, unless a wind springs up from some other quarter."

"I meant till the mast can be got up again."

"Well, this afternoon the captain may set the men at work; but I don't think they would do much good, and there would be a good chance of getting a limb broken. As long as this calm holds there is no hurry one way or the other."

"You mean because we couldn't be sailing even if we had everything set?"

"Well, yes, that is something, but I didn't mean that. I am not thinking so much of our sailing as of other people's; we are not very fit as we are now either for fighting or running, and I should be sorry to see a French privateer coming along; but as long as the calm continues there is no fear of that, and I expect there have been few ships out in this gale who have not got repairs to do as well as we have."

After dinner an effort was made to begin the work, but the captain soon ordered the men to desist.

"It is of no use, Mr. Probert, we shall only be getting some of the men killed; it wouldn't be possible to get half done before dark, and if the sea goes down a bit to-night they will get as much done in an hour's work in the morning as they would if they were to work from now to sunset. The carpenter might get some canvas, and nail it so as to hide those gaps in the bulwark. That will be something done. The boys can give it a coat of paint in the morning. But as for the spar, we must leave it."

All hands were at work next morning with the first gleam of daylight. The rollers were still almost as high as the day before, but there was now a slight breath of wind, which sufficed to give the vessel steerage-way. She was put head to the rollers, changing the motion from the tremendous rolling when she was lying broadside to them for a regular rise and fall that interfered but little with the work. A spare spar was fitted in the place of the bowsprit, the stump of the topmast was sent down and the topgallant mast fitted in its place, and by mid-day the light spars were all in their places again and the brig was showing a fair spread of canvas, and a casual observer would at a distance have noticed but slight change in her appearance.

"That has been a good morning's work," the captain said as they sat down to dinner. "We are a little short of head-sail, but that will make no great difference in our rate of sailing, especially if the wind is aft. We are ready to meet with another storm again if it should come, which is not likely; we are ready for anything, in fact, except a heavily-armed privateer. The loss of four of our guns has crippled us. But there was no choice about the matter; it went against my heart to see them go overboard, but it was better to lose four guns than to lose the ship. I hope we shall meet with nothing till we get through the Straits. I may be able to pick up some guns at Gibraltar; prizes are often brought in there and condemned, and there are sales of stores, so I hope to be able to get her into regular fighting trim again before I clear out from there. I should think you won't be sorry when we drop anchor off the Mole, youngster?"

"I am in no hurry now," Bob said. "I would have given a good deal, if I had had it, two days ago to have been on dry land, but now that we are all right again I don't care how long we are before we get there. It is very warm and pleasant, a wonderful change after what it was when we sailed. Whereabouts are we, captain?"

"We are a good bit farther to the east than I like," the captain replied. "We have been blown a long way into the bay; there is a great set of current in here; we have drifted nearly fifty miles in since noon yesterday. We are in 4·50 west longitude, and 45° latitude."

"I don't think that means anything to me."

"No, I suppose not," the captain laughed. "Well, it means we are nearly due west of Bordeaux, and about one hundred miles from the French coast, and a little more than eighty north of Santander, on the Spanish coast. As the wind is sou'-sou'-west we can lay our course for Cape Ortegal, and once round there we shall feel more comfortable."

"But don't you feel comfortable at present, captain?"

"Well, not altogether. We are a good deal too close

in to the French coast, and we are just on the track of any privateer that may be making for Bordeaux from the west or south, or going out in those directions. So, although I can't say I am absolutely uncomfortable, I shall be certainly glad when we are back again on the regular track of our own line of traffic for the Straits or Portugal. There are English cruisers on that line, and privateers on the look-out for the French, so that the sound of guns might bring something up to our assistance, but there is not much chance of meeting with a friendly craft here, unless it has like ourselves been blown out of its course."

A look-out had already been placed aloft. Several sails were seen in the distance in the course of the afternoon, but nothing that excited suspicion. The wind continued light and although the brig had every sail set she was not making more than five and a half knots an hour through the water. In the evening the wind dropped still more, and by nine o'clock the brig had scarcely steerage-way.

"It is enough to put a saint out of temper," the captain said, as he came down into the cabin and mixed himself a glass of grog before turning in. "If the wind had held we should have been pretty nearly off Finisterre by morning. As it is, we haven't made more than forty knots since we took the observation at noon."

Bob woke once in the night, and knew by the rippling sound of water and by the slight inclination of his berth that the breeze had sprung up again. When he woke again the sun was shining brightly, and he got up and dressed leisurely; but as he went into the cabin he heard some orders given in a sharp tone by the captain on deck, and quickened his pace up the companion to see what was going on.

"Good morning, Mr. Lockett!" he said to the second-mate, who was standing close by looking up at the sails.

"Good morning, Master Repton!" he replied, somewhat more shortly than usual.

"There is a nice breeze this morning," Bob went on. "We seem going on at a good rate."

"I wish she were going twice as fast," the mate said. "There is a gentleman over there who seems anxious to have a talk with us, and we don't want to make his acquaintance."

Bob looked round, and saw over the quarter a large lugger some three miles away.

"What vessel is that?" he asked.

"That is a French privateer, at least there is very little doubt about it. We must have passed each other in the dark, for when we first made him out he was about four miles away, sailing north-east. He apparently sighted us just as we made him out, and hauled his wind at once. He has gained about a mile on us in the last two hours. We have changed our course, and are sailing as you see northwest, so as to bring the wind on our quarter, and I don't think that fellow has come up much since. Still he does come up. We feel the loss of our sail now."

It seemed to Bob, looking up, that there was already an immense amount of canvas on the brig. Stunsails had been set on her, and she was running very fast through the water.

"We seem to have more canvas set than that vessel behind us," he said.

"Yes, we have more; but those luggers sail like witches. They are splendid boats, but they want very big crews to work them. That is the reason why you scarcely ever see them with us except as fishing craft or something of that sort. I daresay that lugger has a hundred men on board, eighty anyhow; so it is no wonder we sometimes get the worst of it. They always carry three hands to our two, and very often two to our one. Of course we are really a trader, though we do carry a letter of marque. If we were a regular privateer we should carry twice as many hands as we do."

Walking to the poop rail, Bob saw that the men were

bringing up shot and putting them in the racks by the guns. The breech covers had been taken off. The first officer was overlooking the work.

"Well, lad," Captain Lockett said, coming up to him, "you see that unlucky calm has got us into a mess after all, and unless the wind drops again we are going to have to fight for it."

"Would the wind dropping help us, sir?"

"Yes; we have more canvas on her than the lugger carries, and, if the breeze were lighter, should steal away from her. As it is, she doesn't gain much; but she does gain, and in another two or three hours she will be sending a messenger to ask us to stop."

"And what will you do, captain?"

"We shall send another messenger back to tell her to mind her own business. Then it will be a question of good shooting. If we can knock out one of her masts we shall get off; if we can't, the chances are we shall see the inside of a French prison. If she once gets alongside, it is all up with us. She can carry us by boarding, for she can throw three times our strength of men on to our deck."

There was but little talking on board the brig. When the men had finished their preparations they stood waiting by the bulwarks watching the vessel in chase of them, and occasionally speaking together in low tones.

"You may as well pipe the hands to breakfast, Mr. Probert. I have told the cook to give them an extra good meal. After that I will say a few words to them. Now, Master Repton, we may as well have our meal, we mayn't get another good one for some time; but I still hope that we shall be able to cripple that fellow. I have great faith in that long eighteen. The boatswain is an old man-o'-war's-man, and is a capital shot. I am a pretty good one myself, and as the sea is smooth, and we have a good steady platform to fire from, I have good hope we shall cripple that fellow before he comes up to us."

There was more talking than usual at breakfast. Captain Lockett and the second-mate both laughed and joked over the approaching fight. Mr. Probert was always a man of few words, and he said but little now.

"The sooner they come up the better," he growled. "I hate this running away, especially when you can't run fastest."

"The men will all do their best, I suppose, Probert? You have been down among them."

The first-mate nodded. "They don't want to see the inside of a prison, captain, no more than I do. They will stick to the guns, but I fancy they know well enough it will be no use if it comes to boarding."

"No use at all, Probert. I quite agree with you there. If she comes up alongside we must haul down the flag. It is of no use throwing away the men's lives by fighting against such odds as that. But we mustn't let her get up."

"That is it, sir. We have got to keep her off if it can be done. We shall have to haul our wind a little when we begin, so as to get that eighteen to bear on her."

"Yes, we must do that," the captain said. "Then we will get the other four guns over on the same side."

After breakfast was over the captain went up and took his station at the poop rail. The men had finished their breakfast, and on seeing that the captain was about to address them, moved aft.

"My lads," he said, "that Frenchman behind will be within range in the course of another hour. What we have got to do is to knock some of her spars out of her, and as she comes up slowly we shall have plenty of time to do it. I daresay she carries a good many more guns than we do, but I do not suppose that they are heavier metal. If she got alongside of us she would be more than our match, but I don't propose to let her get alongside; and, as I don't imagine any of you wish to see the inside of a French prison, I know you will all do your best. Let there be no hurrying in your fire. Aim at her spars, and don't throw a shot away. The chances are all in our favour, for we can fight all our guns, while she can fight only her bow-chasers; at any rate, until she bears up. She doesn't gain on us much now, and when she comes to get a few shot holes in her sails it will make the difference. I shall give ten guineas to be divided among the men at the first gun that knocks away one of her spars, and five guineas besides to the man who lays the gun."

The men gave a cheer.

"Get the guns all over to the port side. I shall haul her wind a little as soon as we are within range."

By five bells the lugger was within a mile and a half. The men were already clustered round the pivot-gun.

"Put her helm down a little," the captain ordered. "That is enough. Now, boatswain, you are well within range. Let us see what you can do. Fire when you have got her well on your sights."

A few seconds later there was a flash and a roar. All eyes were directed on the lugger, which the captain was watching through his glass. There was a shout from the men. The ball had passed through the great foresail a couple of feet from the mast.

"Very good," the captain said. "Give her a trifle more elevation next time. If you can hit the yard it will be just as good as hitting the mast. Ah! there she goes!"

Two puffs of white smoke broke out from the lugger's bow. One shot struck the water nearly abreast of the brig at a distance of ten yards, the other fell short.

"Fourteens!" the captain said. "I thought she wouldn't have eighteens so far forward."

Shot after shot was fired, but so far no serious damage had been caused by them. The brig had been hulled once, and two shots had passed through her sails. The captain went himself to the pivot-gun, and laid it carefully. Bob stood watching the lugger intently, and gave a shout as he saw the foresail run rapidly down.

"It is only the slings cut," the second-mate, who was standing by him, said. "They will have it up again in a minute. If the shot had been the least bit lower it would have smashed the yard."

The lugger came into the wind, and as she did so eight guns flashed out from her side, while almost at the same moment the four broadside guns of the *Antelope* were for the first time discharged. Bob felt horribly uncomfortable for a moment as the shot hummed overhead, cutting one of the stunsail booms in two and making five fresh holes in the sails.

"Take the men from the small guns, Joe, and get that sail in," the captain said. "Its loss is of no consequence."

In half a minute the lugger's foresail again rose, and she continued the chase, heading straight for the brig.

"He doesn't like this game of long bowls, Probert," the captain said. "He intends to come up to board instead of trusting to his guns. Now, boatswain, you try again."

The brig was now sailing somewhat across the lugger's bows, so that her broadside guns, trained as far as possible aft, could all play upon her, and a steady fire was kept up, to which she only replied by her two bow-chasers. One of the men had been knocked down and wounded by a splinter from the bulwark, but no serious damage had so far been inflicted, while the sails of the lugger were spotted with shot holes. Bob wished heartily that he had something to do, and would have been glad to have followed the first-mate's example, that officer having thrown off his coat and taken the place of the wounded man in working a gun, but he felt that he would only be in the way did he try to assist. Steadily the lugger came up until she was little more than a quarter of a mile behind them.

"Now, lads," the captain shouted, "double-shot the guns: this is your last chance. Lay your guns carefully, and all fire together when I give the word. Now, are you all ready? Fire!"

The five guns flashed out together, and the ten shot sped on their way. The splinters flew from the lugger's foremast in two places, but a cry of disappointment rose as it was seen that it was practically uninjured.

"Look, look!" the captain shouted. "Hurrah, lads!" and a cloud of white canvas fell over to leeward of the lugger. Her two masts were nearly in line, and the shot that had narrowly missed the foremast and passed through the foresail, had struck the mainmast, and brought it and its sail overboard. The crew of the brig raised a general cheer. A minute before a French prison had stared them in the face, and now they were free. The helm was instantly put up, and the brig bore straight away from her pursuer.

"What do you say, Probert? Shall we turn the tables now and give her a pounding?"

"I should like to, sir, nothing better; but it would be dangerous work. Directly she gets free of that hamper she will be under command, and will be able to bring her broadside to play on us, and if she had luck and knocked away one of our spars she would turn the tables upon us; besides, even if we made her strike her colours, we could never take her into port. Strong-handed as she is, we should not dare to send a prize crew on board."

"You are right, Probert; though it does seem a pity to let her go scot-free when we have got her almost at our mercy."

"Not quite, sir. Look there."

The lugger had managed to bring her head sufficiently up into the wind for her broadside guns to bear, and the shot came hurtling overhead. The yard of the main-topsail was cut in sunder and the peak halliard of the spanker severed, and the peak came down with a run. They could hear a faint cheer come across the water from the lugger.

"Leave the guns, lads, and repair damages!" the captain

shouted.   "Throw off the throat halliards of the spanker,
get her down, and send a hand up to reef a fresh rope through
the blocks, Mr. Probert.   Joe, take eight men with you
and stow away the topsail.   Send the broken yard down.
Carpenter, see if you have got a light spar that will do
instead of it.   If not, get two small ones and lash them so
as to make a splice of it."

In a minute the guns of the lugger spoke out again, but
although a few ropes were cut away and some more holes
made in the sails no serious damage was inflicted, and before
they were again loaded the spanker was rehoisted.   The
lugger continued to fire, but the brig was now leaving her
fast.   As soon as the sail was up the pivot-gun was again
set to work, and the lugger was hulled several times; but
seeing that her chance of disabling the brig was small, she
was again brought before the wind.   In half an hour a new
topsail-yard was ready, and that sail was again hoisted.   The
Antelope had now got three miles away from the lugger.   As
the sail sheeted home, the second-mate shouted from aloft:
"There is a sail on the weather-bow, sir!   She is close-
hauled, and sailing across our head."

"I see her," the captain replied.   "We ought to have
noticed her before, Mr. Probert.   We have all been so busy
that we haven't been keeping a look-out.   What do you
make her to be, Joe?" he said to the second-mate.

"I should say she was a French frigate, sir."

The captain ascended the shrouds with his glass, remained
there two or three minutes watching the ship, and then returned to the deck.

"She is a frigate certainly, Mr. Probert, and by the cut
of her sails I should say a Frenchman.   We are in an awkward fix.   She has got the weather-gage of us.   Do you
think if we put up helm and ran due north we should come
out ahead of her?"

The mate shook his head.

"Not if the wind freshens, sir, as I think it will.   I

should say we had best haul our wind, and make for one of the Spanish ports. We might get into Santander."

"Yes, that would be our best chance. All hands 'bout ship!"

The vessel's head was brought up into the wind and payed off on the other tack, heading south, the frigate being now on her weather-quarter. This course took the brig within a mile and a half of the lugger, which fired a few harmless shots at her. When she had passed beyond the range of her guns she shaped her course south-east by east for Santander, the frigate being now dead astern. The men were then piped to dinner.

"Is she likely to catch us, sir?" Bob asked as they sat down to table.

"I hope not, lad. I don't think she will, unless the wind freshens a good deal. If it did, she would come up hand over hand. I take it she is twelve miles off now. It is four bells, and she has only got five hours' daylight at most. However fast she is, she ought not to gain a knot and a half an hour in this breeze; and if we are five or six miles ahead when it gets dark we can change our course. There is no moon."

They were not long below.

"The lugger is under sail again, sir," the second-mate, who was on duty, said as they gained the deck.

"They haven't been long getting up a jury-mast," Captain Lockett said, "that is the best of a lug rig. Still, they have a smart crew on board." He directed his glass towards the lugger, which was some five miles away. "It is a good-sized spar," he said, "nearly as lofty as the foremast. She is carrying her mainsail with two reefs in it, and with the wind on her quarter is travelling pretty nearly as fast as she did before. Still, she can't catch us, and she knows it. Do you see, Mr. Probert, she is bearing rather more to the north. She reckons, I fancy, that after it gets dark we may try to throw the frigate out and may make up that way, in which case she would have a good chance of cutting us off. That is awkward, for the frigate will know that, and will guess that instead of wearing round that way we shall be more likely to make the other."

"That is so," the mate agreed. "Still we shall have the choice of either hauling our wind and making south by west, or of running on, and she can't tell which we shall choose."

"That is right enough. It is just a toss up. If we run and she runs she will overtake us, if we haul up close into the wind and she does the same she will overtake us again; but if we do one thing and she does the other, we are safe. Then, again, we may give her more westing after it gets dark, and bear the same course the lugger is taking. She certainly won't gain on us, and I fancy we shall gain a bit on her. Then in the morning, if the frigate is out of sight, we can make for Santander, which will be pretty nearly due south of us then; or if the lugger is left well astern we can make a leg north, and then get on our old course again for Cape Ortegal. The lugger would see it was of no use chasing us any further."

"Yes, I think that is the best plan of the three, captain. I see the frigate is coming up; I can just make out the line of her hull. She must be a fast craft."

The hours passed on slowly. Fortunately the wind did not freshen, and the vessels maintained their respective positions towards each other. The frigate was coming up, but when it began to get dusk she was still some six miles astern. The lugger was five miles away on the lee-quarter, and three miles north-east of the frigate. She was still pursuing a line that would take her four miles to the north of the brig's present position. The coast of Spain could be seen stretching along to the southward. Another hour and it was perfectly dark, and even with the night-glasses the frigate could no longer be made out.

"Starboard your helm," the captain said to the man at the wheel. "Lay her head due east."

"I fancy the wind is dying away, sir," Mr. Probert said.

"So long as it don't come a stark calm, I don't care," the captain replied. "That would be the worst thing that could happen, for we should have the frigate's boats after us; but a light breeze would suit us admirably."

Two hours later the wind had almost died out.

"We will take all the sails off her, Mr. Probert. If the frigate keeps on the course she is steering when we last saw her, she will go two miles to the south of us, and the lugger will go more than that to the north. If they hold on all night they will be hull down before morning, and we shall be to windward of them, and with the wind light the frigate would never catch us, and we know the lugger wouldn't with her reduced sails."

In a few minutes all the sails were lowered, and the brig lay motionless. For the next two hours the closest watch was kept, but nothing was seen of the pursuing vessels.

"I fancy the frigate must have altered her course more to the south," the captain said, "thinking that, as the lugger was up north, we should be likely to haul our wind in that direction. We will wait another hour, and then get up sail again and lay her head for Cape Ortegal."

When the morning broke the brig was steering west. No sign of the lugger was visible, but from the tops the upper sails of the frigate could be seen close under the land, away to the south-east.

"Just as I thought," the captain said, rubbing his hands in high glee. "She hauled her wind as soon as it was dark and stood in for the coast, thinking we should do the same. We are well out of that scrape."

Two days later the brig dropped her anchor in the Tagus, where three English ships of war were lying. A part of the cargo had to be discharged here, and the captain at once went ashore to get a spar to replace the topmast carried away in the gale.

"We may fall in with another Frenchman before we are

through the Straits," he said, "and I am not going to put to sea again like a lame duck."

Bob went ashore with the captain, and was greatly amused at the scenes in the streets of Lisbon.

"You had better keep with me, as I shall be going on board in an hour. To-morrow you can come ashore and see the sights, and spend the day. I would let Joe come with you, but he will be too busy to be spared, so you will have to shift for yourself."

Before landing in the morning the captain advised him not to go outside the town.

"You don't know the lingo, lad, and might get into trouble. You see there are always sailors going ashore from our ships of war, and they get drunk and have sprees, and I don't fancy they are favourites with the lower class here, although the shopkeepers of course are glad enough to have their money; but I don't think it would be safe for a lad like you, who can't speak a word of the language, to wander about outside the regular streets. There will be plenty for you to see without going further."

As Bob was a good deal impressed with the narrow escape he had had from capture, he was by no means inclined to run any risk of getting into a scrape and perhaps missing his passage out. He therefore strictly obeyed the captain's instructions, and when, just as he was going down to the landing-stage where the boat was to come ashore for him, he came upon a party of half-drunken sailors engaged in a vigorous fight with a number of Portuguese civil guards, he turned down a side street to avoid getting mixed up in the fray, repressing his strong impulse to join in by the side of his countrymen. On his mentioning this to the captain when he reached the brig, the latter said:

"It is lucky that you kept clear of the row. It is all nonsense talking about countrymen: it wasn't an affair of nationality at all. Nobody would think of interfering if he saw a party of drunken sailors in an English port fighting with the constables. If he did interfere, it ought to be on the side of the law. Why, then, should anyone take the part of drunken sailors in a foreign port against the guardians of the peace? To do so is an act of the grossest folly. In the first place, the chances are in favour of getting your head laid open with a sword-cut. These fellows know they don't stand a chance against Englishmen's fists, and they very soon whip out their swords. In the second place, you would have to pass the night in a crowded lock-up, where you would be half smothered before morning. And lastly, if you were lucky enough not to get a week's confinement in jail, you would have a smart fine to pay. There is plenty of fighting to be done in days like these; but people should see that they fight on the right side, and not be taking the part of every drunken scamp who gets into trouble simply because he happens to be an Englishman.

"You showed plenty of pluck, lad, when the balls were flying about the other day; and when I see your uncle I am sure he will be pleased when I tell him how well you behaved under fire; but I am equally certain he would not have been by any means gratified at hearing that I had had to leave you behind at Lisbon, either with a broken head or in prison, through getting into a street row, in which you had no possible concern, between drunken sailors and the Portuguese civil guards."

Bob saw that the captain was perfectly right, and said so frankly. "I see I should have been a fool indeed if I had got into the row, captain, and I shall remember what you say in future. Still, you know, I didn't get into it."

"No, I give you credit for that, lad: but you acknowledge your strong impulse to do so. Now, in future you had better have an impulse just the other way, and when you find yourself in the midst of a row in which you have no personal concern, let your first thought be how to get out of it as quickly as you can. I got into more than one scrape myself when I was a young fellow from the conduct of messmates who had got too much liquor in them; but it did them no good, and did me harm. So take my advice: fight your own battles, but never interfere to fight other people's unless you are absolutely convinced that they are in the right. If you are, stick by them as long as you have a leg to stand upon."

CHAPTER VI.

THE ROCK FORTRESS.

ON the third day after her arrival at Lisbon the *Antelope's* anchor was hove up, and she dropped down the river. Half an hour later a barque and another brig came out and joined her, the three captains having agreed the day before that they would sail in company, as they were all bound though the Straits. Captain Lockett had purchased two 14-pounder guns at Lisbon, and the brig, therefore, now carried three guns on each side besides her long 18-pounder. The barque carried fourteen guns, and the other brig ten; so that they felt confident of being able to beat off any French privateer they might meet on the way. One or two suspicious sails were sighted as they ran down the coast, but none of these approached within gun-shot, the three craft being evidently too strong to be meddled with. Rounding Cape St. Vincent at a short distance they steered for the mouth of the Straits. After the bold cliffs of Portugal, Bob was disappointed with the aspect of the Spanish coast.

"Ah! it is all very well," the first-mate replied when he expressed his opinion. "Give me your low sandy shores, and let those who like have what you call the fine bold rocks. Mind, I don't mean coasts with sand-banks lying off them, but a coast with a shelving beach and pretty deep water right up to it. If you get cast on a coast like that of Portugal it is certain death. Your ship will get smashed up like an egg-shell against those rocks you are talking of, and not a soul gets a chance of escape; while if you are blown on a flat coast you may get carried within a ship's length of the beach before you strike, and it is hard if you can't get a line on shore; besides, it is ten to one the ship won't break up for hours. No; you may get a landsman to admire your bold cliffs, but you won't get a sailor to agree with him."

"We seem to be going along fast, although there is not much wind."

"Yes, there is a strong current. You see, the rivers that fall into the Mediterranean ain't sufficient to make up for the loss by evaporation, and so there is always a current running in here. It is well enough for us going east, but it is not so pleasant when you want to come out. Then you have got to wait till you can get a breeze from somewhere about east to carry you out. I have been kept waiting sometimes for weeks, and it is no unusual thing to see two or three hundred ships anchored, waiting for the wind to change."

"Are there any pirates over on that side?" Bob asked, looking across at the African coast.

"Not about here. Ceuta lies over there. They are good friends with us, and Gibraltar gets most of its supplies from there. But once through the Straits we give that coast a wide berth, for the Algerine pirates are nearly as bad as ever, and would snap up any ship becalmed on their coast, or that had the bad luck to be blown ashore. I hope some day we shall send a fleet down and blow the place about their ears. It makes one's blood boil to think that there are hundreds and hundreds of Englishmen working as slaves among the Moors. There, do you see that projecting point with a fort on it, and a town lying behind? That is Tarifa. That used to be a great place in the time when the Moors were masters in Spain."

"Yes," the captain, who had just joined them, said. "'Tarif was a great Moorish commander, I have heard, and the place is named after him. Gibraltar is also named after a Moorish chief called Tarik ibn Zeyad."

Bob looked surprised. "I don't see that it is much like his name, captain."

"No, Master Repton, it doesn't sound much like it now. The old name of the place was Gebel Tarik, which means Tarik's Hill, and it is easy to see how Gebel Tarik got gradually changed into Gibraltar."

In another two hours the Straits were passed, and the Rock of Gibraltar appeared rising across a bay to the left.

"There is your destination, lad," the captain said. "It is a strong-looking place, isn't it?"

"It is, indeed, Captain," Bob said, taking the captain's glass from the top of the skylight and examining the Rock.

"You see," the captain went on, "the Rock is divided from the mainland by that low spit of sand. It is only a few hundred yards wide, and the sea goes round at the back of the Rock and along the other side of that spit, though you can't see it from here; so anything coming to attack it must advance along the spit under the fire of the guns. There, do you see that building standing upon the hill above the town? That is the old Moorish castle, and there are plenty of modern batteries scattered about near it, though you can't see them. You see, the Rock rises sheer up from the spit, and it is only on this side, close to the water's edge, that the place can be entered. The weak side of the place is along this sea face. On the other side the Rock rises right out of the water, but on this side, as you see, it slopes gradually down.

"There are batteries all along by the water's edge; but if the place were attacked by a fleet strong enough to knock those batteries to pieces, and silence their guns, a landing could be effected. At the southern end you see the rocks are bolder, and there is no landing there. That is called Europa Point, and there is a battery there, though you can't make it out from here."

The scene was a very pretty one, and Bob watched it with the greatest interest. A frigate and two men-of-war brigs

AN EAST VIEW OF GIBRALTAR.

A WEST VIEW OF GIBRALTAR.

were anchored at some little distance from the Rock, and around them were some thirty or forty merchantmen waiting for a change in the wind to enable them to sail out through the Straits. White-sailed boats were gliding about among them. At the head of the bay were villages nestled among trees, while the country behind was broken and hilly. On the opposite side of the bay was a town of considerable size, which the captain told him was Algeciras. It was, he said, a large town at the time of the Moors, very much larger and more important than Gibraltar.

The ground rose gradually behind it, and was completely covered with foliage, orchards, and orange groves. The captain said: "You see that rock rising at the end of the bay from among the trees, lad? That is called 'the Queen of Spain's Chair.' It is said that at a certain siege when the Moors were here the then Queen of Spain took her seat on that rock and declared she would never go away till Gibraltar was taken. She also took an oath never to change her linen until it surrendered. I don't know how she managed about it at last, for the place never did surrender. I suppose she got a dispensation, and was able to get into clean clothes again some day. I have heard tell that the Spaniards have a colour that is called by her name—a sort of dirty yellow; it came out at that time. Of course it would not have been etiquette for other ladies to wear white when her majesty was obliged to wear dingy garments; so they all took to having their things dyed so as to match hers, and the tint has borne her name ever since."

"It is a very nasty idea," Bob said; "and I should think she took pretty good care afterwards not to take any oaths. It is hot enough now, and I should think in summer it must be baking here."

"It is pretty hot on the Rock in summer. You know they call the natives of the place Rock scorpions. Scorpions are supposed to like heat, though I don't know whether they do. You generally find them lying under pieces of loose rock, but whether they do it for heat or to keep themselves cool I can't say. Now, Mr. Probert, you may as well take some of the sail off her. We will anchor inside those craft close to the New Mole. They may want to get her alongside to unload the government stores we have brought out, and the nearer we are in the less trouble it will be to warp her alongside to-morrow morning. Of course, if the landing-place is full they will send lighters out to us."

The sails were gradually got off the brig, and she had but little way on when her anchor was dropped a cable's length from the end of the Mole. Scarcely had she brought up when a boat shot out from the end of the pier.

"Hooray!" Bob shouted. "There are my sister and Gerald."

"I thought as much," the captain said. "We hoisted our number as soon as we came round the point, and the signal station on the top of the Rock would send down the news directly they made out our colours."

"Well, Bob, it gave me quite a turn," his sister said after the first greetings were over, "when we saw how the sails were all patched, and everyone said that the ship must have been in action. I was very anxious till I saw your head above the bulwarks."

"Yes, we have been in a storm and a fight, and we came pretty near being taken. Did you get out all right?"

"Yes, we had a very quiet voyage."

The captain then came up and was introduced. "I have a box or two for you, madam, in addition to your brother's kit. Mr. Bale sent them down a couple of days before we sailed. At one time it didn't seem likely that you would ever see their contents, for we had a very close shave of it. In the first place, we had about as bad a gale as I have met with in crossing the bay, and were blown into the bight with the loss of our bowsprit, fore-topmast and four of our guns that we had to throw overboard to lighten her. Then a French lugger, that would have been a good deal more than a match for her at any time, came up. We might have out-sailed her if we could have carried all our canvas, but with only a jury-topmast she was too fast for us. As you may see by our sails, we had a smart fight; but, by the greatest good fortune, we knocked the mainmast out of her. Then we were chased by a French frigate with the lugger to help her. However, we gave them the slip in the night, and here we are. I am afraid you won't get your brother's boxes till to-morrow; nothing can go ashore till the port officer has been on board and the usual formalities gone through. I don't know yet whether we shall discharge into lighters or go alongside, but I will have your boxes all put together in readiness for you the first thing in the morning whichever way it is."

"We shall be very glad if you will dine with us to-morrow," Captain O'Halloran said. "We dine at one o'clock, or if that would be inconvenient for you, come to supper at seven."

"I would rather do that, if you will let me," Captain Lockett replied. "I shall be pretty busy to-morrow, and you military gentlemen do give us such a lot of trouble in the way of papers, documents, and signatures, that I never like leaving the ship till I get rid of the last bale and box with the government brand on it."

"Very well, then; we shall expect you to supper."

"I shall come down first thing in the morning, captain," Bob said, "so I need not say good-bye to anyone now."

"You had better bring only what you may want with you for the night, Bob," his sister put in, as he was about to run below. "The cart will take everything else up together in the morning."

"Then I shall be ready in a minute," Bob said, running below, and it was not much more before he reappeared with a small hand-bag.

"I shall see you again to-morrow, Mr. Probert. I shall be here about our luggage;" and he took his place in the boat beside the others, who had already descended the ladder.

"And you have had a pleasant voyage, Bob?" Captain O'Halloran asked.

"Very jolly, Gerald; first-rate. Captain Lockett was as kind as could be; and the first-mate was very good too, though I did not think he would be when I first saw him; and Joe Lockett, the second-mate, is a capital fellow."

"But how was it that you did not take that French privateer, Bob? With a fellow like you on board, the capturer of a gang of burglars and all that sort of thing, I should have thought that instead of running away you would have gone straight at her, that you would have thrown yourself on her deck at the head of the boarders, would have beaten the Frenchmen below, killed their captain in single combat, and hauled down their flag."

"There is no saying what I might have done," Bob laughed, "if it had come to boarding; but as it was, I did not feel the least wish for a closer acquaintance with the privateer. It was too close to be pleasant as it was, a good deal too close. It is a pity you were not there to have set me an example."

"I am going to do that now, Bob, and I hope you will profit by it. Now, then, you jump out first and give Carrie your hand. That is it." And having settled with the boatman, Captain O'Halloran followed the others' steps.

It was a busy scene. Three ships were discharging their cargoes, and the wharf was covered with boxes and bales, piles of shot and shell, guns, and cases of ammunition. Fatigue parties of artillery and infantry men were piling the goods or stowing them in hand-carts. Goods were being slung down from the ships, and were swinging in the air or run down to the cry of "Look below!"

"Mind how you go, Carrie," Captain O'Halloran said, "or you will be getting what brains you have knocked out."

"If that is all the danger, Gerald," she laughed, "you are

safe, anyhow. Now, Bob, do look out!" she broke off, as while glancing round he tripped over a hawser and fell. "Are you hurt?"

"Never mind him, Carrie,—look out for yourself. A boy never gets hurt. Now, keep your eyes about you, Bob! You can come and look at all this any day."

At last they got to the end of the Mole, then they passed under an archway with a massive gate at which stood a sentry, then they found themselves in a sort of yard surrounded by a high wall, on the top of which two cannon were pointed down upon them. Crossing the yard, they passed through another gateway. The ground here rose sharply, and a hundred yards further back stood another battery, completely commanding the Mole and the defences through which they had passed. The ground here was comparatively level, rising gradually to the foot of the rock, which then rose steeply up. A few houses were scattered about, surrounded by gardens. Hedges of cactus lined the road. Parties of soldiers and sailors, natives with carts, and women in picturesque costumes passed along. The vegetation on the low ground was abundant, and Bob looked with delight at the semi-tropical foliage. Turning to the right they followed the road, passed under an archway in a strong wall, and were in the town itself.

"We are not living in barracks," Carrie said. "Fortunately there was no room there, and we draw lodging allowance, and have taken the upper portion of a Spanish house. It is much more pleasant. Besides, if we had had to live in quarters we should have had no room for you."

"The streets are steep," Bob said. "I can't make out how these little donkeys keep their feet on the slippery stones with those heavy loads. Oh! I say, there are two rum-looking chaps. What are they—Moors?"

"Yes. You will see lots of them here, Bob. They come across from Ceuta, and there are some of them established here as traders. What with the Moors, and Spaniards, and

Jews, and the sailors from the shipping, you can hear pretty nearly every European language spoken in one walk through the streets."

"Oh, I say, isn't it hot!" Bob exclaimed, mopping his face; "and isn't there a glare from all these white walls and houses! How much higher is it?"

"About another hundred yards, Bob. There, you see, we are getting beyond the streets now."

They had now reached a flat shoulder, and on this the houses were somewhat scattered, standing in little inclosures with hedges of cactus and geranium, and embowered in shrubs and flowers.

"This is our house," Carrie said, stopping before a rickety wooden gateway, hung upon two massive posts of masonry. "You see we have got a flight of steps outside, and we are quite cut off from the people below."

They ascended the stairs. At the top there was a sort of wide porch with a wooden roof, which was completely covered with creepers growing from two wooden tubs. Four or five plants covered with blossoms stood on the low walls, and two or three chairs showed that the little terrace was used as an open-air sitting-room.

"In another hour, when the sun gets lower, Bob, we can come and sit here. It is a lovely view, isn't it?"

"Beautiful!" Bob said, leaning on the wall. Below them lay the sea front with its gardens and bright foliage and pretty houses, with Europa Point and the sea stretching away beyond it. A little to the right were the African hills, and then, turning slightly round, the Spanish coast with Algeciras nestled in foliage, and the bay with all its shipping. The head of the bay was hidden, for the ground behind was higher than that on which the house stood.

"Come in, Bob," Captain O'Halloran said. "You had better get out of the sun. Of course it is nothing to what it will be; but it is hot now, and we are none of us acclimatized yet."

The rooms were of a fair size, but the light-coloured walls gave them a bare appearance to Bob's eyes. They were, however, comfortably furnished, matting being laid down instead of carpets.

"It is cooler and cheaper," Carrie said, seeing Bob looking at them. "This is your room, and this is the kitchen," and she opened the door into what seemed to Bob a tiny place indeed. Across one end was a mass of brickwork rather higher than an ordinary table. Several holes a few inches deep were scattered about over this. In some of these small charcoal fires were burning, and pots were placed over them. There were small openings from the front leading to these tiny fireplaces, and a Spanish girl was driving the air into one of these with a fan when they entered.

"This is my brother, Manola," Mrs. O'Halloran said.

The girl smiled and nodded, and then continued her work.

"She speaks English?" Bob said as they went out.

"She belongs to the Rock, Bob. Almost all the natives here talk a little English."

"Where do these steps lead to? I thought we were at the top of the house."

"Come up and see," Carrie said, leading the way.

Following her, Bob found himself on a flat terrace extending over the whole of the house. Several orange-trees in tubs, and many flowers and small shrubs in pots stood upon it, and three or four light cane-work lounging-chairs stood apart.

"Here is where we come when the sun is down, Bob. There is no finer view, we flatter ourselves, anywhere in Gib. Here we receive our guests in the evening. We have only begun yet, but we mean to make a perfect garden of it."

"It is splendid!" Bob said, as he walked round by the low parapet and gazed at the view in all directions; "and we can see what everyone else is doing on their roofs, and no one can look down on us except from the rock over there behind us, and there are no houses there."

"No, the batteries commanding the neutral ground lie over that crest, Bob. We are quite shut in on two sides, but we make up for it by the extent of our view on the others. We are very lucky in getting the place. A regiment went home in the transport that brought us out. Gerald knew some of the officers, and one of them had been staying here and told Gerald of it, and we took it at once. The other officers' wives are all quite jealous of me, and though some of them have very nice quarters, it is admitted that as far as the view goes this is by far the best. Besides, it is a great thing being out of the town, and it does not take Gerald more than three or four minutes longer to get down to the barracks. But now let us go downstairs. I am sure you must want something to eat, and we sha'n't have supper for another three hours."

"I dined at twelve," Bob said, "just before we rounded the point, and I could certainly hold on until supper-time. Still, I daresay I could eat something now."

"Oh, it is only a snack! it is some stewed chicken and some fruit. That won't spoil your supper, Bob?"

"You will be glad to hear, Bob," Captain O'Halloran said as the lad was eating his meal, "that I have secured the services of a Spanish professor for you. He is to begin next Monday."

Bob's face fell. "I don't see that there was need for such a hurry," he said ruefully, laying down his knife and fork. "I don't see there was need for any hurry at all. Besides, of course, I want to see the place."

"You will be able to see a good deal of it in four days, Bob, and your time won't be entirely occupied when you do begin. The days are pretty long here, everyone gets up early. He is to come at seven o'clock in the morning. You have a cup of coffee and some bread-and-butter and fruit before that. He will go at nine, then we have breakfast. Then you will have your time to yourself till dinner at half-past two. The assistant surgeon of our regiment, he is a

Dublin man, will come to you for Latin, and what I may call general knowledge, for two hours. That is all, except I suppose that you will work a bit by yourself of an evening. That is not so bad, is it?"

"What sort of man is the assistant surgeon?" Bob replied cautiously. "It all depends how much he is going to give me to do in the evening."

"I don't think he will give you anything to do in the evening, Bob. Of course the Spanish is the principal thing, and I told him that you will have to work at that."

"I don't think you need be afraid, Bob," his sister laughed. "You won't find Dr. Burke a very severe kind of instructor. Nobody but Gerald would ever have thought of choosing him."

"Sure, and didn't you agree with me, Carrie," her husband said, in an aggrieved voice, "that as we were not going to make the boy a parson, and as it was too much to expect him to learn Spanish and a score of other things at once, that we ought to get someone who would make his lessons pleasant for him, and not be worrying his soul out of his body with all sorts of useless balderdash?"

"Yes, we agreed that, Gerald; but there was a limit, and when you told me you had spoken to Teddy Burke about it, and arranged the matter with him, I thought you had gone beyond that limit altogether."

"He is just the man for Bob, Carrie. That boy will find it mighty dull here after a bit, and will want someone to cheer him up. I promised the old gentleman I would find him someone who could push Bob on in his humanities, and Teddy Burke has taken his degree at Dublin, and I will venture to say will get him on faster than a stiff starched man will do. Bob would always be playing tricks with a fellow like that and be getting into rows with him. There will be no playing tricks with Teddy Burke, for he is up to the whole thing himself."

"I should think he is, Gerald. Well, we will see how

it works, anyhow. Go on with your fowl, Bob. You will see all about it in good time."

Bob felt satisfied that the teacher his brother-in-law had chosen for him was not a very formidable personage, and his curiosity as to what he would be like was satisfied that evening. After he had finished his meal, he went for a stroll with Captain O'Halloran through the town and round the batteries at that end of the Rock, returning to supper. After the meal was over they went up to the terrace above. There was not a breath of wind, and a lamp on a table there burned without a flicker. They had scarcely taken their seats when Manola announced Dr. Burke, and a minute later an officer in uniform made his appearance on the terrace. He wore a pair of blue spectacles, and advanced in a stiff and formal manner. "I wish you a good evening, Mrs. O'Halloran. So this is our young friend! You are well, I hope, Master Repton, and are none the worse for the inconveniences I hear you have suffered on your voyage?"

Carrie, to Bob's surprise, burst into a fit of laughter.

"What is the matter, Mrs. O'Halloran?" Dr. Burke asked, looking at her with an air of mild amazement.

"I am laughing at you, Teddy Burke. How can you be so ridiculous?"

The doctor removed his spectacles.

"Now, Mrs. O'Halloran," he said, with a strong brogue. "Do you call that acting fairly by me? Didn't you talk to me yourself half an hour yesterday, and impress upon me that I ought to be grave and steady now that I was going to enter upon the duties of a pedagogue, and ain't I trying my best to act up to your instructions, and there you burst out laughing in my face and spoil it all entirely?

"Gerald said to me, 'Now mind, Teddy, it is a responsible affair. The boy is up to all sorts of divarsions, and divil a bit will he attend to ye if he finds that you are as bad, if not worse than he is himself.' 'But,' said I, 'it's Latin and such like that you are wanting me to teach him, and not manners at all, at all.' And he says, 'It is all one; it is quiet and well behaved that you have got to be, Teddy. The missis has been houlding out about the iniquity of taking a spalpeen like yourself, and it is for you to show her that she is mistaken altogether.' So I said, 'You trust me, Gerald, I will be as grave as a doctor of divinity.' So I got out these glasses, which I bought because they told me that they would be wanted here to keep out the glare of the sun, and I came here and spoke as proper as might be, and then, Mrs. O'Halloran, you burst out laughing in my face and destroy the whole effect of these spectacles and all.

"Well, we must make the best of a bad business; and we will try for a bit, anyhow. If he won't mind me Gerald must go to the chaplain as he intended to, and I pity the boy then. I would rather be had up before the colonel any day than have any matter in dispute with him."

"You are too bad, Teddy Burke," Mrs. O'Halloran said, still laughing. "It was all very well for you to try and look sensible but to put on that face was too absurd. You know you could not have kept it up for five minutes. No, I don't think it will do;" and she looked serious now. "I always thought that it was out of the question, but this bad beginning settles it."

But Bob, who had been immensely amused, now broke in. "Why not, Carrie? I am sure I should work better for Dr. Burke than I should for anyone who was very strict and stiff. One is always wanting to do something with a man like that: to play tricks with his wig or pig-tail, or something of that sort. You might let us try, anyhow; and if Dr. Burke finds that I am not attentive and don't mind him, then you can put me with somebody else."

"Sure, we shall get on first-rate, Mrs. O'Halloran. Gerald says the boy is a sensible boy, and that he has been working very well under an old uncle of yours. He knows for himself that it's no use his having a master if he isn't going to try his best to get on. When I was at school I used to get larrupped every day, and used to think to myself what a grand thing it would be to have a master just like what Dr. Burke, M.D., Dublin, is now, and I expect it is just about the same with him. We sha'n't work any the worse because maybe we will joke over it sometimes."

"Very well, then, we will try, Teddy; though I know the whole regiment will think Gerald and I have gone mad when they hear about it. But I shall keep my eye upon you both."

"The more you keep your eye upon me the better I shall be plazed, Mrs. O'Halloran, saving your husband's presence," the doctor said insinuatingly.

"Do sit down and be reasonable, Teddy. There are cigars in that box on the table."

"The tobacco here almost reconciles one to living outside Ireland," Dr. Burke said, as he lit a cigar and seated himself in one of the comfortable chairs. "Just about a quarter the price they are at home, and brandy at one shilling per bottle. It is lucky for the country that we don't get them at that price in Ireland, for it is mighty few boys they would get to enlist if they could get tobacco and spirits at such prices at home."

"I have been telling Gerald that it will be much better for him to drink claret out here," Mrs. O'Halloran said.

"And you are not far wrong," the doctor agreed; "but the native wines here are good enough for me, and you can get them at sixpence a quart. I was telling them at mess yesterday that we must not write home and tell them about it, or faith there would be such an emigration that the Rock wouldn't hold the people, not if you were to build houses all over it. Sixpence a quart, and good sound tipple! Sure, it was a mighty mistake of Providence that Ireland was not dropped down into the sea off the coast of Spain. What a country it would have been!"

"I don't know, Teddy," Captain O'Halloran said. "As the people don't kill themselves with overwork now, I doubt if they would ever work at all if they had the excuse of a hot climate for doing nothing."

"There would not have been so much need, Gerald. They needn't have bothered about the thatch when it only rains once in six months or so; while, as for clothes, it is little enough they would have needed. And the bogs would all have dried up, and they would have had crops without more trouble than just scratching the ground and sowing in the seed, and they would have grown oranges instead of praties. Oh, it would have been a great country entirely!"

The doctor's three listeners all went off into a burst of laughter at the seriousness with which he spoke.

"But you would have had trouble with your pigs," Mrs. O'Halloran said. "The Spanish pigs are wild, fierce-looking beasts, and would never be content to share the cottages."

"Ah! but we would have had Irish pigs just the same as now. Well, what do you think—" and he broke off suddenly, sitting upright, and dropping the brogue altogether—"they were saying at mess that the natives declare there are lots of Spanish troops moving down in this direction, and that a number of ships are expected with stores at Algeciras."

"Well, what of that?" Mrs. O'Halloran asked. "We are at peace with Spain. What does it matter where they move their troops or land stores?"

"That is just the thing. We are at peace with them sure enough, but that is no reason why we should be always at peace. You know how they hate seeing our flag flying over the Rock, and they may think that, now we have got our hands full with France and the American colonists, it will be the right time for them to join in the scrimmage, and see if they can't get the Rock back again."

"But they would never go to war without any ground of complaint?"

"I don't know, Mrs. O'Halloran. When one wants to pick a quarrel with a man it is always a mighty easy thing to do so. You can tread on his toe and ask him what he put it there for, or sit down on his hat and swear that he put it on the chair on purpose, or tell him that you do not like the colour of his hair, or that his nose isn't the shape that pleases you. It is the easiest thing in the world to find something to quarrel about when you have a mind for it."

"Are you quite serious, Teddy?"

"Never more serious in my life. Have you heard about it, Gerald?"

"I heard them saying something about it when we were waiting for the colonel on parade this morning, but I did not think much of it."

"Well, of course, it mayn't be true, Gerald; but the colonel and major both seemed to think that there was something in it. It seems from what they said that the governor has had letters that seemed to confirm the news that several regiments are on the march south, and that stores are being collected at Cadiz and some of the other seaports. There is nothing, as far as we know, specially said about Gibraltar; but what else can they be getting ready for, unless it is to cross the Straits and attack the Moors, and they are at peace with them at present, just as they are with us? I mean to think that they are coming here, till we are downright sure they are not. The news is so good I mean to believe that it is true as long as I can."

"For shame, Teddy!" Mrs. O'Halloran said. "You can't be so wicked as to hope that they are going to attack us?"

"And it is exactly that point of wickedness I have arrived at," the doctor said, again dropping into the brogue. "In the first place, sha'n't we need something to kape us from dying entirely of nothing to do at all, at all, in this wearisome old place? We are fresh to it, and we are not tired yet of the oranges and the wine and the cigars, and the quare people you see in the streets; but the regiments that have been here some time are just sick of their lives. Then, in the second place, how am I going to learn my profession if we are going to stop here quiet and peaceful for years? Didn't I come into the army to study gun-shot wounds, and barring duels divil a wound have I seen since I joined. It's getting rusty I am entirely; and there is the elegant case of instruments my aunt gave me that have never been opened. By the same token I will have them out and oil them in the morning."

"Don't talk in that way, Teddy. You ought to be ashamed of yourself. It seems to me that you are making a great to-do about nothing. Some soldiers have been marched somewhere in Spain, and all this talk is made up about it. They must know very well they can't take the Rock. They tried it once, and I should have thought they would not be in a hurry to try it again. I shall believe in it when I see it. You need not look so delighted, Bob. If there should be any trouble—and it seems nonsense even to think about such a thing—but if there should be any, we should put you on board the very first vessel sailing for England, and get you off our minds."

Bob laughed.

"I should go down and ship as a powder-monkey on one of the ships of war, or enlist as a drummer in one of the regiments, and then I should be beyond your authority altogether."

"I begin to think you are beyond my authority already, Bob. Gerald, I am afraid we did a very foolish thing in agreeing to have this boy out here."

"Well, we have got him on our hands now, Carrie, and it is early yet for you to find out your mistake. Well, if there should be a siege—"

"You know there is no chance of it, Gerald."

"Well, I only say if, and we are cut off from all the world, he will be a companion to you, and keep you alive while I am in the batteries."

"I won't hear such nonsense talked any more, Gerald;

and if Teddy Burke is going to bring us every bit of absurd gossip that may be picked up from the peasants, he can stay away altogether."

"Except when he comes to instruct his pupil, Mrs. O'Halloran."

"Oh, that is not likely to last long, Dr. Burke!"

"That is to be seen, Mrs. O'Halloran. It is a nice ex-ample you are setting him of want of respect for his in-structor. I warn you that before another six months have passed you will have to confess that it has been just the very best arrangement that could have been made, and will thank your stars that Dr. Edward Burke, M.D., of Dublin, hap-pened to be here ready to your hand."

CHAPTER VII.

TROUBLES AHEAD.

WHEN Dr. Burke had left, Bob broke into an Indian war-dance expressive of the deepest satisfaction, and Captain O'Halloran burst into a shout of laughter at the contrast between the boy's vehement delight, and the dissatisfaction expressed in his wife's face.

"I am not at all pleased, Gerald, not at all, and I don't see that it is any laughing matter. I never heard a more ridiculous thing. Uncle intrusted Bob to our care, believing that we should do what was best for him, and hear you go and engage the most feather-headed Irishman in the garrison (and that is saying a good deal), Gerald, to look after him."

It was so seldom that Carrie took matters seriously that her husband ceased laughing at once.

"Well, Carrie, there is no occasion to put yourself out about it. The experiment can be tried for a fortnight, and if at the end of that time you are not satisfied, we will get someone else. But I am sure it will work well."

"So am I, Carrie," Bob put in. "I believe Dr. Burke and I will get on splendidly. You see I have been with two people, both of whom looked as grave as judges, and one of them as cross as a bear, and yet they were both first-rate fellows. It seems to me that Dr. Burke is just the other way. He turns everything into fun, but I expect he will be just as sharp when he is at lessons as anyone else. At any rate, you may be sure that I will do my best with him, so as not to get put under some stiff old fellow instead of him."

"Well, we shall see, Bob. I hope that it will turn out well, I am sure."

"Of course it will turn out well, Carrie. Why, didn't your uncle at first think I was the most harum-scarum fellow he ever saw, and now he sees that I am a downright model husband, with only one fault, and that is that I let you have your own way altogether."

"It looks like it on the present occasion, Gerald," his wife laughed. "I will give it, as you say, a fortnight's trial. I only hope that you have made a better choice for Bob's Spanish master."

"I hope so, my dear; that is, if it is possible. The professor, as I call him, has been teaching his language to officers here for the last thirty years. He is a queer, wizened-up little old chap, and has got out of the way of bowing and scraping that the señors generally indulge in; but he seems a cheery little old soul, and he has got to understand English ways, and at any rate there is no fear of his leading Bob into mischief. The Spaniards don't understand that; and if you were to ruffle his dignity he would throw up teaching him at once, and I have not heard of another man on the Rock who would be likely to suit."

On the following Monday Bob began work with the professor, who called himself on his card Don Diaz Martos. He spoke English very fairly, and after the first half-hour Bob found that the lessons would be much more pleasant than he expected. The professor began by giving him a long sentence to learn by heart thoroughly, and when Bob had done this parsed each word with him, so that he perfectly understood its meaning. Then he made the lad say it after him a score of times, correcting his accent and inflection; and when he was satisfied with this, began to construct fresh sentences out of the original one, again making Bob repeat them, and form fresh ones himself. Thus by the time the first lesson was finished, the lad, to his surprise, found himself able without difficulty to frame sentences from the words he had learned. Then the professor wrote down thirty nouns and verbs in common use.

"You will learn them this evening," he said, "and in the morning we shall be able to make up a number of sentences out of them, and by the end of a week you will see we shall begin to talk to each other. After that it will be easy. Thirty fresh words every day will be ample. In a month you will know seven or eight hundred, and seven or eight hundred are enough for a man to talk with on common occasions."

"He is first-rate," Bob reported to his sister, as they sat down to dinner at one o'clock. "You will hardly believe that I can say a dozen little sentences already, and can understand him when he says them. He says in a week we shall be able to get to talk together. I wonder they don't teach Latin like that. Why, I shall know in two or three months as much Spanish, and more, ever so much more, than I do Latin, after grinding away at it for the last seven or eight years."

"Well, that is satisfactory. I only hope the other will turn out as well."

As Mrs. O'Halloran sat that evening with her work in her hand on the terrace, with her husband smoking a cigar beside her, she paused several times as she heard a burst of laughter.

"That doesn't sound like master and pupil," she said sharply, after an unusually loud laugh from below.

"More the pity, Carrie. Why on earth shouldn't a master be capable of a joke? Do you think one does not learn all the faster when the lecture is pleasant? I know I would myself. I never could see why a man should look as if he was going to an execution when he wants to instil knowledge."

"But it is not usual, Gerald," Carrie remonstrated, no other argument occurring to her.

"But that doesn't prove that it's wrong. Why a boy

should be driven worse than a donkey, and thrashed until his life is a burden to him, and he hates his lessons and hates his master, beats me entirely. Some day they will go more sensibly to work. You see, in the old times, Carrie, men used to beat their wives, and you don't think the women were any the better for it, do you?"

"Of course they weren't," Carrie said indignantly.

"But it was usual, you know, Carrie, just as you say that it is usual for masters to beat boys; as if they would do nothing without being thrashed. I can't see any difference between the two things."

"I can see a great deal of difference, sir."

"Well, what is the difference, Carrie?"

But Carrie disdained to give any answer. Still, as she sat sewing and thinking the matter over, she acknowledged to herself that she really could not see any good and efficient reason why boys should be beaten any more than women.

"But women don't do bad things like boys," she said, breaking silence at last.

"Don't they, Carrie? I am not so sure of that. I have heard of women who are always nagging their husbands, and giving them no peace of their lives; I have heard of women who think of nothing but dress, and who go about and leave their homes and children to shift for themselves; I have heard of women who spend all their time spreading scandal; I have heard of—"

"'There, that is enough," Carrie broke in hastily. "But you don't mean to say that they would be any the better for beating, Gerald?"

"I don't know, Carrie; I should think perhaps they might be sometimes. At any rate, I think that they deserve a beating quite as much as a boy does for neglecting to learn a lesson or for playing some prank, which comes just as naturally to him as mischief does to a kitten. For anything really bad I would beat a boy as long as I could stand over him. For lying, or thieving, or any mean, dirty trick

I would have no mercy on him. But that is a very different thing to keeping the cane always going at school as they do now. But here comes Bob. Well, Bob, is the doctor gone? Didn't you ask him to come up and have a cigar?"

"Yes; but he said he had got two or three cases at the hospital he must see, and would wait until this evening."

"How have you got on, Bob?"

"Splendidly. I wonder why they don't teach at school like that."

"It didn't sound much like teaching," Carrie said severely.

"I don't suppose it did, Carrie, but it was teaching for all that. Why, I have learned as much this evening as I did in a dozen lessons in school. He explains everything so that you seem to understand it at once, and he puts things sometimes in such a droll way, and brings in such funny comparisons, that you can't help laughing. But you understand it for all that, and are not likely to forget it. Don't you be afraid, Carrie, if Dr. Burke teaches me for the two years that I am going to be here, I shall know more than I should have done if I had stopped at Tulloch's till I was an old man. I used to learn lessons there and get through them somehow, but I don't think I ever understood why things were so; while Dr. Burke explains everything so that you seem to understand all about it at once. And he is pretty sharp, too. He takes a tremendous lot of pains himself, but I can see he will expect me to take a tremendous lot of pains too."

At the end of a fortnight Carrie made no allusion to the subject of a change of masters. The laughing downstairs still scandalized her a little; but she saw that Bob really enjoyed his lessons, and although she herself could not test what progress he was making, his assurances on that head satisfied her.

The *Brilliant* had sailed on a cruise the morning after Bob's arrival, but as soon as he heard that she had again dropped anchor in the bay, he took a boat and went out to her, and returned on shore with Jim Sankey, who had obtained leave for the afternoon. The two spent hours in rambling about the Rock and talking of old times at Tulloch's. Both agreed that the most fortunate thing that ever happened had been the burglary at Admiral Langton's, which had been the means of Jim's getting into the navy, and Bob's coming out to Gibraltar to his sister. Jim had lots to tell of his shipmates and his life on board the *Brilliant*. He was disposed to pity Bob spending half his day at lessons, and was astonished to find that his friend really enjoyed it, and still more that he should already have begun to pick up a little Spanish.

"You can't help it with Don Diaz," Bob said. "He makes you go over a sentence fifty times until you say it in exactly the same voice he does; I mean the same accent. He says it slow at first so that I can understand him, and then faster and faster till he speaks in his regular voice; then I have to make up another sentence in answer. It is good fun, I can tell you; and yet one feels that one is getting on very fast. I thought it would take years before I should be able to get on anyhow in Spanish: but he says if I keep on sticking to it, I shall be able to speak pretty nearly like a native in six months' time. I quite astonish Manola— that is our servant—by firing off sentences in Spanish at her. My sister Carrie says she shall take to learning with the Don too."

"Have you had any fun since you landed, Bob?"

"No; not regular fun, you know. It has been very jolly. I go down with Gerald—Carrie's husband, you know—to the barracks, and I know most of the officers of his regiment now, and I walk about a bit by myself, but I have not gone beyond the Rock yet."

"You must get a long day's leave, Bob, and we will go across the neutral ground into Spain together."

"Gerald said that as I was working so steadily I might have a holiday sometimes, if I did not ask for it too often.

I have been three weeks at it now. I am sure I can go for a day when I like, so it will depend on you."

"I sha'n't be able to come ashore for another four or five days after having got away this afternoon. Let us see, this is Wednesday, I will try to get leave for Monday."

"Have you heard, Jim, there is a talk about Spanish troops moving down here, and that they think Spain is going to join France and try to take this place?"

"No, I haven't heard a word about it," Jim said, opening his eyes. "You don't really mean it?"

"Yes, that is what the officers say. Of course they don't know for certain, but there is no doubt the country people have got the idea into their heads, and the natives on the Rock certainly believe it."

"Hooray! that would be fun," Jim said. "We have all been grumbling on board the frigate at being stuck down here without any chance of picking up prizes, or of falling in with a Frenchman except we go on a cruise. Why, you have seen twice as much fun as we have, though you only came out in a trader. Except that we chased a craft that we took for a French privateer, we haven't seen an enemy since we came out from England; and we didn't see much of her, for she sailed right away from us. While you have had no end of fighting, and a very narrow escape of being taken to a French prison."

"Too narrow to be pleasant, Jim. I don't think there would be much fun to be got out of a French prison."

"I don't know, Bob. I suppose it would be dull if you were alone, but if you and I were together I feel sure we should have some fun, and should make our escape some-how."

"Well, we might try," Bob said doubtfully. "But, you see, not many fellows do make their escape; and as sailors are up to climbing ropes, and getting over walls, and all that sort of thing, I should think they would do it if it could be managed anyhow."

Upon the following day, when Bob was in the ante-room of the mess with Captain O'Halloran, looking at some papers that had been brought by a ship that had come in that morning, the colonel entered accompanied by Captain Langton. The officers all stood up, and the colonel introduced them to Captain Langton, who was, he told them, going to dine at the mess that evening. After he had done this Captain Langton's eye fell upon Bob, who smiled and made a bow.

"I ought to know you," the captain said. "I have certainly seen your face somewhere."

"It was at Admiral Langton's, sir. My name is Bob Repton."

"Of course it is," the officer said, shaking him cordially by the hand. "But what on earth are you doing here? I thought you had settled down somewhere in the city; with an uncle, wasn't it?"

"Yes, sir; but I have come out here to learn Spanish."

"Have you seen your friend Sankey?"

"Yes, sir. I went on board the frigate to see him yesterday afternoon, and he got leave to come ashore with me for two or three hours."

"He ought to have let me know that you were here," the captain said. "Who are you staying with, lad?"

"With Captain O'Halloran, sir, my brother-in-law," Bob said, indicating Gerald, who had already been introduced to Captain Langton.

"I daresay you are surprised at my knowing this young gentleman," he said, turning to Colonel Cochrane, "but he did my father the admiral a great service. He and three other lads, under his leadership, captured four of the most notorious burglars in London when they were engaged in robbing my father's house. It was a most gallant affair, I can assure you, and the four burglars swung for it a couple of months later. I have one of the lads as a midshipman on board my ship, and I offered a berth to Repton, but very wisely he decided to remain on shore, where his prospects were good."

"Why, O'Halloran, you never told me anything about this," the colonel said.

"No, sir. Bob asked me not to say anything about it. I think he is rather shy of having it talked about, and it is the only thing of which he is shy as far as I have discovered."

"Well, we must hear the story," the colonel said. "I hope you will dine at mess this evening, and bring him with you. He shall tell us the story over our wine. I am curious to know how four boys can have made such a capture."

After mess that evening Bob told the story as modestly as he could.

"There, colonel," Captain Langton said when he had finished. "You see that if these stories I hear are true, and the Spaniards are going to make a dash for Gibraltar, you have got a valuable addition to your garrison."

"Yes, indeed," the colonel laughed. "We will make a volunteer of him. He has had some little experience of standing fire, for O'Halloran told me that the brig he came out in had fought a sharp action with a privateer of superior force, and indeed when she came in here her sails were riddled with shot holes."

"Better and better," Captain Langton laughed. "Well, Repton, remember whenever you are disposed for a cruise I shall be glad to take you as passenger. Sankey will make you at home in the midshipmen's berth. If the Spaniards declare war with us we shall have stirring times at sea as well as on shore, and though you won't get any share in any prize-money we may win while you are on board, you will have part of the honour; and, you see, making captures is quite in your line."

The next day Captain O'Halloran and Bob dined on board the *Brilliant*. Captain Langton introduced the lad to his officers, telling them that he wished him to be considered as being free on board the ship whether he himself happened to be on board or not when he came off. "But you must keep an eye on him, Mr. Hardy, while he is on board," he said to the first lieutenant. "Mr. Sankey," and he nodded at Jim, who was among those invited, "is rather a pickle, but from what I hear Repton is worse. So you will have to keep a sharp eye upon them when they are together, and if they are up to mischief do not hesitate to masthead both of them. A passenger on board one of His Majesty's ships is amenable to discipline like anyone else."

"I will see to it, sir," the lieutenant said laughing. "Sankey knows the way up already."

"Yes. I think I observed him taking a view of the shore from that elevation this morning."

Jim coloured hotly.

"Yes, sir," the lieutenant said. "The doctor made a complaint that his leeches had got out of their bottle and were all over the ship, and I fancy one of them got into his bed somehow. He had given Mr. Sankey a dose of physic in the morning, and remembered afterwards that while he was making up the medicine Sankey had been doing something in the corner where his bottles were. When I questioned Sankey about it he admitted that he had observed the leeches, but declined to criminate himself farther. So I sent him aloft for an hour or two to meditate upon the enormity of wasting His Majesty's medical stores."

"I hope, Captain O'Halloran," the captain said, "that you have less trouble with your brother-in-law than we have with his friend."

"Bob hasn't had much chance yet," Captain O'Halloran said laughing. "He is new to the place as yet, and, besides, he is really working hard and hasn't much time for mischief; but I don't flatter myself that it is going to last."

"Well, Mr. Sankey, you may as well take your friend down and introduce him formally to your messmates," the captain said; and Jim, who had been feeling extremely uncomfortable since the talk had turned on the subject of mastheading, rose and made his escape with Bob, leaving the elders to their wine.

The proposed excursion to the Spanish lines did not come off, as the *Brilliant* put to sea again on the day fixed for it. She was away a fortnight, and on her return the captain issued orders that none of the junior officers when allowed leave were to go beyond the lines, for the rumours of approaching troubles had become stronger, and as the peasantry were assuming a somewhat hostile attitude, any act of imprudence might result in trouble. Jim often had leave to come ashore in the afternoon, and as this was the time that Bob had to himself, they wandered together all over the Rock, climbed up the flagstaff, and made themselves acquainted with all the paths and precipices. Their favourite place was the back of the Rock, where the cliff in many places fell sheer away for hundreds of feet down into the sea. They had many discussions as to the possibility of climbing up on that side, though both agreed that it would be impossible to climb down.

"I should like to try awfully," Bob said one day early in June, as they were leaning on a low wall looking down to the sea.

"But it would never do to risk getting into a scrape here, it wouldn't indeed, Bob. They don't understand jokes at Gib. One would be had up before the big wigs and court-martialled, and goodness knows what. Of course it is jolly being ashore, but one never gets rid of the idea that one is a sort of prisoner. There are the regulations about what time you may come off and what time the gate is closed, and if you are a minute late there you are until next morning. Whichever way one turns there are sentries, and you can't pass one way and you can't go back another way, and there are some of the batteries you can't go into without a special order. It never would do to try any nonsense here. Look at that sentry up there. I expect he has got his eye on us now, and if he saw us trying to get down he would take us for deserters and fire. There wouldn't be any fear of his hitting us, but the nearest guard would turn out, and we should be arrested and reported, and all sorts of things. It wouldn't matter so much for you, but I should get my leave stopped altogether, and should get into the captain's black books. No, no. I don't mind running a little risk of breaking my neck, but not here on the Rock. I would rather get into ten scrapes on board the frigate than one here."

"Yes, I suppose it can't be done," Bob agreed; "but I should have liked to swing myself down to one of those ledges. There would be such a scolding and shrieking among the birds."

"Yes, that would be fun; but as it might bring on the same sort of row among the authorities, I would rather leave it alone. I expect we shall soon get leave to go across the lines again. There doesn't seem to be any chance of a row with the dons; I expect it was all moonshine from the first. Why, they say Spain is trying to patch up the quarrel between us and France. She would not be doing that if she had any idea of going to war with us herself."

"I don't know, Jim. Gerald and Dr. Burke were talking it over last night, and Gerald said just what you do; and then Dr. Burke said, 'You are wrong entirely, Gerald. That is just the dangerous part of the affair. Why should Spain want to put a stop to the war between us and the frog-eaters? Sure, wouldn't she look on with the greatest pleasure in life while we cut each other's throats and blew up each other's ships, and put all the trade of the Mediterranean into her hands? Why, it is the very thing that suits her best.'

"'Then, what is she after putting herself forward for, Teddy?' Gerald said.

"'Because she wants to have a finger in the pie, Gerald. It wouldn't be dacent for her to say to England, It is in a hole you are at present wid your hands full, and so I am going to take the opportunity of pitching into you. So she begins by stipping forward as the dear friend of both parties, and she says, What are you breaking each other's heads for, boys? Make up your quarrel, and shake hands. Then she sets to and proposes terms, which she knows mighty well we shall never agree to—for the letters we had the other day said that it was reported that the proposals of Spain were altogether unacceptable—and then when we refuse she turns round and says you have put yourself in the wrong entirely. I gave you a chance of putting yourself in the right, and it is a grave insult to me for you to refuse to accept my proposals. So there is nothing for me to do now but just to join with France and give you the bating you desarve.'

"'That is Teddy Burke's idea, Jim; and though he is so full of fun he is awfully clever, and has got no end of sense, and I'd take his opinion about anything. You see how he has got me on in these four months in Latin and things. Why, I have learnt more with him than I did all the time I was at Tulloch's. He says most likely the negotiations will be finished one way or the other by the middle of this month, and he offered to bet Gerald a gallon of whisky that there would be a declaration of war by Spain before the end of the month."

"Did he?" Jim said in great delight. "Well, I do hope he is right. We are all getting precious tired, I can assure you, of broiling down there in the harbour. The decks are hot enough to cook a steak upon. When we started to-day we didn't see a creature in the streets. Everyone had gone off to bed for two or three hours, and the shops were all closed as if it had been two o'clock at night instead of two o'clock in the day. Even the dogs were all asleep in the shade. I think we shall have to give up our walks till August is over. It is getting too hot for anything in the afternoon."

"Well, it is hot," Bob agreed. "Carrie said I was mad

coming out in it to-day, and should get sunstroke and all sort of things; and Gerald said at dinner that if it were not against the regulations he would like to shave his head instead of plastering it all over with powder."

"I call it disgusting," Jim said heartily. "That is the one thing I envy you in. I shouldn't like to be grinding away at books as you do, and you don't have half the fun I do, on shore here without any fellows to have larks with, but not having to powder your hair almost makes up for it. I don't mind it in winter, because it makes a sort of thatch for the head, but it is awful now. I feel just as if I had got a pudding crust all over my head."

"Well, that is appropriate, Jim," Bob laughed; and then Jim chased him all along the path till they got within sight of a sentry in a battery; and then his dignity as midshipman compelled them to desist, and the pair walked gravely down into the town.

That evening, after lessons were over, Dr. Burke as usual went up on to the terrace to smoke a cigar with Captain O'Halloran.

"It is a pity altogether, Mrs. O'Halloran," he said as he stood by her side looking over the moonlit bay, with the dark hulls of the ships and the faint lights across at Algeciras, "that we can't do away with the day and have nothing but night of it for four or five months in the year. I used to think it must be mighty unpleasant for the Esquimaux, but faith I envy them now. Fancy five or six months without catching a glimpse of that burning old sun!"

"I don't suppose they think so," Mrs. O'Halloran laughed: "but it would be pleasant here. The heat has been dreadful all day, and it is really only after sunset that one begins to enjoy life."

"You may well say that, Mrs. O'Halloran. Faith, I wish they would let me take off my coat and do my work in my shirt-sleeves down at the hospital. Sure, it is a strange idea these military men have got in their heads, that a man isn't fit for work unless he is buttoned so tightly up to the chin that he is red in the face. If nature had meant it, we should have been born in a suit of scale-armour like a crocodile. Well, there is one consolation, if there is a siege I expect there will be an end of hair-powder and cravats. It's the gineral rule on a campaign, and it is worth standing to be shot at to have a little comfort in one's life."

"Do you think that there is any chance at all of the Spaniards taking the place if they do besiege us?" Bob asked as Dr. Burke took his seat.

"None of taking the place by force, Bob. It has been besieged over and over again, and it is pretty nearly always by hunger that it has fallen. That is where the pinch will come if they besiege us in earnest: it's living on mice and grass you are like to be before it is over."

"But the fleet will bring in provisions surely, Dr. Burke?"

"The fleet will have all it can do to keep the sea against the navies of France and Spain. They will do what they can, you may be sure; but the enemy well know that it is only by starving us out that they can hope to take the place, and I expect they will put such a fleet here that it will be mighty difficult for even a boat to find its way in between them."

"Do you know about the other sieges?" Mrs. O'Halloran asked. "Of course I know something about the last siege, but I know nothing about the history of the Rock before that, and of course Gerald doesn't know."

"And why should I, Carrie? You don't suppose that when I was at school at Athlone they taught me the history of every bit of rock sticking up on the face of the globe? I had enough to do to learn about the old Romans, bad cess to them! and all their bothering doings."

"I can tell you about it, Mrs. O'Halloran," Teddy Burke said. "Bob's professor, who comes to have a talk with me for half an hour every day, has been telling me all about it; and if Gerald will move himself and mix me a glass of grog to moisten my throat I will give you the whole story of it. You know, no doubt, that it was called Mount Calpe by Gerald's friends the Romans, who called the hill opposite there Mount Abyla, and the two together the Pillars of Hercules. But beyond giving it a name they don't seem to have concerned themselves with it; nor do the Phœnicians or Carthaginians, though all of them had cities out in the low country. It was when the Saracens began to play their games over here that we first hear of it. Roderic, you know, was king of the Goths, and seems to have been a thundering old tyrant; and one of his nobles, Julian, who had been badly treated by him, went across with his family into Africa and put up Mousa, the Saracen governor of the province across there, to invade Spain.

"They first of all made a little expedition, that was in 711, with one hundred horse and four hundred foot. They landed over there at Algeciras, and after doing some plundering and burning sailed back again with the news that the country could be conquered. So next year twelve thousand men, under a chief named Tarik, crossed and landed on the flat between the Rock and Spain. He left a party here to build the castle, and then marched away, defeated Roderic and his army at Xeres, and soon conquered the whole of Spain except the mountains of the north. We don't hear much more of Gibraltar for another six hundred years. Algeciras had become a fortress of great strength and magnificence, and Gibraltar was a mere sort of outlying post. Ferdinand IV. of Spain besieged Algeciras for years and could not take it, but a part of his army attacked Gibraltar and captured it.

"The African Moors came over to help their friends, and Ferdinand had to fall back; but the Spaniards still held Gibraltar, a chap named Vasco Paez de Meira being in command. In 1333 Abomelique, son of the Emperor of Fez, came across with an army and besieged Gibraltar. Vasco held out for five months, and was then starved into surrender, just as Alonzo XI. was approaching to his assistance. He arrived before the town five days after it surrendered and attacked the castle; but the Moors encamped on the neutral ground in his rear and cut him off from his supplies, and he was obliged at last to negotiate, and was permitted to retire. He was not long away. Next time he attacked Algeciras, which after a long siege he took in 1343.

"In 1349 there were several wars in Africa, and he took advantage of this to besiege Gibraltar. He was some months over the business, and the garrison was nearly starved out, when pestilence broke out in the Spanish camp, by which the king and many of his soldiers died and the rest retired. It was not until sixty years afterwards, in 1410, that there were fresh troubles, and then they were what might be called family squabbles. The Africans of Fez had held the place till then, but the Moorish king of Grenada suddenly advanced upon it and took it. A short time afterwards the inhabitants rose against the Spanish Moors and turned them out, and the Emperor of Morocco sent over an army to help them; but the Moors of Grenada besieged the place, and took it by famine.

"In 1435 the Christians had another slap at it; but Henry de Guzman, who attacked by sea, was defeated and killed. In 1462 the greater part of the garrison of Gibraltar was withdrawn to take part in some civil shindy that was going on at Grenada; and in their absence the place was taken by John de Guzman, duke of Medina-Sidonia, and son of the Henry that was killed. In 1540 Gibraltar was surprised and pillaged by one of Barossa's captains, but as he was leaving some Christian galleys met him, and the corsairs were all killed or taken. This was really the only affair worth speaking of between 1462, when it fell into the hands of the Spaniards, and 1704, when it was captured by us. Sir George Rooke, who had gone out with a force to attack Cadiz, finding that there was not much chance of success in that direction, resolved, with Prince George of Hesse and

Darmstadt, who commanded the troops on board the fleet, to make an attack on Gibraltar.

"On the 21st of July, 1800, the English and Dutch landed on the neutral ground, and at daybreak on the 23d, the fleet opened fire. The Spaniards were driven from their guns on the Molehead Battery; the boats landed and seized the battery, and held it in spite of the Spaniards springing a mine, which killed two lieutenants and about forty men. The Marquis de Salines, the governor, was then summoned, and capitulated. So you see we made only a day's work of taking a place which the Spaniards thought that they had made impregnable. The professor made a strong point of it that the garrison consisted only of a hundred and fifty men; which certainly accounts for our success, for it is no use having guns and walls if you haven't got soldiers to man them. The Prince of Hesse was left as governor, and it was not long before his mettle was tried; for in October the Spanish army, with six battalions of Frenchmen, opened trenches against the town. Admiral Sir John Leake threw in reinforcements and six months' provisions. At the end of the month a forlorn hope of five hundred Spanish volunteers managed to climb up the Rock by ropes and ladders and surprised a battery, but were so furiously attacked that they were all killed or taken prisoners.

"A heavy cannonade was kept up for another week, when a large number of transports with reinforcements and supplies arrived, and the garrison being now considered strong enough to resist any attack the fleet sailed away. The siege went on till the middle of March, when Sir John Leake again arrived, drove away the French fleet and captured or burnt five of them, and the siege was then discontinued, having cost the enemy ten thousand men. So, you see, there was some pretty hard fighting over it.

"The place was threatened in 1720, and in the beginning of 1727 twenty thousand Spaniards again sat down before it. The fortifications had been made a good deal stronger after the first siege, and the garrison was commanded by Lieutenant-governor Clayton. The siege lasted till May, when news arrived that the preliminaries of a general peace had been signed. There was a lot of firing, but the Spaniards must have shot mighty badly, for we had only three hundred killed and wounded. You would think that that was enough; but when I tell you that the cannon were so old and rotten that seventy cannon and thirty mortars burst during the siege, it seems to me that everyone of those three hundred must have been damaged by our own cannon, and that the Spaniards did not succeed in hitting a single man. That is mighty encouraging for you, Mrs. O'Halloran, for I don't think that our cannon will burst this time; and if the Spaniards do not shoot better than they did before, it is little work enough that is likely to fall to the share of the surgeons."

"Thank you," Mrs. O'Halloran said. "You have told that very nicely, Teddy Burke. I did not know anything about it before, and I had some idea that it was when the English were besieged here that the Queen of Spain sat on that rock which is called after her; but I see now that it was Ferdinand's Isabella, and that it was when the Moors were besieged here hundreds of years before. Well, I am glad I know something about it. It is stupid to be in a place and know nothing of its history. You are rising in my estimation fast, Dr. Burke."

"Mistress O'Halloran," the doctor said, rising and making a deep bow, "you overwhelm me entirely: and now I must say good-night, for I must look in at the hospital before I turn in to my quarters."

CHAPTER VIII.

THE SIEGE BEGINS.

ON the 19th of June General Eliott, accompanied by several of his officers, paid a visit to the Spanish lines to congratulate General Mendoza, who commanded there, on the promotion that he had just received. The visit lasted but a short time, and it was remarked that the Spanish officer seemed ill at ease. Scarcely had the party returned to Gibraltar than a Swedish frigate entered the bay, having on board Mr. Logie, H.M. Consul in Barbary, who had come across in her from Tangier. He reported that a Swedish brig had put in there. She reported that she had fallen in with the French fleet, of twenty-eight sail of the line, off Cape Finisterre, and that they were waiting there to be joined by the Spanish fleet from Cadiz.

The news caused great excitement; but it was scarcely believed, for the Spanish general had given the most amicable assurances to the governor. On the 21st, however, the Spaniards at their lines across the neutral ground refused to permit the mail to pass, and a formal notification was sent in that intercourse between Gibraltar and Spain would no longer be permitted. This put an end to all doubt and discussion. War must have been declared between Spain and England, or such a step would never have been taken. In fact, although the garrison did not learn it until some time later, the Spanish embassador in London had presented what was virtually a declaration of war on the 16th. A messenger had been sent off on the same day from Madrid, ordering the cessation of intercourse with Gibraltar, and had he not been detained by accident on the road he might have arrived during General Eliott's visit to the Spanish lines, a fact of which Mendoza had been doubtless forewarned, and which would account for his embarrassment at the governor's call.

Captain O'Halloran brought the news home when he returned from parade. "Get ready your sandbags, Carrie; examine your stock of provisions; prepare a store of lint and plaster."

"What on earth are you talking about, Gerald?"

"It is war, Carrie. The Dons have refused to accept our mail, and have cut off all intercourse with the mainland."

Carrie turned a little pale. She had never really thought that the talk meant anything, or that the Spaniards could be really intending to declare war without having any ground for quarrel with England.

"And does it really mean war, Gerald?"

"There is no doubt about it. The Spaniards are going to fight, and as their army can't swim across the Bay of Biscay, I take it it is here they mean to attack us. Faith, we are going to have some divarshun at last."

"Divarshun! You ought to be ashamed of yourself, Gerald."

"Well, my dear, what have I come into the army for? To march about for four hours a day in a stiff stock, and powder and pig-tail and a cocked hat, and a red coat? Not a bit of it. Didn't I enter the army to fight, and here have I been without a chance of smelling powder for the last ten years. It is the best news I have had since you told me that you were ready and willing to become Mrs. O'Halloran."

"And to think that we have got Bob out here with us!" his wife said, without taking any notice of the last words. "What will uncle say?"

"Faith and it makes mighty little difference what he says,

Carrie, seeing that he is altogether beyond shouting distance. As for Bob, he will be just delighted. Why, he has been working till his brain must all be in a muddle; and it is the best thing in the world for him, or he would be mixing up the Spaniards and the Romans, and the x's and y's and the tangents, and all the other things into a regular jumble, and it is a nice business that would have been. It is the best thing in the world for him, always supposing that he don't get his growth stopped for want of victuals."

"You don't mean really and seriously, Gerald, that we are likely to be short of food?"

"And that is exactly what I do mean. You may be sure that the Dons know mighty well that they have no chance of taking the place on the land side. They might just as well lay out their trenches against the moon. It is just starvation that they are going to try, and when they get the eighteen French sail of the line that Mr. Logie brought news of, and a score or so of Spanish men-of-war in the bay, you will see that it is likely you won't get your mutton and your butter and vegetables very regularly across from Tangier."

"Well, it is very serious, Gerald."

"Very serious, Carrie."

"I don't see anything to laugh at at all, Gerald."

"I didn't know that I was laughing."

"You were looking as if you wanted to laugh, which is just as bad. I suppose there is nothing to be done, Gerald?"

"Well, yes, I should go down to the town and lay in a store of things that will keep. You see, if nothing comes of it we should not be losers. The regiment is likely to be here three or four years, so we should lose nothing by laying in a big stock of wine and so on; while, if there is a siege, you will see everything will go up to ten times its ordinary price. That room through ours is not used for anything, and we might turn that into a store-room. I don't mean that there is any hurry about it to-day; but we ought

certainly to lay in as large a store as we can of things that will keep. Some things we may get cheaper in a short time than we can now. A lot of the Jew and native traders will be leaving if they see there is really going to be a siege, for you see the town is quite open to the guns of batteries on the other side of the neutral ground. It was a mighty piece of luck we got this house. You see that rising ground behind will shelter us from shot. They may blaze away as much as they like, as far as we are concerned. Ah! there is Bob coming out of his room with the professor."

"Well, take him out and tell him, Gerald. I want to sit down and think; my head feels quite in a whirl."

Bob was of course greatly surprised at the news, and the professor himself was a good deal excited. "We have been living here for three hundred years," he said, "my fathers and grandfathers. When the English came and took this place seventy-five years ago, my grandfather became a British subject, like all who remained here. My father, who was then but a boy, has told me that he remembers the great siege, and how the cannons roared night and day. It was in the year when I was born that the Spaniards attacked the Rock again, and a shell exploded in the house and nearly killed us all. I was born a British subject, and shall do my duty in what way I can if the place is attacked. They call us Rock scorpions. Well, they shall see we can live under fire, and will do our best to sting if they put their finger on us. Ha, ha!"

"The little man is quite excited," Captain O'Halloran said, as the professor turned away and marched off at a brisk pace towards his home. "It is rather hard on these Rock people. Of course, as he says, they are British subjects, and were born so. Still, you see, in race and language they are still Spaniards, and their sympathies must be divided, at any rate at present. When the shot and shell come whistling into the town and knocking their houses about their ears, they will become a good deal more decided in their opinions than they can be now. Come along, Bob, and let us get all the news. I came off as soon as I heard that our communication with Spain was cut off, and therefore it was certain war was declared. There will be lots of orders out soon. It is a busy time we shall have of it for the next month or two."

There were many officers in the ante-room when they entered.

"Any fresh news?" Captain O'Halloran asked.

"Lots of it, O'Halloran. All the Irish officers of the garrison are to be formed into an outlying force to occupy the neutral ground; it is thought their appearance will be sufficient to terrify the Spaniards."

"Get out with you, Grant! If they were to take us at all, it would be because they knew that we were the boys to do the fighting."

"And the drinking, O'Halloran," another young officer put in.

"And the talking," said another.

"Now, drop it, boys, and be serious. What is the news, really?"

"There is a council of war going on at the governor's, O'Halloran. Boyd, of course, and De la Motte, Colonel Green, the admiral, Mr. Logie, and two or three others. They say the governor has been gradually getting extra stores across from Tangier ever since there was first a talk about this business, and of course that is the most important question at present. I hear that Green and the Engineers have been marking out places for new batteries for the last month, and I suppose fatigue work is going to be the order of the day. It is too bad of them choosing this time of the year to begin, for it will be awfully hot work. Everyone is wondering what will become of the officers who are living out with their families at San Roque and the other villages across the Spanish lines; and, besides, there are a lot of officers away on leave in the interior.

"Of course they won't take them prisoners, that would be a dirty trick. But it is likely enough they may ship them straight back to England, instead of letting them return here. Well, it is lucky that we have got a pretty strong garrison. We have just been adding up the last field state. These are the figures—officers, non-commissioned officers, and men—artillery, 485; 12th Regiment, 599; 39th, 586; 56th, 587; 58th, 605; 72d, 1046; the Hanoverian Brigade of Hardenberg's, Reden's, and De la Motte's regiments, 1352; and 122 Engineers under Colonel Green; which makes up altogether 5382 officers and men. That is strong enough for anything, but it would have been better if there had been five hundred more artillerymen; but I suppose they will be able to lend us some sailors to help work the heavy guns. They will turn you into a powder-monkey, Repton."

"I don't care what they turn me into," Bob said, "so long as I can do something."

"I think it is likely," Captain O'Halloran said gravely, "that all women and children will be turned out of the place before fighting begins; except, of course, wives and children of officers."

There was a general laugh at Bob. "Well," he said quietly, "it will lessen the ranks of the subalterns, for there must be a considerable number who are not many months older than I am. I am just sixteen, and I know there are some not older than that."

This was a fact, for commissions were in those days given in the army to mere lads, and the ensigns were often no older than midshipmen. Late in the afternoon a procession of carts was seen crossing the neutral ground from the Spanish lines, and it was soon seen that these were the English officers and merchants from San Roque and the other villages. They had that morning received peremptory orders to leave before sunset. Some were fortunate enough to be able to hire carts to bring in their effects, but several were compelled from want of carriage to leave everything behind them. The guards had all been reinforced at the northern batteries, pickets had been stationed across the neutral ground, the guard at the work known as the Devil's Tower were warned to be specially on the alert, and the artillery in the battery on the rock above it were to hold themselves in readiness to open fire upon the enemy should they be perceived advancing towards it.

It was considered improbable in the extreme that the enemy would attack until a great force had been collected, but it was possible that a body of troops might have been collected secretly somewhere in the neighbourhood, and that an attempt would be made to capture the place by surprise before the garrison might be supposed to be taking precautions against attack. The next morning orders were issued, and large working parties were told off to go on with the work of strengthening the fortifications; and notice was issued that all empty hogsheads and casks in the town would be bought by the military authorities. These were to be filled with earth, and to take the places of fascines, for which there were no materials available on the Rock. Parties of men rolled or carried these up to the heights. Other parties collected earth, and piled it to be carried up in sacks on the back of mules, there being no earth on the rocks where the batteries would be established, a fact which added very largely to the difficulties of the Engineers.

On the 24th, the *Childers* sloop of war brought in two prizes from the west, one of which, an American, she had captured in the midst of the Spanish fleet. Some of the Spanish men-of-war had made threatening demonstrations as if to prevent the sloop from interfering with her, but they had not fired a gun, and it was supposed that they had not received orders to commence hostilities. Two English frigates had been watching the fleet, and it was supposed to be on its way to join the French fleet off Cape Finisterre. The Spaniards were seen now to be at work dragging down guns from San Roque to arm their two forts, St. Philip and St. Barbara which stood at the extremities of their lines—St. Philip on the bay and St. Barbara upon the sea-shore on the eastern side of the neutral side. In time of peace only a few guns were mounted in these batteries. Admiral Duff moved the men-of-war under his command, consisting of the *Panther*, of sixty guns, three frigates, and a sloop, from their usual anchorage off the Water Port, where they were exposed to the fire of the enemy's forts, to the New Mole more to the southward.

Bob would have liked to be out all day watching the busy preparations, and listening to the talk of the natives, who were greatly alarmed at the prospect of the siege, knowing that the guns from the Spanish forts, and especially from Fort St. Philip, could throw their shot and shell into the town. But Captain O'Halloran agreed with his wife that it was much better he should continue his lessons with Don Diaz of a morning, for that it would be absurd for him to be standing about in the sun the whole day.

The evening lessons were, however, discontinued from the first, as Dr. Burke had his hands full in superintending the preparations making at the hospitals for the reception of large numbers of wounded.

Bob did not so much mind this, for he had ceased to regard the time spent with the professor as lessons. After he had once mastered the conjugation of the verbs, and had learned an extensive vocabulary by heart, books had been laid aside altogether, and the three hours with the professor had for the last two months been spent simply in conversation. They were no longer indoors, but sat in the garden on the shady side of the house, or when the sky happened to be clouded and the morning was cool, walked together out to Europa Point, and would sit down there looking over the sea, but always talking. Sometimes it was history—Roman, English, or Spanish, sometimes Bob's school-days and life in London, sometimes general subjects. It mattered little what they talked about, so that the conversation was kept up.

Sometimes when it was found that topics failed them, the professor would give Bob a Spanish book to glance through, and its subject would serve as a theme for talk on the following day; and as it was five months since the lad had landed, he was now able to speak in Spanish almost as fluently as in English. As he had learnt almost entirely by ear, and any word mispronounced had had to be gone over again and again till Don Diaz was perfectly satisfied, his accent was excellent, and the professor had told him a few days before the breaking out of the war that in another month or two he should discontinue his lessons.

"It would be well for you to have one or two mornings a week to keep up your accent. You can find plenty of practice talking to the people. I see you are good at making friends, and are ready to talk to labourers at work, to boys, to the market-women, and to anyone you come across, but their accent is bad, and it would be well for you to keep on with me. But you speak at present much better Spanish than the people here, and if you were dressed up as a young Spaniard, you might go about Spain without anyone suspecting you to be English."

Indeed, by the professor's method of teaching, assisted by a natural aptitude, and three hours' daily conversation for five months, Bob had made surprising progress, especially as he had supplemented his lesson by continually talking Spanish with Manola, with the Spanish woman and children living below them, and with everyone he could get to talk to.

He had seen little of Jim since the trouble began, as leave was, for the most part, stopped, the ships of war being in readiness to proceed to sea at a moment's notice to engage an enemy, or to protect merchantmen coming in, from the attacks of the Spanish ships and gunboats across at Algeciras.

Bob generally got up at five o'clock now and went out

for two or three hours before breakfast, for the heat had become too great for exercise during the day. He greatly missed the market, for it had given him much amusement to watch the groups of peasant women with their baskets of eggs, fowls, vegetables, oranges, and fruit of various kinds, bargaining with the towns-people, and joking and laughing with the soldiers. The streets were now almost deserted, and many of the little traders in vegetables and fruit had closed their shops. The fishermen, however, still carried on their work, and obtained a ready sale for their catch. There had, indeed, been a much greater demand than usual for fish, owing to the falling off in the fruit and vegetable supplies.

The cessation of trade was already beginning to tell upon the poorer part of the population; but employment was found for all willing to labour, either at collecting earth for the batteries, or out on the neutral ground, where three hundred of them were employed by the Engineers in levelling sand hummocks and other inequalities in the ground that might afford any shelter to an enemy creeping up to assault the gates by the water-side. Dr. Burke came in with Captain O'Halloran to dinner ten days after the gates had been closed.

"You are quite a stranger, Teddy," Mrs. O'Halloran said.

"I am that," he replied; "but you are going to be bothered with me again now; we have got everything in apple-pie order, and are ready to take half the garrison under our charge. There has been lots to do. All the medical stores have been overhauled, and lists made out and sent home of everything that can be required—medicines and comforts, and lint and bandages, and splints and wooden legs, and goodness knows what besides. We hope they will be out in the first convoy. There is a privateer going to sail to-morrow, so if you want to send letters home or to order anything to be sent out to you, you had better take the opportunity. Have you got everything you want for the next two or three years?"

"'Two or three years!'" Carrie repeated in tones of alarm. "You mean two or three months."

"Indeed and I don't. If the French and the Dons have made up their mind to take this place, and once set to fairly to do it, they are bound to stick to it for a bit. I should say you ought to provide for three years."

"But that is downright nonsense, Teddy. Why, in three months there ought to be a fleet here that would drive all the French and Spaniards away."

"Well, if you say there ought to be, there ought," the doctor said; "but where is it to come from? I was talking to some of the naval men yesterday, and they all say it will be a long business if the French and Spanish are in earnest. The French navy is as strong as ours, and the Spaniards have got nearly as many ships as the French. We have got to protect our coasts and our trade, to convoy the East Indian fleets, and to be doing something all over the world, and they doubt whether it would be possible to get together a fleet that could hope to defeat the French and Spanish navies combined. Well, have you been laying in stores, Mrs. O'Halloran?"

"Yes, we have bought two sacks of flour and fifty pounds of sugar, ten pounds of tea, and a good many other things."

"If you will take my advice," the doctor said earnestly, "you will lay in five times as much. Say ten sacks of flour, two hundredweight of sugar, and everything else in proportion. Those sort of things haven't got up in price yet, but you will see everything will rise as soon as the blockade begins in earnest."

"No, the prices of those things have not gone up much; but fruit is three times the price it was a fortnight ago, and chickens and eggs are double, and vegetables are hardly to be bought."

"'That is the worst of it," the doctor said. "It's the vegetables that I am thinking of."

"Well, we can do without vegetables," Mrs. O'Halloran laughed, "as long as we have plenty of bread."

"It is just that you can't do. You see we shall be cut off from Tangier; maybe to-morrow, maybe a fortnight hence, but we shall be cut off. A ship may run in sometimes at night, but you can't count upon that; and it is salt meat that we are going to live upon, and if you live on salt meat you have got to have vegetables or fruit to keep you in health.

"Now, I tell you what I should do, Gerald, and I am not joking with you. In the first place I would make an arrangement with the people downstairs, and I would hire their garden from them. I don't suppose they would want much for it, for they make no use of it except to grow a few flowers. Then I would go down the town, and I would buy up all the chickens I could get. There are plenty of them to be picked up if you look about for them, for most of the people who have got a bit of ground keep a few fowls. Get a hundred of them if you can, and turn them into the garden. Buy up twenty sacks, if you like, of damaged biscuits. You can get them for an old song. The commissariat have been clearing out their stores, and there are a lot of damaged biscuits to be sold by auction to-morrow. You would get twenty sacks for a few shillings. That way you will get a good supply of eggs if the siege lasts ever so long, and you can fence off a bit of the garden and raise fowls there. That will give you a supply of fresh meat, and any eggs and poultry you can't eat yourselves you can sell for big prices. You could get a chicken three weeks ago at threepence. Never mind if you have to pay a shilling for them now, they will be worth five shillings before long. If you can rent another bit of garden any-where near I would take it; if not, I would hire three or four men to collect earth and bring it up here. This is a good big place; I suppose it is thirty feet by sixty. Well, I would just leave a path from the door there up to this end, and a spare place here for your chairs, and I would cover the rest of it with earth nine inches or a foot deep, and I would plant vegetables."

"Do you mane we are to grow cabbages here, Teddy?" Captain O'Halloran asked, with a burst of laughter.

"No, I wouldn't grow cabbages; I would just grow mustard and cress and radishes. If you eat plenty of them they will keep off scurvy, and all you don't want for yourselves I will guarantee you will be able to sell at any price you like to ask for them, and if nobody else will buy them the hospitals will. They would be the saving of many a man's life."

"But they would want watering," Captain O'Halloran said more seriously, for he saw how much the doctor was in earnest.

"They will that. You will have no difficulty in hiring a man to bring up water, and to tend to them and to look after the fowls. Men will be glad enough to work for next to nothing. I tell you, Gerald, if I wasn't in the service I should hire every bit of land I could lay hands on, and employ as many labourers as it required, and I should look to be a rich man before the end of the siege. I was speaking to the chief surgeon to-day about it, and he is going to put the convalescents to work on a bit of spare ground there is at the back of the hospital, and to plant vegetables. I was asking down the town yesterday, and I found that at Blount's store you can get as much vegetable seed as you like. You lay in a stock to-day of mustard and cress and radish. Don't be afraid of the expense—get twenty pounds of each of them. You will be always able to sell what you don't want at ten times the price you give for it now. If you can get a piece more garden-ground take it at any price and raise other vegetables, but keep the top of the house here for what I tell you. Well, I said nine inches deep of earth; that is more than necessary. Four and a half will do for the radishes, and two is enough for the mustard and cress. That will grow on a blanket; it is really only water that it wants."

"What do you think, Carrie?" Captain O'Halloran asked.

"Well, Gerald, if you really believe the siege is going to last like that, I should think that it would be really worth while to do what Teddy Burke advises. Of course you will be too busy to look after things, but Bob might do so."

"Of course I would," Bob broke in. "It will give me something to do."

"Well, we will set about it at once then. I will speak to the man downstairs. You know he has got two or three horses and traps down in the town, and lets them to people driving out across the lines; but of course he has nothing to do now, and I should think that he would be glad enough to arrange to look after the fowls and the things up here. The garden is a good size. I don't think anything could get out through that prickly-pear hedge; but, anyhow, any gaps there are can be stopped up with stakes. I think it is a really good idea, and if I can get a couple of hundred fowls, I will. I should think there was plenty of room for them in the garden. I will set up as a poultry merchant."

"You might do worse, Gerald. I will bet you a gallon of whisky they will be selling at ten shillings a couple before this business is over, and there is no reason in the world why you should not turn an honest penny; it will be a novelty to you."

"Well, I will go down the town at once," Gerald said, "and get the seeds and the extra stores you advise, Teddy; and to-morrow I will go to the commissariat sale and buy a ton or two of those damaged biscuits. We will take another room from them downstairs as a store-room for that and the eggs, and I will get a carpenter to come up and put a fence and make some runs and a bit of a shelter

for the sitting hens and the chickens. Bob shall do the
purchasing. You had better get a boy with a big basket to
go with you, Bob. and go round to the cottages to buy up
fowls. Mind, don't let them sell you nothing but cocks—
one to every seven or eight hens is quite enough; and don't
let them foist off old hens on you—the younger they are the
better. I should say that at first you had better take Manola
with you, if Carrie can spare her, then you won't get taken
in, and you will soon learn to tell the difference between an
old hen and a young chicken."

"When you are buying the seed, O'Halloran," said Dr.
Burke, "you would do well to get a few cucumbers, and
melons, and pumpkins; they will grow on the roof splendidly. And you can plant them near the parapet where
they will grow down over the sides, so they won't take up
much room, and you can pick them with a ladder. The
pumpkin is a good vegetable, and the fowls will thank you
for a bit to pick when you can spare one. They will all
want manure, but you get plenty of that from the fowl-yard."

"Why, Teddy, there seems no end to your knowledge,"
Mrs. O'Halloran said; "first of all you turn out to be a
schoolmaster, and now you are a gardener and poultry-
raiser. And to think I never gave you credit for knowing
anything except medicine."

"You haven't got to the bottom of it yet, Mrs. O'Halloran; my head is just stored with knowledge, only it isn't
always that I have a chance of making it useful. I would
be just the fellow to be cast on a desert island; there is no
saying what I wouldn't do towards making myself comfortable there. But I do know about scurvy, for I made a
voyage in a whaler before I got His Majesty's commission
to kill and slay in the army, and I know how necessary
vegetables are. I only wish we had known what the Spaniards were up to a month since, we would have got a cargo
of oranges and lemons; they would have been worth their
weight in silver."

"But they wouldn't have kept, Teddy."

"No, not for long; but we would have squeezed them, and put sugar into the juice and bottled it off. If the general had consulted me that is what he would have been after, instead of seeing about salt meat and biscuits. We shall get plenty of them from ships that run in, I have no fear of that; but it is the acids will be wanting."

As soon as dinner was over Captain O'Halloran went downstairs, and had no difficulty in arranging with the man below for the entire use of his garden. An inspection was made of the hedge, and the man agreed to close up all gaps that fowls could possibly creep through. He was also quite willing to let off a room for storage, and his wife undertook to superintend the management of the young broods and sitting hens. Having arranged this, Captain O'Halloran went down into the town to make his purchases. A quarter of an hour later Bob started with Manola, carrying a large basket, and both were much amused at their errand. Going among the cottages scattered over the hill above the town, they had no difficulty in obtaining chickens and fowls, the former at about fivepence apiece, the latter at sevenpence—such prices being more than double the usual rates. Manola's basket was soon full, and while she was taking her purchases back to the house Bob hired two boys with baskets, and before evening nearly a hundred fowls were running in the garden.

The next day Bob was considered sufficiently experienced to undertake the business alone, and in two more days the entire number of two hundred had been made up. Three of the natives had been engaged in collecting baskets of earth among the rocks, and in a week the terrace was converted into a garden ready for the seeds. As yet vegetables, although very dear, had not risen to famine prices, for although the town had depended chiefly upon the produce of the mainland, many of the natives had grown small patches of vegetables in their gardens for their own use, and these they now disposed of at prices that were highly satisfactory to themselves. O'Halloran's farm, as they called it as soon as they heard from him what he was doing, became quite a joke in the regiment, but several of the other married officers who had similar facilities for keeping fowls adopted the idea to some extent, and started with a score or so of fowls.

"I wonder you didn't think of pigs, O'Halloran," one of the captains said laughing, as they were talking over the farm in the mess ante-room; "pigs and potatoes. The idea of you and Burke, both from the sod, starting a farm and not thinking first of the two chief national products."

"There is not room for praties, Sinclair; and as for pigs, there are many reasons against it. In the first place, I doubt whether I could buy any; in the second, there isn't room for them; in the third, what should I give them to keep them alive? in the fourth, pigs are illigant bastes, but in a hot country like this I should not care for a stye of them under my drawing-room window; in the fifth—"

"That will do, that will do, O'Halloran; we give way. We allow that you could not keep pigs, but it is a pity."

"It is that, Sinclair; there is nothing would please me better than to see a score of nice little pigs with a nate stye, and a magazine of food big enough to keep them, say for a year."

"Three months, O'Halloran, would be ample."

"Well, we shall see, Sinclair. Teddy Burke says three years, but I do hope it is not going to be as long as that."

"Begorra!" another Irish officer, Captain O'Moore, exclaimed: "if it is three years we are going to be here we had best be killed and buried at once. I have been all the morning in the Queen's Battery, where my company has been slaving like haythens, with the sun coming down as if it would fry your brain in your skull-pan; and if that is to go on day after day for three years, I should be dead in a month."

"That is nothing, O'Moore; if the siege goes on they say the officers will have to help at the work."

"I shall protest against it. There is not a word in the articles of war about officers working. I am willing enough to be shot by the Spaniards, but not to be killed by inches. No, sir, there is not an O'Moore ever did a stroke of work since the flood, and I am not going to demean myself by beginning. What are you laughing at, young Repton?"

"I was only wondering, Captain O'Moore, how your ancestors got through the flood. Unless, indeed, Noah was an O'Moore."

"There is reason to believe that he was," the captain said seriously. "It must have been that, if he hadn't a boat of his own or found a mountain that the water didn't cover. I have got the tree of the family at home, and an old gentleman who was learned in these things came to the house when I was a boy, and I remember right well that he said to my father, after reckoning them up, that the first of the house must have had a place there in Ireland well-nigh a thousand years before Adam. I don't think my father quite liked it, but for the life of me I couldn't see why. It was just what I should expect from the O'Moores. Didn't they give kings to Ireland for generations, and what should they want to be doing out among those rivers in the East when there was Ireland ready to receive them."

Captain O'Moore spoke so seriously that Bob did not venture to laugh, but listened with an air of gravity equal to that of the officer.

"You will kill me altogether, Phelim!" Captain O'Halloran exclaimed amid a great shout of laughter, in which all the others joined. The O'Moore looked round, speechless with indignation.

"Gentlemen," he said, "I shall expect satisfaction for this insult. The word of an O'Moore has never been doubted. Captain O'Halloran, my friend will call upon you first."

"He may call as often as he likes, O'Moore, and I shall

be happy to converse with any friend of yours, but at present that is all the satisfaction you will get out of me. Duelling is strictly forbidden on the Rock, and there is no getting across the Spanish lines to fight, unless, indeed, you can persuade the governor to send out a flag of truce with us. So we must let the matter rest till the siege is over, and then if both of us are alive and you have the same mind we will talk about it."

"I think, O'Moore," Dr. Burke, who had entered the room two or three minutes before, said persuasively, "you will see that you are the last man who ought to maintain that the first of your race lived here as far back as Adam. You see, we are all direct descendants of Adam—I mean all the rest of us."

"No doubt you are," Captain O'Moore said stiffly.

"And one has just as much right as another to claim that he is the heir in a direct line."

"I suppose so, Burke," the officer said, "though for the life of me I can't see what you are driving at."

"What I mean is this. Suppose Adam and the O'Moore started at the same time, one in Ireland and the other in Eden, and they had an equal number of children, as was likely enough, half the people in the world would be descendants of Adam and the other half of the O'Moore; and, you see, instead of your being the O'Moore, the genuine descendant in the direct line from the first of the family, half the world would have an equal claim to the title."

Captain O'Moore reflected for a minute or two.

"You are right, Dr. Burke," he said. "I never saw it in that light. It is clear enough that you are right, and that the less we say about the O'Moores before the first Irish king of that name, the better. There must have been some mistake about that tree I spoke of. Captain O'Halloran, I apologize; I was wrong."

The two officers shook hands, and peace was restored; but Captain O'Moore was evidently a good deal puzzled and mortified by the problem the doctor had set before him, and after remaining silent for some time evidently in deep thought, he left the room. Some of the others watched him from the window until he had entered the door of his own quarters, and then there was a general shout of laughter.

"The O'Moore will be the death of me!" Teddy Burke exclaimed, as he threw himself back in a chair exhausted. "He is one of the best fellows going, but you can lead him on into anything. I don't suppose he ever gave a thought to the O'Moores anywhere further back than those kings. He had a vague idea that they must have been going on, simply because it must have seemed to him that a world without an O'Moore in it would be necessarily imperfect. It was Bob Repton's questions as to what they were doing at the time of the flood that brought him suddenly up, then he didn't hesitate for a moment in taking them back to Adam or before him. Just on the ancestry of the O'Moores Phelim has got a tile a little loose, but on all other points he is as sensible as anyone in the regiment."

"I wonder you didn't add, 'and that is not saying much,' doctor," one of the lieutenants said.

"I may have thought it, youngster; but, you see, I must have made exceptions in favour of myself and the colonel, so I held my tongue. The fact that we are all here under a sun hot enough to cook a beef-steak, and that for the next two or three years we are going to have to work like niggers, and to be shot at by the Spaniards, and to be pretty well if not quite starved, speaks for itself as to the amount of sense we have got between us. There go the drums! Now, gentlemen, you have got the pleasure of a couple of hours' drill before you, and I am due at the hospital."

CHAPTER IX.

THE "ANTELOPE."

ON the 3d of July a hundred and eighty volunteers from the infantry joined the artillery, who were not numerous enough to work all the guns of the batteries, and two days later a Spanish squadron of two men-of-war, five frigates, and eleven smaller vessels hove in sight from the west, and lay to off the entrance to the bay. Three privateers came in, and one of the Spanish schooners stood across to reconnoitre them, and a shot was fired at her from the batteries on Europa Point. The *Enterprise* frigate had gone across to Tetuan to bring Mr. Logie over again. On her return she was chased by the enemy's squadron, but succeeded in giving them the slip in the dark. As she neared the Rock the captain fearing to be discovered by the enemy, did not show the usual lights, and several shots were fired at the ship, but fortunately without effect. On the following day letters were received from England with the official news that hostilities had commenced between Great Britain and Spain, and the same evening a proclamation was published authorizing the capture of Spanish vessels, and letters of marque were given to the privateers in the bay, permitting them to capture Spanish as well as French vessels. Among the privateers was the *Antelope*, which was one of those that had come in on the previous afternoon. Bob had not heard of her arrival when he ran against Captain Lockett in the town next morning. They had not met since Bob had landed six months before.

"Well, Master Repton," the captain said after they had shaken hands, "I was coming up to see you after I had managed my business. I have letters from Mr. Bale for you and Mrs. O'Halloran."

"You are all well on board, I hope, captain?"

"Joe is well. He is first-mate now. Poor Probert is on his back in hospital at Portsmouth. We had a sharp brush with a French privateer, but we beat her off. We had five men killed, and Probert had his leg taken off by an eighteen-pound shot. We clapped on a tourniquet, but he had a very narrow escape of bleeding to death. Fortunately it was off Ushant, and the wind being favourable we got into Portsmouth on the following morning, and the doctors think that they will pull him round. You have grown a good bit since I saw you last."

"Not much, I am afraid," Bob replied dolefully, for his height was rather a sore point with him. "I get wider, but I don't think I have grown half an inch since I came here."

"And how goes on the Spanish?"

"First-rate. I can get on in it almost as well as in English."

"So you are in for some more fighting?"

"So they say," Bob replied; "but I don't think I am likely to have as close a shave of a Spanish prison as I had of a French one coming out here."

"No; we had a narrow squeak of it that time."

"Was war declared when you came away?"

"No; the negotiations were broken off, and everyone knew that war was certain, and that the proclamation might be issued at any hour. I have not had a very fast run, and expected to have learned the news when I got here, but you are sure to hear it in a day or two. That was why I came here. Freights were short, for with the ports of France and Spain both closed there was little enough doing, so the owners agreed to let me drop trading and make straight for Gibraltar, so as to be ready to put out as soon as we get the declaration of war. There ought to be some first-rate pickings along the coast. It isn't here as it is with France, where they have learned to be precious cautious, and where one daren't risk running in close to their coast on the chance of picking up a prize, for the waters swarm with their privateers. The Spaniards are a very slow set, and there is not much fear of their fitting out many privateers for months to come, and the coasters will be a long time before they wake up to the fact that Spain is at war with us, and will go lumbering along from port to port without the least fear of being captured. So it is a rare chance of making prize-money. If you like a cruise I shall be very happy to take you with me. I have seen you under fire, you know, and know that you are to be depended upon."

"I should like to go above all things," Bob said; "but I don't know what my sister would say. I must get at her husband first. If I can get him on my side I think I shall be able to manage it with her. Well, will you come up to dinner?"

"No, I shall be busy all day. Here are the letters I was speaking of."

"Well, we have supper at seven. Will you come then?"

"With pleasure."

"Will Joe be able to come too?"

"No; it wouldn't do for us both to leave the brig. The Spanish fleet may be sending in their boats to try and cut some of our vessels out, and I should not feel comfortable if we were both ashore; but he will be very glad to see you on board. We are anchored a cable-length from the Water Port. You are pretty sure to see one of our boats alongside. The steward came off with me to buy some soft tack and fresh meat. I saw him just before I met you. He told me he had got some bread, but that meat was at a ruinous price. I told him that he must get it whatever price it was, and I expect by this time he has done so; so if you look sharp you will get to the boat before it puts off with him."

The steward was in the act of getting into the boat as Bob ran down. "Glad to see you, Mister Repton," the man said, touching his hat. "Have you seen the captain, sir?"

"Yes, I have just left him. He told me I should catch you here."

"Thinking of having another cruise with us, sir?"

"I am thinking about it, Parker, but I don't know whether I shall be able to manage it."

They were soon alongside the *Antelope*.

"I thought it was you, Mister Repton, when I saw you run down to the boat," Joe Lockett said as he shook hands with Bob.

"I am glad to see you again, Joe, and I am glad to hear you are first-mate now; though, of course, I am sorry for Mr. Probert."

"Yes, a bad job for him, a very bad job; but it won't be so bad in his case as in some. He has been talking for the last two or three voyages of retiring. An old uncle of his died and left him a few acres of land down in Essex, and he has saved a bit of money out of his pay and his share of the prizes we have made, and he talked about giving up the sea and settling down on shore. So now he will do it. He said as much as that the night he was wounded. 'Well,' he said, 'there won't be any more trouble about making up my mind, Joe. If I do get over this job, I have got to lay up as a dismantled hulk for the rest of my life. I have been talking of it to you, but I doubt whether I should ever have brought myself to it if it had not been for them Frenchmen's shot.' Well, will you come into the cabin and take something?"

"No, thank you, Joe."

"Have they got the news about the declaration of war yet, Mister Repton?"

"No, it hasn't arrived yet."

"I expect we shall get some good pickings along the coast directly it comes. We have been trading regularly this last year, and we all of us want the chance of earning a bit of prize-money. So I can tell you we were very glad when we heard that we were going to take to that again for a bit."

"Yes, the captain was telling me about it, and he has asked me to go for a trip with you."

"Well, I hope that you will be able to come, Mister Repton."

"I hope so, Joe. But there is one thing, if I do come you must call me Bob; I hate being called Mister Repton."

"Well, it would be different if you come with us like that," the young mate said. "You see you were a passenger before, but if you came like this you will be here as a friend like. So it will come natural to call you Bob. And how do you like the place?"

"Oh, I like it well enough! I have been working very hard—at least pretty hard—so I haven't had time to feel it dull; and of course I know all the officers in my brother-in-law's regiment. But I shall be very glad indeed of a cruise, especially as we are likely presently, by all they say, to be cut off here, some say for months, some say for years."

"But still I expect there will be some lively work," the mate said, "if the Spaniards really mean to try and take this place."

"They will never take it," Bob said, "unless they are able to starve us out; and they ought not to be able to do that. Ships ought to be able to run in from the east at any time, for the Spaniards dare not come across within range of the guns, and if the wind was strong, they could not get out from their side of the bay."

"That is true enough, and I expect you will find fast-sailing craft, privateers and such like will dodge in and out; but a merchantman won't like to venture over this side of the Straits, but will keep along the Moorish coasts. You see they can't keep along the Spanish side without the risk of being picked up by the gunboats and galleys with the blockading fleet. There are a dozen small craft lying over there now with the men-of-war. Still I don't say none of them will make their way in here, because I daresay they will. They well know they will get big prices for their goods if they can manage to run the blockade. We are safe to pick up some of the native craft and bring them in, and so will the other privateers. I expect there will be a good many down here before long. The worst of it is, there won't be any sale for the craft we capture."

"Except for firewood, Joe. That is one of the things I have heard we are sure to run very short of if there is a long siege."

"Well, that will be something, and of course any prizes we take laden with things likely to be useful and sell here we shall bring in; but the rest we shall have to send over to the other side, so as to be out of sight of their fleet, and then take them straight back to England. You see we have shipped twice as many hands as we had on the voyage when you were with us. We had only a trader's crew then, now we have a privateer's. Look there! There is a craft making in from the south. It is like enough she has got the despatches on board. There are two or three of those small Spanish craft getting under sail to cut her off, but they won't do it. They could not head her without getting under the fire of the guns of those batteries on the point."

"Well, I will go ashore now, Joe, if you will let me have the boat. The captain is going to have supper with us to-night. I wanted you to come too, but he said you could not both come on shore together. I hope we shall see you to-morrow."

On landing Bob made his way to the barrack, so as to intercept Gerald when he came off duty.

"Look here, Gerald," he said when Captain O'Halloran came out of the orderly-room, "I want you to back me up."

"Oh, you do? Then I am quite sure that you are up to

some mischief or other, Bob, or you wouldn't want me to help you with Carrie."

"It is not mischief at all, Gerald. The *Antelope* came in last night, and I saw Captain Lockett this morning, and I have asked him to come to supper."

"Well, that is all right, Bob. We have plenty of food at present."

"Yes, but that is not it, Gerald. He has invited me to go for a cruise with him. He is going to pick up some prizes along the Spanish coast."

"Oh, that is it, is it? Well, you know very well Carrie won't let you go."

"Well, why shouldn't I, Gerald? You know that I have been working very well here, and I am sure I have learnt as much Spanish in six months as uncle expected me to learn in two years, besides lots of Latin and other things from the doctor. Now, I do think that I have earned a holiday. A fellow at school always has a holiday. I am sure I have worked as hard as I did at school. I think it only fair that I should have a holiday. Besides, you see, I am past sixteen now, and being out here I think I ought to have the chance of any fun there is, especially as we may be shut up here for ever so long."

"Well, there may be something in that, Bob. You certainly have stuck at it well; and you have not got into a single scrape since you came out, which is a deal more than I expected of you."

"Besides, you see, Gerald, if I had not made up my mind to stick to uncle's business I might have been on board the *Brilliant* now with Jim Sankey, and I think after my giving up that chance it would be only fair that I should be allowed to have a cruise, now that there is such a splendid opportunity."

"Well, Bob, I will do my best to persuade Carrie to let you go; but as far as you are concerned, you know, she is commanding officer."

Bob laughed, for he knew well enough that not only in that but in all other matters his sister generally had her own way.

"Well, I am very much obliged to you, Gerald. I am sure I should enjoy it awfully."

"Don't thank me too soon, Bob. You have your sister to manage yet."

"Oh, we ought to be able to manage her between us!" Bob said confidently. "Look how you managed to have Dr. Burke for me, and you know how well that turned out."

"Yes, that was a triumph, Bob. Well, we will do our best."

"Why, Bob, where have you been all the morning?" his sister said. "The professor came at ten o'clock. He said he had arranged with you that he should be an hour later than usual, as he had another engagement early."

"I forgot all about him, Carrie; he never came into my mind once since breakfast. I met Captain Lockett down in the town as soon as I went out, and I wanted him to come here to dinner. I knew you would be glad to see him, for you said you liked him very much; but he said he should be too busy, but he is coming up to supper at seven. Then I went on board the *Antelope* and had a chat with his cousin Joe, who is first-mate now."

When dinner was finished Bob said: "Don't you think, Carrie, I am looking pale? What with the heat, and what with my sticking in and working so many hours a day, I begin to feel that it is too much for me."

His sister looked anxiously at him. "Well, Bob, you are looking a little pale, but so is everybody else; and no wonder, with this heat. But I have not been noticing you particularly. What do you feel, Bob?"

"I think Bob feels as if he wants a holiday," Captain O'Halloran put in.

"Well, then, we must tell the professor that we don't want him to come for a bit. Of course Teddy Burke has given up coming already. But if you have a holiday, Bob, what will you do with yourself?"

"I don't think I shall get any better here, Carrie. I think I want change of air."

"Nonsense, Bob! You can't be as bad as all that, and you never said anything about it before. If he is not well you must ask Teddy Burke to come up to see him, Gerald. Besides, how can he have change of air? The only place he could go would be Tetuan, and it would be hotter there than it is here."

"I think, Carrie," Captain O'Halloran said, "I can prescribe for him without calling Teddy Burke in. I fancy the very thing that would get Bob set up would be a sea voyage."

"A sea voyage!" his wife repeated. "Do you mean that he should go back to England? I don't see anything serious the matter with him. Surely there cannot be anything serious enough for that."

"No, not so serious as that, Carrie. Just a cruise for a bit, on board the *Antelope* for example."

Mrs. O'Halloran looked from one to the other, and then, catching a twinkle in Bob's eye, the truth flashed across her.

"You ought to be ashamed of yourself, Gerald," she said, laughing in spite of herself. "You have quite frightened me. I see now. Captain Lockett has invited Bob to go for a cruise with him, and all this about his being ill is nonsense from beginning to end. You don't mean to say that you have been encouraging Bob in this ridiculous idea?"

"I don't know about encouraging, Carrie; but when he put it to me that he had been working very steadily for the last six months, and that he had got into no scrapes, and that he had really earned a holiday, and that this would be a very jolly one, I did not see any particular reason why he shouldn't have it."

"No particular reason! Why, the *Antelope* is a privateer;

and if she is going to cruise about, that means that she is going to fight, and he may get shot."

"So he may here, Carrie, if a ball happens to come the right way. I think Bob certainly deserves a reward for the way he has stuck to his lessons. You know you never expected he would do as he has done; and I am sure his uncle would be delighted if he heard how well he speaks Spanish. As to his health the boy is well enough, but there is no denying that this hot weather we are having takes it out of us all, and that it would be a mighty good thing if every soul on the Rock had the chance of a month's cruise at sea to set him up. But seriously, Carrie, I don't see any reason whatever why he should not go. We didn't bring the boy out here to make a mollycoddle of him. He has got to settle down some day in a musty old office, and it seems to me that he ought to have his share in any fun and diversion that he has a chance of getting at now. As to danger, sure you are a soldier's wife; and why shouldn't he have a share of it just the same as if he had gone into the navy? You wouldn't have made any hullabaloo about it if he had done that. This is Bob's good time, let him enjoy it. You are not going to keep a lad of his age tied to your apron strings. He has just got the chance of having two or three years of fighting and adventure. It will be something for him to talk about all his life; and my opinion is, that you had best let him go his own way. There are hundreds and hundreds of lads his age knocking about the world, and running all sorts of risks, without having elder sisters worrying over them."

"Very well, Gerald, if you and Bob have made up your minds about it, it is no use my saying no. I am sure I don't want to make a mollycoddle, as you call it, of him. Of course uncle will blame me if any harm comes of it."

"No he won't, Carrie. Your uncle wants the boy to be a gentleman and a man of the world. If you had said that a year ago I would have agreed with you; but we know him better now, and I will be bound he will like him to see as much life as he can during this time. He has sent him out into the world. I will write to your uncle myself, and tell him it is my doing entirely, and that I think it is a good thing Bob should take every chance he gets, and that I will answer for it that he won't be any the less ready when the time comes for buckling to at business."

"Well, if you really think that, Gerald, I have nothing more to say. You know I should like Bob to enjoy himself as much as he can, only I seem to have the responsibility of him."

"I don't see why you worry about that, Carrie. If he had gone out to Cadiz or Oporto, as your uncle intended, you don't suppose the people there would have troubled themselves about him. He would just have gone his own way. You went your own way, didn't you? and it is mighty little you troubled yourself about what your uncle was likely to say when you took up with an Irishman in a marching regiment, and I don't see why you should trouble now. The old gentleman means well with the boy, but, after all, he is not either his father or his mother. You are his nearest relation, and though you are a married woman, you are not old enough yet to expect that a boy of Bob's age is going to treat you as if you were his mother instead of his sister; there is not one boy in fifty would have minded us as he has done."

"Well, Bob, there is nothing more for me to say after that," Carrie said half laughing, though there were tears in her eyes.

"No, no, Carrie; I won't go if you don't like," Bob said impetuously.

"Yes, you shall go, Bob. Gerald is quite right. It is better you should begin to think for yourself, and I am sure I should like you to see things, and to enjoy yourself as much as you can. I don't know why I should fidget about you, for you showed you had much more good sense than I credited you with, when you gave up your chance of going to sea and went into uncle's office. I am sure I am the last person who ought to lecture you, after choosing to run about all over the world, and to take the risk of being starved here," and she smiled at her husband. "You do as you like, Bob," she went on, "I won't worry about you in future; only if you have to go back to England without a leg or an arm, don't blame me; and be sure you tell uncle that I made as good a fight against it as I could."

And so it was settled.

"By the way," Bob exclaimed presently, "I have got a letter from uncle to you in my pocket, and one for myself also. Captain Lockett gave them to me this morning, but I forgot all about them."

"Well, you are a boy!" his sister exclaimed. "This is a nice sample, Gerald, of Bob's thoughtfulness. Well, give me the letter. Perhaps he writes saying you had better be sent home by the first chance that offers itself."

Bob's face fell. He had indeed himself had some misgiving ever since the troubles began that his uncle might be writing to that effect.

"Well, look here, Carrie," he said, "here is the letter, but I think you had better not open it till I have started on this cruise. Of course, if he says I must go back, I must, but I may as well have this trip first."

Carrie laughed. "What do you think, Gerald, shall I leave it till Bob has gone?"

"No, open it at once, Carrie. If he does say, send Bob on by the first vessel, there is not likely to be one before he goes in the *Antelope*. Besides, that is all the more reason why he should go for a cruise before he starts back for that grimy old place in Philpot Lane. We may as well see what the old gentleman says."

"I won't open mine till you have read yours, Carrie," Bob said. "I mean to go the cruise anyhow; but if he says

I must go after that, I will go.   If he had been the old bear I used to think him, I would not mind it a snap, but he has been so kind that I shall certainly do what he wants."

Bob sat with his hands deep in his pockets watching his sister's face with the deepest anxiety as she glanced through the letter, Gerald standing by and looking over her shoulder.

"The old gentleman is a brick!" Gerald, who was the first to arrive at the end, exclaimed. "I wish I had had such a sensible old relative myself; but barring an aunt who kept three parrots and a cat, and who put more store on the smallest of them than she did on me, never a relative did I have in the world."

"Oh, tell me that afterwards!" Bob broke in.   "Do tell me what uncle says, Carrie."

His sister turned to the beginning again and read aloud: "My dear niece—"

"Where does he write from?" Bob interrupted.   "Is it from Philpot Lane or from somewhere else?"

"He writes from Matlock, Derbyshire."

"That is all right," Bob said.   "I thought by what Gerald said he could not have written from Philpot Lane."

"My dear niece," Carrie began again, "I duly received your letter saying that Bob had arrived out safely, and also his more lengthy epistle giving an account of the incidents of the voyage.   I should be glad if you would impress upon him the necessity of being more particular in his punctuation, as also in the crossing of his t's and the dotting of his i's.   I have also received your letter bearing date June 1st, and note with great satisfaction your statement that he has been most assiduous in his studies, and that he is already able to converse with some fluency in Spanish.   Since that time the state of affairs between the two countries has much occupied my attention, both from its commercial aspect, which is serious, and in connection with Bob.

"As the issue of a declaration of war is hourly expected as I write, the period of uncertainty may be considered as

over, and the two countries may be looked upon as at war. I have reason to congratulate myself upon having followed the advice of my correspondent, and of having laid in a very large supply of Spanish wine, from which I shall, under the circumstances, reap considerable profits. I have naturally been debating with myself whether to send for Bob to return to England, or to proceed to Lisbon and thence to Oporto to the care of my correspondent there. I have consulted in this matter my junior partner, Mr. Medlin, who is staying with me here for a few days, and I am glad to say that his opinion coincides with that at which I had finally arrived, namely, to allow him to remain with you.

"His conduct when with me, and the perseverance with which, as you report, he is pursuing his studies, has shown me that he will not be found wanting in business qualities when he enters the firm. I am therefore all the more willing that he should use the intervening time in qualifying himself generally for a good position in the city of London; especially for that of the head of a firm in the wine trade, in which an acquaintance with the world and the manners of a gentleman, if not of a man of fashion—a matter in which my firm has been very deficient heretofore—are specially valuable. It is probable from what I hear that Gibraltar will be besieged, and the event is likely to be a memorable one. It will be of advantage to him, and give him a certain standing to have been present on such an occasion. And if he evinces any desire to place any services he is able to render, either as a volunteer or otherwise, at the disposal of the military authorities—and I learn from Mr. Medlin that it is by no means unusual for the civil inhabitants of a besieged town to be called upon to aid in its defence—I should recommend that you should place no obstacle in his way.

"As a lad of spirit he would naturally be glad of any opportunity to distinguish himself. I gathered from him that one of his school-fellows was serving as a midshipman in a ship-of-war that would not improbably be stationed at

Gibraltar, and Bob would naturally dislike remaining inactive when his school fellow, and many other lads of the same age, were playing men's parts in an historical event of such importance. Therefore you will fully understand that you have my sanction beforehand to agree with any desire he should express in this direction if it seems reasonable and proper to you and Captain O'Halloran. As it is probable that the prices of food and other articles will be extremely high during the siege, I have written by this mail to Messrs. James & William Johnston, merchants of Gibraltar, with whom I have had several transactions, authorizing them to honour drafts duly drawn by Captain O'Halloran upon me to the extent of £500, such sum being of course additional to the allowance agreed upon between us for the maintenance and education of your brother.—I remain, my dear niece, your affectionate uncle, JOHN BALE."

"Now I call that being a jewel of an uncle," Captain O'Halloran said, while Bob was loud in his exclamations of pleasure. "Now you see what you brought on yourself, Bob, by your forgetfulness. Here we have had all the trouble in life to get Carrie to agree to your going, while, had she read this letter first, she would not have had a leg to stand upon, at least metaphorically speaking, practically no one would doubt it for a minute."

"Practically you are a goose, Gerald; metaphorically uncle is an angel. But I am very, very glad. That has relieved me from the responsibility altogether, and you know at heart I am just as willing that Bob should enjoy himself as you are. Now, what does your uncle say to you, Bob?"

Bob opened and read his uncle's letter, and then handed it to his sister. "It is just the same sort of thing, Carrie. I can see Mr. Medlin's hand in it everywhere. He says that for the time I must regard my connection with the firm as of secondary importance, and take any opportunity that offers to show the spirit of an English gentleman by doing

all in my power to uphold the dignity of the British flag,
and taking any becoming part that may offer in the defence
of the town.   Of course he says he has heard with pleasure
of my progress in Spanish, and that he and his junior
partner look forward with satisfaction to the time when I
shall enter the firm."

"My dear Carrie," Captain O'Halloran said, "I will get
a bottle of champagne from the mess, and this evening at
supper we will drink your excellent uncle's health with all
the honours.   I will ask Teddy Burke to come up and join
us."

"Then I think, Gerald," his wife said smiling, "that as
Captain Lockett will be here too, one bottle of champagne
will not go very far."

"I put it tentatively, my dear; we will say two bottles,
and we will make the first inroad on our poultry-yard.   We
had twenty eggs this morning, and the woman downstairs
reports that two of the hens want to sit, though how they
explained the matter to her is more than I know; anyhow,
we can afford a couple of chickens."

It was a very jovial supper, especially as it was known that
the news of the proclamation of war had been brought in
by the ship that had arrived that morning.

"By the way, Mrs. O'Halloran," Captain Lockett said,
"I have a consignment for you.   I will land it the first
thing in the morning, for I shall sail in the evening.   We
are to get our letters of marque authorizing the capture of
Spanish vessels at ten o'clock in the morning."

"What is the consignment, captain?"

"It is from Mr. Bale, madam.   I saw him in town a week
before I sailed, and told him I was likely to come on here
direct, and he sent off at once three cases of champagne and
six dozen of port directed to you and an eighteen-gallon
cask of Irish whisky for Captain O'Halloran."

"My dear," Captain O'Halloran said solemnly, "I believe
that you expressed to-day the opinion that your uncle was

metaphorically an angel. I beg that the word metaphori
cally be omitted. If there was ever an angel in a pig-tail
and a stiff cravat that angel is Mr. John Bale of Philpot
Lane."

"It is very good of him," Carrie agreed. "We could
have done very well without the whisky, but the port-wine
and the champagne may be very useful if this siege is going
to be the terrible thing you all seem to fancy."

"A drop of the craytur is not to be despised, Mrs. O'Halloran," Dr. Burke said; "taken with plenty of water it is a
fine digestive, and when we run short of wine and beer you
will not be despising it yourself."

"I did not know, Teddy Burke, that you had any experience whatever of whisky mixed with plenty of water."

"You are too hard on me altogether," the doctor laughed.
"There is no soberer man in the regiment than your
humble servant."

"Well, it will do you all good if you get on short allowance of wine for a time. I can't think why men want to
sit after dinner and drink bottle after bottle of port-wine.
It is all very well to say that everyone does it, but that is
a very poor excuse. Why should they do it? Women
don't do it, and I don't see why men should. I hope the
time will come when it is considered just as disgraceful for
a man to drink as it is for a woman. And now, Captain
Lockett, about Bob. What time must he be on board?"

"He must be on board before gun-fire, Mrs. O'Halloran,
unless you get a special order from the town-major. I was
obliged to get one myself for this evening. The orders are
strict now; all the gates are closed at gun-fire."

"Yes, and mighty strict they are," Captain O'Halloran
said. "There was Major Corcoran of the 72d and the
doctor of the regiment were out fishing yesterday, and the
wind fell, and the gun went just as they were landing, and
divil a bit could they get in. The major is a peppery little
man, and I would have given anything to have seen him.

One of the Hanoverian regiments furnished the guard at the water-batteries, and the sentry told him if he came a foot nearer in the boat they would fire, and in the end he and the doctor had to cover themselves up with a sail and lie there all night.   I hear the major went to lodge a complaint when he landed, but of course the men were only doing their duty; and I hear Eliott gave him a wigging for endeavouring to make him disobey orders."

"I will be on board before gun-fire, Captain Lockett. There is no fear of my missing it."

"How long do you expect to be away, Captain Lockett?" Mrs. O'Halloran asked.

"That depends on how we get on.   If we are lucky and pick up a number of prizes we may bring them in in a week, if not we may be three weeks, especially if this calm weather lasts."

"I am sure I hope you won't be too lucky at first captain," Bob put in.   "I don't want the cruise to finish in a week."

"Oh, I sha'n't consider the cruise is finished merely because we come in, Bob!" the captain said.   "We shall be going out again, and only put in here to bring in our prizes. The cruise will last as long as Captain O'Halloran and your sister will allow you to remain on board.   I expect that I shall be able to make you very useful.   I shall put you down in the ship's books as third-mate.   You won't be able to draw prize-money as an officer, because the number of officers entitled to prize-money was entered when the crew signed articles; but if I put you down as supercargo you will share with the men in any prizes we take while you are away with us."

"That will be jolly, captain; not because of the money, you know, but because it will give one more interest in the cruise.   Besides, I shall like something to do."

"Oh, I will give you something to do.   I shall put you in Joe's watch, and then you will learn something.   It is always as well to pick up knowledge when you get a chance;

and if we do take any prizes it will be your duty as supercargo to take an inventory of what they have on board."

The next morning Bob packed his trunks the first thing, then he went round to the professor's and told him that he was going away for a fortnight or so for a cruise, then he went down to the port and met Joe Lockett when he landed and brought him up to breakfast, as had been arranged with the captain the night before. After that he went with him up the Rock to look at the Spaniards, whose tents were a good deal more numerous than they had been, and who were still at work arming the forts.

"If I were the general," Joe said, "I would go out at night with two or three regiments, and spike all those guns and blow up the forts. The Dons wouldn't be expecting it, and it would be a good beginning, and would put the men in high spirits. Do you see, the Spanish fleet has drifted away almost out of sight to the east. I thought what it would be at sunset yesterday when I saw that they did not enter the bay, for the current would be sure to drive them away if the wind didn't spring up. Well, I hope we shall get a little this evening. And now I must be going down, for there is a good deal to do before we sail."

CHAPTER X.

A CRUISE IN A PRIVATEER.

BOB was on board the *Antelope* a quarter of an hour before gun-fire. No movement was made until after sunset, for some of the gun-boats over at Algeciras might have put out had they seen any preparations for making sail; but as soon as it became dark the anchor was hove, the sails dropped and sheeted home, and the brig began to move slowly through the water. As she breasted Europa Point her course was altered to west by north, and the Rock faded from sight in the darkness. The first-mate was on watch, and Bob walked up and down the deck with him.

"There is no occasion for you to keep up," Joe Lockett said; "you may just as well turn in."

"Oh no, I mean to keep the watch with you!" Bob said. "The captain said that I was to be in your watch, and I want you to treat me just the same way as if I were a midshipman under you."

"Well, if you were a midshipman there wouldn't be anything for you to do now; still if you like to keep up of course you can do so, I shall be glad of your company, and you will help keep a sharp look-out for ships."

"There is no chance of our coming across any Spanish traders to-night, I suppose, Joe?"

"Not in the least: they would keep a deal farther out than we shall if they were bound either for Algeciras or through the Straits. We are not likely to meet anything till we get near Malaga. After that of course we shall be in the line of coasters. There are Almeria, and Cartagena, and Alicante, and a score of small ports between Alicante and Valencia."

"We don't seem to be going through the water very fast, Joe."

"No, not more than two or two and a half knots an hour. However, we are in no hurry. With a light wind like this we don't want to get too close to the shore, or we might have some of their gun-boats coming out after us. I expect that in the morning, if the wind holds light, the captain will take in our upper sails, and just drift along. Then after it gets dark he will clap on everything, and run in so as to strike the coast a few miles above Malaga. Then we will take in sail, and anchor as close in as we dare. Anything coming along then will take us for a craft that has come out from Malaga."

At midnight the second-mate, whose name was Crofts, came up to relieve watch, and Bob, who was beginning to feel very sleepy, was by no means sorry to turn in. It hardly seemed to him that he had closed an eye when he was aroused by a knocking at the cabin door.

"It's two bells, sir, and Mr. Lockett says you are to turn out."

Bob hurried on his things and went up, knowing that he was an hour late.

"I thought you wanted to keep watch, Bob. You ought to have been on deck at eight bells."

"So I should have been if I had been woke," Bob said indignantly. "I am not accustomed to wake up just after I go to sleep; it doesn't seem to me that I have been in bed five minutes. If you wake me to-morrow morning, you will see I will be up sharp enough. There is hardly any wind."

"No, we have been only crawling along all night. There is Gib, you see, behind us."

"Why, it doesn't look ten miles off," Bob said in surprise.

"It is twice that; it is two- or three-and-twenty, I should

say. Now, the best thing you can do is to go down to the waist, slip off your togs, and have a few buckets of water poured over you. That will wake you up, and you will feel ever so much more comfortable afterwards. I have just told the steward to make us a couple of cups of coffee, they will be ready by the time you have had your wash."

Bob followed the advice, and after a bath, a cup of coffee, and a biscuit, he no longer felt the effects from the shortness of the night. The sun had already risen, and there was not a cloud upon the sky. "What are those over there?" he asked, pointing to the south-east; "they look like sails."

"They are sails. They are the upper sails of the Spanish fleet. I expect they are trying to work back into the bay again, but they won't do it unless they get more wind. You see I have taken the topgallant sails off the brig so as not to be seen. There is the Spanish coast, you see, twelve or fourteen miles away to port. If you like you can take the glass and go up into the main-top, and see if you can make anything out on shore."

Bob came down in half an hour. "There are some fishing-boats," he said, "at least they look like fishing-boats, close inshore just abreast of us."

"Yes, there are two or three little rivers on this side of Malaga. There is not water in them for craft of any size, but the fishing-boats use them. There is a heavy swell sets in here when the wind is from the east with a bit south in it, and they run up there for shelter."

Captain Lockett now came on deck. "Good-morning, Bob, I did not see you here when watch was changed."

"No, sir, I wasn't woke; but I mean to be up another morning."

"That is right, Bob. Joe and I agreed to give you an extra hour this morning. Four hours are very short measure to one who is not accustomed to it; but you will soon find that you can turn in and get a sleep when your watch is over whatever the time of day."

"It seems to me that this watch has the worst of it, Captain Lockett. We had from eight to twelve, and now from four to eight, and the other had only four hours on deck."

"Yours is considered the best watch, Bob; the middle watch, as the one that comes on at twelve o'clock is called, is always the most disliked. You see at eight bells you go off and have your breakfast comfortably, and can then turn in till twelve o'clock, and you can get another caulk from five or six till eight in the evening. Of course if there is anything to do, bad weather or anything of that sort, both watches are on deck all day."

"Well, I am almost sure I should like the other watch best," Bob said.

"You are wrong, lad, especially in summer. You see it is not fairly dark till nine, and you wouldn't turn in till ten anyhow, so that really you are only kept two hours out of your bunk at that watch. It is getting light when you come up at four, and at five we begin to wash decks, and there is plenty to occupy you, so that it doesn't seem long till eight bells. The others have to turn out at twelve o'clock, just when they are most sleepy, and to be on watch for the four dark hours, and then go down just as it is getting light. On a cold night in winter in the channel I think perhaps the advantage is the other way. But, in fact, men get so accustomed to the four hours in and the four hours out, that it makes very little difference to them how it goes."

All day the brig kept on the same course, moving very slowly through the water, and passing the coast as much by aid of the current as by that of her sails.

"We are pretty well off Malaga," Captain Lockett said in the afternoon. "If there had been any wind we should have had a chance of picking up something making from there to the Straits; but there is no chance of that to-day. People like making quick voyages when there is a risk of falling in with an enemy, and they won't be putting out from port until there is some change in the weather. However, it looks to me as if there is a chance of a little breeze from the south when the sun goes down. I have seen a flaw or two on the water that way."

"Yes, it seems to me darker over there," the mate said. "I will go up and have a look round. Yes, sir, there is certainly a breeze stirring down to the south," he shouted from aloft.

"That will just suit us," the captain said. "We must be twenty miles off the coast at least, and even if they had noticed us from above the town, we are too far off for them to make us out at all, so it will be safe for us to run in to the land. We shall rely upon you, Bob, if we are hailed."

"I will do my best to throw dust in their eyes, captain. You must tell me beforehand all particulars, so that I can have the story pat."

"We will wait till we see what sort of craft is likely to hail us. A tale may be good enough for the skipper of a coaster, that might not pass muster with the captain of a gun-boat."

"What are the coasters likely to be laden with?"

"There is never any saying. Mostly fruit and wine, grain and olives. Then some of them would be taking goods from the large ports to the small towns and villages along the coast. Some of the coasters are well worth picking up; but of course the craft we shall be chiefly on the look-out for will be those from abroad. Some of these have very valuable cargoes. They bring copper and lead, and sometimes silver from the mines of Mexico and South America. Some of them carry a good lot of silver, but it is too much to hope that we should run across such a prize as that. They bring over hides too; they are worth money. Then of course there are ships that have been trading up the Mediterranean with France and Italy or the Levant. So you see there is a considerable variety in the chances of what we may light upon. Coasters are of course the staple, so to speak.

If we have anything like luck we shall not do badly with them. The others we must look upon as the prizes in the lottery."

Before the sun set the breeze came up to them, and the brig was at once headed for the land. At ten o'clock the lights of Malaga were made out on the port-beam, and the brig bore away a little to the east. Two hours later the land was looming not far ahead. Sail was got off her, and a man placed in the chains and soundings taken. This was continued until the water shoaled to eight fathoms, when the brig was brought up head to wind, and the anchor let go. Then an anchor watch of four men was set, and the rest of the crew allowed to turn in. At daybreak the officers were out again, and it was found that the brig was lying within a quarter of a mile of the land in a slight indentation of the coast. The wind had died away, and the sails were loosed and suffered to fall against the masts.

"It could not be better," Captain Lockett said. "We look now as if we had been trying to make up or down the coast, and had been forced to come to anchor here. Fortunately there don't seem to be any villages near, so we are not likely to have anyone coming out to us."

"How far do you think we are from Malaga, captain?"

"About ten miles I should say, Bob. Why do you ask?"

"I was only thinking whether it would be possible for me to make my way there and find out what vessels there are in harbour, and whether any of them are likely to be coming this way. But if it is ten miles I am afraid it is too far. I should have to pass through villages, and I might be questioned where I came from and where I was going. I don't know that my Spanish would pass muster if I were questioned like that. I should be all right if I were once in a seaport. No one would be likely to ask me any questions. Then I could stroll about and listen to what was said, and certainly I could talk quite well enough to go in and get a meal and all that sort of thing."

"I couldn't let you do that, Bob," the captain said. "It is a very plucky idea, but it wouldn't be right to let you carry it out. You would get hung as a spy if you were detected."

"I don't think there is the least fear in the world of my being detected in a seaport," Bob said, "and I should think it great fun; but I shouldn't like to try to cross the country. Perhaps we may have a better chance later on."

The captain shook his head.

"You might go on board some ship if one brings up at anchor anywhere near us, Bob. If you got detected there we would take her and rescue you. But that is a different thing to letting you go ashore."

Presently the sails of two fishing-boats were seen coming out from beyond a low point three miles to the east.

"I suppose there is a fishing village there," the mate said. "I am glad they are no nearer." He examined the boats with a glass. "They are working out with sweeps. I expect they hope to get a little wind when they are in the offing."

Just as they were at breakfast the second-mate, who was on deck, called down the sky-light:

"There are three craft to the west, sir. They have just come out from behind the point there. They are bringing a little breeze with them."

"What are they like, Mr. Crofts?"

"One is a polacre, another a xebec, and a third looks like a full-rigged craft; but as she is end-on I can't say for certain."

"All right, Mr. Crofts, I will be up in five minutes. We can do nothing until we get the wind anyhow."

Breakfast was speedily finished, and they went on deck. The Spanish flag was already flying from the peak. The three craft were about two miles away.

"How are they sailing, Mr. Crofts?"

"I fancy the xebec is the fastest, sir. She was astern just now, and she is abreast of the polacre now, as near as I can make out. The ship or brig, whichever it is, seems to me to be dropping astern."

"Heave away at the anchor, Joe. Get in all the slack, so as to be ready to hoist as soon as the breeze reaches us. I don't want them to come up to us. The line they are taking now will carry them nearly half a mile outside us, which is fortunate. Run in six of the guns, and throw a tarpaulin over the eighteen-pounder. Three guns on each side are about enough for us to show."

The breeze caught them when the three Spanish craft were nearly abeam.

"They have more wind out there than we shall have here," the captain said: "which is an advantage, for I don't want to run away from them. Now get up the anchor, Joe. Don't take too many hands."

The watch below had already been ordered to sit down on the deck, and half the other watch were now told to do the same.

"Twelve or fourteen hands are quite enough to show," the captain said.

"The anchor's up, sir," Joe shouted.

"Let it hang there; we will get it aboard presently. Now haul that fore-staysail across, ease off the spanker-sheet. Now, as she comes round, haul on the braces and sheets one by one. Do it in as lubberly a way as you can."

The brig, which had been riding with her head to the west, came slowly round, the yards being squared in a slow fashion, in strong contrast to the active way in which they were generally handled. The captain watched the other craft carefully.

"The xebec and polacre are gaining on us, but we are going as fast through the water as the three-master. When we get the wind a little more we shall have the heels of them all. Get a sail overboard, Joe, and tow it under her port-quarter. Don't give her too much rope, or they might catch sight of it on board the ship. That will bring us down to her rate of sailing. I want to keep a bit astern of them. We dare not attack them in the daylight, they mount too many guns for us altogether. That big fellow has got twelve on a side, the polacre has eight, and the xebec six, so between them they have fifty-two guns. We might try it if they were well out at sea, but it would never do here. There may be galleys or gun-boats within hearing, so we must bide our time. I think we are in luck this time, Joe. That ship must have come foreign, at least I should say so by her appearance; though she may be from Cadiz. As to the other two, they may be anything. The xebec, no doubt, is a coast trader; the polacre may be one thing or another, but I should hardly think she has come across the Atlantic. Likely enough she is from Bilbao or Santander. The ship is the fellow to get hold of, if we get a chance. I shall be quite content to leave the others alone."

"I should think so," Joe agreed. "The ship ought to be a valuable prize wherever she comes from. If she is sound and pretty new she would fetch a good sum, if we can get her into an English port."

The wind continued to hold light, and the four vessels made but slow progress through the water. The two leaders, however, gradually improved their position. They were nearly matched in point of sailing, and their captains were evidently making a race of it, hoisting every stitch of canvas they were able to show. By the afternoon they were fully two miles ahead of the ship, which was half a mile on the starboard-bow of the brig. The wind died away to nothing as the sun set. The three Spanish vessels had all been edging in towards shore, and the polacre anchored just before sunset.

The ship held on for another hour, but was a mile astern of the other two when she also dropped her anchor. The sail that had been towing overboard from the brig had been got on board again when the wind began to drop, and she had come up to within little more than a quarter of a mile of the ship. The anchor was let go as soon as it was seen that the crew of the ship were preparing to anchor, so that the brig should be first to do so. Whether there had been any suspicions on board the Spaniards as to the character of the brig, they could not tell; but watching her closely, Captain Lockett saw that the order to anchor was counter-manded as soon as it was seen that the brig had done so. A few minutes after the men again went forward, and the anchor was dropped, for the vessel was making no way whatever through the water.

"Well, Joe, there we are close to her now. The question is, what are we to do next? If there was any wind it would be simple enough. We would drop alongside in the middle watch, and carry her by boarding before the Dons had time to get out of their hammocks; but as it is that is out of the question, and of course we can't think of towing her up; on such a still night as this will be, they would hear the slightest noise."

"We might attack her in the boats," the mate said.

"Yes, that would be possible; but their watch would hear the oars the instant we began to row. You see by the number of guns she carries she must be strongly manned."

"I expect most of them are small," Joe said, "and meant for show rather than use. It is likely enough she may have taken half of them on board at Cadiz or Malaga, so as to give her a formidable appearance in case she should fall in with any craft of our description. If she has come across the Atlantic she would never have carried anything like that number of guns, for Spain was not at war with any-one."

"No; but craft flying the black flag are still to be found in those waters, Joe, and she might carry her guns for defence against them. But it is not a question of guns at present, it is a question of the crew. It isn't likely that she carries many more than we do, and if we could but get alongside her there would be no fear about it at all; but I own I don't like the risk of losing half my men in an attack on a craft like that, unless we can have the advantage of a surprise."

"What do you say to my swimming off to her as soon as it gets quite dark, captain?" Bob said. "I am a very good swimmer. We used to bathe regularly at Putney where I was at school, and I have swum across the Thames and back lots of times. There is sure to be a little mist on the water presently, and they won't be keeping a very sharp look-out till it gets later. I can get hold of a cable and climb up, and get in over the bow if there is no look-out there, and see what is going on. There is no danger in the thing, for if I am discovered I have only got to dive and swim back again. There is no current to speak of here, and there wouldn't be the least chance of their hitting me in the dark. I should certainly be able to learn something by listening to their talk."

"It would be a very risky thing, Bob," Captain Lockett said, shaking his head. "I shouldn't like to let you do it, though of course it would be a great thing if we could learn something about her. I own I don't like her appearance, though I can't say why. Somehow or other I don't think she is all right. Either all those guns are a mere pretence and she is weak-handed, or she must carry a very big crew."

"Well, I don't see there can be any possible harm in my trying to get on board her, captain. Of course if I am hailed as I approach her I shall turn and come back again. The night will be dark, but I shall have no difficulty in finding her from the talking and noise on board.

"Well, Joe, what do you think?" the captain said doubtfully.

"I think you might let Bob try," Joe said. "I should not mind trying at all, but as I can't speak Spanish I should be able to learn nothing. They are not likely to be setting a watch and keeping a sharp look-out for some time, and I should think that he might possibly get on board unobserved. If they do make him out he has only to keep on diving, and in the dark there would be little chance of their hitting him. Besides, they certainly couldn't make out that it was a swimmer; if they noticed a ripple in the water, they would be sure to think it was a fish of some sort."

Bob continued to urge that he should be allowed to try it, and at last Captain Lockett agreed to his doing so. It was already almost dark enough for the attempt to be made, and Bob prepared at once for the swim. He took off his coat, waistcoat, and shirt, and put on a dark knitted jersey, fastened a belt tightly round his waist over his breeches, and took off his shoes.

"If I am seen," he said, "you are sure to hear them hailing or shouting, and then please show a lantern over the stern;" for slight as the current was it sufficed to make the vessel swing head to west. A rope was lowered over the side, and by this he slipped down quietly into the water, which was perfectly warm. Then he struck off noiselessly in the direction of the ship. He kept the two masts of the brig in one as long as he could make them out, but owing to the mist on the water he soon lost sight of her; but he had no difficulty in keeping a straight course, as he could plainly hear the sound of voices ahead of him. Taking the greatest pains to avoid making the slightest splash, and often pausing to listen, Bob swam on until he saw a dark mass looming up in front of him. He now did little more than float, giving a gentle stroke occasionally and drifting towards it until he grasped the cable. He now listened intently. There were voices on the fo'castle above him, and he determined, before trying to climb up there, to swim round the vessel, keeping close to her side, so that he could not be seen unless someone leaned far over the bulwark.

Half-way along he came upon a projection, and, looking up, saw that slabs of wood three inches wide were fixed against the side at intervals of a foot apart, so as to form an accommodation ladder when it was not considered necessary to lower a gangway. Two hand-ropes hung by the side of

BOB SWIMS OFF TO THE SPANISH WARSHIP.

it. His way was now easy. He drew himself out of the water by the ropes and ascended the ladder, then crawled along outside the bulwark until he came to a port-hole, from which a gun projected; then he crawled in there, and lay under the cannon. Two or three lanterns were suspended above the deck, and by their light Bob could at once see that he was on board a ship-of-war. Groups of sailors were sitting on the deck among the guns, and he saw that most of these were run in and that they were of heavy calibre, several of them being 32-pounders.

As the captain and Joe had both agreed that the guns were only 14-pounders, Bob had no difficulty in arriving at the fact that these must have been mere dummies thrust out of the port-holes to deceive any stranger as to her armament. He lay listening for some time to the talk of the sailors, and gathered that the ship had been purposely disguised before putting out from Malaga, in order to deceive any English privateers she might come across as to her strength. He learned also that considerable doubts were entertained as to the brig, and that the xebec and polacre had been signalled to go on ahead so as to induce the brig, if she should be an enemy, to make an attack.

The reason why she had not been overhauled during the day was that the captain feared she might escape him in a light wind, for the watch had been vigilant, and had made out that she was towing something to deaden her way. It was considered likely that, taking the ship for a merchantman, an attack would be made in boats during the night, and the men joked as to the surprise their assailants would get. Boarding-pikes were piled in readiness, shot had been placed in the racks ready to throw down into the boats as they came alongside, and the ship's boats had been swung out in readiness for lowering, as it was intended to carry the brig by boarding after the repulse and destruction of her boats.

"We have had a narrow escape of catching a tartar,"

Bob said to himself. "It is very lucky I came on board to reconnoitre; the Spaniards are not such duffers as we thought them. We fancied we were taking them in, and very nearly fell into a trap ourselves."

Very quietly he crawled back under the port-hole, made his way along outside the bulwark until his hand touched the rope, and then slid down by it into the water. As he knew there was more chance of a sharp watch being kept in the eyes of the ship than elsewhere, he swam straight out from her side until she became indistinct, and then headed for the brig. The lights on board the Spaniard served as a guide to him for some time, but the distance seemed longer to him than it had before, and he was beginning to fancy he must have missed the brig when he saw her looming up on his right. In three or four minutes he was alongside.

"The brig there!" he hailed. "Drop me a rope overboard."

There was a stir overhead at once.

"Where are you, Bob?" Captain Lockett asked, leaning over the side.

"Just below you, sir."

A rope was dropped. Bob grasped it, and was hauled up.

"Thank God you are back again!" the captain said. "I have been blaming myself ever since you started, though, as all was quiet, we felt pretty sure they hadn't made you out. Well, have you any news? Did you get on board?"

"You will get no prize-money this time, captain. The Spaniard is a ship-of-war mounting twenty-four guns, none of them smaller than eighteens, and ten of them thirty-twos."

"Impossible, Bob! We could not have been so mistaken. Joe and I were both certain that they were fourteens."

"Yes, sir; but those things you saw were dummies. The guns themselves are almost all drawn in; all the thirty-twos are, and most of the eighteens. She has been specially disguised at Malaga in hopes of tempting a craft like yours to attack her, and, what is more, she has a shrewd suspicion of what you are;" and he related the whole of the conversation he had heard, and described the preparations for repulsing a boat attack and in turn carrying the brig in the ship's boats.

Captain Lockett was thunderstruck. "The Spanish officer who commands her must be a smart fellow," he said, "and we have had a narrow escape of running our head into a noose. Thanks to you, Bob; for Joe and I had quite made up our minds to attack her in the middle watch. Well, the only thing for us to do is to get away from here as soon as we can. If she finds we don't attack her to-night she is sure to send a boat to us in the morning, and then if we have an engagement we could hardly hope to get off without losing some of our spars, even if we were not sunk, with such heavy metal as she carries. We should have the other two craft down on us too, and our chances of getting away would be worth nothing. Well, I suppose, Joe, our best plan will be to tow her away?"

"I should think so, sir. When they hear us at it they may send their boats out after us, but we can beat them off; and I should hardly think that they would try it, for they will be sure that if we are a privateer we have been playing the same game as they have, and hiding our guns, and will guess that we carry a strong crew."

"Send the crew aft, Joe; I will tell them how matters stand. We have had a narrow escape of catching a tartar, my lads," he said when the men went aft. "You all know Mr. Repton swam off an hour ago to try and find out what the ship was like. Well, he has been on board, and brings back news that she is no trader, but a ship-of-war disguised, and that she carries twenty-four guns, eighteen-pounders and thirty-twos. If we met while out at sea we might make a fight of it, but it would never do here, especially as her two consorts would be down upon us. She suspects what we are, although she is not certain, and everything is in readiness to repel a boat attack, her captain's intention being, if we tried, to sink or cripple the boats and then to attack us with her guns. So you may thank Mr. Repton that you have had a narrow escape of seeing the inside of a Spanish prison.

"Now, what I propose to do is to tow her out. Get the four boats in the water as quietly as you can; we have greased the falls already. We will tow her straight ahead, at any rate for a bit. That craft won't be able to bring any guns to bear upon us, except perhaps a couple of bow-chasers; and as she won't be able to see us, there is not much chance of our being hit. Pass the hawser along from boat to boat and row in a line ahead of her, the hull will shelter you. Then lay out heartily, but be ready if you are hailed to throw off the hawser and get back on board again as soon as you can, for they may send their boats out after us. We shall get a start anyhow, for when they hear you rowing they will think you are putting off to attack them, and it will be some minutes before they will find out their mistake. Joe, do you go in charge of the boats; I will take the helm. You must cut the cable, they would hear the clank of the windlass."

The operation of lowering boats was conducted very silently. Bob had taken his place at the taffrail, and stood listening for any sound that would show that the Spaniards had heard what was doing. The oars were scarcely dipped in the water when he heard a sudden lull in the distant talking. A minute later it broke out again.

"They have orders to pay no attention to the noises," Captain Lockett said, "so as to lead us to think that we shall take them unawares. There she is moving now," he added as he looked down into the water.

Four or five minutes elapsed, and then in the stillness of the evening they could hear a loud hail in Spanish: "What ship is that? Cease rowing or we will sink you!"

"Don't answer," Captain Lockett said. "They have nothing but the confused sound of the oars to tell them where we are."

The hail was repeated, and a minute later there was the flash of a gun in the darkness, and a shot hummed through the air.

"Fire away," the captain muttered. "You are only wasting ammunition."

For some minutes the Spaniard continued to fire her two bow guns. Then after a pause there was a crash, and twelve guns were discharged together.

"We are getting farther off every minute," the captain said, "and unless an unlucky shot should strike one of her spars we are safe." The broadside was repeated four times, and then all was silent. "We are a mile away from them now, Bob, and though I daresay they can hear the sound of the oars it must be mere guesswork as to our position."

He went forward to the bows, and hailed the boats.

"Take it easy now, Mr. Lockett; I don't think she will fire any more. When the men have got their wind row on again. I shall head her out now. We must give her a good three miles offing before we stop."

The men in the four boats had been exerting themselves to their utmost, and it was five minutes before they began rowing again. For an hour and a half they continued their work, and then Captain Lockett said to the second-mate: "You can go forward and hail them to come on board. I think we have been moving through the water about two knots an hour, so we must be three miles seaward of him."

As soon as the men came on board a tot of grog was served out all round. Then the watch below turned in.

"You won't anchor, I suppose, captain?"

"No, there is a considerable depth of water here and a rocky bottom. I don't want to lose another anchor, and it would take us something like half an hour to get it up again; besides, what current there is will drift us eastward. There is more of it here than we had inshore. I should say there must be nearly a knot an hour, which will take us a good distance away from those gentlemen before morning. Now, Bob, you had better have a glass of grog and then turn in. Joe will excuse you keeping watch to-night."

"Oh, I feel all right," Bob said. "The water was quite warm, and I slipped down and changed my clothes directly they left off firing."

"Never mind, you turn in as you are told. You have done us good service to-night, and have earned your keep on board the brig if you were to stop here till she fell to pieces of old age."

When Bob went up in the morning at five o'clock the three Spanish vessels were still lying at anchor under the land, seven or eight miles away.

"There is a breeze coming," Joe said, "and it is from the south, so we shall get it long before they do. We shall see no more of them."

As soon as the breeze reached them the sails were braced aft, and the brig kept as close to the wind as she would sail, lying almost directly off from the land.

"I want them to think that we are frightened," Captain Lockett said, in answer to a question from Bob as to the course, "and that we have decided to get away from their neighbourhood altogether. I expect they are only going as far as Alicante. We will run on till we are well out of sight, then hold on for the rest of the day east, and in the night head for land again beyond Alicante. It would never do to risk those fellows coming upon us again when we are quietly at anchor. We might not be so lucky next time."

An hour later the look-out in the top hailed the deck, and said there was a sail in sight.

"What does she look like, Halkett?" Joe Lockett shouted, for the captain was below.

"As far as I can make out she is a two-master—I should say a brig."

"How is she heading?"

"About north-east, sir. I should say if we both hold on our courses she will pass ahead of us."

The captain was now on deck, and he and the first-mate went up to the top. "Starboard your helm a bit!" the captain shouted, after examining the distant sail through his telescope. "Keep her about east."

"What do you think she is, captain?" Bob asked when the two officers came down again to the poop.

"I should say that she was a craft about our own size, Bob, and I fancy she has come through the Straits, keeping well over the other side so as to avoid our cruisers from Gib, and is now heading for Alicante. Now we are on our course again, parallel to the coast, there is no reason why she should suspect us of being anything but a trader. If she doesn't take the alarm I hope we shall be alongside her in a few hours."

CHAPTER XI.

CUTTING OUT A PRIZE.

THE distant sail was anxiously watched from the *Antelope*. She closed in with them fast, running almost before the wind. In two hours her hull could be seen from the deck. Efforts had been made, by slacking the ropes and altering the set of the sails, to give the brig as slovenly an appearance as possible. The guns had been run in and the port-holes closed, and as the Spaniard approached, the crew, with the exception of five or six men, were ordered to keep below the bulwarks. The course that the Spaniard was taking would have brought her just under the stern of the *Antelope*, when suddenly she was seen to change her course and to bear up into the wind.

"Too late, my lady," the captain said; "you have blundered on too long. There is something in our cut that she doesn't like. Haul down that Spanish flag and run the Union Jack up. Open ports, lads, and show them our teeth. Fire that bow gun across her forefoot!"

The guns were already loaded, and as soon as they were run out a shot was fired as a message to the Spaniard to heave to. A minute later, as she paid no attention, a broadside followed. Three of the shots went crashing into the side of the Spaniard, and one of her boats were smashed. A moment later the Spanish flag fluttered down, and a hearty cheer broke from the crew of the *Antelope*. The Spaniard was thrown up into the wind, and in a few minutes the brig ranged up alongside within pistol shot. The gig was lowered, and the captain rowed alongside her, taking Bob with him as interpreter.

The prize proved to be a brig of about the same tonnage as the *Antelope*. She was from Cadiz, bound first to Alicante and then to Valencia. She carried only six small guns and a crew of eighteen men; her cargo consisted of grain and olive-oil.

"Not a bad prize," Captain Lockett said, as Bob read out the items of her bill of lading. "It is a pity that it is not full up instead of only half laden. Still it is not a bad beginning, and the craft herself is of a handy size, and if she won't sell at Gibraltar will pay very well to take on to England. I should say she was fast."

An hour later the two brigs parted company, the second-mate and twelve hands being placed on board the Spaniard. There was some discussion as to the prisoners, but it was finally agreed to leave them on board their ship.

"Keep them down in the hold, Mr. Crofts; see that you don't leave any knives with them. Keep a couple of sentries over the hatchway. If the wind holds you will be in the bay by to-morrow evening. Keep pretty well inshore, and slip in as close to the point as you can. If you do that you need not have much fear of their gun-boats. I don't suppose the authorities will want to keep the prisoners, but of course you will report them on your arrival, and can give them one of the boats to land across the bay if they are not wanted. If the governor wants to buy the cargo for the garrison let him have it at once; don't stand out for exorbitant terms, but take a fair price. It is just as well to be on good terms with the authorities; we might have to put in to refit, and want spars, &c., from the naval yard. If the governor doesn't want the cargo don't sell it to anyone else till we return; there is no fear of prices going down, the longer we keep it the more we shall get for it."

"Hadn't I better bring the ship's papers on board with us, Captain Lockett?"

"What for, Bob? I don't see that they would be any use to us, and the bills of lading will be useful for selling the cargo.'

"I can copy them, sir, for Mr. Crofts. What I thought was this: the brig is just our own size, and if we should get becalmed anywhere near the shore and a boat put off, we might possibly be able to pass with her papers."

"That is a capital idea, Bob; capital! I will have a bit of canvas painted '*Alonzo*, Cadiz,' in readiness to nail over our stern should there be any occasion for it. Well, good-bye Mr. Crofts, and a safe journey to you. I needn't tell you to keep a sharp look-out."

"You may trust us for that, sir; we have no desire to rot in one of their prisons till the end of the war."

The captain's gig took him back to the *Antelope*, the weather-sheets of the fore-staysail were eased off, and the square sails swung round; as they drew the two brigs got under way, heading in exactly opposite directions. Before nightfall the captain pronounced that they were now abreast of Alicante, and under easy sail the vessel's head was turned towards the land, and the next morning she was running along the shore at a distance of three miles. Beyond fishing-boats and small craft hugging the land, nothing was met with until they neared Cartagena. Then the sound of firing was heard ahead, and on rounding a headland they saw a vessel of war chasing some five or six craft nearer inshore.

"That is a British frigate," the captain exclaimed; "but I don't think she will get them. There is Cartagena only three or four miles ahead, and the frigate will not be able to cut them off before they are under the guns of the batteries."

"They are not above a mile ahead of her," the first-mate said; "if we could knock away a spar with our long eighteen we might get one of them."

"We shouldn't make much prize-money if we did, Joe,

for the frigate would share; and as she has five or six times as many men and officers as we have got, it is not much we should get out of it. Hallo!" he broke out, as a shot came ricochetting along the water; "she is trying a shot at us. I forgot we had the Spanish colours up. Get that flag down and run up the Union Jack, Joe."

"One moment, captain," Bob said.

"Well, what is it, Bob?"

"Well, it seems to me, sir, that if we keep the Spanish flag up—"

"We may be sunk," the captain broke in.

"We might, sir, but it is very unlikely, especially if we run in more to the shore; but you see if we are fired at by the frigate it will never enter the minds of the Spaniards that we are anything but what we seem, and if we like we can anchor right under their batteries in the middle of their craft. It will be dark by the time we get in, and we might take our pick of them."

"That is a splendid idea, Bob! This boy is getting too sharp for us altogether, Joe; he is as full of ideas as a ship's biscuit is of weevils. Keep her off, helmsman; that will do." Again and again the frigate fired, but she was two miles away, and though the shot went skipping over the water near the brig, none of them struck her. The men, unable to understand why they were running the gauntlet of the frigate's fire, looked inquiringly towards the poop.

"It is all right, lads," the captain said; "there is not much fear of the frigate hitting us, and it is worth risking it. The Spaniards on shore will never dream that we are English, and we can bring up in the thick of them."

There was a good deal of laughing and amusement among the men as they understood the captain's motive in allowing the brig to be made a target of. As she drew in towards shore the frigate's fire ceased and her course was changed off shore.

"No nearer," the captain said to the helmsman. "Keep

her a little farther off shore. There is not much water here, Joe;" for a man had been heaving the lead ever since they had changed their course. "We have not got a fathom under her keel. You see the frigate did not like to come any closer. She would have cut us off if there had been deep water right up."

An hour later the brig dropped anchor off Cartagena, at little more than a quarter of a mile from one of the batteries that guarded the entrance to the port, and close to two or three of the craft that had been first chased by the frigate. These, as they were going on in the morning, had not entered the harbour with their consorts, for it was already getting dusk.

"Not much fear of their coming to ask any questions this evening," Joe Lockett said. "The Spaniards are not given to troubling themselves unnecessarily, and as we are outside the port we are no one's business in particular."

At this moment a hail came from the vessel anchored ahead of them. Bob went to the bulwark. The brig had swung head to wind, and was broadside on with the other craft.

"You have not suffered from the fire of that accursed ship, I hope?" the captain of the barque shouted.

"No, señor; not a shot struck us."

"You were fortunate. We were hulled twice, and had a man killed by a splinter. This is a rough welcome home to us. We have just returned from Lima, and have heard nothing about the war till we anchored off Alicante yesterday. We heard some firing as we came through the Straits, but thought it was only one of the ships or forts practising at a mark. It was lucky we put in at Alicante, or we should have had no suspicion, and should have let that frigate sail up alongside of us without trying to escape."

"You were fortunate indeed," Bob shouted back. "We had ourselves a narrow escape of being captured by a ship-of-war near Malaga. The *Alonzo* is only from Cadiz with grain and olive-oil."

"Do you think there is any fear of that rascally Englishman trying to cut us out with his boats to-night?"

"Not the slightest," Bob replied confidently. "They would never venture on that. Those batteries on shore would blow them out of the water, and they would know very well they would not have a shadow of chance of taking us out; for even if they captured us the batteries would send us to the bottom in no time. Oh, no; you are perfectly safe from the frigate here."

The Spanish captain raised his hat, Bob did the same, and both left the side of their ships.

"Well, what does he say, Bob?" the captain asked.

"I think you are in luck this time, captain, and no mistake."

"How is that, Bob?"

"She is from Lima."

"You don't say so!" the captain and Joe exclaimed simultaneously. "Then she is something like a prize. She has got hides, no doubt; but the chances are she has a lot of lead too, and maybe some silver. Ah! he is getting one of his boats in the water. I hope he is not coming off here. If he does, Joe, Bob must meet him at the gangway and take him into the cabin. As he comes in you and I will catch him by the throat, gag and bind him, and then Bob must go and tell the men to return to their ship, that the captain is going to spend the evening with us, and that we will take him back in our boat."

"That would be the best thing that could happen," Joe said, "for in that way we could get alongside without suspicion."

"So we could, Joe. I didn't think of that. Yes, I hope he is coming now."

They saw, however, the boat row to a large polacre lying next to the Spaniard on the other side. It remained there two or three minutes, and then rowed away towards the mouth of the harbour.

"Going to spend the evening on shore," the captain observed. "I am not surprised at that. It is likely enough they have been six months on their voyage from Lima. It is unlucky, though; I wish he had come here. Well, Bob, as you have got the best head among us, what scheme do you suggest for our getting on board that craft?"

"I think we could carry out Joe's idea, though in a different way," Bob said. "I should say we had better get a boat out, and put say twenty men on board. It is getting dark, but they might all lie down in the bottom except six oarsmen. Then we should pull in towards the mouth of the harbour just as they have done, and lay up somewhere under the rocks for a couple of hours, then row off again and make for the barque. Of course they would think it was the captain returning. Then ten of the men should spring on board, and they ought to be able to silence any men on deck before they could give the alarm. Directly the ten men got out the boat would row across to the polacre, as there is no doubt her captain went ashore with the other. They would take her in the same way."

"You ought to be made Lord High Admiral of the Fleet, Bob! That will succeed if anything will, only we must be sure to put off again before the Spaniards do.

"Well, Joe, you had better take charge of this expedition. You see, however quietly it is done there is almost sure to be some shouting, and they will take the alarm at the batteries, and when they make out three of us suddenly getting up sail they will be pretty certain that something is wrong, and will open fire on us. That, of course, we must risk; but the thing to be really afraid of is their gun-boats. They are sure to have a couple of them in the port. They may be some little time in getting out, but they will come out. The wind has died away now, but the land breeze is just springing up; but we shall hardly get off before the gun-boats can come to us, they row a lot of oars, you know. You must clap on all sail on the prizes, and I shall hang behind a bit and tackle the gun-boats. You will see what guns there are on board the prizes, and may perhaps be able to lend me a hand; but that you will see. Of course you will take Bob with you to answer the hails from the two Spaniards. Be careful when you bring up ashore. Let the men row very gently after they once get away, so as not to attract any attention. Let them take cutlasses, but no pistols. If a shot were fired the batteries would be sure at once there was some mischief going on. A little shouting won't matter so much; it might be merely a quarrel. Of course the instant you are on board you will cut the cables and get up sail. You will remain on board the barque, Joe. Bob will have command of the party that attack the polacre. You had better take the jolly-boat, and pick out twenty active fellows. Tell them to leave their shoes behind them; the less trampling and noise there is the better. Tell them not to use their cutlasses unless driven to it. There are not likely to be above four or five men on deck; they ought to be able to knock them down and bind them almost before they know what has happened."

In a few minutes the boat was lowered and manned, and rowed away for the shore. As soon as they got well past the ships the men were ordered to row as quietly and noiselessly as possible. Joe had brought with him six strips of canvas, and handed these to the men, and told them to wrap them round the oars so as to muffle them in the rowlocks. This was done, and the boat glided along silently. Keeping in the middle of the channel, they passed through the passage between the shore and the rocky island that protects the harbour, and then, sweeping round, stole up behind the latter and lay-to close to the rocks.

"So far so good," Joe said in a low voice. "I don't think the sharpest eyes could have seen us. Now the question is how long to wait here. The longer we wait the more of the Spaniards will have turned into their bunks; but, upon the other hand, there is no saying how long the captains will remain on shore. There is a heavy dew falling, and that will help to send the sailors below. I should think an hour would be about the right time; the Dons are not likely to be off again before that. It is some distance up the harbour to the landing-place, and they would hardly have taken the trouble to go ashore unless they meant to stay a couple of hours. What time is it now, Bob?"

Bob opened his watch-case and felt the hands. "It is just a quarter past nine."

"Well, we will move at ten," Joe said.

The three-quarters of an hour passed very slowly, and Bob consulted his watch several times before the minute-hand got to twelve.

"Ten o'clock," he said at last.

The oars had not been got in, so the boat glided off again noiselessly out through the entrance. There were lights burning at the sterns of the two Spanish ships as a guide to the boat coming off, and when the boat had tra-versed half the distance Joe ordered the oars to be un-muffled, and they rowed straight for the barque. There was no hail at their approach, but a man appeared at the top of the ladder. As the boat came alongside ten of the men rose noiselessly from the bottom of the boat and followed the first-mate up the ladder. As he reached the top Joe sprang on the Spanish sailor and seized him by the throat. The two sailors following thrust a gag into the man's mouth, bound his arms, and laid him down.

This was effected without the slightest noise. The other sailors had by this time clambered up from the boat and scattered over the deck. A group of seven or eight Spaniards were seated on the deck forward, smoking by the light of a lantern which hung above the fo'castle. They did not notice the approach of the sailors with their naked feet, and the latter sprang upon them, threw them down, bound and gagged them, without a sound save a few short excla-mations of surprise being uttered. Three or four of the

"THEY FOUND THE TWO SPANISH MATES PLAYING AT CARDS."

sailors now coiled a rope against the fo'castle door to prevent its being opened. In the meantime Joe with two men entered the cabin aft, where they found the two Spanish mates playing at cards. The sudden apparition of three men with drawn cutlasses took them so completely by surprise that they were captured without any attempt at resistance, and were, like the rest, bound and gagged.

"You take the helm, Halkett," Joe said, and then hurried forward. "Have you got them all?" he asked as he reached the fo'castle.

"Every man-Jack," one of the sailors said.

"Is there nobody on watch in the bows?"

"No, sir, not a man."

"Very well. Now then to work. Cut the cable, Thompson. The rest of you let fall the sails."

As these had only been loosely furled when the vessel came to anchor, this was done in a very short time, and the vessel began to move through the water before the light breeze, which was dead aft.

The capture of the polacre had not been effected so silently. Bob had allowed the boatswain, who accompanied him, to mount the ladder first; but the man at the top of the gangway had a lantern, and as its light fell upon the sailor's face he uttered an exclamation of surprise, which called the attention of those on deck, and as the sailors swarmed up the ladder shouts of alarm were raised. But the Spaniards could not withstand the rush of the English, who beat them to the deck before they had time to seize their arms. The noise, however, alarmed the watch below, who were just pouring up from the hatchway when they were attacked by the sailors with drawn cutlasses, and were speedily beaten below and the hatches secured over them. Bob had posted himself with two of the men at the cabin door, and as the officers rushed out on hearing the noise they were knocked down and secured. As soon as this was effected Bob looked over the side.

"Hurrah!" he said, "the barque is under way already. Get the sails on her, lads, and cut the cable."

While this was being done Bob mounted the poop, placed one of the sailors at the helm, and then turned his eyes towards the battery astern. He heard shouts, and had no doubt that the sound of the scuffle had been heard. Then lights appeared in several of the casements; and just as the sails were sheeted home, and the polacre began to move through the water, a rocket whizzed up from the battery and burst overhead. By its light Bob saw the *Antelope* and the Spanish barque two or three hundred yards ahead, with their crews getting up all sail rapidly.

A minute later twelve heavy guns flashed out astern, one after another. They were pointed too high and the shot flew overhead, one or two passing through the sails. The boatswain's voice was heard shouting: "Never mind the shot, lads! Look alive! Now, then, up with those topgallant sails! The quicker you get them up the quicker we shall be out of range!" Another battery higher up now opened fire, but the shot did not come near them. Then rocket after rocket was sent up, and the battery astern again fired. One of the shot cut away the main-topsail yard, another struck the deck abreast of the foremast, and then tore through the bulwarks; but the polacre was now making good way. They felt the wind more as they got farther from the shore, and had decreased their distance from the craft ahead. The boatswain now joined Bob upon the poop.

"We have got everything set that will draw now," he said; "she is walking along well. Another ten minutes and we shall be safe, if they don't knock away a spar. She is a fast craft, Mr. Repton; she is overhauling the other two hand over hand."

"We had better bear away a bit, boatswain. The captain said we were to scatter as much as we could so as to divide their fire."

"All right, sir;" and the boatswain gave the orders

to the helmsman, and slightly altered the trim of the sails.

"I suppose we can do nothing with that broken yard, boatswain?"

"No, sir; and it don't matter much, going pretty nearly before the wind as we are. The sails on the foremast draw all the better, so it don't make much difference. Look out, below!" he shouted as there was a crash above and the mizzen-mast was cut in sunder by a shot that struck it just above the topsail blocks, and the upper part came toppling down, striking the bulwark, and falling overboard.

"Lay aft, lads, and out knives!" the boatswain shouted. "Cut away the wreck! It is lucky it wasn't two feet lower," he said to Bob, "or it would have brought the topsail down, and that would have been a serious loss now the main-top-sail is of no use."

He sprang to assist the men, when a round shot struck him, and almost carried off his head. Bob caught at the knife that fell from his hand, and set to work with the men.

"That is it, lads, cut away!" he shouted. "We sha'n't have many more of them on board, we are a good mile away now."

Just as the work of getting rid of the wreck was accomplished, one of the men said, as a rocket burst overhead, "There are two of their gun-boats coming out of the harbour, sir."

"We had better close with the others, then," Bob said. "The brig will engage them when they come up. We shall be well beyond reach of the batteries before they do. Now, lads, see what guns she carries. Break open the magazine and get powder and ball up. We must lend the captain a hand if we can."

The polacre mounted eight guns, all 14-pounders, and in a few minutes these were loaded. The batteries continued to fire, but their shooting was no longer accurate, and in another ten minutes ceased altogether. The craft had now closed to within hailing distance of the brig.

"Hallo, the polacre!" Captain Lockett shouted. "What damages?"

"The boatswain is killed, sir," Bob shouted back, "and we have lost two spars; but, in spite of that, I think we are sailing as fast as you."

"What guns have you got?"

"Eight fourteen-pounders, sir. We are loaded and ready."

"Keep a little ahead of me," the captain shouted. "I am going to shorten sail a bit. We have got to fight those gun-boats."

As he spoke a heavy gun boomed out from the bow of one of the gun-boats, and the shot went skipping between the two vessels. Directly after, the other gun-boat fired, and the shot struck the quarter of the brig. Then there was a creaking of blocks as the sheets were hauled upon, and as the yards swung round, she came up into the wind, and a broadside was fired at the two gun-boats. Then the helm was put down, and she payed off before the wind again.

The gun-boats ceased rowing for a minute. The discharge had staggered them, for they had not given the brig credit for carrying such heavy metal. Then they began to row again. The swivel-gun of the brig kept up a steady fire on them. Two of the guns of the polacre had been by this time shifted to the stern, and these opened fire, while the first-mate's crew on board the barque were also at work. A fortunate shot smashed many of the oars of one of the gun-boats, and while she stopped rowing in disorder, the brig was again rounded to and opened a steady fire with her broadside guns upon them. As the gun-boats were now little more than a quarter of a mile away, the effect of the brig's fire, aided by that of the two prizes, was very severe, and in a short time the Spaniards put round and rowed towards the shore, while a hearty cheer broke from the brig and her prizes.

There had been no more casualties on board the polacre, the fire of the gun-boats having been directed entirely upon the brig, as the Spaniards knew that if they could but destroy or capture her they would be able to recover the prizes. The polacre was soon brought close alongside of the brig.

"Have you suffered much, Captain Lockett?"

"I am sorry to say we have had six men killed and five wounded. We have got a dozen shot in our stern. They were evidently trying to damage the rudder, but beyond knocking the cabin fittings to pieces, there is no more harm done than the carpenter can repair in a few hours' work. You have not been hit again, have you?"

"No, sir; none of their shots came near us."

"Well, examine the papers and have a talk with the officers you made prisoners, and then come on board to report. I shall want you to go on board the barque with me and see what she is laden with."

Bob went below. The two Spanish mates were unbound. "I am sorry, señors," Bob said, "that we were obliged to treat you rather roughly, but you see we were in a hurry, and there was no time for explanations. I shall be obliged if you will show me which is the captain's cabin, and hand me over the ship's papers and manifesto. What is her name?"

"The *Braganza.*"

"Where are you from? and what do you carry?"

"We are from Cadiz, and are laden principally with wine. We were bound for Barcelona. You took us in nicely, señor. Who could have dreamt that you were English when that frigate chased you under the guns of the battery?"

"She thought we were Spanish as you did," Bob said.

By this time the other Spaniard had brought the papers out of the captain's cabin. Bob ran his eye down over the bill of lading, and was well satisfied with the result. She contained a very large consignment of wine.

"I am going on board the brig," he said, as he put the

papers together. "I must ask you to give me your parole not to leave the cabin until I return. I do not know whether my captain wishes you to remain here or will transfer you to his own craft."

"Well, Master Bob, what is your prize?" the captain asked.

"It is a valuable one, sir. The polacre herself is, as I see by her papers, only two years old, and seems a fine craft. She is laden with wine from Cadiz to Barcelona."

"Capital, Bob; we are in luck indeed! How many prisoners have you got?"

"The crew is put down at eighteen, sir, and there are the two mates."

"You had better send them on board here presently. Where are they now?"

"They are in the cabin, captain. They gave me their promise not to leave it till I return; but I put a man on sentry outside, so as to make sure of them."

"Well, perhaps you had better go back again now, and we will shape our course for Gibraltar at once. All this firing would have attracted the attention of any Spanish war-vessel there might be about. We must leave the barque's manifesto till the morning. As you have lost the boatswain, I will send one of my best hands back with you to act as your first-mate. He must get that topsail yard of yours repaired at once. It does not matter about the mizzen-mast, but the yard is of importance. We may meet with Spanish cruisers outside the Rock and may have to show our heels."

"Yes, I shall be glad of a good man, captain. You see I know nothing about it, and don't like giving any orders. It was all very well getting on board and knocking down the crew, but when it comes to sailing her, it is perfectly ridiculous my giving orders when the men know that I don't know anything about it."

"The men know you have plenty of pluck, Bob, and they know that it was entirely due to your swimming off to that

Spanish ship that we escaped being captured before, and they will obey you willingly as far as you can give them orders. Still, of course, you do want somebody with you to give orders as to the setting and taking in of the sails."

As soon as the last gun had been fired the three vessels had been laid head to wind, but when Bob's boat reached the side of the polacre they were again put on their course and headed south-west, keeping within a short distance of each other. Bob's new first-mate, an old sailor named Brown, at once set the crew to work to get up a fresh spar in place of the broken yard. The men all worked with a will. They were in high spirits at the captures they had made, and the news which Brown gave them that the polacre was laden with wine, assured to each of them a substantial sum in prize-money.

Before morning the yard was in its place and the sail set, and except for the shortened mizzen and a ragged hole through the bulwark forward the polacre showed no signs of the engagement of the evening before. Two or three men were slung over the stern of the brig, plugs had been driven through the shot holes, and over these patches of canvas were nailed and painted black. Nothing, however, could be done with the sails, which were completely riddled with holes. The crew were set to work to shift some of the worst, cutting them away from the yards and getting up spare sails from below. Bob had put a man on the look-out to give him notice if any signal was made to him from the brig, which was a quarter of a mile ahead of him, the polacre's topgallant sails having been lowered after the main-topsail had been hoisted, as it was found that with all sail set she sailed considerably faster than the brig.

Presently the man came aft and reported that the captain was waving his hat from the taffrail.

"We had better get up the main-topgallant sail, Brown, and run up to her," Bob said. The sail was soon hoisted, and in a quarter of an hour they were alongside the brig.

"That craft sails like a witch," Captain Lockett said, as they came abreast of him.

"Yes, sir, she seems very fast."

"It is a pity she is rigged as she is," the captain said. "It is an outlandish fashion; if she were barque-rigged I should be tempted to shift on board her. We will leave the barque alone at present, Mr. Repton; our curiosity must keep a bit. I don't want to lose any of this breeze. We will keep right on as long as it lasts, if it drops we will overhaul her."

The barque was the slowest craft of the three, and Joe Lockett had every stitch of canvas set to enable him to keep up with the others. At noon a large craft was seen coming off from the land. Bob examined her with the telescope, and then handed the glass to Brown. "She is a frigate," the sailor said. "It's the same that blazed away at us yesterday; it's the *Brilliant*, I think."

"You are sure she is the same that chased us yester-day?"

"Quite sure."

Captain Lockett was evidently of the same opinion, as no change was made in the course he was steering. "We may as well speak the captain again," Bob said; and the polacre, closed again with the brig. "Brown says that is the same frigate that fired at us yesterday, Captain Lockett," Bob said when they were within hailing distance.

"Yes, there is no doubt about that. I don't want to lose time or I would stand out and try our speed with her."

"Why, sir?"

"Because I am afraid she will want to take some of our hands. Those frigates are always short of hands. Still she may not, as we have got twelve men already away in a prize and ten in each of these craft."

"I don't think you need be uneasy, sir. I know the captain of the *Brilliant* and all the officers. If you like I will keep the polacre on that side, so that they will come up to us first, and will go on board and speak to the captain. I don't think then he would interfere with us."

"Very well, Mr. Repton; we will arrange it so."

The polacre had now taken its place to leeward of the other two vessels, and they held on in that order until the frigate was within half a mile, when she fired a gun across their bows as signal for them to heave to. The brig was now flying the British colours, her prizes the British colours with the Spanish underneath them. At the order to heave to they were all thrown up into the wind. The frigate reduced her sail as she came up, and as she neared the polacre the order was shouted, "Send a boat alongside!" The boat was already prepared for lowering; four seamen got into her and rowed Bob alongside the frigate. The first person he encountered as he stepped on to the deck was Jim Sankey, who stared at him in astonishment.

"Hullo, Bob! What in the world are you doing here?"

"I am in command of that polacre, Mr. Sankey," Bob replied.

"Eh—what?" Jim stammered in astonishment, when the captain's voice from the quarter-deck came sharply down:

"Now, Mr. Sankey, what are you waiting for? Bring that gentleman here."

Jim led the way up to the poop. Bob saluted, "Good-morning, Captain Langton."

"Why, it's Repton!" the captain exclaimed in surprise. "Why, where did you spring from, and what craft are these?"

"I am in command at present, sir, of the polacre, which, with the barque, is a prize of the brig the *Antelope*, privateer."

But what are you doing on board, Repton? and how is it that you are in command?"

"Well, sir, I was out on a cruise in the *Antelope*. The second-mate was sent with a prize crew back to Gibraltar in a craft we picked up off Malaga. We cut out the other two prizes from under the guns of Cartagena. The first-mate was in command of the party that captured the barque; and as there was no one else to send, the captain put me in command of the party that captured the polacre."

"But how on earth did you manage it?" the captain asked. "I see the brig has been cut up a good deal about the sails and rigging. You don't mean to say that she sailed right into Cartagena? Why, they would have blown her out of the water!"

"We didn't go in, sir; we anchored outside the port. We were not suspected, because one of His Majesty's frigates fired at us as we were going in; and the consequence was the Dons never suspected that we were anything but a Spanish trader."

"Why, you don't mean to say," the captain exclaimed, "that this was the brig flying Spanish colours which we chased in under the guns of Cartagena yesterday?"

"It is, sir," Bob said smiling. "You did us a very good turn, although your intentions were not friendly. We were under Spanish colours when you made us out, and it struck us that running the gauntlet of your fire for a little while would be an excellent introduction for us to the Spaniards. So it proved. We brought up close to those other two vessels, and I had a talk with the captain of one of them. The two captains both went ashore after dark; so we put twenty men into a boat and rowed in to the mouth of the port, waited there for a bit, and then rowed straight out to the ships. They thought, of course, it was their own officers returning; so we took them by surprise and captured them pretty easily. Unfortunately there was some noise made, and they took the alarm on shore. However, we were under way before the batteries opened. It was rather unpleasant for a bit, but we got safely out. Two gun-boats came out after us, but the brig beat them off, and we helped as well as we could. The brig had five men killed, we had one, and there are several wounded."

"Well, it was a very dashing affair," the captain said; "very creditable indeed. I hope you will get a share of the prize-money."

"I only count as a hand," Bob said laughing; "and I am sure that is as much as I deserve. But here comes the captain, sir; he will tell you more about it."

Captain Lockett now came on board, and Bob, seeing that he was not farther required, went off with Jim down to the cockpit. The captain had a long talk with Captain Lockett. When the latter had related in full the circumstances of his capture of his two prizes he said:

"There is a Spanish ship-of-war, sir, somewhere off Alicante at present. She is got up as a merchantman and took us in thoroughly, and we should probably have been caught if it had not been for Mr. Repton," and he then related how Bob had swum on board and discovered the supposed merchantman to be a ship-of-war.

"Thank you, Captain Lockett. I will go in and have a look after her. It is fortunate that you told me, for if I had seen her lying at anchor under the land I might have sent some boats in to cut her out, and might, as you nearly did, have caught a tartar. He is an uncommonly sharp young fellow, that Repton. I offered him a midshipman's berth here when I first came out, but he refused it. By what you say he must be a good officer lost to the service."

"He would have made a good officer, sir; he has his wits about him so thoroughly. It was his doing our keeping the Spanish flag flying when you came upon us. I had ordered the colours to be run down, when he suggested our keeping them up and running boldly in to Cartagena."

"I suppose you can't spare us a few hands, Captain Lockett?"

"Well, sir, I shall be very short as it is. You see I have a score away in a prize, I have had six killed, and some of the wounded won't be fit for work for some time, and I mean to take these two prizes back with me to England.

They are both valuable, and I should not get anything like a fair price for them at Gibraltar. I don't want to run the risk of their being picked up by privateers on the way back, so I shall convoy them; and I certainly sha'n't have a man too many to fight my guns when I have put crews on board them."

"No, I suppose not," the captain said. "Well, I must do without them, then. Now, as I suppose you want to be on your way, I will not detain you any longer."

Bob was sent for.

"Captain Lockett has been telling me that you were the means of preventing his getting into a nasty scrape with that Spanish man-of-war, Mr. Repton. I consider there is great credit due to you. It is a pity you didn't come on to my quarter-deck."

"I should not have got the chances then, sir," Bob said.

"Well, no; I don't know that you would, lad; there is something in that. Well, good-bye. I shall write and tell the admiral all about it. I know he will be glad to hear of your doings."

A few minutes later the privateer and her prizes were on their way towards Gibraltar, while the frigate was standing inshore again to search for the Spanish ship-of-war.

CHAPTER XII.

A RICH PRIZE.

IN the evening the wind died away, and the three vessels were becalmed. Captain Lockett rowed to the polacre and examined his prize, and then taking Bob in his boat rowed to the barque.

"Well, Joe, have you made out what you have got on board?" the captain said, when he reached the deck.

"No, sir. Neither of the officers can speak a word of English. I have opened the hatches and she is chock-full of hides, but what there is underneath I don't know."

"Come along, Bob, we will overhaul the papers," the captain said, and going to the cabin they examined the bill of lading.

"Here it is, sir," Bob said triumphantly. "Two hundred tons of lead."

"Splendid!" the captain exclaimed. "That is a prize worth having. Of course that is stowed away at the bottom, and then she is filled up with hides, and they are worth a lot of money; but the lead alone is worth six thousand pounds, at twenty pounds per ton. Is there anything else, Bob?"

"Yes, sir. There are fifty boxes; it doesn't say what is in them."

"You don't say so, Bob! Perhaps it is silver. Let us ask the officers."

The Spanish first-mate was called down. "Where are these boxes?" Bob asked; "and what do they contain?"

"They are full of silver," the man said sullenly. "They are stowed in the lazaretto under this cabin."

"We will have one of them up and look into it," the captain said. "Joe, call a couple of hands down."

The trap-door of the lazaretto was lifted; Joe and the two sailors descended the ladder, and with some difficulty one of the boxes was hoisted up.

"That weighs over two hundredweight, I'm sure," Joe said.

The box was broken open, and it was found to be filled with small bars of silver.

"Are they all the same size, Joe?" the captain asked.

"Yes, as far as I can see."

The captain took out his pocket-book and made a rapid calculation.

"Then they are worth between thirty-two and thirty-three thousand pounds, Joe. Why, lad, she is worth forty thousand pounds without the hides or the hull. That is something like a capture," and the two men shook hands warmly.

"The best thing to do, Joe, will be to divide these boxes between the three ships; then even if one of them gets picked up by the Spaniards or French, we shall still be in clover."

"I think that would be a good plan," Joe agreed.

"We will do it at once. There is nothing like making matters safe. Just get into the boat alongside and row to the brig, and tell them to lower the jolly-boat and send it alongside. We will get some of the boxes up by the time you are back."

In an hour the silver was divided between the three ships, and the delight of the sailors was great when they heard how valuable had been the capture.

"How do you divide?" Bob asked Captain Lockett, as they were watching the boxes lowered into the boat.

"The ship takes half," he said. "Of the other half I take twelve shares, Joe eight, the second-mate six, the boatswain three, and the fifty hands one share each. So you may say there are eighty shares; and if the half of the

THEY FIND BOXES OF SILVER IN THE LAZARETTO

prize is worth twenty thousand pounds, each man's share will be two hundred and fifty. It will be worth having, Bob; though it is a great shame you should not rate as an officer."

"I don't want the money," Bob laughed. "I should have no use for it if I had it. My uncle has taken me in hand, and I am provided for."

"Yes, I understand that," the captain said. "If it were not so I should have proposed to the crew that they should agree to your sharing the same as the second officer. I am sure they would have agreed willingly, seeing that it is due to you that we were not captured ourselves in the first place, and entirely to your suggestion that we should keep the Spanish flag flying and run into Cartagena, that we owe the capture of the prizes."

"Oh, I would much rather not, captain. I only came for a cruise, and it has been a splendid one; and it seems to be quite absurd that I should be getting anything at all. Still, it will be jolly, because I shall be able to make Carrie and Gerald nice presents with my own money, and to send some home to Mr. Medlin and his family, and something to uncle too, if I can think of anything he would like."

"Yes, it is all very well, Bob, for you; but I feel that it is not fair. However, as you really don't want the money and are well satisfied, we will say nothing more about it now."

The ships lay becalmed all night, but a brisk breeze from the east sprang up in the morning, and at noon the Rock was visible in the distance. They held on for four hours, and then lay to till after midnight. After that, sail was again made, and soon after daybreak they passed Europa Point, without having been seen by any of the Spanish cruisers. They were greeted by a hearty cheer from the vessels anchored near the new Mole as they brought up amongst them with the British flags flying above the Spanish on board the prizes. As soon as the morning gun was fired and the gates opened, Bob landed and hurried up to his sister's. She and her husband were just partaking of their early coffee.

"Hallo, Bob!" Captain O'Halloran exclaimed. "What, back again? Why, I didn't expect you for another fortnight. You must have managed very badly to have brought your cruise to an end so soon."

"Well, I am very glad you are back, Bob," his sister said. "I have been fidgetting about you ever since you were away."

"I am as glad to see you as your sister can be," Gerald put in. "If she has fidgetted when you had only gone a week, you can imagine what I should have to bear before the end of a month. I should have had to move into barracks. Life would have been insupportable here."

"I am sure I have said very little about it, Gerald," his wife said indignantly.

"No, Carrie, you have not said much, but your aspect has been generally tragic. You have taken but slight interest in your fowls, and there has been a marked deterioration in the meals. My remarks have been frequently unanswered, and you have got into a Sister Anne sort of way of going upon the roof and staring out to sea. Your sister is a most estimable woman, Bob, I am the last person who would deny it, but I must admit that she has been a little trying during the last week."

Carrie laughed. "Well, it is only paying you back a little in your own coin, Gerald. But what has brought you back so soon, Bob? We heard of you three days ago; for Gerald went on board a brig that was brought in, as he heard that it was a prize of the *Antelope's*, and the officer told him about your cruise up to when he had left you."

"Well, there wasn't much to tell up till then," Bob said, "except that I was well and my appetite was good. But there has been a good lot since. We have come in with two more good prizes this morning, and the brig is going to convoy them back to England."

"Oh, that is all right," Carrie said in a tone of pleasure. So far she had been afraid that Bob's return was only a temporary one, and that he might be setting out again in a day or two.

"Well, let us hear all about it, Bob," her husband said. "I could see Carrie was on thorns lest you were going off again. Now that she is satisfied she may be able to listen to you comfortably."

"Well, we really had some adventures, Gerald. We had a narrow escape from being captured by a Spanish ship-of-war ever so much stronger than we were. She was got up as a merchantman, and regularly took us in. We anchored close to her, intending to board her in the dark. I thought I would swim off and reconnoitre a bit before we attacked her, and, of course, I saw at once what she was, and we cut our cable and were towed out in the dark. She fired away at us but didn't do us any damage. The next day, late in the afternoon, we came upon the *Brilliant* chasing some Spanish craft into Cartagena, and as we had Spanish colours up she took us for one of them, and blazed away at us."

"But why didn't you pull down the Spanish colours at once, Bob? I never heard of anything so silly," Carrie said indignantly.

"Well, you see, Carrie, they were some distance off, and weren't likely to damage us much, and we ran straight in and anchored with the rest under the guns of the battery outside Cartagena. Seeing us fired at, of course they never suspected we were English. Then at night we captured the two vessels lying next to us and put out to sea. The batteries blazed away at us, and it was not very pleasant till we got outside their range. They did not do us very much damage. Two gun-boats came out after us, but the brig beat them back, and we helped."

"Who were we?" Captain O'Halloran asked.

"We were the prizes, of course. I was in command of one."

"Hooray, Bob!" Gerald exclaimed with a great laugh, while Carrie uttered an exclamation of horror.

"Well, you see, the second-mate had been sent off in the first prize, and there was only Joe Lockett and me; so he took the biggest of the two ships we cut out, and the captain put me in command of the men that took the other. I had the boatswain with me, and, of course, he was the man who really commanded in getting up the sails and all that sort of thing. He was killed by a shot from the battery, and was the only man hit on our vessel, but there were five killed on board the brig in the fight with the gun-boats. We fell in with the *Brilliant* on the way back, and I went on board; and you should have seen how Jim Sankey opened his eyes when I said that I was in command of the prize. They are awfully good prizes too, I can tell you. The one I got is laden with wine; and the big one was a barque from Lima, with hides, and two hundred tons of lead and fifty boxes of silver—about thirty-three thousand pounds' worth. Just think of that! The captain said she was worth altogether at least forty thousand pounds. That is something like a prize, isn't it?"

"Yes, that is. What do you think, Carrie? I propose that I sell my commission, raise as much as I can get on the old place in Ireland, and fit out a privateer. Bob will, of course, be captain, you shall be first-mate, and I will be content with second-mate's berth; and we will sail the salt ocean, and pick up our forty-thousand-pound prizes."

"Oh, what nonsense you do talk, to be sure, Gerald! Just when Bob's news is so interesting too."

"I have told all my news, Carrie; now I want to hear yours. The Spaniards haven't began to batter down the Rock yet?"

"We have been very quiet, Bob. On the 11th a great convoy of about sixty sail, protected by five xebecs of from twenty to thirty guns each, came along. They must have come out from Malaga the very night you passed there.

They were taking supplies for the use of the Spanish fleet; and the privateers captured three or four small craft, and the *Panther*, the *Enterprise*, and the *Childers* were kept at their anchor all day. Why, no one but the admiral could say. We were all very much disappointed, for everyone expected to see pretty nearly all the Spanish vessels brought in."

"Yes," Captain O'Halloran said, "it has caused a deal of talk, I can tell you. The navy were furious. There they were, sixty vessels all laden with the very things we wanted, pretty well becalmed, not more than a mile off Europa Point, with our batteries banging away at them, and nothing in the world to hinder the *Panther* and the frigates from fetching them all in. Half the town were out on the hill, and every soul who could get off duty at the Point, and there was the admiral wasting the whole mortal day in trying to make up his mind. If you had heard the bad language that was used in relation to that old gentleman, it would have made your hair stand on end. Of course, just as it got dark the ships-of-war started, and equally of course the convoy all got away in the dark, except six bits of prizes which were brought in in the morning. We have heard since, that it was on purpose to protect this valuable fleet that the Spanish squadron arrived before you went away; but as it didn't turn up the squadron went off again, and we had nothing to do but just to pick it up."

After breakfast Captain O'Halloran went off with Bob to the *Antelope*. He found all hands busy bending on sails in place of those that had been damaged, taking those of the brig first captured for the purpose."

"They fit very well," Joe Lockett said, "and we have not time to lose. We sail again this afternoon. The captain says there is nothing to prevent our going out now, and as the Spanish squadron may be back any day, we might have to run the gauntlet to get out if we lost the present chance. So he is not going to waste an hour. Crofts has already sold the grain and discharged it; the hull is worth but little, and the captain has sold her as she stands to a trader for two hundred pounds. I expect he has bought her to break up for firewood if the siege goes on. If it doesn't he will sell her again afterwards at a good profit. Of course it is a ridiculous price; but the captain wanted to get her off his hands, and would have taken a ten-pound note rather than be bothered with her. So by to-night we shall be across at Ceuta, and if the wind holds east but another day we shall be through the Straits on our way home. They are going to shift two of our 18-pounders on board the barque, and I am going to command her, and to have fifteen men on board. Crofts commands the polacre with ten men; the rest, of course go in the brig. We shall keep together, and steer well out west into the Atlantic, so as to give as wide a berth as possible to Spaniards and Frenchmen. If we meet with a privateer we ought to be able to give a good account of him; if we run across a frigate we shall scatter; and it will be hard luck if we don't manage to get two out of the three craft into port. We have been shifting some more of the silver again this morning from the barque into the other two vessels, otherwise, as she has the lead on board, she would be the most valuable prize. As it is, now the three are of about equal value."

"Well, we wish you a pleasant voyage," Captain O'Halloran said. "I suppose we shall see you back again before long."

"Yes, I should think so; but I don't know what the captain means to do. We have had no time to talk this morning. I daresay you will meet him on shore; he has gone to the post-office to get his papers signed. We have been quite pestered this morning by men coming on board to buy wine out of the polacre, but the captain wouldn't have the hatches taken off. The Spaniards may turn up at any moment, and it is of the greatest importance our getting off while the coast is clear. It is most unfortunate now that we did not run straight in yesterday, instead of laying-to to wait for night."

They did not meet the captain in the town; and from the roof Bob saw the three vessels get up sail early in the afternoon and make across for the African coast. The doctor came in in the evening.

"Well, Bob, so I hear you have been fighting and commanding ships and doing all sorts of things. I saw Captain Lockett in the town, and faith if you had been a dozen admirals rolled into one he couldn't have spoken more highly of you. It seems, Mrs. O'Halloran, that Bob has been the special angel who has looked after poor Jack on board the *Antelope*."

"What ridiculous nonsense, doctor!" Bob exclaimed hotly.

"Not at all, Bob; it is too modest you are entirely. It is yourself is the boy who has done the business this time, and it is a silver tay-service, or some such trifle as that, that the owners will be sending you; and small blame to them. Captain Lockett tells me he owns a third of the ship, and he reckons the ship's share of what they have taken this little cruise won't be less than five-and-twenty thousand. Think of that, Mrs. O'Halloran, five-and-twenty thousand pounds! and here is Edward Burke, M.D., working his sowl out for a miserable eight or ten shillings a day."

"But what has Bob done?"

"I hadn't time to learn it all, Mrs. O'Halloran, for the captain was in a hurry. It seems to me that the question ought to be, what is it that he hasn't done? It all came in a heap together, and I am not sure of the exact particulars; but it seems to me that he swam out and cut the cable of a Spanish sloop of war, and took the end in his mouth and towed her out to sea, while the guns were blazing in all directions at him. Never was such an affair! Then he humbugged the captain of an English frigate, and the commander of the Spanish forts, and stole a vessel chockfull of silver, and did I don't know what besides."

Bob went off into a shout of laughter, in which the others joined.

"But what is the meaning of all this nonsense, Teddy?" Carrie asked as soon as she recovered her composure. "Is there anything in it, or is it all pure invention?"

"Is there anything in it! Haven't I been telling you that there is twenty-five thousand pounds in it to the owners, and as much more to the crew, and didn't the captain vow and declare that if it hadn't been for Bob, instead of going home to divide all this treasure up between them, every man-Jack of them would be at this moment chained by the leg in a dirty Spanish prison at Malaga!"

"Well, what does it all mean, Bob? There is no getting any sense out of Dr. Burke."

"It is exactly what I told you, Carrie. We anchored close to a craft that we thought was a merchantman, and that we meant to attack in our boats. I swam on board her in the dark, to see if they were keeping a good watch and that sort of thing, and when I got on board I found she was a ship-of-war, with a lot of heavy guns, and prepared to take us by surprise when we attacked her; so of course when I swam back again with the news, Captain Lockett cut his cable and towed the brig out in the dark. As to the other affair that the doctor is talking about, I told you that too, and it is exactly as I said it was. The only thing I had to do with it, was that it happened to be my idea to keep the Spanish colours flying and let the frigate keep on firing at us. The idea turned out well; but of course if I had not thought of it somebody else would; so there was nothing in it at all."

"Well, Bob, you may say what you like," Doctor Burke said; "but it is quite evident that the captain thought there was a good deal in it, and I think really, Gerald, that you and Mrs. O'Halloran have good reason to feel quite proud of him. I am not joking at all when I say that Captain Lockett really spoke as if he considered that the good fortune they had had is very largely due to him.   He said he hoped he should have Bob on board for another cruise."

"I certainly shall not go any more with him," Bob said indignantly, "if he talks such nonsense about me afterwards. As if there was anything in swimming two or three hundred yards on a dark night, or in suggesting the keeping a flag up instead of pulling it down."

When the *Brilliant*, however, came in two days later, Captain Langton called upon Mrs. O'Halloran, and told her that he did so in order to acquaint her with the extremely favourable report Captain Lockett had made to him of Bob's conduct, and that from what he had said, it was evident that the lad had shown great courage in undertaking the swim to the Spanish vessel, and much promptness and ready wit in suggesting the device that had deceived him as well as the Spaniards.

Captain Langton told the story that evening at General Eliott's dinner-table, and said that although it was certainly a good joke against himself, that he should have thus assisted a privateer to carry off two valuable prizes that had slipped through the frigate's hands, the story was too good not to be told.   Thus Bob's exploit became generally known among the officers of the garrison, and Captain O'Halloran was warmly congratulated upon the sharpness and pluck of his young brother-in-law.

Captain Lockett's decision to be off without any delay was fully justified by the appearance of a Spanish squadron in the bay three days after his departure.   It consisted of two seventy-fours, two frigates, five xebecs, and a number of galleys and small armed vessels.   The men-of-war anchored off Algeciras, while the rest of the squadron kept a vigilant patrol at the mouth of the bay, and formed a complete blockade.   Towards the end of the month the troops were delighted by the issue of an order that the use of powder for the hair was henceforth to be abandoned.

Vessels were now continually arriving from Algeciras with

troops and stores, and on the 26th the Spaniards began to form a camp on the plain below San Roque, three miles from the garrison. This increased in size daily as fresh regiments arrived by land. Orders were now issued that all horses in the garrison, except those whose owners had a store of at least one thousand pounds of grain, were either to be shot or turned out through the gates.

There was much excitement when two Dutch vessels, laden with rice and dried fruit, made their way in at night through the enemy's cruisers. Their cargoes were purchased for the troops, and these vessels, and a Venetian that had also got through, carried off with them a large number of Jewish, Genoese, and other traders, with their families, to ports in Barbary or Portugal. Indeed from this time every vessel that went out carried away some of the inhabitants.

The position of these poor people was indeed serious. The standing order on the Rock was, that every inhabitant, even in time of peace, should have in store six months' provisions; but the order had never been enforced, and few of them had any supplies of consequence. As they could not expect to be supplied from the garrison stores, the greater number had no resource but to leave the place. Some, however, who were better provided, obtained leave to erect wooden huts at the southern end of the Rock, so as to have a place of shelter to remove to in case the enemy bombarded the town.

The Spaniards had by this time mounted their cannon in forts St. Philip and St. Barbara. Vast quantities of stores were landed at Point Mala, at the end of the bay. Some fifteen thousand men were under canvas in their camp, and strong parties were constantly employed in erecting works near their forts. The garrison on their side were continually strengthening and adding to their batteries, erecting palisades and traverses, filling the magazines in the works, and preparing for an attack; and on the 11th of September some of the guns were opened upon the enemy's working parties, and for a time compelled them to desist.

From the upper batteries on the Rock a complete view was obtainable of all the enemy's operations, and as they were seen to be raising mortar batteries, preparations were made to diminish the effects of a bombardment of the town. For this purpose the pavement of the streets was removed and the ground ploughed up, the towers and most conspicuous buildings taken down, and traverses carried across the streets to permit communications to be carried on. Early in October the Engineers and Artillery managed with immense labour to mount a gun on the summit of the Rock, and as from this point an almost bird's-eye view was obtained of the Spanish works, the fire of the gun annoyed them greatly at their work. This was maintained, however, steadily; but in spite of this interference with their operations, the Spaniards on the 20th of October opened thirty-five embrasures, in three batteries in a line between their two forts.

Provisions of every kind were now becoming very dear, fresh meat was from three to four shillings a pound, chickens twelve shillings a couple, ducks from fourteen to eighteen.

Fish was equally dear, and vegetables hardly to be bought at any price. Flour was running very short, and rice was served out instead of it.

On the 14th of November the privateer *Buck*, armed with twenty-four 9-pounders, was seen making into the bay. Two Spanish ships of the line, a frigate, two xebecs, and twenty-one small craft set out to intercept her. The cutter, seeing a whole Spanish squadron coming out, tacked and stood across towards the Barbary shore, pursued by the Spaniards. The wind was from the west, but the cutter, lying close-hauled, was able just to stem the current and hold her position: while the Spaniards, being square-rigged, and so unable to stand near the wind, drifted bodily away to leeward with the current, but the two men-of-war, perceiving what was happening, managed to make back into the bay.

As soon as the privateer saw the rest of the squadron

drift away to leeward, she again headed for the Rock. The Spanish admiral, Barcelo, in a seventy-four gun-ship, endeavoured to cut her off, firing two broadsides of grape and round shot at her, but with the other man-of-war was compelled to retire by the batteries at Europa, and the cutter made her way in triumphantly, insultingly returning the Spanish admiral's fire with her two little stern guns. The Spanish men-of-war drifted away after their small craft, and thus for the time the port was open again, thanks to the pluck of the little privateer, which had, it was found on her arrival, been some time at sea, and simply came in to get provisions.

As it could be seen from the African coast that the port was again open, two or three small craft came across with bullocks and sheep. Four days later, the wind veering round to the southward, Admiral Barcelo with his fleet returned to the bay, and the blockade was renewed.

Already Captain O'Halloran and his wife had the most ample reasons for congratulating themselves that they had taken Dr. Burke's advice in the matter of vegetables and fowls. The little garden on the roof was the envy of all Carrie's female friends, many of whom indeed began imitations of it on a small scale. Under the hot sun, and with careful watering, everything made astonishing progress. The cutting of the mustard and cress had of course begun in a little more than a week from the time when the garden had been completed and the seeds sown. The radishes were fit for pulling three weeks later, and as constant successions were sown, they had been amply supplied with an abundance of salad; and each morning a trader in town came up and took all that they could spare, at prices that would, before the siege began, have appeared fabulous. Along the edge of the parapet, and trailing over almost to the ground, covering the house in a bower of rich green foliage, the melons, cucumbers, and pumpkins blossomed and fruited luxuriantly, and for these prices were obtained as high as those that the fruit would fetch in Covent Garden when out of season. But as melons, cucumbers, and pumpkins alike produce great quantities of seed, by the end of the year they were being grown on a considerable scale, by all who possessed any facilities for cultivating them.

Later on, indeed, the governor, hearing from the principal medical officer how successful Captain O'Halloran had been, issued an order recommending all inhabitants to grow vegetables, and granting them every facility for so doing. All who chose to do so were allowed to fence in any little patches of earth they could discover among the rocks or on unused ground, and it was not long before the poorer inhabitants spent much of their time in collecting earth and establishing little garden plots, or in doing so for persons who could afford to pay for their labour.

The poultry venture was equally satisfactory. Already a considerable piece of rough and rocky ground next to the garden had been enclosed, thereby affording a much larger run for the fowls, and enabling a considerable portion of the garden to be devoted to the young broods.

The damaged biscuits had been sold at a few shillings a ton, and at this price Captain O'Halloran had bought the whole of the condemned lot, amounting to about ten tons; and there was consequently an ample supply of food for them for an almost indefinite time. After supplying the house amply, there were at least a hundred eggs a day to sell; and Carrie, who now took an immense interest in the poultry-yard, calculated that they could dispose of ten couple a week, and still keep up their number from the young broods.

"The only thing you have to be afraid of is disease, Mrs. O'Halloran," the doctor, who was her greatest adviser, said; "but there is little risk of that. Besides, you have only to hire one or two lads of ten or twelve years old, and then you can put them out when you like from the farther inclosure, and let them wander about."

"But people don't generally watch fowls," Mrs. O'Halloran said. "Surely they would come back at night to roost."

"I have no doubt they would; when chickens are well fed they can be trusted to find their way home at night. But you must remember that they are worth from twelve to fourteen shillings a couple, and what with the natives and what with soldiers off duty, you would find that a good many would not turn up at all unless they were watched. A couple of boys at sixpence a day each would keep them from straying too far and prevent their being stolen, and would relieve you of a lot of anxiety about them."

So after this the fowls were turned out on to the Rock, where they wandered about, narrowly watched by two native boys, and were able to gather no small store of sustenance from the insects they found among the rocks or on the low shrubs that grew among them.

Bob had, after his return from his cruise, fallen into his former habits, spending two hours every morning with Don Diaz, and reading for an hour or two in the evening with the doctor. It was now cool enough for exercise and enjoyment in the day, and there were few afternoons when he did not climb up to the top of the Rock and watch the Spanish soldiers labouring at their batteries, and wondering when they were going to begin to do something. Occasionally they obtained news of what was passing in the enemy's lines, and the Spaniards were equally well informed of what was going on in the fortress, for desertions from both sides were not infrequent. Sometimes a soldier with the working parties out in the neutral ground would steal away and make for the Spanish lines, pursued by a musketry fire from his comrades, and saluted perhaps with a round or two of shot from the batteries above. But more frequently they made their escape from the back of the Rock, letting themselves down by ropes, although at least half the number who made the attempt were dashed to pieces among the precipices.

The majority of the deserters belonged to the Hanoverian regiments, but a good many British soldiers also deserted. In all cases these were reckless men who, having been punished for some offence or other, preferred risking death to remaining in the garrison. Some were caught in the attempt, while several by getting into places where they could neither descend further nor return, were compelled at last by hunger and thirst to shout for assistance, preferring death by hanging to the slower agony of thirst. The deserters from the Spanish lines principally belonged to the Walloon regiments in the Spanish service, or to regiments from Biscaya and other northern provinces. The troops were raised on the principle of our own militia, and objected strongly to service outside their own provinces; and it was this discontent that gave rise to their desertions to us.

Some of them made their way at night from the works where they were employed, through the lines of sentries; others took to the water, either beyond Fort Barbara or at the head of the bay, and reached our lines by swimming.

Bob heartily congratulated himself, when he heard of the fate of some of the deserters who tried to make their way down at the back of the Rock, that he and Jim Sankey had not carried out their scheme of descending there in search of birds. By this time he had come to know most of the young officers of the garrison, and although the time passed without any marked events, he had plenty of occupation and amusement. Sometimes they would get up fishing parties, and although they could not venture very far from the Rock on account of the enemy's galleys and row-boats, they had a good deal of sport, and fish were welcome additions to the food, which consisted principally of salt rations, for Bob very soon tired of a diet of chicken.

There were some very heavy rains in the last week of the year; these, they learned from deserters, greatly damaged the enemy's lines, filling their trenches and washing down their banks. One advantage was that a great quantity of wood, cork, and other floating rubbish was washed down by the rain into the two rivers that fell into the bay, and as the wind was from the south this was all blown over towards the Rock, where it was collected by boats, affording a most welcome supply of fuel, which had been for some time extremely scarce.

On the 8th of January a Neapolitan polacre was driven in under the guns by the wind from the other side of the bay and was obliged to drop anchor. Six thousand bushels of barley were found on board her, which was of inestimable value to the inhabitants, who were now suffering extremely, as were also the wives and children of the soldiers, whose rations, scanty for one, were wholly insufficient for the wants of a family. Fowls had now risen to eighteen shillings a couple, eggs were sixpence each, and small cabbages fetched eighteenpence.

On the 12th the enemy fired ten shots into the town from Fort St. Philip, causing a panic among the inhabitants, who at once began to remove to their huts at the other end of the Rock. A woman was wounded by a splinter of stone from one of the houses, being the first casualty that had taken place through the siege. The next day the admiral gave orders to the men-of-war that they should be in readiness in case a convoy appeared, to afford protection to any ships that might attempt to come in. This order caused great joy among the garrison and inhabitants, as it seemed to signify that the governor had received information in some manner that a convoy was on its way out to relieve the town.

Two days later a brig that was seen passing through the Straits to the east suddenly changed her course and made for the Rock, and although the enemy tried to cut her off she succeeded in getting into port. The welcome news soon spread that the brig was one of a large convoy that had sailed late in December for the relief of the town. She had parted company with the others in the Bay of Biscay, and on her way had seen a Spanish squadron off Cadiz, which was supposed to be watching for the convoy. This caused much anxiety, but on the 16th a brig laden with flour arrived with the news that Sir George Rodney had captured off the coast of Portugal six Spanish frigates, with seventeen merchantmen on their way from Bilbao to Cadiz, and that he had with him a fleet of twenty-one sail of the line and a large convoy of merchantmen and transports.

The next day one of the prizes came in, and the midshipman in charge of her reported that when he had left the convoy on the previous day, a battle was going on between the British fleet and the Spanish squadron. Late in the evening the convoy was in sight, and the *Apollo* frigate and one or two merchantmen got in after dark with the news that the Spaniards had been completely defeated, their admiral's flag-ship with three others captured, one blown up in the engagement, another driven ashore, and the rest dispersed. The preparations for relieving the town had been so well concealed that the Spaniards had believed that the British men-of-war were destined for the West Indies, and had thought that the merchantmen would have fallen easy prizes to their squadron, which consisted of eleven men-of-war.

CHAPTER XIII.

ORANGES AND LEMONS.

THERE was great anxiety in Gibraltar that night, for the wind was very light and from the wrong direction, and in the morning it was seen that the greater portion of the convoy had drifted far away to the east. Soon after noon, however, the *Edgar* managed to get in with the Spanish admiral's flag-ship the *Phœnix*, of eighty guns; and in the evening the *Prince George*, with eleven or twelve ships, worked in round Europa Point; but Admiral Rodney, with the main body of the fleet and the prizes, was forced to anchor off Marbella, a Spanish town, fifteen leagues east of Gibraltar. It was not until seven or eight days later that the whole of the fleet and convoy arrived in the port.

On the 29th a transport came in with the 2d battalion of the 73d Regiment, with 944 rank and file. A large number of heavy cannon from the prizes were landed, and several hundreds of barrels of powder in addition to those brought out with the convoy. Great stores of salt provisions and supplies of flour had been brought out, but unfortunately little could be done towards providing the garrison with a supply of fresh meat. Had Admiral Rodney been able to remain with his fleet at Gibraltar, supplies could have been brought across from the African coast, but the British fleet was required elsewhere, and the relief afforded was a temporary one. The garrison was, however, relieved by a large number of the soldiers' wives and children being put on board the merchantmen and sent home to England; many of the poor inhabitants were also taken either to Barbary or Portugal.

While the fleet were in port the Spanish blockading squadron was moored close under the guns of Algeciras, and booms were laid round them to prevent their being attacked by the boats of the British fleet. An opportunity was taken of the presence of the Spanish admiral in Gibraltar to arrange for an exchange of prisoners, and on the 13th of February, the fleet sailed away, and the blockade was renewed by the Spaniards.

After the departure of the fleet many months passed monotonously. The enemy were ever increasing and strengthening their works, which now mounted a great number of cannon; but beyond an occasional interchange of a few shots, hostilities were carried on languidly.

The enemy made two endeavours to burn the British vessels anchored under the guns of the batteries, by sending fireships down upon them; but the crews of the ships-of-war manned the boats, and going out to meet them, towed them ashore, where they burned out without doing damage, and the hulls being broken up afforded a welcome supply of fuel. The want of fresh meat and vegetables operated disastrously upon the garrison; even before the arrival of the relieving fleet scurvy had shown itself, and its ravages continued and extended as months went on. The hospitals became crowded with sufferers; a third of the force being unfit for any duty, while there were few but were more or less affected by it.

As soon as it became severe, Captain O'Halloran and his wife decided to sell no more vegetables, but sent the whole of their supply, beyond what was needed for their personal consumption, to the hospitals.

During these eight months only a few small craft had managed to elude the vigilance of the enemy's cruisers, and frequently for many weeks at a time no news of any kind from without reached the besieged. The small supplies of fresh meat that had, during the early part of the siege, been brought across in small craft from Barbary, had for some-time ceased altogether, for the Moors of Tangiers had, under pressure of the Spaniards, broken off their alliance with us and joined them, and in consequence not only did supplies cease to arrive, but English vessels entering the Straits were no longer able to anchor as they had before done under the guns of the Moorish batteries for protection from the Spanish cruisers.

Several times there were discussions between Bob, his sister, and Captain O'Halloran, as to whether it would not be better for him to take the first opportunity that offered of returning to England. Their argument was that he was wasting his time, but to this he would not at all agree. "I am no more wasting it here than if I were in Philpot Lane," he said. "It will be plenty of time for me to begin to learn the routine of the business when I am two- or three-and-twenty. Uncle calculated I should be four years abroad learning the languages and studying wine. Well, I can study wines at any time; besides, after all, it is the agents out here that choose them. I can speak Spanish now like a native, and there is nothing further to be done in that way; I have given up lessons now with the doctor, but I get plenty of books from the garrison library and keep up my reading; as for society, we have twenty times as much here with the officers and their families as I should have in London, and I really don't see there would be any advantage whatever in my going back. Something must be done here some day. And after all, the siege does not make much difference in any way, except that we don't get fresh meat for dinner. Everything goes on just the same, only, I suppose, in peace time we should make excursions some-times into Spain. The only difference I can make out is, that I am able to be more useful to you now with the garden and poultry than I could have been if there had been no siege."

There was indeed no lack of society. The O'Hallorans' was perhaps the most popular house on the Rock. They were making quite a large income from their poultry, and spent it freely. Presents of eggs, chicken, and vegetables were constantly being sent to all their friends where there was any sickness in the family; and as even at the high prices prevailing they were able to purchase supplies of wine, and such other luxuries as were obtainable, they kept almost open house, and twice a week had regular gatherings with music; and the suppers were vastly more appreciated by their guests than is usually the case at such entertainments. Early in September, when scurvy was still raging, the doctor was one day lamenting the impossibility of obtaining oranges and lemons.

"It makes one's heart ache," he said, "to see the children suffer. It is bad enough that strong men should be scarcely able to crawl about; but soldiers must take their chances, whether they come from shot or from scurvy, but it is lamentable to see the children fading away. We have tried everything—acids and drugs of all sorts—but nothing does any good. As I told you, I saw the scurvy on the whaling trip I went, and I am convinced that nothing but lemon juice, or an absolutely unlimited amount of vegetables, will do any good."

A week previously a small privateer had come in with some mail bags which she had brought on from Lisbon. Among them was a letter to Bob from the owners of the *Antelope*. It had been written months before, after the arrival of the brig and her two prizes in England. It said that the two vessels and their cargoes had been sold and the prize-money divided, and that his share amounted to three hundred and thirty-two pounds, for which sum an order upon a firm of merchants at Gibraltar was inclosed. The writers also said that after consultation with Captain Lockett, from whom they had heard of the valuable services he had rendered, the owners of the *Antelope* had decided, as a very small mark of their appreciation and gratitude, to present him with a service of plate to the value of five hundred pounds, and in such form as he might prefer on his return to England. He had said nothing to his sister of this letter, as his intention was to surprise her with some present. But the doctor's words now determined him to carry into effect an idea that had before occurred to him upon seeing so many sickly children among the families of the officers of their acquaintance.

"Look here, doctor," he said, "I mean to go out and try and get a few boxes of oranges and lemons; but mind, nobody but you and I must know anything about it."

"How on earth do you mean to do it, Bob?"

"Well, I have not settled yet: but there can't be any difficulty about getting out. I might go down to the old Mole and swim from there to the head of the bay, or I might get some of the fishermen to go round the point and land me to the east well beyond the Spanish lines."

"You couldn't do that, Bob; there is too sharp a look-out kept on the batteries. No craft is allowed to go any distance from the Rock, as they are afraid of the Spaniards learning the state to which we are reduced by illness. If you did swim to the head of the bay as you talk about, you would be certain to be captured at once by the Spaniards; and in that case you would as likely as not be shot as a spy."

"Still deserters do get out, you know, doctor. There is scarcely a week that two or three don't manage to get away. I mean to try, anyhow. If you like to help me, of course it will make it easier; if not, I shall try by myself."

"Gerald and your sister would never forgive me if anything happened to you, Bob."

"There is no occasion for them to know anything about it. Anyhow I shall say nothing to them. I shall leave a note behind me saying that I am going to make an attempt to get out and bring back a boat full of oranges and lemons. I am past seventeen now, and am old enough to act for myself. I don't think, if the thing is managed properly, there is any particular risk about it. I will think it over by to-morrow, and tell you what plan I have fixed on."

On the following day Bob told the doctor that there were two plans. "The first is to be lowered by a rope down at the back of the Rock. That is ever so much the simplest. Of course there is no difficulty about it if the rope is long enough. Some of the deserters have failed because the rope has been too short, but I should take care to get one long enough. The only fear is the sentries; I know that there are lots of them posted about there on purpose to prevent desertion."

"Quite so, Bob; and no one is allowed to go along the paths after dark except on duty."

"Yes. Well, the other plan is to go out with the party that furnishes the sentries down on the neutral ground, choose some dark night, manage to get separated from them as they march out, and then make for the shore and take to the water. Of course if one could arrange to have the officer with the party in the secret it would make it easy enough."

"It might be done that way," the doctor said thoughtfully. "Have you quite made up your mind to do this thing, Bob?"

"I have quite made up my mind to try, anyhow."

"Well, if you mean to try, Bob, it is just as well that you shouldn't get shot at the start. I have just been round to the orderly-room. Our regiment furnishes the pickets on the neutral ground to-night. Captain Antrobus commands the party. He is a good fellow; and as he is a married man, and all four of his children are bad with scurvy, he would feel an interest in your attempt. You know him as well as I do. If you like I will go with you to his quarters and see what we can do with him."

They at once set out.

"Look here, Antrobus," the doctor said, after asking that officer to come out for a chat with him, "if we don't get some lemon-juice I am afraid it will go very hard with a lot of the children."

"Yes, we have known that for some time, doctor."

"Well, Repton here has made up his mind to try to get out of the place and make his way to Malaga, and get a boat-load of fruit and try to bring it in. Of course he will go dressed as a native, and he speaks Spanish well enough to pass anywhere without suspicion. So once beyond the lines, I don't see much difficulty in his making his way to Malaga. Whether he will get back again is another matter altogether. That is his business. He has plenty of money to purchase the fruit when he arrives there, and to buy a boat and all that sort of thing. The difficulty is in getting out. Now, nobody is going to know how he does this except our three selves."

"But why do you come to me, Burke?"

"Because you command the guard to-night on the neutral ground. What he proposes is that he should put on a soldier's greatcoat and cap and take a firelock, and in the dark fall in with your party. When you get well out on the neutral ground he could either slip away and take his chance, or, what would be better still, he might be in the party you take forward to post as sentries, and you could take him along with you, so that he would go with you as far as the shore, and could then slip away, come back a bit so as to be out of sight of the farthest sentry, and then take to the water. He can swim like a fish, and what current there is will be with him, so that before it began to be light he could land two or three miles beyond the Spanish lines. He is going to leave a note behind for O'Halloran saying he has left, but no one will know whether he got down at the back of the Rock or swam across the bay, or how he has gone. I have tried to dissuade him, but he has made up his mind to try it: and seeing that if he succeeds it may save the lives of scores of children, I really cannot refuse to help him."

"Well, I don't know," Captain Antrobus said. "There certainly does not seem much risk in his going out, as you say. I should get a tremendous wigging no doubt if he is discovered and it was known that I had a hand in it, but I would not mind risking that for the sake of the children. But don't take a firelock, Repton; the sergeants would be sure to notice that there was an extra man. You had better join us just as we set out. I will say a word or two to you, then do you follow on in the dark. The men will suppose you are one of the drummers I am taking with me to serve as a messenger or something of that sort. That way you can follow close behind me while I am posting the sentries after leaving the main body at the guard-house. After posting the last man at the sea-shore I can turn off with you for a few yards as if giving you an order. Then I will go back and stay for a time with the last sentry, who will naturally think that the drummer has been sent back to the guard-house. I will recommend him to be vigilant, and keep by him for some time till I am pretty sure you have taken to the water and swam past, so that if the sentry should hear a splash or anything, I can say it can only be a fish, and that at any rate it would not do to give an alarm, as it cannot be anything of consequence. You see you don't belong to the garrison, and it is no question of assisting a deserter to escape. Anyhow I will do it."

Thanking Captain Antrobus greatly for his promise of assistance, Bob went off into the town, where he bought a suit of Spanish clothes such as would be appropriate for a small farmer or trader; he then presented his letter of credit at the merchant's and drew a hundred pounds, which he obtained in Spanish gold. This money and the clothes he put in an oil-skin bag, of which the mouth was securely closed. This he left at the doctor's. As soon as it became dark he went down again. The doctor had a greatcoat and hat in readiness for him—there being plenty of effects of men who had died in the hospital—and as soon as Bob had put them on, walked across, with Bob following him, to the spot where Captain Antrobus' company were falling in. Just as they were about to march the doctor went up to the captain, who after a word or two with him said to Bob, in a voice loud enough to be heard by the non-commissioned officer close to him: "Well, you will keep by me."

The night was a dark one, and the party made their way down to the gate, where the pass-words were exchanged, and the company then moved along by the narrow pathway between the artificial inundation and the foot of the Rock. They continued their way until they arrived at the building that served as the main guard of the outlying pickets. Here two-thirds of the company were left, and the captain led the others out, an officer belonging to the regiment whose men he was relieving accompanying him. As the sentries were posted the men relieved fell in under the orders of their officer, and as soon as the last had been relieved they marched back to the guard-house.

A minute later Captain Antrobus turned to Bob.

"You need not wait," he said; "go back to the guard-house. Mind how you go."

Bob saluted and turned off, leaving the officer standing by the sentry. He went some distance back, then walked down the sand to the water's-edge, and waded noiselessly into the water. The oil-skin bag was, he knew, buoyant enough to give him ample support in the water. When he was breast-deep he let his uniform cloak slip off his shoulders, allowed his shoes to sink to the bottom and his three-cornered hat to float away. The doctor had advised him to do this.

"If you leave the things at the edge of the water, Bob, it will be thought that somebody has deserted, and then there will be a lot of questions and inquiries. You had better take them well out into the sea with you, and then let them go. They will sink and drift along under water, and if they are ever thrown up it will be far beyond our lines. In that way, as the whole of the guard will answer to their names when the roll is called to-morrow, no one will ever give a thought to the drummer who fell in at the last moment, or if one of them does think of it he will suppose that the captain sent him into the town with a report."

The bag would have been a great encumbrance had Bob wanted to swim fast. As it was he simply placed his hands upon it and struck out with his feet, making straight out from the shore. This he did for some ten minutes, and then, being certain that he was far beyond the sight of any-one on shore, he turned, and as nearly as he could followed the line of the coast. The voices of the sentries calling to each other came across the sea, and he could make out a light or two in the great fort at the water's edge. It was easy work; the water was as nearly as possible the temperature of his body, and he felt that he could remain for any time in it without inconvenience. The lights in the fort served as a mark by which he could note his progress, and an hour after starting he was well abreast of them, and knew that the current must be helping him more than he had expected it would do.

Another hour and he began to swim shorewards, as the current might, for aught he knew, be drifting him somewhat out into the bay. When he was able to make out the dark line ahead of him he again resumed his former course. It was just eight o'clock when the guard had passed through the gate. He had started half an hour later. He swam what seemed to him a very long time, but he had no means of telling how the time passed. When he thought it must be somewhere about twelve o'clock he made for the shore. He was sure that by this time he must be at least three miles beyond the fort, and as the Spanish camps lay princi-pally near San Roque at the head of the bay, and there were no tents anywhere by the sea-shore, he felt sure that he could land now without the slightest danger.

Here then he waded ashore, stripped, tied his clothes in a bundle, waded a short distance back again, and dropped them in the sea. Then he returned, took up the bag, and carried it up the sandy beach; opening it, he dressed himself in the complete set of clothes he had brought with him, put on the Spanish shoes and round turned-up hat, placed his money in his pocket, scraped a shallow hole in the sand, put the bag in it and covered it, and then started walking briskly along on the flat ground beyond the sand-hills. He kept on until he saw the first faint light in the sky, then he sat down among some bushes until it was light enough for him to distinguish the features of the country.

Inland the ground rose rapidly into hills, in many places covered with wood, and half an hour's walking took him to one of these. Looking back, he could see the Rock rising, as he judged, from twelve to fourteen miles away. He soon found a place with some thick undergrowth, and entering this, lay down and was soon sound asleep. When he woke it was already late in the afternoon. He had brought with him in the bag some biscuits and hard boiled eggs, and of a portion of these he made a hearty meal. Then he pushed up over the hill, until after an hour's walking he saw a road before him. This was all he wanted, and he sat down and waited until it became dark. A battalion of infantry passed along as he sat there, marching towards Gibraltar. Two or three long lines of laden carts passed by in the same direction.

He had consulted a map before starting, and knew that the distance to Malaga was more than twenty leagues, and that the first place of any importance was Estepona, about eight leagues from Gibraltar, and that before the siege a large proportion of the supplies of fruit and vegetables were brought to Gibraltar from this town. Starting as soon as it became dark, he passed through Estepona at about ten o'clock, looked in at a wine-shop and sat down to a pint of wine and some bread, and then continued his journey until, taking it quietly, he was in sight of Marbella. He slept in a grove of trees until daylight, and then entered the town, which was charmingly situated among orange groves. Going into a fonda or tavern, he called for breakfast; when he had eaten this, he leisurely strolled down to the port, and taking his seat on a block of stone on the pier, watched the boats. As while walking down from the fonda he had passed several shops with oranges and lemons, it seemed to him that it would in some respects be better for him to get the fruit here instead of going on to Malaga.

In the first place the distance to return was but half that from Malaga, and in the second it would probably be easier to get out from a quiet little port like this than from a large town like Malaga. The question which puzzled him was how he was to get his oranges on board. Where could he reasonably be going to take them?

Presently a sailor came up and began to chat with him.

"Are you wanting a boat, señor?"

"I have not made up my mind yet," he said. "I suppose you are busy here now?"

"No; the times are dull. Usually we do a good deal of trade with Gibraltar, but at present that is all stopped. It is hard on us; but when we turn out the English hereticos I hope we shall have better times than ever. But who can say? They have plenty of money, the English, and are ready to pay good prices for everything."

"But I suppose you take things to our camp?"

The fisherman shook his head. "They get their supplies direct from Malaga by sea. There are many carts go through here, of course; but the roads are heavy, and it is cheaper to send things by water. If our camp had been on the sea-shore instead of at San Roque we might have taken fish and fruit to them; but it is a long way across, and of course in small boats we cannot go round the great Rock and run the risk of being shot at or taken prisoners. No; there is nothing for us to do here now but to carry what fish and fruit we do not want at Marbella across to Malaga, and we get poor prices there to what we used to get at Gibraltar, and no chance of turning an honest penny by smuggling away a few pounds of tobacco as we come back. There was as much profit in that as there was in the sale of the goods; but one had to be very sharp, for they were always suspicious of boats coming back from there, and used to search us so that you would think one could not bring so much as a cigar on shore. But you know there are ways of managing things. Are you thinking of going across to Malaga, señor?"

"Well, I have a little business there. I want to see how the new wines are selling, and whether it will be better for me to sell mine now or to keep them in my cellars for a few months. I am in no hurry; to-morrow is as good as to-day. If there had been a boat going across I might have taken a passage that way instead of riding."

"I don't know, señor. There was a man asking an hour ago if anyone was going. He was wanting to take a few boxes of fruit across, but he did not care about hiring my boat for himself. That, you see, was reasonable enough; but if the señor wished to go too it might be managed if you took the boat between you. I would carry you cheaply if you would be willing to wait for an hour or two, so that I could go round to the other fishermen and get a few dozen fish from one and a few dozen from another, to sell for them over there. That is the way we manage."

"I could not very well go until the afternoon," Bob said.

"If you do not go until the afternoon, señor, it would be as well not to start until evening. The wind is very light, and we should have to row. If you start in the afternoon we should get to Malaga at two or three o'clock in the morning, when everyone was asleep: but if you were to start in the evening we should be in in reasonable time, just as the people were coming into the markets. That would suit us for the sale of our fish and the man with his fruit. The nights are warm, and with a cloak and an old sail to keep off the night dew the voyage would be more pleasant than in the heat of the day."

"That would do for me very well," Bob said; "nothing could be better. What charge would you make for taking me across and bringing me back to-morrow?"

"At what time would you want to return, señor?"

"It would matter little. I should be done with my business by noon, but I should be in no hurry. I could wait until evening, if that would suit you better."

"And we might bring other passengers back, and any cargo we might pick up?"

"Yes, so that you do not fill the boat so full that there would be no room for me to stretch my legs."

"Would the señor think four dollars too much? There will be my brother and myself, and it will be a long row."

"It is dear," Bob said decidedly; "but I will give you three dollars, and if everything passes to my satisfaction maybe I will make up the other dollar."

"Agreed, señor. I will see if I can find the man who was here asking for a boat for his fruit."

"I will come back in an hour and see," Bob said, getting up and walking leisurely away.

The fisherman was waiting for him. "I can't find the man, señor, though I have searched all through the town. He must have gone off to his farm again."

"That is bad. How much did you reckon upon making from him?"

"I should have got another three dollars from him."

"Well, I tell you what," Bob said; "I have a good many friends, and people are always pleased with a present from the country. A box of fruit from Marbella is always welcome, for their flavour is considered excellent. It is well to throw a little fish to catch a big one, and a present is like oil on the wheels of business. How many boxes of fruit will your boat carry? I suppose you could take twenty and still have room to row?"

"Thirty, sir; that is the boat," and he pointed to one moored against the quay. She was about twenty feet long, with a mast carrying a good-sized sail.

"Very well, then. I will hire the boat for myself. I will give you six dollars, and another dollar for drink-money if all goes pleasantly. You must be ready to come back to-morrow evening, or the first thing next morning if it should suit you to stay till then. You can carry what fish you can get to Malaga, and may take in a return cargo if you can get one; that will be extra profit for yourselves. But you and your brother must agree to carry down the boxes of fruit and put them on board here. I am not going to pay porters for that. At what time will you start?"

"Shall we say six o'clock, señor?"

"That will suit me very well. You can come up with me now and bring the fruit down and put it on board; or I will be down here at five o'clock, and you can go up and get it then."

The man thought for a moment. "I would rather do it now, señor, if it makes no difference to you. Then we can have our evening meals at home with our families, and come straight down here and start."

"Very well; fetch your brother and we will set about the matter at once, as I have to go out to my farm and make some arrangements, and tell them they may not see me again for three days."

In two or three minutes the fisherman came back with his brother. Bob went with them to a trader in fruit, and bought twenty boxes of lemons and ten of oranges, and saw them carried down and put on board. Then he handed a dollar to the boatman.

"Get a loaf of white bread and a nice piece of cooked meat and a couple of bottles of good wine, and put them on board; we shall be hungry before morning. I will be here at a few minutes before six."

Highly satisfied with the good fortune that had enabled

him to get the fruit on board without the slightest difficulty,
Bob returned into the town. It was but eleven o'clock now,
so, having had but a short sleep the night before, and no
prospect of sleep the next night, he walked a mile along the
road by the sea, then turned off among the sand-hills and
slept till four in the afternoon, after which he returned to
Marbella and partook of a hearty meal. Having finished
this he strolled out, and was not long in discovering a shop
where arms were sold. Here he bought a brace of long
heavy pistols and two smaller ones, with powder and bullets,
and also a long knife. They were all made into a parcel
together; and on leaving the shop he bought a small bag.
Then he went a short distance out of the town again,
carefully loaded the four pistols, and placed them and the
knife in the bag.

As he went back the thought struck him that the voyage
might probably last longer than they expected, and buying
a basket he stored it with another piece of meat, three loaves,
and two more bottles of wine, and gave it to a boy to carry
down to the boat. It was a few minutes before six when he
got there. The two sailors were standing by the boat, and
a considerable pile of fish in the bow showed that they had
been successful in getting a consignment from the other
fishermen of the port. They looked surprised at the second
supply of provisions.

"Why, señor, we have got the things you ordered."

"Yes, yes, I do not doubt that; but I have heard before
now of head-winds springing up, and boats not being able
to make their passage and being blown off land, and I am
not fond of fasting. I daresay you won't mind eating to-
morrow anything that is not consumed by the time we reach
port."

"We will undertake that, señor," the man said laughing,
highly satisfied at the liberality of their employer.

"Is there wind enough for the sail?" Bob asked as he
stepped into the stern of the boat.

"It is very light, señor, but I daresay it will help us a bit. We shall get out the oars."

"I will take the helm if you sail," Bob said. "You can tell me which side to push it; it will be an amusement, and keep me awake."

The sun was just setting as they started. There was scarcely a breath of wind. The light breeze that had been blowing during the day had dropped with the sun, and the evening breeze had not yet sprung up. The two fishermen rowed, and the boat went slowly through the water; for the men knew that they had a long row before them, and were by no means inclined to exert themselves, especially as they hoped that in a short time they would get wind enough to take them on their way without the oars. Bob chatted with them until it became dark. As soon as he was perfectly sure that the boat could not be seen from the land, he quietly opened his bag and changed the conversation.

"My men," he said, "I wonder that you are content with earning small wages here when you could get a lot of money by making a trip occasionally round to Gibraltar with fruit. It would be quite easy, for you could keep well out from the coast till it became dark, and then row in close under the Rock, and keep along round the Point and into the town without the least risk of being seen by any of our cruisers. You talked about making money by smuggling in tobacco from there, but that is nothing to what you could get by taking fruit into Gibraltar. These oranges cost a dollar and a half a box, and they would fetch ten dollars a box easily there; indeed I think they would fetch twenty dollars a box. Why, that would give a profit on the thirty boxes of six or seven hundred dollars. Just think of that!"

"Would they give such a price as that?" the men said in surprise.

"They would. They are suffering from want of fresh meat, and there is illness among them, and oranges and lemons are the things to cure them. It is all very well for men to suffer, but no one wants women and children to do so; and it would be the act of good Christians to relieve them, besides making as much money in one little short trip as you would make in a year's work."

"That is true," the men said; "but we might be sunk by the guns going there, and we should certainly be hung when we got back if they found out where we had been."

"Why should they find out?" Bob asked. "You would put out directly it got dark, and row round close under the Rock, and then make out to sea, and in the morning you would be somewhere off Marbella, but eight or ten miles out, with your fishing-nets down, and who is to know that you have been to Gibraltar?"

The men were silent. The prospect certainly seemed a tempting one. Bob allowed them to turn it over in their minds for a few minutes, and then spoke again.

"Now, my men, I will speak to you frankly; it is just this business that I am bent upon now. I have come out from Gibraltar to do a little trade in fruit. It is sad to see women and children suffering; and there is, as I told you, lots of money to be made out of it. Now, I will make you a fair offer. You put the boat's head round now and sail for Gibraltar. If the wind helps us a bit we shall be off the Rock by daylight. When we get there I will give you a hundred dollars apiece."

"It is too much risk," one of the men said after a long pause.

"There is no risk at all," Bob said firmly. "You will get in there to-morrow, and you can start again as soon as it becomes dark, and in the morning you will be able to sail into Marbella, and who is to know that you haven't been across to Malaga as you intended? I tell you what, I will give you another fifty dollars for your fish, or you can sell them there yourselves; they will fetch you quite that."

The men still hesitated, and spoke together in a low voice.

"Look here, men," Bob said as he took the two heavy

pistols from his bag, "I have come out from the Rock to do this, and I am going to do it. The question is, Which do you choose—to earn two hundred and fifty dollars for a couple of day's work, or to be shot and thrown overboard? This boat is going there, whether you go in her or not. I don't want to hurt you, I would rather pay the two hundred and fifty dollars; but that fruit may save the lives of many women and little children, and I am bound to do it. You can make another trip or not, just as you please. Now I think you will be very foolish if you don't agree, for you will make three times as much as I offer you every thirty boxes of fruit that you can take in there; but the boat has got to go there now, and you have got to take your choice whether you go in her or not."

"How do we know that you will pay us the money when we get there?" one of the Spaniards asked.

Bob put his hand into his pocket. "There," he said; "there are twenty gold pieces, that is a hundred dollars. That is a proof I mean what I say. Put them into your pockets. You shall have the rest when you get there. But, mind, no nonsense; no attempts at treachery. If I see the smallest sign of that I will shoot you down without hesitation. Now row, and I'll put her head round."

The men said a few words in an undertone to each other. "You guarantee that no harm shall come to us at Gibraltar, and that we shall be allowed to leave again?"

"Yes, I promise you that faithfully. Now you have got to row a good bit harder than you have been rowing up till now. We must be past Fort Santa Barbara before daylight."

The boat's head was round by this time, and the men began to row steadily. At present they hardly knew whether they were satisfied or not. Two hundred and fifty dollars was to them an enormous sum, but the risk was great. It was not that they feared that any suspicion would fall upon them on their return. They had often smuggled tobacco from Gibraltar, and had no high opinion of the acuteness of the authorities.   What really alarmed them was the fear of being sunk either by the Spanish or British guns.   However, they saw that for the present at any rate they had no option but to obey the orders of a passenger possessed of such powerful arguments as those he held in his hands.

CHAPTER XIV.

AFTER the men had been rowing for an hour Bob felt a
slight breeze springing up from off the land, and said:
"You may as well get up the sail, it will help you along a
bit." The sail was a large one for the size of the boat, and
Bob felt a distinct increase in her pace as soon as the men
began to row again. He could make out the line of the hills
against the sky, and had therefore no difficulty in keeping
the course. They were soon back opposite Marbella, the
lights of which he could clearly make out. Little by little
the breeze gathered strength, and the rowers had comparatively easy work of it as the boat slipped away lightly before
the wind.

"What do you make it—twelve leagues from Marbella
to the Rock?"

"About that," the man replied. "If the wind holds like
this we shall not be very far from the Rock by daylight. We
are going along about a league an hour."

"Well, stretch out to it, lads, for your own sakes. I have
no fear of a shot from Santa Barbara. The only thing I am
afraid of is that we should be seen by any Spanish boats
that may be cruising round that side before we get under
shelter of the guns of the Rock."

The fishermen needed no warning as to the danger of
being caught, and bent again more strongly to their oars.

After they had rowed two hours longer Bob told them to
pull the oars in.

"You had better have a quarter of an hour's rest and some supper and a bottle of wine," he said. "You have got your own basket forward, I will take mine out of this by my side."

As their passenger had paid for it, the boatmen had got a very superior wine to that they ordinarily drank. After eating their supper—bread, meat, and onions—and drinking half a bottle of wine each, they were disposed to look at the situation in a more cheerful light. Two hundred and fifty dollars was certainly well worth running a little risk for. Why, it would make them independent of bad weather, and they would be able to freight their boat themselves with fish or fruit, and to trade on their own account.

They were surprised at the enterprise of this young trader, whom they supposed to be a native of Gibraltar; for Bob thought that it was as well that they should remain in ignorance of his nationality, as they might have felt more strongly that they were rendering assistance to the enemy did they know that he was English. Hour after hour passed. The wind did not increase in force, nor on the other hand did it die away; there was just enough to keep the sail full, and take much of the weight of the boat off the arms of the rowers. The men, knowing the outline of the hills, were able to tell what progress they were making, and told Bob when they were passing Estepona. Two or three times there was a short pause for the men to have a draught of wine. With that exception they rowed on steadily.

"It will be a near thing, señor," one of them said towards morning. "The current counts for three or four miles against us. If it hadn't been for that we should certainly have done it. As it is, it is doubtful."

"I think we are about a mile off shore, are we not?" Bob asked. "That is about the distance I want to keep. If there are any cruisers they are sure to be further out than that; and as for Santa Barbara, if they see us and take the trouble to fire at us, there is not much chance of their hitting such a mark as this a mile away. Besides, almost all their guns are on the land side."

The men made no reply. To them the thought of being fired at by big guns was much more alarming than that of being picked up by a cruiser of their own nation, although they saw there might be a good deal of difficulty in persuading the authorities that they had taken part perforce in the attempt to get fruit into the beleaguered garrison. Daylight was just beginning to break, when one of the fishermen pointed out a dark mass inshore, but somewhat ahead of them.

"That is Santa Barbara," he said.

They had already for some time made out the outline of the Rock, and Bob gazed anxiously seaward, but could as yet see no signs of the enemy's cruisers.

"Row away, lads," he said. "They won't see us for some time, and in another half hour we shall be safe."

The Spaniards bent to their oars with all their strength now, from time to time looking anxiously over their shoulders at the fort. Rapidly the daylight stole across the sky, and they were just opposite Santa Barbara when a gun boomed out and a shot flew over their heads and struck the water a quarter of a mile beyond them. With a yell of fear the two Spaniards threw themselves at the bottom of the boat.

"Get up, you fools!" Bob shouted. "You will be no safer down there than if you were rowing. If a shot strikes her she will be smashed up whether you are rowing or lying down. If you stay there it will be an hour before we get out of range of their guns, while if you row like men we shall get further and further away every minute, and be safe in a quarter of an hour."

It was only, however, after he threatened to shoot them if they did not set to work again that the Spaniards resumed their oars, but when they did they rowed desperately. Another shot from the fort struck the water a short distance astern, exciting a fresh yell of agony from the men.

"There, you see," Bob said; "if you hadn't been sending her faster through the water that would have hit us. Ah! they are beginning from that sloop out at sea."

This was a small craft that Bob had made out as the light increased, a mile and a half seaward. She had changed her course, and was heading in their direction. Retaining his hold of his pistols Bob moved forward, put out a spare oar, and set to to row. Shot after shot came from the fort and several from the sloop; but a boat at that distance presents but a small mark, and although a shot went through the sail none struck her. Presently a gun boomed out ahead of them high in the air, and a shot fell near the sloop, which at once hauled her wind and stood out to sea.

"We have got rid of her," Bob said, "and we are a mile and a half from the fort now. You can take it easy, men. They won't waste many more shot upon us."

Indeed only one more gun was fired by the Spaniards, and then the boat pursued her course unmolested, Bob re turning to his seat at the helm.

"They will be on the look-out for us as we go back," one of the Spaniards said.

"They won't see you in the dark," Bob replied. "Besides, as likely as not they will think that you are one of the Rock fishing-boats that has ventured out too far and failed to get back by daylight."

Once out of reach of the shot from the fort the sailors laid in their oars, having been rowing for more than ten hours, and the boat glided along quietly at a distance of a few hundred feet from the foot of the cliff.

"Which are you going to do?" Bob asked them; "take fifty dollars for your fish, or sell them for what you can get for them?"

The fishermen at once said they would take the fifty dollars; for although they had collected all that had been brought in by the other fishermen, amounting to some five hundred pounds in weight, they could not imagine that fish for which they would not have got more than ten dollars at the outside at Malaga could sell for fifty at Gibraltar. As they rounded Europa Point there was a hail from above, and looking up Bob saw Captain O'Halloran and the doctor.

"Hulloa, Bob!"

"Hulloa!" Bob shouted back, and waved his hat.

"All right, Bob!"

"All right. I have got thirty boxes!"

"Hurrah!" the doctor shouted, waving his hat over his head. "We will meet you at the New Mole. That is something like a boy, Gerald!"

"It is all very well for you," Captain O'Halloran said. "You are not responsible for him, and you are not married to his sister."

"Put yourself in the way of a cannon-ball, Gerald, and I will be married to her a week after—if she will have me."

His companion laughed.

"It is all very well, Teddy; but it is just as well for you that you did not show your face up at the house during the last three days. It is not Bob who has been blamed. It has been entirely you and me, especially you. The moment she read his letter she said at once that you were at the bottom of it, and that it never would have entered Bob's mind to do such a mad thing if you had not put him up to it; and of course when I came back from seeing you, and said that you admitted that you knew what he was doing, it made the case infinitely worse. It will be a long time before she takes you into favour again."

"About an hour," the doctor said calmly. "As soon as she finds that Bob has come back again with the fruit, and that he has as good as saved the lives of scores of women and children, she will be so proud of him that she will greet me as part author of the credit he has gained; though really, as I told you, I had nothing to do with it, except that when I saw that Bob had made up his mind to try, whether I helped him or not, I thought it best to help him, as far as I could, to get away. Now, we must get some porters to carry the boxes up to your house, or wherever he wants them sent. Ah! here is the governor. He will be pleased to hear that Bob has got safely back."

Captain O'Halloran had, when he found Bob's letter in his room on the morning after he had left, felt it his duty to go to the town-major's office to mention his absence, and it had been reported to the general, who had sent for Gerald to inquire about the circumstances of the lad's leaving. Captain O'Halloran had assured him that he knew nothing whatever of his intention, and that it was only when he found the letter on his table saying that he had made up his mind to get beyond the Spanish lines somehow, and to bring in a boat-load of oranges for the use of the women and children who were suffering from scurvy, that he knew his brother-in-law had any such idea in his mind.

"It is a very gallant attempt, Captain O'Halloran; although, of course, I should not have permitted it to be made had I been aware of his intentions."

"Nor should I, sir," Captain O'Halloran said. "My wife is naturally very much upset."

"That is natural enough," the governor said. "Still, she has every reason to be proud of her brother. A man could risk his life for no higher object than that for which Mr. Repton has undertaken this expedition. How do you suppose he got away?"

"I have no idea, sir. He may have got down by ropes from the back of the Rock, the way the deserters generally choose."

"Yes; but if he got down without breaking his neck he would still have to pass our line of sentries, and also through the Spaniards'."

"He is a very good swimmer, general, and may have struck out and landed beyond the Spanish forts. Of course he may have started from the old Mole, and swam across to the head of the bay. He is sure to have thought the matter well out. He is very sharp, and if anyone could get through I should say Bob could. He speaks the language like a native."

"I have heard of him before," the governor said smiling. "Captain Langton told us of the boy's doings when he was away in that privateer brig, and how he took in the frigate, and was the means of the brig capturing those two valuable prizes, and how he had swam on board a Spanish sloop of war. He said that no officer could have shown greater pluck and coolness. I sincerely hope that no harm will come to him; but how, even if he succeeds in getting through the Spanish lines, he can manage single-handed to get back here in a boat, is more than I can see. Well, I sincerely trust that no harm will come to him."

As the governor with two or three of his staff now came along, Captain O'Halloran went up to him.

"I am glad to say, sir," he said, "that young Repton has just returned, and that he has brought in thirty cases of fruit."

"I am extremely glad to hear it, Captain O'Halloran," the governor said warmly. "When it was reported to me an hour since that the Spanish fort and one of their cruisers were firing at a small boat that was making her way in from the east, the thought struck me that it might be your brother-in-law. Where is he?"

"He is just coming round to the Mole, sir. Doctor Burke and myself are going to meet him."

"I will go down with you," the governor said. "Those oranges are worth a thousand pounds a box to the sick."

The party reached the Mole before the boat came in, for after rounding the Point she had been becalmed, and the fishermen had lowered the sail and betaken themselves to their oars again. Bob felt a little uncomfortable when, as the boat rowed up to the landing-stairs, he saw General Eliott, with a group of officers, standing at the top. He was relieved when on ascending the steps the governor stepped forward and shook him warmly by the hand.

"I ought to begin by scolding you for breaking out of the fortress without leave, but I am too pleased with the success of your venture, and too much gratified at the spirit that prompted you to undertake it, to say a word. Captain O'Halloran tells me that you have brought in thirty cases of fruit."

"Yes, sir. I have ten cases of oranges and twenty of lemons. I propose, with your permission, to send half of these up to the hospitals for the use of the sick there; the others I intend for the use of the women and children of the garrison and townspeople. Doctor Burke will see for me that they are distributed where they will do most good."

"Well, my lad, I thank you most cordially for your noble gift to the troops, and there is not a man here who will not feel grateful to you for the relief it will afford to the women and children. I shall be very glad if you will dine with me to-day, and you can then tell me how you have managed what I thought, when I first heard of your absence, was a sheer impossibility. Captain O'Halloran, I trust that you and Mrs. O'Halloran will also give me the pleasure of your company at dinner to-day."

"If you please, sir," Bob said, "will you give these two boatmen a pass permitting them to go out after dark to-night. I promised them that they should not be detained. It is of the greatest importance to them that they should get back before their absence is discovered."

"Certainly," the governor said, and at once ordered one of the officers of the staff to see that the pass was given, and orders issued to the officers of the batteries to allow the boat to pass out in the dark unquestioned. As soon as the governor walked away with his staff, Bob was heartily greeted by Captain O'Halloran and the doctor.

"You have given us a fine fright, Bob," the former said,

"and your sister has been in a desperate way about you. However, now that you have come back safe I suppose she will forgive you. But what about all those fish? Are they yours? Why, there must be half a ton of them!"

"No; the men say there are five or six hundred pounds. Yes, they are mine. I thought of keeping a few for ourselves, and dividing the rest between the ten regiments, and sending them up with your compliments to their messes."

"Not with my compliments, Bob; that would be ridiculous. Send them up with your own compliments, it will be a mighty acceptable present. But you had better pick out two or three of the finest fish and send them up to the governor. Now, then, let us set to work. Here are plenty of porters, but first of all we had better get ten men from the officer of the guard here, and send one off with each of the porters with the fish to the regiments, or the chances are that these baskets will be a good bit lighter by the time they arrive there than when they start. I will go and ask the officer while you are getting the fish up here and divided."

In a quarter of an hour the ten porters started, each with about half a hundredweight, and under the charge of a soldier. The doctor took charge of the porters with the fifteen boxes of fruit for the various hospitals, and then after Bob had paid the boatmen the two hundred and fifty dollars due to them, and had told them they would get the permit to enable them to sail again as soon as it became dark, he and Captain O'Halloran started for the house, with the men in charge of the other fifteen boxes, and with one carrying the remaining fish, which weighed about the same as the other parcels.

"How did you and the doctor happen to be at Europa Point, Gerald?" Bob asked, as they went along.

"The doctor said he felt sure that whenever you did come, that is, if you came at all, you would get here somewhere about daylight, and he arranged with the officer in charge of the upper battery to send a man down with the news if there was a boat in sight. Directly he heard that the Spaniards were firing at a boat he came over and called me, and we went round to the back of the Rock. We couldn't be sure that it was you from that height; but as we could make out the boxes, we thought it must be you, and so walked down to the Point to catch you there."

"Does Carrie know that a boat was in sight?"

"No, I wouldn't say anything to her about it. She had only just dropped off to sleep when I was called. She woke up and asked what it was, but I said that I supposed I was wanted on duty, and she went off again before I was dressed. I was glad she did, for she hadn't closed her eyes before since you started."

Carrie was on the terrace when she saw Bob and Gerald, followed by a procession of porters, coming up the hill. With a cry of joy she ran down into the house and out to meet them.

"You bad boy!" she cried, as she threw her arms round Bob's neck. "How could you frighten us so? It is very cruel and wicked of you, Bob, and I am not going to forgive you; though I can't help being glad to see you, which is more than you deserve."

"You mustn't scold him, Carrie," her husband said. "Even the governor didn't scold him, and he has thanked him in the name of the whole garrison, and he has asked him to dine with him; and you and I are to dine there too, Carrie. There is an honour for you! But what is better than honour is, that there isn't a woman and child on the Rock who won't be feeling deeply grateful to Bob before the day is over."

"Has he really got some fruit?"

"Yes. Don't you see the boxes, Carrie?"

"Oh, I saw something coming along, but I didn't see anything clearly but Bob. What are these boxes—oranges?"

"Oranges and lemons, five of oranges, and ten of lemons,

and there are as many more that have gone up to the hospital for the use of the men. There, let us see them taken into the store-room. You can open two of them at once, and send Manola off with a big basket, and tell her to give half a dozen of each with your love to each of the ladies you know. The doctor will take charge of the rest, and see about their division among all the women on the Rock. It will be quite a business, but he won't mind it."

"What is all this—fish?"

"Well, my dear, you are to take as much as you want, and you are to pick out two or three of the best and send them to the governor with your compliments, and the rest you can divide and send out with the fruit to your special friends."

"But how has Bob done it?" Carrie asked, quite overwhelmed at the sight of all those welcome stores.

"Ah, that he must tell you himself. I have no more idea than the man in the moon."

"It has all been quite simple," Bob said. "But see about sending these things off first, Carrie; Doctor Burke will be here after he has seen the others taken safely to the hospital, and I shall have to tell it all over again then."

"I am very angry with the doctor," Mrs. O'Halloran said.

"Then the sooner you get over being angry the better, Carrie. The doctor had nothing whatever to do with my going; but when he saw that I had made up my mind to go, he helped me, and I am extremely obliged to him. Now you may have an orange for yourself if you are good."

"That I won't," Carrie said. "Thanks to our eggs and vegetables we are perfectly well, and when there are so many people really in want of the oranges, it would be downright wicked to eat them merely because we like them."

In a short time Manola, with two of the children from downstairs carrying baskets, started with the presents of fruit and fish to all the ladies of Carrie's acquaintance. Soon after she had left, Doctor Burke arrived.

"I was not going to speak to you, Teddy Burke," Mrs. O'Halloran said, shaking her head at him. "I had lost confidence in you; but with Bob back again, and all this fruit for the poor creatures who want it, I will forgive you."

"I am glad you have grace enough for that, Mrs. O'Halloran. It is down on your knees you ought to go to thank me, if I had my rights. Isn't Bob a hero, and hasn't he received the thanks of the governor, and hasn't he saved scores of lives this blessed day, and although it is little enough I had to do with it, isn't it the thanks of the whole garrison ought to be given me for even the little bit of a share I had in it?"

"We have been waiting for you to come, Teddy," Captain O'Halloran said, "to hear Bob's story."

"Well, then, you will have to wait a bit longer," the doctor said. "I have sent orderlies from the hospital to all the regiments, including of course the Artillery and Engineers, asking them to send me lists of the numbers of the women and children of the non-commissioned officers and privates, and also of officers' wives and families, and to send with the lists here two orderlies from each regiment with baskets. I have been down to the town-major, and got a list of the number of women and children in the town. When we get the returns from the regiments we will reckon up the totals, and see how many there will be for each. I think that each of the boxes holds about five hundred."

The work of counting out the oranges and lemons for the various regiments and the townspeople occupied some time, and it was not until the orderlies had started with their supplies that Bob sat down to tell his story.

"Nothing could have been easier," he said when he finished.

"It was easy enough, as you say, Bob," the doctor said; "but it required a lot of coolness and presence of mind. Events certainly turned out fortunately for you, but you took advantage of them. That is always the point. Nobody could have done it better, and most people would have done worse. I have been wondering myself a great deal since you have been gone what plan you could possibly hit on to get the oranges into a boat, and how, when you had got them in, you would manage to get them here. It seems all easy enough now you have done it; but that is all the more creditable to you for hitting on a plan that worked so well."

Similar praise was given to Bob when he had again to tell his story at the governor's.

"So you managed, you say, to slip out with the reliefs?" the governor said.

"Yes, sir. I had got a military cloak and hat."

"Still it is curious that they did not notice an addition to their party. I fancy you must have had a friend there?"

"That, general, is a point that I would rather not say anything about. That is the way that I did go out; and when I took to the water I let the coat and hat float away, for had they been found it might have been supposed that somebody had deserted."

"I wish you could have brought in a ship-load instead of a boat-load of fruit, Mr. Repton. They will be of immense benefit to the sick; but unfortunately there is scarcely a person on the Rock that is not more or less affected, and if your thirty boxes were multiplied by a hundred it would be none too much for our needs."

The oranges and lemons did, however, for a time have a marked effect in checking the progress of the scurvy, especially among the children, who came in for a larger share than that which fell to the sick soldiers, but in another month the condition of those in hospital, and indeed of many who still managed to do duty, was again pitiable. On the 11th of October, however, some of the boats of the fleet went out during a fog and boarded a Danish craft from Malaga laden with oranges and lemons and brought her in. The cargo was at once bought by the governor and distributed. The beneficial effects were immediate. Cases which had but a few days before appeared hopeless, were cured as if by magic, and the health of the whole garrison was re-established. Heavy rains setting in at the same time, the gardens, upon which for months great attention had been bestowed, came rapidly into bearing, and henceforth throughout the siege the supply of vegetables, if not ample for the needs of the garrison and inhabitants, was sufficient to prevent scurvy from getting any strong hold again.

A few days after the ship with oranges was brought in, an orderly came in to Captain O'Halloran with a message that the governor wished to speak to Mr. Repton. Bob was out at the time, but went up to the castle as soon as he returned, and was at once shown in to the governor.

"Mr. Repton," the latter began, "after the spirit you showed the other day I shall be glad to utilize your services still farther, if you are willing."

"I shall be very glad to be useful in any work upon which you may think fit to employ me, sir."

"I wish to communicate with Mr. Logie at Tangiers," the governor said. "It is a month now since we have had any news from him. At the time he last wrote he said that the Emperor of Morocco was manifesting an unfriendly spirit towards us, and that he was certainly in close communication with the Spaniards, and had allowed their ships to take more than one English vessel lying under the guns of the town. His own position was, he said, little better than that of a prisoner, for he was closely watched. He still hoped, however, to bring the emperor round again to our side, as he had for years exercised a considerable influence over him. If he would grant him an interview, Mr. Logie thought that he might still be able to clear up any doubts of us that the Spaniards might have infused in his mind.

"Since that letter we have heard nothing from him, and we are ignorant how matters stand over there. The matter is important; for although, while the enemy's cruisers are as vigilant as at present, there is little hope of our getting fresh meat over from there, I am unable to give any directions to such privateers or others as may find their way in here. It makes all the difference to them whether the Morocco ports are open to them or not. Until lately, when chased they could run in there, wait for a brisk east wind, and then start after dark, and be fairly through the Straits before morning. I am very desirous, therefore, of communicating with Mr. Logie. I am also anxious, not only about his safety, but of that of several English families there, among whom are those of some of the officers of the garrison, who, thinking that they would be perfectly safe in Tangiers, and avoid the hardships and dangers of the siege, despatched them across the Straits by the native craft that came in when first the port was closed.

"Thinking it over, it appeared to me that you would be far more fitted than most for this mission, if you would accept it. You have already shown yourself able to pass as a Spaniard; and should you find that things have gone badly in Tangiers, and that the Moors have openly joined the Spaniards, you might be able to get a passage to Lisbon in a neutral ship, and to return thence in the first privateer or ship-of-war bound for this port. I could of course provide you with a document requesting the officer in command of any such ship to give you a passage. Should no such neutral ship come along, I should trust to you to find your way across to Tarifa or Algeciras, and thence to manage in some way, which I must leave to your own ingenuity, to make your way in. I do not disguise from you that the commission is a very dangerous as well as an honourable one, as, were you, an Englishman, detected on Spanish soil, you would almost certainly be executed as a spy."

"I am ready to undertake the commission, sir, and I am much obliged to you for affording me the opportunity of being of service. It is irksome for me to remain here in idleness when there are many young officers of my own age doing duty in the batteries. As to the risk, I am quite prepared to run it. It will be exactly such an adventure as I should choose."

"Very well, Mr. Repton. Then I will send you the despatches this evening, together with a letter recommending you to all British officers and authorities. Both will be written on the smallest pieces of paper possible, so that you may conceal them more easily. Now, as to the means. There are many of the fishermen here would be glad to leave. The firing in the bay has frightened the greater part of the fish away, and, besides, the boats dare not go any distance from the Rock. I have caused inquiries to be made, and have given permits to three men to leave the Rock in a boat after nightfall, and to take their chances of getting through the enemy's cruisers. It is likely to be a very dark night. I have arranged with them to take a passenger across to Tangiers, and have given them permission to take two others with them.

"We know that there are many Jews and others most anxious to leave the town before the enemy begin to bombard it, and the men will doubtless get a good price from two of these to carry them across the Straits. You will form an idea for yourself whether these boatmen are trustworthy. If you conclude that they are you can make a bargain with them, or with any others, to bring you back direct. I authorize you to offer them a hundred pounds for doing so. Come up here at eight o'clock this evening. I will have the despatches ready for you then. You will understand that if you find the Moors have become absolutely hostile, and have a difficulty in getting at Mr. Logie, you are not to run any risk in trying to deliver the despatches, as the information you will be able to obtain will be sufficient for me without any confirmation from him."

After further conversation Bob took his leave of the governor. On his return home Carrie was very vexed when she heard the mission that Bob had undertaken, and at first it needed all her husband's persuasions to prevent her going off to the governor's to protest against it.

"Why, my dear, you would make both yourself and Bob ridiculous. Surely he is of an age now to go his own way without petticoat government. He has already gained great credit both in his affair with the privateer and in fetching in the oranges the other day. This is far less dangerous. Here he has only got to smuggle himself in, there he had to bring back something like a ton of oranges. It is a great honour for the governor to have chosen him. And as to you opposing it, the idea is absurd!"

"I shall go round to Major Harcourt," Bob said. "Mrs. Harcourt is terribly anxious about her daughter, and I am sure she will be glad to send a letter over to her."

"Carrie," Captain O'Halloran said gravely, "I have become a sudden convert to your opinion regarding this expedition. Suppose that Bob, instead of coming back, were to carry Amy Harcourt off to England, it would be terrible! I believe that Mr. Logie, as His Majesty's consul, could perform the necessary ceremony before they sailed."

Bob laughed.

"I should doubt whether Mr. Logie would have power to officiate in the case of minors. Besides, there is an English church where the banns could be duly published. No. I think we must put that off, Gerald."

Amy Harcourt was the daughter of one of the O'Hallorans' most intimate friends, and the girl, who was about fifteen years old, was often at their house with her mother. She had suffered much from the heat early in June, and her parents had, at a time when the Spanish cruisers had somewhat relaxed their vigilance, sent her across to Tangiers in one of the traders. She was in the charge of Mrs. Colomb, the wife of an officer of the regiment, who was also going across for her health. They intended to stay at Tangiers only for a month or six weeks, but Mrs. Colomb had become worse, and was, when the last news came across, too ill to be moved. Major and Mrs. Harcourt had consequently become very anxious about Amy, the feeling being much heightened by the rumours of the hostile attitude of the emperor towards the English. Mrs. Harcourt gladly availed herself of the opportunity that Bob's mission offered.

"I shall be glad indeed if you will take a letter, Mr. Repton. I am in great trouble about her. If anything should happen to Mrs. Colomb her position would be extremely awkward. I know that Mr. Logie will do the best he can for her, but for aught we know he and all the English there may at present be prisoners among the Moors. I need not say how bitterly her father and I have regretted that we let her go, and yet it seemed by far the best thing at the time, for she would get an abundance of fresh meat, food, and vegetables. Of course you will see how she is situated when you get there, and I am sure you will give her the best advice you can as to what she is to do. Not knowing how they are placed there we can do literally nothing, and you managed that fruit business so splendidly that I feel very great confidence in you."

"I am sure I shall be glad to do anything that I can, Mrs. Harcourt, and if it had been a boy I daresay we could have managed something between us, but you see girls are different."

"Oh, you won't find any difficulty with her. I often tell her she is as much of a boy at present as she is a girl. Amy has plenty of sense. I shall tell her in my letter about your going out to fetch in the fruit for the women and children. She is inclined to look up to you very much already, owing to the share you had in the capture of those Spanish vessels, and I am sure she will listen to any advice you give her."

"Well, I will do my best, Mrs. Harcourt," Bob said meekly; "but I have never had anything to do with girls except my sister, and she gives the advice always and not me."

"By what she says, Bob, I don't think you always take it," Mrs. Harcourt said smiling.

"Well, not quite always," Bob admitted. "Women are constantly afraid that you are going to hurt yourself or something, just as if a boy had got no sense. Well, I will do what I can, Mrs. Harcourt. I am sure I hope that I shall find them all right over there."

"I hope so, too," Mrs. Harcourt said. "I will see Captain Colomb. He will be sure to give you a letter for his wife. I shall talk it over with him, and if he thinks that she had better go straight home if any opportunity offers I shall tell Amy to go with her, and stay with my sister at Gloucester till the siege is over and then she can come out again to us. I will bring you down the letters myself at seven o'clock."

From her Bob went to Dr. Burke.

"I have just come from your house, Bob. I found your sister in a despondent state about you. I assured her you had as many lives as a cat, and could only be considered to have used up two or three of them yet, and were safe for some years to come. I hinted that you had more to fear from a rope than either drowning or shooting. That made her angry, and did her good. However, it was better for me to be off, and I thought most likely that you would be coming round for a talk. So you are going officially this time. Well, what disguise are you going to take?"

"That is what I have been thinking of. What would you recommend, doctor?"

"Well, the choice is not a very extensive one. You can hardly go as you are, because if the Moors have joined the Spaniards you would be arrested as soon as you landed. Gerald tells me that probably two of the Jew traders will go away with you. If so I should say you could not do better than dress in their style. There are many of them Rock scorpions and talk Spanish and English equally well; but I should say that you had better take another disguise."

"That is what I was thinking," Bob said. "The boatman will know that I have something to do with the governor and the two Jews will certainly know that I don't belong to the Rock. If they find that the Moors have joined the Spaniards these Jews may try to get through themselves by denouncing me. I should say I had better get clothes with which I can pass as a Spanish sailor or fisherman. There are almost sure to be Spanish ships in there; there is a good deal of trade between Tangiers and Spain. Then again I shall want my own clothes if I have to take passage in a neutral to Lisbon. So I should say that I had better go down to the town and get a sort of trader's suit and a fisherman's at one of the low slop-shops. Then I will go as a trader to start with and carry the other two suits in a bag."

"That will be a very good plan, Bob. You are not likely to be noticed much when you land. There are always ships anchored there waiting for a wind to carry them out. They must be accustomed to sailors of all sorts of nationalities in the streets. However, I hope you will find no occasion for any clothes after you land but your own. The Moors have always been good friends of ours, and the emperor must know that the Spaniards are very much more dangerous neighbours than we are, and I can hardly believe he will be fool enough to throw us over. I will go down with you to buy these things."

Bob had no difficulty in procuring the clothes he required at a second-hand shop, and then took the lot home with him. Carrie had by this time become more reconciled to what could not be avoided, and she laughed when Dr. Burke came in.

"You are like a bad penny, Teddy Burke. It is no use trying to get rid of you."

"Not the least bit in the world, Mrs. O'Halloran. Fortunately, I know that, however hard you are upon me, you don't mean what you say."

"I do mean it very much, but after you are gone I say to myself, 'It is only Teddy Burke,' and think no more of it."

That evening at nine o'clock Bob embarked on board the

fishing-boat at the New Mole. One of the governor's aides-de-camp accompanied him to pass him through all the guards, and orders had been sent to the officers in command of the various batteries that the boat was not to be challenged. It was to show a light from a lantern as it went along, in order that it might be known. The other two passengers and the boatmen had been sitting there since before gun-fire, and they were glad enough when Bob came down and took his seat in the stern, taking the tiller ropes. The oars had been muffled, and they put off noiselessly. When they got past Europa Point they found a light breeze blowing, and at once laid in their oars and hoisted sail. A vigilant look-out was kept. Once or twice they thought they made out the hulls of anchored vessels, but they gave these a wide berth, and when the morning broke were half-way across the Strait, heading directly for Tangiers. In another six hours they entered the port.

There were half a dozen vessels lying in the harbour. Four of these were flying Spanish colours, one was a Dane, and the other a Dutchman. From the time morning broke Bob had been narrowly examining his fellow-passengers and the boatmen, and came to the conclusion that none of them were to be trusted. As soon as he stepped ashore with his bag in his hand he walked swiftly away, and passing through the principal streets, which were crowded with Moors, held steadily on without speaking to anyone until he reached the outskirts of the town, and then struck off among the hedges and gardens.

CHAPTER XV.

AS soon as he found a secluded spot he stripped off the clothes he wore and put on those of a Spanish sailor, and then, placing the others in the bag, buried it in the sandy soil, taking particular note of its position in regard to trees and surrounding objects, so as to be able to find it again. Then he turned to the right, and skirted the town till he came down to the sea-shore again, and then strolled quietly back to the quays. In passing by the ships at anchor he had noticed the names of the four Spaniards, and after wandering about for a short time he entered a wine-shop, and seated himself at a table near one at which three Spanish sailors sat drinking.

From their talk he learned that the British were shortly to be turned out of Tangiers, that the town was to be given up to the Spaniards, and that the British consul had the day before been taken to Sallee, where the emperor now was. The English in the town had not yet been made prisoners, but it was believed that they would be seized and handed over to the Spaniards without delay. Having obtained this information, Bob saw that, at any rate for the present, he might if he chose appear in his own character, and regretted that he had buried his clothes before knowing how matters stood. However, there was no help for it but to go back to the place where he had hidden them. This he did, and having put on his own clothes he went straight to the consulate, which was a large house facing the port. A clerk was sitting in the office.

"I understand Mr. Logie is away," Bob said.

The clerk looked surprised, for he knew the whole of the small body of British residents well, and he could not understand how Bob could have arrived.

"I am the bearer of letters to him from Governor Eliott," Bob said. "I came across by boat, and landed two hours ago; but I was in disguise, not knowing how matters stood here, and have but now ascertained that so far the English are not prisoners."

"Not at present," the clerk said. "But will you come into the house, sir? We may be disturbed here."

"In the first place," Bob asked when they were seated in an inner room, "when do you expect Mr. Logie back, and what is the real situation? My orders are, if I cannot see Mr. Logie himself, that I am to obtain as accurate a statement as possible as to how matters are going on here, as it is important that the governor should be able to inform vessels sailing from Gibraltar east whether they can or can not put safely into the Moorish ports. Of course we know that vessels have been several times taken by the Spaniards while at anchor close to the towns, but they might risk that if there were no danger from the Moors themselves; but if the reports last sent by Mr. Logie are confirmed, the Moors would be openly at war with us, and would themselves seize and make prizes of vessels anchoring. The danger would, of course, be vastly greater than that of merely running the risk of capture if a Spanish vessel of war happened to come into a port where they were at anchor. Of course I am merely expressing the views of the governor."

"I am sorry to say," the clerk said, "that there is no doubt the Moors are about to join the Spaniards in formal alliance against us. Englishmen are liable to insult as they go through the street. This, however, would not go for much by itself, but last week a number of soldiers rushed into the office, seized Mr. Logie, violently assaulted him, spat upon him, and otherwise insulted him, acting, as they said, by the express order of the emperor himself. He is now practically a prisoner, having been taken under an escort to Sallee, and at any moment the whole of the British colony here may be seized and thrown into prison; and if you know what Moorish prisons are, you would know that that would mean death to most of them, certainly I should say to all the ladies."

"But can they not leave in neutral vessels?"

"No. The strictest orders have been issued against any Englishman leaving; they are, in fact, so far prisoners, although nominally at liberty to move about the town. I believe that the greater part of the Moors regret extremely the course their emperor has taken. Many have come in here after dark to assure Mr. Logie how deeply averse they were to this course, for that the sympathies of the population in general were naturally with the English in their struggle against the Spaniards, who had for all time been the deadly foe of the Moors. Unfortunately, the emperor has supreme power, and anyone who ventured to murmur against his will would have his head stuck up over a gate in no time; so that the sympathy of the population does not count for much."

"How many English are there altogether?"

"A hundred and four; we made up the list last week. Of course that includes men, women, and children. There are some ten merchants, most of whom have one or two clerks, the rest of the men are small traders and shopkeepers. Some of them make their living by supplying ships that put in here with necessaries; a few, at ordinary times, trade with the Rock in live stock; half a dozen or so keep stores, where they sell English goods to the natives."

"I have a mission to discharge to a Mrs. Colomb, or at least to a young lady living with her."

"Mrs. Colomb, I regret to say, died three weeks ago," the clerk said. "Miss Harcourt, who is, I suppose, the young lady you mean, is now, with Mrs. Colomb's servant, staying here. Mr. Logie had placed them in lodgings in the house of a Moorish trader just outside the town, but the young lady could not remain there alone after Mrs. Colomb's death. I will ring the bell and tell the servant to inform her that you are here."

Ten minutes later Bob was shown into a large sitting-room on the first floor, with a verandah overlooking the sea.

"Oh, Bob Repton, I am glad to see you!" Amy Harcourt exclaimed, coming forward impulsively with both hands held out. "It is dreadfully lonely here. Mr. Logie is away, and poor Mrs. Colomb is dead, and as for Mrs. Williams she does nothing but cry, and say we are all going to be shut up and starved in a Moorish prison. But first, how are father and mother, and everyone at the Rock?"

"They are all quite well, Amy, though your mother has been in a great state of anxiety about you since she got your letter saying how ill Mrs. Colomb was. Here is a letter she has given me for you." He handed the girl the letter and went out on to the verandah while she read it.

"Mamma says I am to act upon Mr. Logie's advice, and that, if by any means he should not be in a position to advise me, I am to take your advice if Mrs. Colomb is dead."

"I don't think I am in a position to give you advice, Amy. What did Mr. Logie say about the state of affairs before he went away?"

"He seemed to think things were going on very badly. You know the soldiers rushed in here and assaulted him one day last week. They said they had orders from the emperor to do so; and Mr. Logie said they certainly would not have dared to molest the British consul if it hadn't been by the emperor's orders. He was talking to me about it the day before they took him away to Sallee, and he said he would give anything if he could get me away to the Rock, for that the position here was very precarious, and that the emperor might at any moment order all the English to be thrown into prison, and I know that the servants expect we shall all be killed by the populace. They have frightened Mrs. Williams nearly out of her senses. I never saw such a foolish woman. She does nothing but cry. She is the wife, you know, of Captain Colomb's soldier servant. Well, what do you advise, Bob?"

"I am sure I don't know what to advise, Amy. This seems a regular fix, doesn't it?"

"But you are just as badly off as I am," she said. "If they seize everyone else, of course they will seize you now you are here."

"Oh, I could get away easily enough," Bob said. "I should dress myself up as a Spanish sailor. I have got the clothes here, and should boldly go on board one of the Spanish ships and take passage across to any port they are going to, and then manage to work round into Gibraltar again. But of course you can't do that."

"I couldn't go as a Spanish sailor, of course," the girl said, "but I might dress up and go somehow; anything would be better than waiting here, and then being thrown into one of their dreadful prisons. They say they are awful places. Do take me, Bob Repton. I do so want to get back to father and mother again, and I am quite well and strong now—as well as ever I was."

Bob looked at the girl with a puzzled expression of face. He had promised her mother to do the best thing he could for her. The question was, What was the best thing? It certainly seemed that the position here was a very perilous one. If he left her here and harm befell her, what would her parents say to him? But, on the other hand, how on earth was he to get her away?

"I tell you what, Amy," he said, after a time. "Who were the ladies Mrs. Colomb saw most of? I suppose she knew some of the people here?"

"Oh, yes, she knew several; but she was most intimate with Mrs. Hamber. She is the wife of one of the principal merchants, and is very kind. She offered to take me in when Mrs. Colomb died; but her husband lives out of the town, and Mr. Logie had promised Mrs. Colomb that he would look after me until he could send me across; besides, Mrs. Hamber's child is very ill with fever, and so he brought me here."

"Well, I will go and consult her," Bob said. "I daresay the clerk downstairs will send a man with me to show me her house."

Mrs. Hamber listened to Bob's account of his mission, asking a question now and again in a straightforward and decided way, which gave Bob an idea that she was a resolute sort of woman, with plenty of common sense.

"Well, Mr. Repton," she said, when he had finished, "it is a difficult matter for anyone but the girl's mother to form an opinion upon. I remember hearing from Mrs. Colomb about your going out and bringing in fruit when the scurvy was so bad two months ago. She had received the news no doubt from her husband, and therefore it seems to me that you must be a very capable young gentleman, with plenty of courage and coolness. The fact that Mrs. Harcourt gave you such a message as she did regarding her daughter, shows that she has every confidence in you. If the girl were a year or two older, I should say it would be quite out of the question for her to attempt to make her way back to Gibraltar under your protection; but she is still a mere child, and as you possess her mother's confidence, I don't see that this matters so much.

"If you are both taken prisoners, there is no reason for supposing that she would not be treated honourably by the Spaniards. They must have taken numbers of women in the vessels they have captured lately, and, I suppose, the girl would be placed with them; she would, at any rate, be far better off in a Spanish prison than in a Moorish one. Besides, I really consider that all our lives are in danger here. After the assault on Mr. Logie, it is just as likely the emperor may order us all to be massacred as thrown into prison; or he might sell us as slaves, as they do at Algiers. There is no saying. I think that if I were in the position of the girl's mother at Gibraltar, I should say that it was better for her to run the risk of capture with you, than to remain here where there is no saying what may happen, she having every confidence in your honour, young gentleman."

"I thank you, Mrs. Hamber. I have no idea at present what plan I shall form. I may not see any possible way of getting out, but if I do we will certainly attempt it. Major Harcourt belongs to the same regiment as my brother-in-law, and his wife and my sister are great friends, which is why, I suppose, she has confidence in me. I have known Amy now for a year and a half, and she is very often at my sister's. I will take care of her just the same as if she were a young sister of my own. I don't see how I could go back and tell her mother that I left her here with things in the state they are. I only hope they may not turn out so badly as you fear, and that, at the worst, the Moors will only hand you over as prisoners to the Spaniards."

Bob went back to the consulate and told Amy the result of his conversation with Mrs. Hamber.

"I consider that has taken the responsibility off my shoulders, Amy. You referred me to Mrs. Hamber as the lady you knew best here. She is of opinion that if she were your mother she would advise your trying to get away with me. So now we have only to decide how it is to be done, that is, if you still wish to try."

"Certainly I do," the girl said. "Anything is better than waiting here expecting the Moors to rush in, as they did the other day, and carry one off to prison or kill one. Mr. Parrot, that is the gentleman you saw downstairs, said that you would stay here, and ordered a room to be prepared for you: and dinner is ready. I am sure you must be terribly hungry."

Bob remembered now that he had had nothing to eat, save

some biscuits on board the boat, and a piece of bread at the wine shop, since he left Gibraltar, and that he really was desperately hungry. Amy had already had her dinner; but she sat by him, and they talked about their friends at the Rock.

"Now," he said when he had finished, "let us have a regular council of war. It was my intention to get a passage to Malaga if I could, because I know something of the road back from there; but I could not do that with you."

"Why not, Bob?"

"Because the voyage is too long. Someone would be certain to speak to you before you got across, and as you can't talk Spanish the cat would be out of the bag directly. If possible, we must manage to cross to Tarifa; it is only a few hours across to there, even if we go in an open boat; and now that the Spaniards are friends with the Moors there ought to be no difficulty in getting a passage across there or to Algeciras. Of course you can't go as you are," he said, looking at her rather ruefully.

"No, of course not," she said; "I am not so silly as that. I should think I had better dress up like a boy, Bob."

"That would be a great deal the best plan, if you would not mind it," Bob said, greatly relieved that the suggestion came from her. "It is the only thing that I can think of. There didn't seem any story one could invent to account for a Spanish girl being over here, but a ship's-boy will be natural enough. If asked questions, of course our story will be that we had been left behind here. There could be lots of reasons for that. Either we might have been on shore and the vessel gone on without us, or you might have been sent ashore ill, and I might have been left to nurse you. That wouldn't be a bad story. What we must do when we get to the other side must depend upon where we land. I mean, whether we try to get straight in by boat, or to wait about until a chance comes. Once over there, you will have to pretend to be deaf and dumb, and then you can dress up

as a Spanish girl—of course a peasant, which will be much
more pleasant than going about as a boy, and better in lots
of ways.   So if I were you I should take a bundle of things
with me, so that we should have nothing to buy there.   It
is all very well buying disguises for myself, but I could
never go into a shop to ask for all sorts of girls' clothes."

Amy went off in a fit of laughter at the thought of Bob
having to purchase feminine garments.

"It is all very well to laugh," Bob said.   "These are the
sort of little things that are so difficult to work in.   It is
easy enough to make a general plan, but the difficulty is to
get everything to fit in.   I will have a talk with Mr. Parrot
in the morning about the boats.   He will know what boats
have been trading with the Rock, and what men to trust."

"You can talk to him now if you like," the girl said.
"He and Mr. Logie's other clerk have the top storey of the
house."

"Oh, then, I will go up and see him at once: the sooner
it is arranged the better.   If things are in the state that
everyone says, you might all be seized and imprisoned any
day."

Bob went up at once to Mr. Parrot's rooms, and had a long
talk with him.   The clerk quite agreed that anything would
be better than for a young girl to be shut up in a Moorish
prison, but he did not see how it was possible for them to find
their way across to Gibraltar.   "Many of our fishermen are
most courageous fellows, and have run great risks in taking
letters from Mr. Logie across to Gibraltar.   I do not suppose
that the blockade is very much more strict than it was, and
indeed the fact that you got through shows that with good
luck the thing is possible enough.   But that is not the difficulty.   The strictest order has been issued that no boat is to
take Englishmen across to the Rock, or is to cross the Straits
on any pretence whatever; and that anyone evading this
law will be executed and his goods forfeited to the state.
That is how it is Mr. Logie has been able to send no letters

for the last month, and why none of the merchants here have tried to get across to the Rock. No bribe would be sufficient to tempt the boatmen. It would mean not only death to themselves if they ever returned, but the vengeance of the authorities would fall on their relations here. I am afraid that there is nothing to be done that way at all."

"There are the three men who brought me across this morning," Bob said. "They might be bribed to take us back. The governor authorized me to offer a hundred pounds. I own that I don't like their looks."

"You would have some difficulty in finding them to begin with," Mr. Parrot said; "and I don't think a hundred pounds would be likely to tempt them to run the risk."

"I would not mind giving them two hundred more," Bob said. "I have got that money of my own at Gibraltar, and I am sure if it were necessary Major Harcourt would gladly pay as much more to get his daughter back."

"Three hundred would be ample. If they would not run the risk for a hundred a piece, nothing would tempt them. I should say your best plan would be to go down early to-morrow and see if you can find one of them. They are likely to be loitering about by the quays, as they have their boat there. The question is, are they to be trusted? They know that you have been sent out by the governor, and that you are here on some special business, and they may very well think that the Spaniards will give a higher reward for you than you can give, to be taken back. They will by this time know of the order against boats crossing, and might betray you to the Moors. If you were going by yourself, of course you could take all sorts of risks; but with this young lady under your protection, it would be different."

"Yes, I see that, Mr. Parrot. Rather than run any risk, I should prefer being put ashore at any Spanish port by one of the ships in the harbour. If you give me the name of any Spanish merchantman who was here say a fortnight ago, my story that we were left behind, owing to one of us being ill, would be so simple that there need be no suspicion whatever excited. Tarifa or Algeciras would of course be the best places, as we should only be on board a few hours; and Miss Harcourt could very well pretend to be still ill and weak, and could lie down in a corner, and I could cover her up with a blanket till we got there. Once across, I don't so much mind. Even if we were detected, we should simply be two fugitives from here, trying to make our way to Gibraltar; and I don't think there would be any question of my being a spy. We should probably be sent to wherever they keep the English prisoners they have taken in ships, and there would be nothing very dreadful in that, even for her. We should probably be exchanged before long. There have been several batches sent in to the Rock in exchange for prisoners taken in prizes brought in by privateers."

"Well, I really think that that would be the best way, Mr. Repton. As you say, there will be nothing very dreadful in detention for a while with the Spaniards, while there is no saying what may happen here. If you like I will send one of the consulate servants out the first thing in the morning to inquire what ports the Spanish craft are bound for, and when they are likely to sail. They seldom stop more than two or three days here. Most of them are taking live-stock across for the use of the Spanish army, and though Algeciras would be an awkward place for you to land at, because if detected there you would be more likely to be treated as a spy, still in a busy place like that no one would notice a couple of young sailors, and it would be no great distance for you to walk over to Tarifa or any of the villages on the Straits. But how do you propose to get in from there? That is what seems to me the great difficulty."

"Well, I got in before," Bob said, "and do not think that there ought to be much difficulty in getting hold of a boat. If I did I should sail round the Point, and keeping well outside the line of cruisers, come down on the coast the other side of Gibraltar, and so work along at night, just as I did before. If I found it absolutely impossible to get a boat, of course I could not, with the girl with me, try to swim across from the head of the bay to the Rock, which is what I should have done had I been alone. So I should then go to the authorities and give myself up, and say that being afraid that the Moors intend to massacre all the English at Tangiers, I had come across with this young lady, who is the daughter of an officer of the garrison, to put her into Spanish hands, knowing that there she would receive honourable treatment till she could be passed in at the next exchange of prisoners."

"I think that would be your very best course to pursue, unless you find everything turn out just as you would wish, Mr. Repton."

When Bob came down in the morning he at once went into the office below, and Mr. Parrot told him that one of the Spanish craft would start for Algeciras at noon.

"Then I must ask you to send one of the servants out to buy some clothes, such as are worn by a Spanish sailor-boy, Mr. Parrot. I have my own suit upstairs, and will go off and arrange for a passage across directly after breakfast."

"I will see to it," Mr. Parrot said. "The ship's decks will be crowded up with cattle. She is a small craft, and I hear she will take as many as can be packed on her deck. She is alongside now, taking them in. There is not much likelihood of any attention whatever being paid to you and your companion."

Amy turned a little pale when Bob told her that the attempt was to be made at once, but she said bravely: "I am glad there is to be no waiting, I do so long to be out of this town. I daresay I shall be a little nervous at first, but I shall try not to show it; and I sha'n't be really frightened, for I know that you will take care of me."

As soon as breakfast was over Bob changed his things and went down to the quay. He stopped at the vessel taking cattle on board. She was a polacre brig of about a hundred and fifty tons. The captain was smoking a cigar aft, while the mate was seeing to the storing of the cattle. Bob went on board and told his story to the captain.

"I was left behind in charge of a cabin-boy from the *Esmeralda* a fortnight ago. The boy had fever, and the captain thought it might be infectious and put him ashore, but he soon got well. We want to be taken across, as our friends live not many miles from Tarifa. We will pay a dollar a piece for our passage."

The captain nodded. "Be on board by noon; we shall not be a minute later."

Bob went ashore and told Amy that everything was arranged without the slightest difficulty. He then went down to inspect the clothes.

"They will do very well," he said, "except that they are a good deal cleaner than anything ever seen on a Spanish sailor. Those canvas trousers will never do as they are." He accordingly took some ashes and rubbed them well into the canvas, got some grease from the kitchen, and poured two or three large patches over the trousers.

"That is more like it," he said. "The shirt will do well enough, but there must be a patch or two of grease upon the jacket, and some smears of dirt of some kind." When he had done them to his satisfaction he took them upstairs.

"What horrid, dirty-looking things!" Amy exclaimed in disgust.

"They are clean enough inside, child. They are quite new, but I have been dirtying them outside to make them look natural. You must be dressed by half-past eleven, and you can tuck your hair up under that red night-cap; but you must manage to dirty your face, neck, and hands. You really ought to have some brown stain, but I don't suppose it is to be got. I will speak to Mr. Parrot."

"There is no stain that I know of," Mr. Parrot said; "but I know Mr. Logie paints a little. I think you will find a box of colours upstairs. If you mix some Vandyke brown in water, and paint her with it and let it dry on, I should think it would do very well, though of course it wouldn't stand washing."

Bob found the paint-box and soon mixed some paint. At half-past eleven Amy came into the room, laughing a little shyly.

"That will do very well," Bob said encouragingly, "except that you are a great deal too fair and clean. Look here, I have been mixing some paint. I think a wash of that will make all the difference. Now, sit down while I colour you. That will do capitally!" he said when he finished. "I think when it dries it will be just about the right shade for a Spanish sailor-boy. Have you got your bundle? That is right. Now here is my bag and a couple of black Moorish blankets. I will bring Mr. Parrot up to say good-bye. Have you told your servant?"

"No; I said nothing to her about it. She would make such a terrible fuss there would be no getting away from her. We must ask Mr. Parrot to tell her after the vessel has set sail."

Mr. Parrot pronounced the disguise excellent, and said that he should not have the slightest suspicion that she was anything but what she seemed to be. Amy felt very shy as she sallied out with Bob, but she gained courage as she saw that no one noticed her.

When they arrived at the brig, the cattle were nearly all on board. Bob led the way across the gangway, and went up on to the fo'castle. There he laid one of the blankets down against a stanchion, wrapped Amy in the other so that her face was almost hidden, and told her to sit down and close her eyes as if weak or asleep. Then he took up his post beside her. In a quarter of an hour the last bullock was on board. The gangway was at once hauled in, the hawsers thrown off, and the sails let drop, and in another minute the vessel was gliding away from the wharf.

The wind was nearly due west, and the sheets were hauled in as she was headed across the Straits. It was half an hour before the sailors' work was all done. Several of them came up on to the fo'castle and began twisting cigarettes, and one at once entered into conversation with Bob.

"Is the boy ill?" he said.

"Yes, he has been ill, but is better now. It would have been better if he could have stopped a few days longer, but he was pining to get home. He won't have far to go when we get to Algeciras, and no doubt I shall be able to get him a lift in some cart that will be bringing provisions to the camp."

The talk at once turned on the siege, the sailors expressing their certainty that the Rock would soon be taken. Bob had moved away from Amy as if to allow her to sleep undisturbed by the conversation.

"There is a brig running down the Straits at a good speed," one of the sailors said when they were half-way across. "It is a nice breeze for her."

Bob looked at the craft. She was about a mile away, and by the course they were steering—almost at right angles— would come very near to them. There was something familiar in her appearance, and he looked at her intently, examining every sail and shroud. Then doubt became certainty as his eye fell upon a small patch in one of the cloths of the topgallant sail.

It was the *Antelope*. One of the Spanish shot had passed through the topgallant sail, and as that was the only injury that sail had received, the bit had been cut out and a fresh one put in before she sailed again from Gibraltar. She was flying Spanish colours. His heart beat fast. Would she overhaul them, or pass without taking notice of them, seeing that the polacre was a small one and not likely to be a valuable prize? The vessels approached each other quickly. The course the *Antelope* was taking would carry her some length or two behind the Spaniard. Bob hesitated whether

to hail her as she came along.   If his hail was not heard he
would of course be detected and his plans entirely spoilt,
and with the wind blowing straight across and he in the
bow it would be by no means certain that his hail would be
distinguished.   Suddenly, to his delight, when the brig was
within a hundred yards of the polacre, he saw her head come
up, while the crew began to haul upon the sheets.

An exclamation of surprise and alarm broke from the
Spaniards, as in another minute the *Antelope* was running
parallel with them, a cable's length to windward.   Then the
port-holes were opened, and eight guns run out.   The Spanish flag was run down and the British hoisted to the peak,
and a summons to strike their flag shouted to the Spaniards.
As the latter carried only four small guns, resistance was
out of the question.   The Spanish flag was lowered, and in
obedience to the gesticulations rather than the words of an
officer on board the English brig, the halliards were thrown
off and the sails came down with a run.

The Spanish sailors were frantic with rage, swearing by all
the saints in the calendar.   Bob had moved at once across to
Amy.

"Lie still, Amy.   We are going to be captured by an
English ship.   It is the same privateer that I was in before.
Don't make any sign until they come on board.   In the fury
that these Spaniards are in they might stick their knives
into us if they knew we were English."

The brig had been thrown up into the wind as soon as
the polacre's sails had been lowered, and in three minutes
a boat came alongside.   Then Joe Lockett, followed by half
a dozen sailors armed with pistol and cutlass, scrambled on
board.

"Now, follow me, Amy."   And descending the ladder Bob
made his way along the narrow gangway between the lines
of cattle, and then mounted to the poop.

"Well, Joe, how are you?"   The first-mate of the
Antelope started back in astonishment.

"Why, Bob Repton!" he exclaimed. "What on earth are you doing here masquerading as a Spanish sailor?"

"I am trying to get across to Gibraltar," he said.

"Why, is this fellow bound for Gibraltar? In that case we have not got a prize, as we fancied."

"She is a fair prize, Joe; she is bound for Algeciras. I was going to make my way in from there as best I could."

"That is all right then. What has she got on board?"

"Nothing beyond these cattle and some vegetables, I expect; but they are worth a lot of money on the Rock."

"Well, you will be able to tell us all about things, Bob. I will hail the captain to send Crofts on board with a dozen men to take charge here, and then I will take you on board."

"I have a friend here," Bob said turning to Amy, who was standing timidly behind him, "so you must take him with me."

"All right!" Joe said carelessly.

In five minutes Bob stood again on the deck of the *Antelope*, and a hearty greeting was exchanged between him and Captain Lockett.

"Before I tell you anything, Captain, which cabin am I to have? I will tell you why afterwards. I suppose it will be my old one?"

"Yes; that is our one spare cabin, Bob. But I don't know why you are in such a hurry about it."

"I will tell you presently," Bob laughed, and led the way below.

"There, Amy," he said, "you can go in there and put on your own things again. I thought it would be more comfortable for you, for them not to know it until you are properly dressed in your own clothes. You have brought a frock, of course?"

"Yes; I thought I had better bring one in case we should be made prisoners."

"That is all right. When you are dressed come upon deck. I will explain all about it before you appear."

Bob as briefly as possible told his story to Captain Lockett and Joe, who were much amused to find that Bob's friend was a young lady.

"You are coming out in quite a new light, Bob, as a

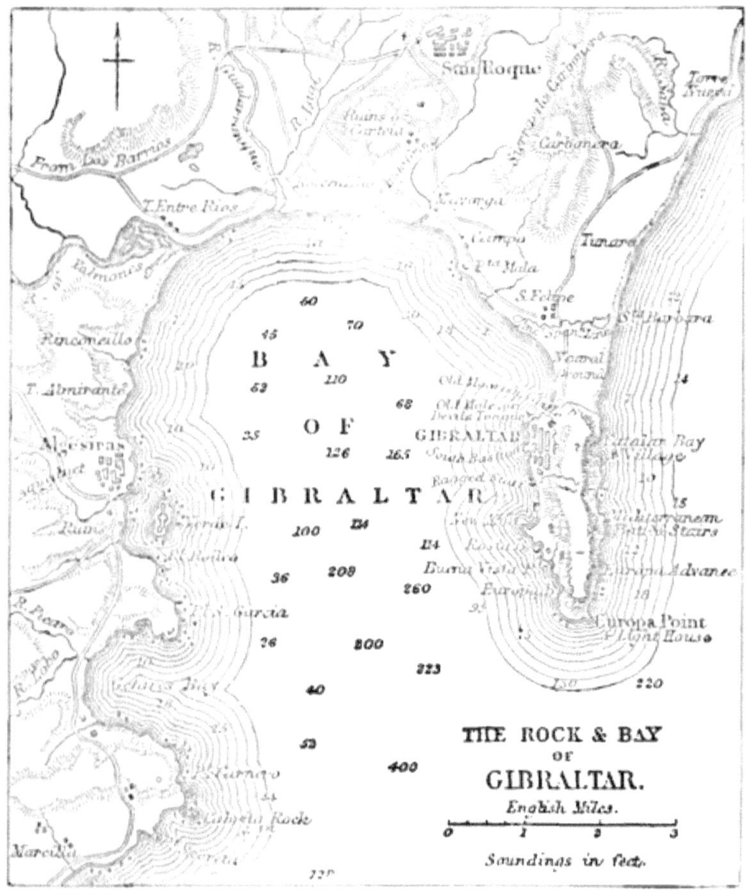

squire of dames. But I won't laugh at you now; I want to hear the last news. I overhauled that craft not so much to capture her as to get the last news. There were reports before I started that the Moors were joining the Spaniards, and that their ports were closed to us, and what you say confirms that. That was one of the points I wanted to know, as I could not tell whether I could run in there safely were I chased. Now, as to getting into the Rock, are their cruisers active at present?"

"Well, there are lots of them about. I think your best plan will be to run in close to the Point and hold on as if you were going into Algeciras. In that way they won't suspect you. Then, when you get right up the bay, haul across to the town. The wind is in your favour, because you will have to tack to work up the bay, and if you make pretty long tacks, they won't suspect you when you start across until you have got pretty well away, and with this breeze there will be no chance of their catching you before you are under our guns."

"That seems hopeful enough. At any rate we will try it. I will send six more men on board the polacre. They will want to be handy with her sails. I will go myself and give Crofts orders. He had better keep ahead of us, for if we are chased by their gun-boats we can protect him."

Just as sail was again got up and the two vessels were under way, Amy Harcourt came on deck, and was soon laughing and chatting merrily with the captain. At four in the afternoon they rounded the Point, the polacre a few hundred yards ahead, and both flying Spanish colours. There were several Spanish cruisers and some gun-boats outside them; but these paid no attention to their movements, and both beat up the bay, keeping close into the Spanish shore, but holding somewhat farther out at each tack.

"Now," Captain Lockett said when they were within half a mile of Algeciras, "we will run out this tack. There are two gun-boats in our way, I see, but we must take our chance of them. Go and wave a handkerchief from the bow, Joe. Mr. Crofts will be on the look-out for the signal."

The two vessels held away on the port tack. As the polacre approached the gun-boats a sudden bustle was observed on board them.

"They begin to smell a rat," Captain Lockett said, "hoist the topgallant sails," for the brig had been under easy sail to enable her to hold her place with the polacre. The men were already at quarters, and the ports were opened and the guns run out. Just as the gun-boat nearest the polacre, finding the hail for her to bring to unheeded, fired a shot into her, the brig's head paid off, and she poured a broadside into the two gun-boats. One of them was struck amidships. For a minute there was great confusion on board, and then she made for her companion, evidently in a sinking condition. Several shots were now fired from the forts, but though they fell near, the brig was uninjured. The second gun-boat did not venture to attack so formidable an opponent, and half an hour later the *Antelope* and her prize dropped anchor off the Mole.

Bob had already run down and put on his usual clothes, and he and Amy were at once rowed ashore and made their way to Major Harcourt's quarters. The delight of Amy's father and mother, as she rushed into the room, was extreme. Bob did not enter with her, but left her to tell her own story, and proceeded straight to the governor's, to whom he reported the state of affairs at Tangier.

"It is bad news," the governor said. "However, I am extremely obliged to you for the valuable service that you have rendered; and, as I had the pleasure of before doing when you brought in the oranges, I shall place your name in the orders of the day, for having, as a volunteer, rendered signal service by carrying despatches at great risk across to the Barbary coast."

Bob then returned home. Captain Lockett had already been to the house and informed the O'Hallorans of his arrival.

"There you see, Carrie," Bob said after his sister's first greetings were over ; "there was nothing to have been so terribly alarmed about."

"It isn't because you got through it safely, Bob, that there was no danger," his sister replied. "It was a very foolish thing to do, and nothing will change my opinion as to that. Captain Lockett tells me you brought Amy Harcourt back with you, dressed up as a boy. I never heard of such a thing, Bob! The idea of a boy like you, not eighteen yet, taking charge in that way of a young girl!"

"Well, there was nothing else to do, Carrie, that I could see. I went to Mrs. Hamber, who was Mrs. Colomb's most intimate friend, and asked her opinion as to what I had better do, and she advised me to get Amy away if I possibly could do so. I can't see what difference it makes whether it is a boy or a girl. It seems to me that people are always so stupid about that sort of thing."

Carrie laughed. "Well, never mind, Bob. Amy Harcourt is a very nice girl. A little too boyish, perhaps; but I suppose that is natural, being brought up in the regiment. I am very glad that you have brought her back again, and it will be an immense relief to her father and mother. Her mother has been here three or four times during these two days you have been away, and I am in no way surprised at her anxiety. They will be in here this evening certainly, to thank you."

"Very well; then I shall be round smoking a cigar with the doctor," Bob said. "I am very glad to have been of use to them, and to have got Amy back again; but I don't want to be thanked, and you tell them so. I hate being made a fuss about."

And so, beyond a warm grasp of the hand on the part of Major Harcourt, and two or three words of hearty thanks on that of his wife, the next time they met, Bob escaped any expression of gratitude. But the occurrence drew the two families together more closely, and Amy often came round with her father and mother in the evening, and there were many little confidential talks between Carrie and Mrs. Harcourt.

It was some time before the anxiety as to the fate of the English inhabitants at Tangier was allayed. They were at the beginning of December forced to remove to Marteen, a few miles from Tetuan, abandoning their houses and all their property, which was estimated at the value of sixty thousand pounds, and three days afterwards were handed over as prisoners to the Spaniards. They were then put on board a ship, and taken to Algeciras, where they were kept, for nearly a month, prisoners on board ship, but were, on the 11th of January, 1781, sent across to Gibraltar.

The next five months passed slowly and heavily. Occasionally privateers and other craft ran through the blockade of the Spanish cruisers and succeeded in getting into port. Some of these brought wine and sugar, of both of which the garrison was extremely short, and occasionally a few head of cattle and other provisions. All of these were sold by public auction, the governor considering that to be the fairest way of disposing of them.

On the 12th of April another great convoy, under Admiral Darby, entered the port. It consisted of about a hundred merchantmen under the protection of a powerful fleet. The joy of the garrison and inhabitants was intense, although among the latter this was mingled with a certain feeling of uneasiness. Deserters had at various times brought in reports that, should Gibraltar be again relieved, it was the purpose of the Spaniards to bombard the town. Hopes were entertained that so wanton an act of cruelty would not be carried out, for the entire destruction of the town would not advance in the smallest degree the progress of the siege.

At a quarter to eleven, just as the van of the convoy came to an anchor off the New Mole, Fort San Philip opened fire upon the town, and at the signal the whole of the batteries in the forts and lines followed suit. A hundred and fourteen guns and mortars rained their shot and shell upon the town, and the guns of the batteries of the garrison at once responded. Several of the officers of the 58th and their wives had come up to Captain O'Halloran's to enjoy from the terrace the view of the great convoy entering the port. All were in the highest spirits at the thought of the abundant supplies that would now be at their disposal, and in the belief that the Spaniards, seeing that the garrison was again amply provisioned, would abandon the siege, which had now lasted for twenty-two months. Suddenly there came upon the air the deep sound of the guns of San Philip, followed by a prolonged roar as the whole of the Spanish batteries opened fire. The hum of shot could be heard, followed by the explosion of shells, the fall of masonry, and screams and cries.

"The bombardment has begun at last!" Captain O'Halloran exclaimed.

The greatest consternation reigned among the ladies. Several of them had left children in their quarters; and although the barracks were so placed as to be to a great extent sheltered from the enemy's fire from the land side, they were still terribly anxious as to their safety. Two of them had, like the O'Hallorans, quarters in the town itself; and the husbands of these ladies, accompanied by Captain O'Halloran and Bob, at once set out to bring the children up to the house, which was perfectly sheltered.

The scene in the town was a pitiful one. Men, women, and children were flying in the wildest alarm towards the gate looking south, and thence out to the huts that the more prudent ones had erected many months before near Europa Point. Shot and shell were raining down, while chimneys and portions of masonry fell clattering in the streets. Sick people were being carried out on doors or planks, and most of the inhabitants were laden with what few articles of value they could snatch up at the first alarm. The children were soon brought up to the O'Halloran's, and then for a time there was nothing to do but to listen to the roar of artillery.

The officers and Bob ascended the Rock to a point near

one of the batteries, whence they could command a view of the Spanish lines. The flashes of smoke were bursting forth almost incessantly, but were answered shot for shot from the English batteries, which had already almost silenced the San Carlos Battery, which mounted a large number of mortars, and against which the fire of the English guns was concentrated. Between one and two o'clock the Spanish fire abated, and soon ceased altogether. The inhabitants took advantage of the lull to hurry back to their houses, whence they removed the lighter and more portable articles; but the heavy stores, of which it now appeared many of them had large quantities concealed, they were of course unable to take away.

The discovery of these stores excited much indignation among the troops. The inhabitants had been constantly representing themselves as reduced to the last point of hunger, and had frequently received provisions from the scanty supplies of the garrison; and the soldiers were exasperated on finding that all this time they possessed great stores of wine, flour, and other articles, which they were hoarding to produce and sell when prices should rise to even more exorbitant heights than they had already reached.

At five o'clock the enemy's batteries opened again, and the firing continued without intermission all that night. As several casualties had taken place in the barracks and quarters, marquees were on the following morning served out to all the officers whose quarters were exposed to fire, and these were pitched near Europa Point, as were also a large number of tents for the use of the inhabitants.

A considerable body of troops were kept under arms near the northern gate, in case the Spaniards should attempt to make an assault under cover of their fire; and five hundred officers and men were told off to assist in the work of getting the supplies up from the wharves, as fast as they were landed from the transports. The bombardment continued during the whole of the next two days. The mortars still

poured their shells upon the town; but the guns were now
directed at our batteries, and their fire was remarkably
accurate.

On the 14th the unloading parties were increased to a
thousand men, and strong detachments of troops were told
off to extinguish the fires in the town, as the enemy were
now discharging shell filled with a composition that burned
with great fury, igniting everything with which it came
in contact. The troops engaged upon this duty were not
long in broaching the casks of wine found in such abundance
in many of the ruined houses. For two years they had been
living almost entirely on salt provisions, and wine had been
selling at prices vastly beyond their means. It was scarcely
surprising, then, that they should take advantage of this
opportunity.

The stores were practically lost, for the whole town was
crumbling to pieces beneath the fire of the enemy's mortars
and was on fire in several places, and little if any of the liquor
and stores consumed could in any case have been saved.
However, for a time insubordination reigned. The troops
carried off liquors to their quarters, barricaded themselves
there, and got drunk, and it was two or three days before
discipline was restored. Up to this time the conduct of the
soldiers had been most exemplary, and they had borne their
prolonged hardships without a murmur; and this outbreak
was due as much to a spirit of revenge against the inhabitants, for hiding away great stores of provisions and liquor
with a view to making exorbitant profits, as from a desire
to indulge in a luxury of which they had been so long
deprived.

On the 15th the enemy's fire was hotter than ever, and
the guns were withdrawn from our batteries, as they pro-
duced but little effect upon the Spanish batteries, and the
men working them suffered a good deal from the besieger's
fire. Two officers were dangerously wounded in one of the
casemates of the King's Bastion, and the fire was so heavy

around some of the barracks that all the troops who could not be disposed of in the casemates and bomb-proofs were sent out of the town and encamped southward, and the next day all the women and children who had gone with their husbands and fathers into the casemates were also removed and placed under canvas.

All this gave incessant work to the troops, for there was no level ground upon which the tents could be pitched; and as it was therefore necessary to level all the ground into terraces, it was some days before the camps were ranged in anything like order. Each day the enemy sent out their gun-boats to harass the merchantmen, but these were always driven back by the guns of the fleet. On the 17th the besieger's shells set fire to the Spanish church, which had been used as a store-house. Strong parties were sent down to remove the provisions, which consisted largely of barrels of flour. These were carried up and piled so as to afford protection to the casemates, which had been frequently entered by the enemy's shots, several men having been killed there.

They proved a valuable defence, and afforded, moreover, great amusement to the soldiers, who, whenever a barrel was smashed by a shell, carried off the contents and quickly converted them into pancakes, until so many casks had been emptied that the whole structure came toppling down.

On the 18th a shell came through the arch of one of the casemates, killing two and wounding four men, and in consequence a good many more of the troops were sent under canvas. On the 20th the work of unloading the greater portion of the transports was completed, and the admiral, who was most anxious to take advantage of the easterly wind that was blowing to sail out of the Straits, gave the signal for departure. Many of the merchantmen whose cargoes were consigned to merchants and traders on the Rock carried them back to England, as the merchants, having no place whatever in which to store goods—for the town was now almost entirely destroyed,—refused to accept them.

The transports with ordnance stores were brought in behind the New Mole to be discharged at leisure, while several colliers were run close in and scuttled, so that their cargoes could be removed as required. A great many of the inhabitants and of the officers' wives and families embarked on board the fleet before it left.

The enemy's fire still continued very heavy, and their guns and mortar-boats on the 23d came boldly out and opened fire upon the working parties who were stacking the barrels and stores at the south end of the Rock. The wife of a soldier was killed and several men wounded.

On the 26th the governor determined sternly to repress the drunkenness that still prevailed, owing to the soldiers going down among the ruins of the town, where they occasionally discovered uninjured casks of wine. An order was therefore issued on that day, that any soldier convicted of being drunk, asleep at his post, or marauding, should be immediately shot. On the 27th a convoy of twenty ships, in charge of the *Brilliant* and three other frigates, came in from Minorca, where the governor had ordered provisions to be purchased, in case the convoy expected from England did not arrive. The arrival of these ships largely added to the stores at the disposal of the garrison.

CHAPTER XVI.

A CRUISE IN THE "BRILLIANT."

WHILE the bombardment continued, Bob had been constantly occupied. He had some time before put down his name as a volunteer for service if required, and he and several others who had similarly enrolled themselves had been appointed to assist in looking after the removal of the soldiers' wives and children to the tents erected for them, and to seeing to their comfort there. He had also been in charge of bodies of labourers employed by the governor in the work of levelling the ground and transporting stores. Captain O'Halloran was constantly away on duty; and soon after the bombardment began it was found necessary to drive the whole of the poultry into the lower part of the house, the Spaniards retaining only one room for their own accommodation.

Had not this step been taken the chickens would speedily have been stolen by marauders, as in the absence of Captain O'Halloran and Bob there was no one to protect them. After the issue of the governor's proclamation discipline was speedily restored, and there was no longer any occasion to keep them under shelter. The bombardment was followed by heavy rains, which caused very great discomfort to the troops. The water pouring in torrents down the face of the hills swept away the newly raised banks, and brought down the tents, the soldiers having to turn out in the wet; and as the troops, owing to their heavy duties, were only one night out of three in bed, the discomfort and annoyance were very great.

Great quantities of the provisions, too, were damaged, as these were all stacked in the open air, with no other covering than that afforded by the sails of the colliers, which were cut off and used for the purpose. Until the end of the month the downfall of rain was incessant, and was accompanied with heavy storms of thunder and lightning. The batteries required constant repair, and the labours of the troops were very severe. Since the departure of Admiral Darby's fleet the enemy appeared to have given up all hopes of compelling the place to surrender by hunger. The convoy from Minorca had not been interfered with, and on the 2d of May two native craft came in from Algiers with sheep, wine, and brandy unmolested by the enemy's cruisers.

The enemy's fire had never entirely ceased since the commencement of the bombardment, and now amounted to about fifteen hundred rounds every twenty-four hours, the gun-boats generally coming out every day and sending their missiles into the town and batteries, the latter being specially the mark of the enemy's land guns, which reached even the highest batteries on the Rock. All through May and June the enemy's fire continued, dropping towards the end of the latter month to about five hundred shot and shell a day. The gun-boats were specially annoying, directing their fire against the south end of the Rock, and causing great alarm and distress among the fugitives from the town encamped there.

Occasionally they directed their fire towards the houses that had escaped the fire of the land batteries, and several shot and shell fell near the O'Hallorans', but, fortunately, without hitting the house. The volunteers had now been released from duty, and Bob was free to wander about as he pleased. As, since his exploit in fetching in the fruit, he had become known to every officer in the garrison, he was a privileged person and was able to enter any of the batteries, and to watch the effects of their fire against the enemy's forts and lines. He often spent the day on board the *Brilliant*,

At the end of June the frigate went away for a fortnight's cruise, and the captain invited Bob to accompany them.

"We shall all expect great things from you, Mr. Repton. As you managed to capture some fifty thousand pounds' worth of prizes when you were on board that privateer brig, you ought to put the frigate into the way of taking at least four times as much."

"It is easy to turn a brig into anything, Captain Langton, but there is no making one of His Majesty's frigates look other but what she is. The mere sight of your topsails is enough to send every Spanish craft into port."

For three or four days the frigate sailed along the coast, keeping well out during the day and closing with the land in the evening. Two or three small coasters were picked up by the boats, but they were scarcely worth sending into Gibraltar. On the fifth day a large barque was seen making in from the south. All sail was made, but the barque had the weather gauge, and crossing her ran into the shore and anchored under the shelter of a battery.

"That would be a prize worth having, Bob," Jim Sankey said. "I wonder what she has got on board? Perhaps she is like that craft you captured chock-full of lead and silver from Lima."

"I think I can tell you what she is full of," Bob, who had been examining her through a glass he had borrowed from the third lieutenant, replied.

"How do you mean you can tell, Bob? She has not got her bill of lading stuck upon her broadside, I suppose?"

"She has not, Jim. But I can tell you without that."

"Well, what has she got on board?"

"She has got a very strong crew, Jim, and twenty-four guns."

"Why, how on earth did you know that, Bob?" he asked, staring at his friend in surprise.

"Because, Jim, I have been on board, and counted the guns. That is the craft I swam off to nearly two years ago. You hunted for her then, you know; but I suppose she had gone into one of the ports. But that is her, I can almost swear. I don't know whether there is a better glass than this on board, but if there is I should be glad to have a look through it. Yet I feel certain without that; her stern is of rather peculiar shape, and that stern gallery looks as if it was pinched out of her instead of being added on. We particularly noticed that when we were sailing with her. I can't be mistaken about it."

"I think the captain ought to know, then," Jim said. "I will speak to Mr. Rawdon; he is in charge of the watch."

Jim went up on to the quarter-deck, touched his hat, and informed the second lieutenant what Bob had told him. Mr. Rawdon went up at once to the captain, who was talking to the first lieutenant, and examining the barque and battery through his glass.

"Mr. Sankey has reported to me, sir, that Mr. Repton is very strongly of opinion that the barque there is the Spanish ship-of-war he boarded by night just after the beginning of hostilities. He told us about it, sir, and we spent two or three days in looking for her."

"Of course I remember," the captain said. "Have the kindness to pass the word for Mr. Repton to come aft."

Bob soon stood before the captain.

"Mr. Rawdon tells me that you are of opinion that the barque in there is the disguised Spanish sloop you boarded two years ago?"

"Yes, sir, I am almost sure of it; but I should like to have another look at her through your glass before I speak with certainty."

The captain handed his glass, which was a remarkably good one, to Bob.

"That is her," Bob said after a minute's examination. "I could swear to her anywhere;" and he then pointed out to the captain the peculiarities he had noticed. "I can make out her figure-head too," he said. "It is a saint, though I don't know what saint; but if you notice, sir, you will see that, instead of standing nearly upright, he leans much more forward than usual. I remember the captain saying he looked as if he was going to take a header. So with that and the stern gallery there is no possibility of mistaking her.

The captain again examined the barque through his glass. "Yes. I notice both the points you mention. Well, I am much obliged to you for the news; it is very important. I was thinking of cutting her out to-night, and should have fallen into the same error you so nearly did in the privateer."

Bob bowed and retired. "We should have caught a tartar, Mr. Lyons, if we had sent the force we were talking about to cut her out; but I think we must have her somehow."

"I hope so, sir. We have had a very dull time of it, with nothing to do but to exchange shots occasionally with those gun-boats, and to get under sail now and then to escort some craft or other into port. The navy hasn't done much to boast of during this siege, and it has been very hard on us being cooped up there in Gibraltar while the fleet all over the world are picking up prizes and fighting the French and Spanish. Why, we haven't made enough prize-money in the last two years to pay for pipe-clay and powder."

"Yes, we all feel that, Mr. Lyons. We have certainly been terribly out of luck. That privateer Mr. Repton was on board did more in her week's cruise than all His Majesty's ships in Gibraltar have done in the last two years. We must take that craft inshore if we can. There is no doubt she is ably commanded, for she is so well disguised that we never suspected her for a moment; therefore there is not the least chance of our catching her napping. She is a formidable craft to cut out with the boats, even if she hadn't the aid of the battery."

"There is no doubt about that, sir. I think Mr. Repton

reported before that she carried twenty-four guns, and all heavy metal. As far as I can make out with the glass the battery mounts twelve guns."

"Yes, that is the number. Besides, you see, we dare not take the frigate in nearer than a mile; and a mile and a quarter would be safer. So that we could not be of any assistance beyond annoying the battery with long shot. It seems to me that there is only one chance."

"What is that, sir?"

"We must land a strong party some distance along the shore, and make an attack upon the battery and carry it by surprise. I can make out some huts behind it. I suppose they wouldn't have less than a hundred soldiers there—perhaps a hundred and fifty. If we can drive them off and capture the battery, we can open fire down upon the ship. At that distance we could fairly sweep her deck with grape. The rest of our boats would be lying ahead and astern of her, and as soon as the battery opened they could make a dash for her. The crew of the barque would be so disorganized by the fire of the battery that they should hardly be able to make very much of a fight of it."

"That seems a capital plan, sir. The only question is the number of hands. Suppose you send eighty to take the battery, we should only have as many more to spare for the boat attack on the ship, and that would leave us with only a hundred on board. I should think she would carry a fighting crew of two hundred at least. The Spaniards are always very strongly manned."

"I should think that would be about it. They are long odds, but not too long, I think, Mr. Lyons. At any rate, we will try. Lay her off the land, Mr. Lyons, then we will go into my cabin and make all the arrangements."

There was much talk and excitement among the crew, for the general opinion was that the captain would try to cut out the craft lying under the Spanish battery. The navy had for a long time been very sore at their inactivity, and had fretted that no attempts had been made to cut out the Spanish vessels across the bay. The admiral had steadily set his face against all such attempts, considering that the benefits to be gained did not justify the risks; for had any of his small squadron been damaged or sunk by the guns of the batteries the consequences would have been very serious, as the Spanish gun-boats would then have been able to carry on their operations without check, and it would have been next to impossible for vessels to run the blockade.

The information Bob had given was soon known to all the officers, and was not long before it permeated through the crew and added to their anxiety to cut the Spaniard out; for although the prize-money would be less than if she had been a richly-laden merchantman, the honour and glory was proportionately greater. The undertaking would be a serious one, but the prospect of danger is never deterrent to a British sailor.

There was great satisfaction when, presently, it became known that the crews of the whole of the boats were to muster. Arms were inspected, cutlasses ground, and everything prepared. It was early in the morning when the Spanish barque had been first discovered, and ten o'clock when the frigate had sailed away from land, as if considering the Spanish craft too strongly protected to be attacked. When five miles away from land her course was laid east, and under easy sail she maintained the same distance on the coast.

The plan of operation was, that the first lieutenant, with thirty marines and as many sailors, should land at a spot some two miles from the battery, and should make their way inland and come down upon the position from the rear. A hundred men in the rest of the boats should make for the barque direct. This party was to act in two divisions, under the second and third lieutenants respectively, and were to lie one to the east and the other to the west of the barque, and remain there until the guns of the battery opened upon he1 ; then they were to row for her at all speed, a blue light being burned by each division when they were within a hundred yards of the enemy, as a warning to their friends in the battery, who were then to fire round-shot instead of grape. The frigate was to venture in as closely as she dared, anchor broadside on, and open fire at the enemy. Jim Sankey was told off to the landing-party, and Bob went up to the captain and requested leave to accompany him as a volunteer.

"You see, sir," he said, "we may fall in with peasants, or be challenged by sentries as we approach the battery, and my ability to speak Spanish might be an advantage."

"It would undoubtedly," the captain said. "Well, Mr. Repton, I shall be very glad to accept your services."

At four in the afternoon the frigate's head was again turned west, and at ten o'clock the boats for the landing-party were lowered, and the men taking their places in them rowed away for the shore, which was some two miles distant. The night was dark, but Mr. Lyons had with him a pocket-compass, and had before embarking taken the exact bearings of the battery from the spot where they would land. He was therefore able to shape his course to a point half a mile in its rear. The strictest silence had been enjoined, and the little body of sailors made their way inland until they came upon a road running parallel with the shore. They followed this for about half a mile, and then struck off inland again. The country was highly cultivated, with orchards, vineyards, and orange groves. Their progress was slow, for they had many times to cut a passage through the hedges of prickly-pear. At last they reached a spot where they believed themselves to be directly behind the battery. Here there was a path leading in the direction which they wished to follow. In a quarter of an hour they made out some lights ahead of them, and the lieutenant halted his men and again repeated the orders they had before received.

"You are to go straight at the huts. As you approach

them you are to break up into parties of ten, as already formed. Each party is to attack one hut, cut down all who resist, seize and carry away all arms. Never mind the men if you have once got their arms; they cannot trouble us afterwards. Waste no time; but directly you have got all the firelocks in one hut make for another. As soon as all have been cleared out make for the battery. Now let the officers told off to command parties, each fall in at the head of his ten men. Mr. Repton, you will keep beside me to answer a challenge."

They were within fifty yards of the huts when a sentinel challenged. "Who goes there?"

"Soldiers of the king," Bob answered in Spanish, "with reinforcements for you."

"Halt till I call an officer," the sentry said. But the lieutenant gave the word, and the whole party dashed forward at a run. The sentry hesitated in surprise for a moment, and then discharged his piece. The sailors gave a cheer and rushed at the huts. Taken utterly by surprise, the Spaniards at first offered no resistance whatever as the sailors rushed in; indeed few of them attempted to get out of bed. The blue lights with which one man in each party was provided were lighted as they entered, and the arms were collected without a moment's delay, and they were off again before the Spaniards were fairly awake to what had happened.

There were ten huts, each containing twenty men. Two or three shots were fired as they entered the last two huts; but the Spaniards were overpowered in an instant, as they were here vastly outnumbered. The officers were made prisoners, and ten men being placed over them, the rest of the force, now carrying three muskets each, ran down into the battery. The sentries here threw down their arms at once, and were allowed to go where they pleased.

"Pile the arms you have captured!" Lieutenant Lyons ordered. "Run the ram-rods down them, and see if they are loaded. The Spaniards are not likely to rally, but if they do we can give them a hot reception. Now, gunner, break open the magazine there, and load with grape."

By this time the drum was beating to arms in the vessel below, the shots fired having given the alarm, and lights were seen to flash along the deck. In two minutes the guns were loaded, and these opened with a fire of grape upon the deck of the vessel, which was near enough to be distinctly seen by the glare of the blue lights. As the first gun was fired an answering flash came from sea as the frigate also opened fire. For five minutes the guns were worked fast, then two lights burst out in close succession ahead and astern of the barque.

"Cease firing grape; load with round shot!" the lieutenant shouted; but a moment later a loud cheer broke from the sailors, as by the lights in the boats the Spanish ensign was seen to run up to the peak of the barque, and then at once to fall again to the deck. The barque had surrendered.

"Now, gunner, spike the guns," the lieutenant ordered, "and then tumble them off the carriages."

This was soon done.

"Now let each man take one of the muskets, and throw the rest of them over the parapet down the rocks. That is right. Now, fall in!"

The sailors fell in and marched back to the huts. The Spanish officers were placed in the midst, and twenty men were told off to fire the huts. This was soon done. The lieutenant waited until they were well alight, and then gave the order to march. They took the coast road this time for two miles and then struck off to the shore, and saw, a few hundred yards away, the lantern that had been hoisted on one of the boats as a signal. They were challenged by the boat-keeper, who had moored the boats twenty yards from the shore. A cheer broke out as the answer was given. The grapnels were pulled up and the boats were soon alongside. The party embarking rowed out in the direction where they knew the frigate to be, and as soon as they were fairly out from the shore they saw the three lights she had hoisted as a signal.　In half an hour they were alongside.

"I need not ask if you have succeeded, Mr. Lyons," the captain said as the boats came up, "for we have seen that. You have not had many casualties, I hope?"

"Only one, sir.　One of the marines has a ball in his shoulder.　There were only five or six shots fired in all, and no one else has as much as a scratch."

"I am truly glad to hear it," the captain said.　"It has been a most successful surprise.　I don't think the boats can have suffered either."

"I don't think there was a shot fired at them, sir," the lieutenant said.　"The Spaniard ran up his colours and dropped them again directly the boats showed their lights. I fancy they must have suffered very heavily from our fire. You see, they were almost under our guns, and we must have pretty well torn up their decks."

"We shall soon hear," the captain said.　"The boats are towing the Spaniard out, she will be alongside in a few minutes."

The wind had entirely dropped now, and in a short time the Spaniard was brought close alongside the frigate, and Mr. Rawdon came on board to report.

"The ship is the *San Joaquin*, mounting twenty-four guns, with a crew of two hundred and twenty men, sir.　Her casualties are very heavy.　The men had just poured up on deck, it seems, when the battery opened fire.　The captain, first lieutenant, and fifty-six men are killed, and there are forty-three wounded.　We have no casualties.　Their flag came down just as we got alongside."

"Then as far as we are concerned," the captain said, "this is one of the most bloodless victories on record.　There will be no death promotions this time, gentlemen, but I am sure you won't mind that.　It has been a most admirably managed affair altogether, and I am sure that it will be appreciated by my lords of the admiralty. You will take command of her at present, Mr. Lyons, with the crew now on board. Dr. Colfax and his assistant will go off with you to attend to the wounded, and will remain on board until we get into Gibraltar. Mr. Rawdon, you will be acting first, and I can only say that I hope you will be confirmed."

The frigate and her prize at once sailed for Gibraltar. On their arrival there the captain took some pains, by sending up larger yards and by repainting the broad white streaks showing the port-holes, to restore the prize to its proper appearance as a ship-of-war.

"We should not get half so much credit for her capture if you took her into Portsmouth looking like a lubberly merchantman," the captain said to Mr. Lyons. "I don't care about patching up all those shot-holes in the bulwarks. That gives her the appearance of having been taken after a sharp action; and the deck looks almost like a ploughed field. I shall give you fifty men, Mr. Lyons, I can't spare more than that."

"That will do, sir. Nothing smaller than ourselves is likely to interfere with us, and if a large frigate engaged us we should not have more chance with a hundred men on board than with fifty. In that case we shall have to trust to our legs. Of course if we fall in with two or three of the enemy's ships I should run up the Spanish flag. I will find out if I can from the prisoners what is her private number; if I hoist that and a Spanish flag it ought to deceive them. I will get her back to England if possible, sir."

"You will, of course, take home my report, Mr. Lyons. It is sure to give you your step, I think."

Next day the *San Joaquin* sailed, and six weeks later a sloop of war brought despatches to the admiral. Among them was a letter from the admiralty to Captain Langton, expressing their gratification at the very able arrangements by which he had captured and silenced a Spanish battery, and cut out the sloop of war, *San Joaquin*, anchored under its guns, without any loss of life. It was, they said, a feat almost without parallel. They stated that they had, in accordance with his recommendation, promoted Mr. Lyons to the rank of commander, and they confirmed Mr. Rawdon in rank of first lieutenant, the third lieutenant becoming second, and the senior passed midshipman, Mr. Outram, being promoted to that of third lieutenant.

No change of any importance had taken place at Gibraltar during the absence of the *Brilliant*, except that the governor had determined to retaliate for the nightly annoyance of the gun-boats, and accordingly six guns were fixed at a very considerable elevation, behind the Old Mole, and shells fired from them. These reached the enemy's camp, and caused, as could be seen from the heights, great alarm and confusion. It was determined that in future, when the enemy's gun-boats bombarded our camps and huts, we should retaliate by throwing shells into their camp.

The day after the *Brilliant* returned, the *Helena* sloop of war, with fourteen small guns, was seen working in towards the Rock. The wind, however, was so light that she scarcely moved through the water. Fourteen Spanish gun-boats came out to cut her off. For a time she maintained a gallant contest against odds that seemed overwhelming, although the garrison gave her up as lost. But when the wind suddenly freshened, she sailed through her opponents into the port, where she was received with ringing cheers by the soldiers lining the batteries.

Week after week passed in minor hostilities. There was a constant exchange of fire between our batteries and those of the enemy. The gun-boats continued their operations, and we in return shelled their camp. Fresh works were erected on both sides. Casualties took place almost daily, but both troops and inhabitants were now so accustomed to the continual firing that they went about their ordinary avocations without paying any attention to the shot and shell, unless one of the latter fell close at hand. November came in, and in spite of the heavy fire maintained by our batteries the enemy's works continually advanced towards the Rock, and when, in the middle of the month, it was seen that the new batteries were being armed and placed in readiness to open fire, the governor determined to take the offensive.

Accordingly, after gun-fire on the evening of the twenty-sixth, an order was issued for all the grenadier and light infantry companies, with the 12th and Hardenberg's Regiment, to assemble at twelve o'clock at night, with a party of Engineers and two hundred workmen from the line regiments, for a sortie upon the enemy's batteries. The 39th and 59th Regiments were to parade at the same hour to act as support to the attacking party. A hundred sailors from the ships-of-war were to accompany them. The attacking party numbered 1014 rank and file, besides officers and non-commissioned officers; this was exclusive of the two regiments forming the supports. The attacking force was divided into three columns.

At a quarter to three in the morning the column moved out. The enemy's pickets discovered the advance as soon as it passed the outlying work known as Forbes' Barrier, and after firing fell back. Lieutenant-colonel Hugo's column, which was in front, pushed on rapidly and entered the enemy's lines without opposition, when the pioneers began to dismantle the work. Hardenberg's Regiment and the central column attacked and carried the tremendous work known as the San Carlos Battery. The enemy were unable to withstand for a moment the fierce attack of the troops, and in a very short time the whole of the advanced works were in our hands.

The leading corps formed up to resist any attempt the enemy might make to repel the sortie, and the working parties began to destroy the enemy's work. Faggots dipped in tar were laid against the facines and gabions, and in a short time columns of fire and smoke rose from all parts of the works occupied. In an hour the object of the sortie was effected. Trains were laid to the magazines and the troops fell back. Just as they reached the town the principal magazine blew up with a tremendous explosion.

The enemy appeared to have been wholly confounded at this sudden attack upon their advanced works, the fugitives from which created a panic throughout the whole army; and although the main Spanish lines, mounting a hundred and thirty-five heavy pieces of artillery, were but a few hundred yards behind the works attacked, not a single shot was fired at the troops engaged.

The batteries continued burning for three days, and when they ceased to smoke nothing but heaps of sand remained of the works that had cost the enemy months of labour to erect. It was some days before the Spaniards appeared to come to any definite conclusion as to their next step. Then large numbers of men set to work to re-establish their batteries, and things fell into their old routine again. Every day shots were exchanged occasionally. Vessels made their way in and out, being sometimes briskly chased by the enemy's gun-boats, sometimes passing in with little interference; for by this time the Spaniards must have recognized that there was no hope whatever of reducing Gibraltar by blockade. There was a great deal of sickness in the garrison; but comparatively little of this was due to scurvy, for every available corner of ground was now cultivated, and the supply of vegetables, if not absolutely sufficient to counteract the effects of so long and monotonous a diet of salt meat, was yet ample to prevent any serious outbreak of scurvy recurring.

In February fresh activity was manifested among the besiegers. Vast numbers of mules were seen bringing facines to their works. At the end of March the *Vernon* store-ship arrived, and a few hours later four transports with the 97th Regiment, under the convoy of two frigates, came in. A singular series of casualties was caused by a single shot, which entered an embrasure in Willis's Battery, took both legs off two men, one leg off another, and wounded another man in both legs; thus four men had seven legs taken off or wounded by one shot. These casualties were caused by the inattention of the men to the warning of a boy who was looking out for shot. There were two boys in the garrison whose eyesight was so keen that they could see the enemy's shot coming, and both were employed in the batteries especially exposed to the enemy's fire, to warn the men to withdraw themselves into shelter when shot were coming.

This quickness of eyesight was altogether exceptional. Standing behind a gun, and knowing therefore the exact course the shot will take, it is comparatively easy for a quick-sighted man to follow it, but there are few indeed who can see a shot coming towards them. In this respect the ear is a far better index than the eye. A person possessed of a fair amount of nerve can judge to within a few yards the line that a shot coming towards him will take. When first heard the sound is as a faint murmur, increasing as it approaches to a sound resembling the blowing off of steam by an express engine as it rushes through a station. At first the keenest ear could not tell the direction in which the shot is travelling, but as it approaches the difference in the angle becomes perceptible to the ear, and a calm listener will distinguish whether it will pass within twenty or thirty yards to the right or left. It would require an extraordinary acute ear to determine more closely than this, the angle of flight being so very small until the shot approaches almost within striking distance.

The garrison had been trying experiments with carcasses and red-hot shot. A carcass is a hollow shot or shell pierced with holes, but instead of being charged with powder to explode it either by means of a fuse or by percussion, it is filled with a fierce-burning composition, so that upon falling it will set on fire anything inflammable near it. Red-hot shot are fired by putting a wet wad in over the dry wad next to the powder. The red-hot shot is then run into the gun and rammed against the wet wad, and the gun fired in the usual way. The carcasses several times set fire to the enemy's works, but the use of the red-hot shot was reserved for a pressing emergency. A number of furnaces were constructed in the various batteries for heating the shot, which necessarily required a considerable amount of time to bring them to a white heat.

News came in April that great preparations were making at Cadiz and other Mediterranean ports, for a fresh and vigorous attack on Gibraltar, and that the Duc de Crillon, who had lately captured Minorca, would bring twenty thousand French and Spanish troops in addition to those at present engaged in the siege; that a large fleet would also be present, and that the principal attack would be made by means of ships turned into floating batteries and protected by an immense thickness of cork or other wood. On the 9th of May the ships began to arrive. Among them were seven large vessels, which appeared to be old men-of-war. A large number of workmen immediately went on board them and began to lower the topmasts. This confirmed the news in respect to the floating batteries.

About this time three store-ships fortunately arrived from England with powder, shell, and other stores. As there could be no longer any doubt that the attack was this time to be delivered on the seaface, strong working parties were employed in strengthening the water batteries, in erecting lines of palisades to prevent a landing from boats, and in building furnaces for the heating of shot in these batteries also. At this time the Engineers began to drive a gallery through the Rock facing the neutral ground in order to place guns there. This work was carried on to the end of the siege, and the batteries thus erected are now among the strongest of the defences of Gibraltar. At the end of the month a great fleet, consisting of upwards of a hundred sail, entered the bay and anchored off Algeciras, some nine or ten thousand troops were landed, and from that time scarce a day passed without fresh vessels laden with stores and materials for the siege arriving in the bay.

Early in May twelve gun-boats that had been sent out in pieces from England were completed and launched. Each carried one gun, and was manned by twenty-one men. Six of these drew their crews from the *Brilliant*, five from the *Porcupine*, and one from the *Speedwell* cutter. These craft had been specially designed for the purpose of engaging the enemy's gun-boats and for convoying ships into the port. On the 11th of June a shell from the enemy burst just at the door of one of the magazines of Willis's Battery. This instantly blew up, and the explosion was so violent that it seemed to shake the whole Rock. Fourteen men were killed and fifteen wounded, and a great deal of injury done to the battery; but strong parties at once set to work to repair it. A few days later a French convoy of sixty sail and three frigates anchored in the bay, and from these another five thousand French troops landed.

At the end of the month the Duc de Crillon arrived and took command of the besiegers. A private letter that was brought in by a privateer that had captured a merchantman on her way, gave the garrison an idea of the method in which the attack was to be made. It stated that ten ships were to be fortified six or seven feet thick with green timber bolted with iron, and covered with cork, junk, and raw hides. They were to carry guns of heavy metal, and to be bomb-proof on the top, with a descent for the shells to slide off. These vessels, which they supposed would be impregnable, were to be moored within half gunshot of the walls with iron chains, and large boats with mantlets were to lie off at some distance full of troops ready to take advantage of occurrences; that the mantlets of these boats were to be formed with hinges to fall down to facilitate their landing. There would by that time be forty thousand men in camp, but the principal attack was to be made by sea, to be covered by a squadron of men-of-war with bomb-ketches, floating batteries, gun and mortar boats, &c.; and that the Comte D'Artois, brother to the King of France, with other great personages, was to be present at the attack.

At this time the enemy fired but little, and the garrison were able to turn their whole attention to strengthen the points most threatened. The activity of the enemy on their offensive works on the neutral ground continued, and in one night a strong and lofty work five hundred yards long, with a communication thirteen hundred yards long to the works, was raised. It was calculated that ten thousand men at least must have been employed upon it, and no less than a million and a half sand-bags used in its construction. There could be no doubt now that the critical moment was approaching, and that ere long the garrison would be exposed to the most tremendous fire ever opened upon a besieged place.

CHAPTER XVII.

THE FLOATING BATTERIES.

IN spite of the unremitting work, of the daily cannonade, of illness and hardship, life on the Rock had not been unpleasant to the O'Hallorans. Although many of the officers' wives had at one time or another taken advantage of ships sailing from the port to return home, or rather to endeavour to do so, for a considerable number of the vessels that left were captured by the Spaniards before getting through the Straits, there still remained sufficient for agreeable society, and the O'Hallorans' was, more than any other house, the general meeting-place.

From its position in the hollow it was sheltered from the fire of all the shore batteries, whose long-distance shots searched all the lower parts of the Rock, while the resources of the establishment enabled the O'Hallorans to afford an open-handed hospitality that would have been wholly beyond the means of others. They had long since given up selling any of their produce, distributing all their surplus eggs among families where there was illness or sending them up to the hospitals, and doing the same with their chickens and vegetables. The greatest care was bestowed upon the poultry, fresh broods being constantly raised, so that they could kill eight or ten couple a week and still keep up their stock to its full strength. Thus, with gatherings two evenings a week at their own house and usually as many at the houses of their friends, while Captain O'Halloran and Bob frequently dined at the mess of their own or other regiments, the time passed pleasantly.

While Carrie was fully occupied with the care of the house and a general superintendence of what they called their farm, Bob was never at a loss for amusement. There was always something to see, some fresh work being executed, some fresh development in the defences, while he was on terms of friendship with almost every officer in the garrison. It was two years and a half since he had come out, and he was now eighteen. His constant intercourse with people older than himself and with the officers of the garrison, together with the exceptional position in which he found himself, made him in some respects seem older than he was, but he still retained his liveliness and love of fun. His spirits never flagged, and he was a general favourite with all who knew him.

On the 19th of August a boat with a flag of truce brought in a complimentary letter from the Duc de Crillon to the governor, informing him of the arrival of the Comte D'Artois and the Duc de Bourbon in his camp, and sending him a present of ice, fruit, partridges, and other delicacies. The governor returned a letter in similar complimentary terms, thanking the Duke for his letter and the presents, but declining with thanks the supplies that had been offered, saying that he never received for himself anything beyond what was common to the garrison.

The sailors of the ships-of-war now pitched tents ashore for their use when they should be ordered to land to take part in the defence, and the heavy guns were for the most part moved down from the upper batteries to the sea lines.

Day after day passed, the bombardment being constantly expected, but the damage inflicted by fire on the enemy's works by our carcasses delayed the attack. On the 8th of September a tremendous fire was suddenly opened with red-hot shot and carcasses upon the enemy's works. The Mahon Battery was burned, while the San Carlos and San Marten Batteries so damaged that they had almost to be rebuilt. The enemy, as on previous occasions, showed extreme bravery in their efforts to extinguish the fire and to repair damages, and it was afterwards known that the French troops alone had a hundred and forty killed and wounded. The damage done probably convinced the Duc de Crillon that no advantage could be hoped for by trying further to increase his works, and at half-past five next morning a volley of sixty shells was fired by their mortar batteries, followed by the discharge of one hundred and seventy pieces of heavy artillery.

This tremendous fire was kept up for some time, while nine line-of-battle ships, supported by fifteen gun and mortar boats, passed to and fro along the seaface, pouring in their fire upon us. At nightfall the enemy's guns ceased firing, but their mortars kept up their shell fire all night. The next day the ships-of-war renewed their attack, as did the land batteries. In the course of the day the *Brilliant* and *Porcupine* frigates were scuttled by the navy, alongside the New Mole, and their crews landed. On the following day the enemy's fire was principally directed against the barrier and *chevaux de frise* in front of the land port, and in the afternoon these barriers and palisades were all in flames, and the troops at that end of the Rock got under arms in case an attack should be made.

On the morning of the 12th the combined fleets of France and Spain, consisting of thirty-eight men-of-war, three frigates, and a number of smaller craft, sailed into the bay and anchored near Algeciras. Their fleet now consisted of forty-seven men-of-war, ten battering-ships—considered invincible, and carrying two hundred and twelve guns—and innumerable frigates and small ships-of-war; while on the land side were batteries mounting two hundred heavy guns, and an army of forty thousand men. Tremendous odds, indeed, against a fortress whose garrison consisted of seven thousand effective men, including the Marine Brigade.

For some days past Bob had been engaged with their landlord and some hired labourers in bringing in earth and filling up the lower rooms four feet deep, in order to render the cellars bomb-proof. Some beds and furniture were taken below, so that Carrie, the servants, and the Spanish family could retire there in case the enemy's shells fell thickly round the house.

It was noticed as a curious incident, that just as the combined fleet entered the bay, an eagle, after circling round it, perched for a few minutes upon the summit of the flag-post on the highest point of the Rock, an omen of victory which would have been considered decisive by the Romans, and which did, in fact, help to raise the spirits and confidence of the garrison.

On the morning of the 13th the enemy's battering-ships got under way, with a gentle breeze from the north-west, and at a little past nine o'clock anchored in admirable order in line of the seaface. The nearest was about nine hundred yards from the King's Bastion, the most distant being about eleven hundred yards. Not a shot was fired before the enemy anchored, and then the whole of the batteries that commanded them opened fire, to which the battering-ships and the artillery in their lines at once replied.

Bob was standing on the roof of the house with his sister.

"What a magnificent sight, Carrie!" he exclaimed. "It is well worth all the waiting to be here to see it."

"It is terrible!" Carrie said. "It is like one great roar of thunder. How awfully the men must be suffering in the batteries!"

"I don't suppose it is as bad as it looks," Bob said. "At any rate you needn't be uneasy about Gerald. All the troops except those working the guns are in shelter, and won't be called out unless the enemy attempt to land. I wonder their fleet don't come across to help their batteries. I suppose they are afraid of the carcasses and red-hot shot. Well, there is one comfort, Carrie: none of their shot are coming this way. Their floating batteries, evidently, are firing only at our batteries by the water. As to the others, we know that we are safe enough from them, though certainly the shot do make a most unpleasant noise as they fly overhead. I wish there was a little more wind to blow away the smoke so that we could see what effect our fire is having on those hulks. I shouldn't think that we had begun with red-hot shot yet. It takes three hours to get them hot enough. As far as I can see, whenever the wind blows the smoke away a little, our shot and shell roll off the roofs and sides without doing any damage to speak of."

About noon the enemy's mortar-boats and ketches attempted to come across and assist their battering-ships, but the wind had changed and had worked round to the south-west, blowing a smart breeze and bringing in a heavy swell, so that they were prevented from taking part in the action. Our own gun-boats were hindered by the same cause from putting out and opening a flanking fire upon the battering-ships. The northern batteries by the water suffered heavily from the fire of the Spanish lines, which took them in flank, and, indeed, some of the batteries in reverse, causing many casualties. The Artillery, however, refused to let their attention be diverted from the battering-ships.

By two o'clock the furnaces had heated the shot in all the batteries, and although some of them had been firing these missiles for upwards of an hour, it was not until two that their use became general. Soon afterwards, when the wind cleared away the smoke from the ships, men could be seen on their sloping roofs directing streams of water from the pumps upon small wreaths of smoke that curled up here and there. Up to this time the defenders had begun to fear that the craft were indeed as invulnerable as the Spaniards believed them to be; but these evidences that the red-hot shot were doing their work greatly roused their spirits, and cheers frequently rose as the men toiled at their heavy guns.

As the afternoon went on the smoke from the upper part of the Spanish admiral's flag-ship rose more and more thickly, and although numbers of men continued to bring up and throw water over the roof, working with extraordinary bravery in spite of the hail of projectiles poured upon them, it was clear that the fire was making steady progress. Bob had long before this gone down to the works by the seaface, where considerable bodies of troops were lying in the bomb-proof casemates in readiness for action if called upon, and from time to time he went out with Captain O'Halloran and other officers to see how matters were going on.

In sheltered places behind the batteries some of the surgeons were at work, temporarily binding up the wounds of artillerymen struck with shell or splinters, after which they were carried by stretcher-parties of the infantry up to the hospitals. Dr. Burke was thus engaged in the battery where his regiment was stationed. He had, since the first bombardment commenced, ceased to complain of the want of opportunities for exercising himself in his professional work, and had been indefatigable in his attendance on the wounded. Among them he was an immense favourite. He had a word and a joke for every man who came under his hands, while his confident manner and cheery talk kept up the spirits of the men. He was, too, a very skilful operator, and many of the poor fellows in hospital had urgently requested that if they must lose a limb it should be under the hands of Dr. Burke.

"It is much better to make men laugh than to make them cry," he would say to Bob. "It is half the battle gained when you can keep up a patient's spirit. It is wonderful how some of them stand pain. The hard work they have been doing is all in their favour."

Bob several times went out to him and assisted him as far as he could by handing him bandages, sponges, &c.

"You ought to have been an assistant from the beginning, Bob," he said. "By this time you would have been quite a decent surgeon; only you have a silly way of turning pale. There, hand me that bandage. All right, my man; we will have you patched up in no time. No, I don't think you can go back to your gun again. You will have to eat and drink a bit and make fresh blood before you will be much use at a thirty-two pounder again. What is this—a scalp wound? Splinter of a shell, eh? Well, it is lucky for you, lad, that you have been hardening your skull a bit before you enlisted. A few clips from a blackthorn are capital preparation. I don't think you will come to much harm. You are not more hurt than you would be in a good lively faction fight. There, you had better put down that sponge, Bob, and go into the casemate for a bit; you are getting white again. I think we are over the worst now; for if, as you tell me, the smoke is beginning to come up from some of those floating batteries their fire will soon slacken a bit. As long as they keep out the shot those defences of theirs are first-rate; but as soon as the shot begin to embed themselves in the roof they are worse than nothing, for they can neither dig out the shot nor get at them with the water. Once establish a fire and it is pretty sure to spread."

Bob was glad to get back again into the bomb-proof case-mates; for there was comparative quiet, while outside the constant roar of the guns, the howl of shot, the explosion of shell, and the crash of masonry created a din that was almost bewildering. Presently a cheer was heard in the battery, and Bob went out to see what it was, and returned with the news that the ship next to the Spanish admiral's was also smoking in several places. As the afternoon went on confusion was apparent on board several of the battering-ships, and by evening their fire had slackened considerably. Before eight o'clock it had almost entirely ceased except from one or two ships to the northward of the line, which being somewhat farther from the shore had suffered less than the others. At sunset the Artillery in our batteries were relieved, the Naval Brigade taking their place, and the fire was continued without relaxation.

As soon as it became dark rockets were fired by several of the battering-ships; these were answered by the Spanish men-of-war, and many boats rowed across to the floating batteries. By ten o'clock the flames began to burst out from the admiral's battering-ship, and by midnight she was completely in flames. The light assisted our gunners, who were able to lay their cannon with as much accuracy as during the daytime, and the whole Rock was illuminated by the flames. These presently burst out vigorously from the next ship, and between three and four o'clock points of light appeared upon six of the other hulks.

At three o'clock Brigadier Curtis, who commanded the Naval Brigade encamped at Europa Point, finding that the sea had gone down, manned the gun-boats, and rowing out for some distance opened a heavy flanking fire upon the battering-ships, compelling the boats that were lying in shelter behind them to retire. As the day broke he captured two of the enemy's launches, and finding from the prisoners that there were still numbers of men on board the hulks, rowed out to rescue them. While he was employed at this work at five o'clock one of the battering-ships to the northward blew up with a tremendous explosion, and a quarter of an hour later another in the centre of the line also blew up. The wreck was scattered over a wide extent of water. One of the gun-boats was sunk and another seriously injured, and the Brigadier, fearing other explosions, ordered the boats to draw off towards the town.

On the way, however, he visited two of the other burning ships, and rescued some more of those left behind— landing in all nine officers, two priests, and three hundred and thirty-four soldiers and seamen. Besides these one officer and eleven Frenchmen had floated ashore the evening before on the shattered fragments of a launch. While the boats in the navy were thus endeavouring to save their foes, the land batteries, which had ceased firing on the previous evening, again opened on the garrison; but as from some of the camps the boats could be perceived at their humane work, orders were despatched to the batteries to cease fire, and a dead silence succeeded the din that had gone on for nearly twenty-four hours.

Of the six battering-ships still in flames, three blew up before eleven o'clock. The other three burned to the water's-edge, the magazines having been drowned by the Spaniards before they left the ships in their boats. The garrison hoped that the two remaining battering-ships might be saved to be sent home as trophies of the victory, but about noon one of them suddenly burst into flames and presently blew up. The other was examined by the men-of-war boats, and found to be so injured that she could not be saved. She was accordingly set fire to and also destroyed. Thus the whole of the ten vessels that were considered by their constructors to be invincible were destroyed.

The loss of the enemy in killed and prisoners was estimated at two thousand, while the casualties of the garrison were astonishingly small, consisting only of one officer and fifteen non-commissioned officers and men killed, and five officers and sixty-three men wounded. Very little damage was done to the works. It is supposed that the smoke enveloping the vessels prevented accurate aim. The chief object of the attack was to silence the King's Bastion, and upon this two of the largest ships concentrated their fire, while the rest endeavoured to effect a breach in the wall between that battery and the battery next to it.

The enemy had three hundred heavy cannon engaged, while the garrison had a hundred and six cannon and mortars. The distance at which the batteries were moored from the shore was greatly in favour of the efforts of our artillery, as the range was almost point blank, and the guns did not require to be elevated. Thus the necessity for using two wads between the powder and the red-hot balls was obviated, and the gunners were able to fire much more rapidly than they would otherwise have done. The number of the Spanish soldiers on board the battery-ships was 5260, in addition to the sailors required to work the ships.

Great activity was manifested by the Spaniards on the day following the failure of their bombardment, and large numbers of men were employed in bringing up fresh ammunition to their batteries. Many of the men-of-war also got under way. Major Harcourt, Doctor Burke, and two or three other officers stood watching the movements from the O'Hallorans' terrace.

"I should have thought that they had had enough of it," Doctor Burke said. "If those battering-ships couldn't withstand our fire, what chance would their men-of-war have? See! they are just as busy on the land side, and the 71st has been ordered to send down extra guards to the land-port. I should have thought they had given it up as a bad job this time."

"I have no doubt they have given it up, doctor," Major Harcourt said; "but they are not likely to say so just yet. After all the preparations that have been made, and the certainty expressed about our capture by the allied armies and navies of France and Spain, and having two or three royal princes down here to grace the victory, you don't suppose they are going to acknowledge to the world that they are beaten. I should have thought you would have known human nature better than that, doctor. You will see De Crillon will send a pompous report of the affair, saying that the battering-ships were found, owing to faults in their construction, to be of far less utility than had been expected, and that therefore they had been burned. They had, however, inflicted enormous loss upon the garrison and defences, and the siege would now be taken up by the army and fleet, and vigorously pushed to a successful termination.

"That will be the sort of thing, I would bet a month's pay. The last thing a Spanish commander will confess is that he is beaten, and I think it likely enough that they will carry on the siege for months yet, so as to keep up appearances. In fact, committed as they are to it, I don't see how they can give it up without making themselves the laughing-stock of Europe. But now that they find they have no chance of getting the object for which they went to war, I fancy you will see before very long they will begin to negotiate for peace."

The major's anticipations were verified. For some time the siege was carried on with considerable vigour—from a thousand to twelve hundred shots being fired daily into the fortress. Their works on the neutral ground were pushed forward, and an attempt was made at night to blow out a portion of the face of the Rock by placing powder in a cave, but the attempt was detected.

The position of the garrison became more comfortable after a British fleet arrived with two more regiments and a large convoy of merchantmen; but nothing of any importance took place till, on the 2d of February, 1782, the Duc de Crillon sent in to say that the preliminaries of a general peace had been signed by Great Britain, France, and Spain, and three days later the blockade at sea was discontinued, and the port of Gibraltar again open.

Bob Repton, however, was not present at the concluding scenes of the great drama. Satisfied after the failure of the bombardment that there would be no more serious fighting, and that the interest of the siege was at an end, he took advantage of the arrival of the *Antelope* in the bay a few days after the engagement to return in her to England. He had now been two years and eight months on the Rock, and felt that he ought to go home to take his place with his uncle. He had benefited greatly by his stay in Gibraltar. He had acquired the Spanish language thoroughly, and in other respects had carried on his studies under the direction of Doctor Burke, and had employed much of his leisure time with instructive reading.

Mixing so much with the officers of the garrison he had acquired a good manner and address. He had been present at the most memorable siege of the times, and had gained the credit of having, though but a volunteer, his name twice placed in general orders for good services. He had landed a school-boy, he was now a well-built young fellow of medium height and powerful frame; but he had retained his boyish, frank good humour, and his love of fun.

"I trust that we shall be back in England before long," his sister said to him. "Everyone expects that Spain will make peace before many months are over, and it is likely that the regiments who have gone through the hardships of the siege will soon be relieved, so I hope that in a year or two we may be ordered home again."

There was a great deal of regret expressed when it was known that Bob Repton was going home, for he had always been ready to do any acts of kindness in his power, especially to children, of whom he was very fond, and it was not forgotten that his daring enterprise in going out alone to fetch in fruit had saved many of their lives. Amy Harcourt's eyes were very red when he went up to say good-bye to her and her mother an hour before he sailed, and the farewells were spoken with quivering lips.

The *Antelope* evaded the enemy's cruisers near the Rock, and made a quick passage to England without adventure. She had made two or three good prizes up the Spanish coast before she put into Gibraltar on her way home. Captain Lockett therefore did not go out of his way to look for more. On arriving at Portsmouth Bob at once went up to London by coach. He had no lack of clothes, having purchased the effects of an officer of nearly his own build and stature who had been killed a short time before. On alighting from the coach he walked to Philpot Lane, and went straight into the counting-house. His old acquaintance, Jack Medlin, was sitting on the stool his father had formerly occupied, and Bob was greatly amused at the air of gravity on his face.

"Do you wish to see Mr. Bale or Mr. Medlin, sir?" he asked, "or can I take your orders?"

"You are a capital imitator of your father, Jack," Bob

said, as he brought his hand down heavily on the shoulder
of the young clerk, who stared at him in astonishment.

"Why, it is Bob—I mean Mr. Repton!" he exclaimed.

"It's Bob Repton, Jack, sure enough, and glad I am to
see you. Why, it is nearly three years since we met, and
we have both altered a good bit since then. Well, is my
uncle in?"

"No, he is out at present, but my father is in the inner
office."

Bob strode into the inner office, and greeted Mr. Medlin
as heartily as he had done his son, and Mr. Medlin, for the
first time since he had entered Philpot Lane as a boy,
forgot that he was within the sacred precincts of the city,
and for at least ten minutes laughed and talked as freely
and unrestrainedly as if he had been out at Highgate.

"Your uncle will be delighted to see you back," he said.
"He is for ever talking about you, and there wasn't a
prouder man in the city of London than he was when the
despatches were published and your name appeared twice
as having rendered great service. He became a little afraid
at one time that you might take to soldiering altogether.
But I told him that I thought there was no fear of that.
After you had once refused to take a midshipman's berth,
with its prospect of getting away from school, I did not think
it likely that you would be tempted now."

"No; the General told Captain O'Halloran that he would
get me a commission if I liked, but I had not the least
ambition that way. I have had a fine opportunity of seeing war, and have had a jolly time of it, and now I am quite
ready to settle down here."

Mr. Bale was delighted on his return to find Bob. It was
just the hour for closing, and he insisted upon Mr. Medlin
stopping to take supper with him. Bob had written whenever there was an opportunity of sending letters; but many
of these had never come to hand, and there was much to tell
and talk about.

"Well, I am thoroughly satisfied with the success of our experiment, Mr. Medlin," Mr. Bale said next day. "Bob has turned out exactly what I hoped he would—a fine young fellow and a gentleman. He has excellent manners, and yet there is nothing foppish or affected about him."

"I had no fear of that with Bob, Mr. Bale; and, indeed, Gibraltar during the siege must have been a bad school for anyone to learn that sort of thing. Military men may amuse themselves with follies of that kind when they have nothing better to do; but it is thrown aside and their best qualities come out when they have such work to do as they have had there. Yes, I agree with you, sir. The experiment has turned out capitally, and your nephew is in every respect a far better man than he would have been if he had been kept mewed up here these three years. He is a young fellow that anyone—I don't care who he is—might feel proud of."

So Bob took up his duties in the office, and his only complaint there was, that he could hardly find enough to do. Mr. Bale had relaxed his close attention to the business since he had taken Mr. Medlin into the firm, but as that gentleman was perfectly capable of carrying it on single-handed, Bob's share of it was easy enough. It was not long before he complained to his uncle that he really did not find enough to do.

"Well, Bob, you shall come down with me to a place I have bought out by Chislehurst; it is a tidy little estate. I bought it a year ago. It is a nice distance from town; just a pleasant ride or drive up; I am thinking of moving my establishment down there altogether, and as you will have it some day, I should like your opinion of it. It isn't quite ready yet. I have been having it thoroughly done up, but the men will be out in a week or two."

Bob was greatly pleased with the house, which was a fine one, and very pleasantly situated in large grounds.

"There are seventy or eighty acres of land," Mr. Bale said. "They are let to a farmer at present. He only has them by the year, and I think it will be an amusement to you to take them in hand and look after them yourself. I know a good many people living about here, and I have no doubt we shall have quite as much society as we care for."

Another month and they were established at Chislehurst, and Bob found the life there very pleasant. He generally drove his uncle up to town in the morning, getting to the office at ten o'clock and leaving it at five in the afternoon. On his return home there was the garden to see about and the stables. Very often his uncle brought a city friend or two home with him for the night, and they soon had a large circle of acquaintances in the neighbourhood.

"I should like you to marry young, Bob," Mr. Bale said to him one day. "I did not marry young, and so you see I have never married at all, and have wasted my life shockingly in consequence. When you are ready to marry I am ready to give you the means. Don't forget that."

"I won't forget it, sir," Bob said smiling ; "and I will try to meet your wishes."

Mr. Bale looked at him sharply. Carrie's letters were long and chatty, and it may be that Mr. Bale had gleaned from them some notion of an idea that Carrie and Mrs. Harcourt had in their heads.

Three years later Mr. Bale remarked, as they were driving home : "By the way, Bob, I was glad to see in the paper to-day that the 58th is ordered home."

"Is it, sir?" Bob asked eagerly. "I have not looked at the paper to-day. I am glad to hear that. I thought it wouldn't be long. But there is never any saying, they might have been sent somewhere else instead of being sent home."

"I hope they will be quartered somewhere within reach," Mr. Bale said. "If they are stationed at Cork, or some outlandish place in Ireland, they might almost as well be at Gibraltar for anything we shall see of them."

"Oh, we can manage to run over to Cork, uncle."

"There will be no occasion to do that, Bob. Captain

O'Halloran will be getting leave soon after he comes over, and then he can bring Carrie here." And he smiled slily to himself.

"He mayn't be able to get leave for some time," Bob said. "I think, uncle, I shall run over directly they arrive."

"Perhaps the firm won't be able to spare you," Mr. Bale remarked.

"It is my opinion the firm would get on just as well without me for an indefinite time, uncle."

"Not at all, Bob. Mr. Medlin was saying only a few days ago that you do quite your share of the work, and that he generally leaves it to you now to see country customers when I am out, and thinks the change has been an advantage to the business. However, if the regiment does go to Ireland, as is likely enough, I suppose we must manage to spare you."

It was indeed soon known that the 58th were in the first place to be disembarked at Cork, and one day Mr. Bale came into the office. "I have just seen your friend Lockett, Bob; I mean the younger one. He commands the *Antelope* now, you know. His uncle has retired and bought a place near Southampton, and settled down there. Young Lockett came up from Portsmouth by the night coach. He put in at Gibraltar on his way home, and the 58th were to embark three days after he left. So if you want to meet them when they arrive at Cork you had better lose no time, but start by the night coach for Bristol, and cross in the packet from there."

It was a month before Bob returned. The evening that he did so he said to his uncle : "I think, uncle, you said that you were anxious that I should marry young."

"That is so, Bob," Mr. Bale said gravely.

"Well, uncle, I have been doing my best to carry out your wishes."

"You don't mean to say, Bob," Mr. Bale said in affected alarm, "that you are going to marry a soldier's daughter?"

"Well—yes, sir," Bob said a little taken aback; "but I don't know how you guessed it. It is a young lady I knew in Gibraltar."

"What, Bob! Not that girl who went running about with you dressed up as a boy?"

As this was a portion of his adventures upon which Bob had been altogether reticent, he sat for a moment confounded.

"Don't be ashamed of it, Bob," Mr. Bale said with a smile, laying his hand kindly on his shoulder. "Your sister Carrie is an excellent young woman, and it is not difficult to read her thoughts in her letters. Of course she told me about your adventure with Miss Harcourt, and she has mentioned her a good many times since; and it did not need a great deal of discernment to see what Carrie's opinion was regarding the young lady. Carrie has her weak points—as, for example, when she took up with that wild Irishman—but she has plenty of good sense, and I am sure by the way she wrote about this Miss Harcourt that she must be a very charming girl; and I think, Bob, I have been looking forward almost as much to the regiment coming home as you have. Regarding you as I do, as my son, there is nothing I should like so much as having a bright, pretty daughter-in-law; so you have my hearty consent and approval, even before you ask for it. And you found her very nice, Bob —eh?"

"Very nice, sir," Bob said smiling.

"And very pretty, Bob?"

"Very pretty, sir. I never thought that she would have grown up so pretty."

"And her head has not been turned by the compliments that she has of course received?"

"I don't think so, sir. She said her mind has been made up ever since I brought her back to Gibraltar; so, you see, the compliments did not go for much."

"Well, Bob, I will write to Major Harcourt. I shall hand you over this place altogether and settle down in my old quarters in Philpot Lane."

"No, no, sir," Bob said.

"But I say yes, Bob. I shall keep a room here, and I dare say I shall often use it. But I have been rather like a fish out of water since I came here, and shall be well content to fall into my old ways again, knowing that if I want any change and bright society I can come down here. If I find I am restless there, which is not likely, I can buy a little place and settle down beside you. As I told you long ago, I am a rich man—I have been doing nothing but save money all my life—and though, as I then said, I should like you to carry on the firm after I am gone, there will, as far as money goes, be no occasion for you to do so."

Two months later the three members of the firm went over to Cork, and there a gay wedding was celebrated ; and when, at the termination of the honeymoon, Bob returned to Chislehurst, he found Captain O'Halloran and Carrie established there on a month's leave ; and a day or two later the party was increased by the arrival of Doctor Burke.

Mr. Bale lived for twenty years after Bob's marriage, the last fifteen of which were passed in a little place he bought adjoining that of the Reptons ; and before he died he saw four grandchildren, as he called them, fast growing up.

General and Mrs. Harcourt also settled down in the neighbourhood, to be near their only daughter, a few years before Mr. Bale's death. Doctor Burke remained with the regiment for some years and then bought a practice in Dublin, but to the end of his life he paid a visit every three or four years to his former pupil. Captain O'Halloran obtained the rank of colonel ; but, losing an arm at the capture of Martinique, in 1794, he retired from the army and settled at Woolwich —where Carrie was within easy reach of Chislehurst— having his pension and a comfortable income which Mr. Bale settled upon Carrie. At Mr. Bale's death it was found that he had left his house at Chislehurst to Carrie, and she and her husband accordingly established themselves there. Bob to the end of his life declared that, although in all things he had been an exceptionally happy and fortunate man, the most fortunate occurrence that ever happened to him was that he should have taken part in the famous Siege of Gibraltar.

THE END.

A LIST OF BOOKS
FOR
YOUNG PEOPLE
By G. A. HENTY

BY CONDUCT AND COURAGE

A Story of Nelson's Days.   Illustrated. $1.50 net.

This, the last of the celebrated Henty Books ever to be published, is a rattling story of the battle and the breeze in the glorious days of Parker and Nelson. The hero is brought up in a Yorkshire fishing village, and enters the navy as a ship's boy.

In the course of a few months after joining he so distinguishes himself in action with French ships and Moorish pirates that he is raised to the dignity of midshipman. His ship is afterward sent to the West Indies. Here his services attract the attention of the Admiral, who gives him command of a small cutter. In this vessel he cruises about among the islands, chasing and capturing pirates, and even attacking their strongholds. He is a born leader of men, and his pluck, foresight, and resource win him success where men of greater experience might have failed. He is several times taken prisoner: by mutinous negroes in Cuba, by Moorish pirates who carry him as a slave to Algiers, and finally by the French. In this last case he escapes in time to take part in the battles of Cape St. Vincent and Camperdown. His adventures include a thrilling experience in Corsica with no less a companion than Nelson himself.

WITH THE ALLIES TO PEKIN

A Tale of the Relief of the Legations. Illustrated by WAL PAGET. $1.50 net.

In this book the writer re-tells the story of the Siege of Pekin in a way that is sure to grip the interest of his young readers. The experiences of Rex Bateman, the son of an English merchant at Tientsin, and of his cousins, two girls whom Rex rescues from the Boxers just after the first outbreak, offer a variety of heroic incident sufficient to fire the loyalty of the most indifferent lad.

THROUGH THREE CAMPAIGNS

A Story of Chitral, Tirah, and Ashanti. Illustrated by WAL PAGET. $1.50 net.

The exciting story of a boy's adventures in the British Army. Lisle Bullen, left an orphan, is to be sent home by the colonel of the regiment on the eve of the Chitral campaign. The boy's patriotism compels him, instead, to secretly join the regiment. He early distinguishes himself for conspicuous bravery. His disguise is discovered and his promotions follow rapidly.

BY G. A. HENTY

" Mr. Henty is the king of story-tellers for boys."—*Sword and Trowel.*

AT ABOUKIR AND ACRE

A Story of Napoleon's Invasion of Egypt. With 8 full-page
Illustrations by WILLIAM RAINEY, and 3 Plans. 12mo,
$1.50 net.

The hero, having saved the life of the son of an Arab chief, is taken
into the tribe, has a part in the battle of the Pyramids and the revolt
at Cairo. He is an eye-witness of the famous naval battle of Aboukir,
and later is in the hardest of the defense of Acre.

BOTH SIDES THE BORDER

A Tale of Hotspur and Glendower. With 12 full-page Illustrations by RALPH PEACOCK. 12mo, $1.50 net.

This is a brilliant story of the stirring times of the beginning of the
Wars of the Roses, when the Scotch, under Douglas, and the Welsh,
under Owen Glendower, were attacking the English. The hero of the
book lived near the Scotch border, and saw many a hard fight there.
Entering the service of Lord Percy, he was sent to Wales, where he
was knighted, and where he was captured. Being released, he returned
home, and shared in the fatal battle of Shrewsbury.

WITH FREDERICK THE GREAT

A Tale of the Seven Years' War. With 12 full-page Illustrations. 12mo, 75 cents net.

The hero of this story while still a youth entered the service of
Frederick the Great, and by a succession of fortunate circumstances
and perilous adventures, rose to the rank of colonel. Attached to the
staff of the king, he rendered distinguished services in many battles, in
one of which he saved the king's life. Twice captured and imprisoned,
he both times escaped from the Austrian fortresses.

A MARCH ON LONDON

A Story of Wat Tyler's Rising. With 8 full-page Illustrations by W. H. MARGETSON. 12mo, $1.50 net.

The story of Wat Tyler's Rebellion is but little known, but the hero
of this story passes through that perilous time and takes part in the
civil war in Flanders which followed soon after. Although young he
is thrown into many exciting and dangerous adventures, through which
he passes with great coolness and much credit.

BY G. A. HENTY

"Surely Mr. Henty should understand boys' tastes better than any man living."—*The Times.*

WON BY THE SWORD

A Tale of the Thirty Years' War. With 12 Illustrations by CHARLES M. SHELDON, and four Plans.   12mo, $1.50 net.

The scene of this story is laid in France, during the time of Richelieu, of Mazarin and Anne of Austria. The hero, Hector Campbell, is the orphaned son of a Scotch officer in the French Army. How he attracted the notice of Marshal Turenne and of the Prince of Conde; how he rose to the rank of Colonel; how he finally had to leave France, pursued by the deadly hatred of the Duc de Beaufort—all these and much more the story tells with the most absorbing interest.

A ROVING COMMISSION

Or, Through the Black Insurrection at Hayti.   With 12 Illustrations by WILLIAM RAINEY.   12mo. $1.50 net.

This is one of the most brilliant of Mr. Henty's books. A story of the sea, with all its life and action, it is also full of thrilling adventures on land. So it holds the keenest interest until the end. The scene is a new one to Mr. Henty's readers, being laid at the time of the Great Revolt of the Blacks, by which Hayti became independent. Toussaint l'Overture appears, and an admirable picture is given of him and of his power.

NO SURRENDER

The Story of the Revolt in La Vendée.   With 8 Illustrations by STANLEY L. WOOD.   12mo, $1.50 net.

The revolt of La Vendée against the French Republic at the time of the Revolution forms the groundwork of this absorbing story. Leigh Stansfield, a young English lad, is drawn into the thickest of the conflict. Forming a company of boys as scouts for the Vendéan Army, he greatly aids the peasants. He rescues his sister from the guillotine, and finally, after many thrilling experiences, when the cause of La Vendée is lost, he escapes to England.

UNDER WELLINGTON'S COMMAND

A Tale of the Peninsular War.   With 12 Illustrations by WAL PAGET.   12mo, $1.50 net.

The dashing hero of this book, Terence O'Connor, was the hero of Mr. Henty's previous book, "With Moore at Corunna," to which this is really a sequel. He is still at the head of the "Minho" Portuguese regiment. Being detached on independent and guerilla duty with his regiment, he renders invaluable service in gaining information and in harassing the French. His command, being constantly on the edge of the army, is engaged in frequent skirmishes and some most important battles.

BY G. A. HENTY

"Mr. Henty is one of the best story-tellers for young people."
—*Spectator.*

WHEN LONDON BURNED

A Story of the Plague and the Fire. By G. A. HENTY. With 12 full-page Illustrations by J. FINNEMORE. Crown 8vo, olivine edges, 75 cents net.

The hero of this story was the son of a nobleman who had lost his estates during the troublous times of the Commonwealth. During the Great Plague and the Great Fire, Cyril was prominent among those who brought help to the panic-stricken inhabitants.

WULF THE SAXON

A Story of the Norman Conquest. By G. A. HENTY. With 12 full-page Illustrations by RALPH PEACOCK. Crown 8vo, olivine edges, $1.50 net.

The hero is a young thane who wins the favor of Earl Harold and becomes one of his retinue. When Harold becomes King of England Wulf assists in the Welsh wars, and takes part against the Norsemen at the Battle of Stamford Bridge. When William of Normandy invades England, Wulf is with the English host at Hastings, and stands by his king to the last in the mighty struggle.

ST. BARTHOLOMEW'S EVE

A Tale of the Huguenot Wars. By G. A. HENTY. With 12 full-page Illustrations by H. J. DRAPER, and a Map. Crown 8vo, olivine edges, 75 cents net.

The hero, Philip Fletcher, has a French connection on his mother's side. This induces him to cross the Channel in order to take a share in the Huguenot wars. Naturally he sides with the Protestants, distinguishes himself in various battles, and receives rapid promotion for the zeal and daring with which he carries out several secret missions.

THROUGH THE SIKH WAR

A Tale of the Conquest of the Punjaub. By G. A. HENTY. With 12 full-page illustrations by HAL HURST, and a Map. Crown 8vo, olivine edges.

Percy Groves, a spirited English lad, joins his uncle in the Punjaub, where the natives are in a state of revolt. Percy joins the British force as a volunteer, and takes a distinguished share in the famous battles of the Punjaub.

BY G. A. HENTY

" The brightest of the living writers whose office it is to enchant boys.—*Christian Leader.*

da

A JACOBITE EXILE

Being the Adventures of a Young Englishman in the Service of Charles XII. of Sweden. By G. A. HENTY. With 8 full-page Illustrations by PAUL HARDY, and a Map. Crown 8vo, olivine edges, $1.50 net.

Sir Marmaduke Carstairs, a Jacobite, is the victim of a conspiracy, and he is denounced as a plotter against the life of King William. He flies to Sweden, accompanied by his son Charlie. This youth joins the foreign legion under Charles XII., and takes a distinguished part in several famous campaigns against the Russians and Poles.

CONDEMNED AS A NIHILIST

A Story of Escape from Siberia. By G. A. HENTY. With 8 full-page Illustrations. Crown 8vo, olivine edges, $1.50 net.

The hero of this story is an English boy resident in St. Petersburg. Through two student friends he becomes innocently involved in various political plots, resulting in his seizure by the Russian police and his exile to Siberia. He ultimately escapes, and, after many exciting adventures, he reaches Norway, and thence home, after a perilous journey which lasts nearly two years.

BERIC THE BRITON

A Story of the Roman Invasion. By G. A. HENTY. With 12 full-page Illustrations by W. PARKINSON. Crown 8vo, olivine edges, $1.50 net.

This story deals with the invasion of Britain by the Roman legionaries. Beric, who is a boy-chief of a British tribe, takes a prominent part in the insurrection under Boadicea ; and after the defeat of that heroic queen (in A. D. 62) he continues the struggle in the fen-country. Ultimately Beric is defeated and carried captive to Rome, where he is trained in the exercise of arms in a school of gladiators. At length he returns to Britain, where he becomes ruler of his own people.

IN GREEK WATERS

A Story of the Grecian War of Independence (1821–1827). By G. A. HENTY. With 12 full-page Illustrations by W. S. STACEY, and a Map. Crown 8vo, olivine edges, $1.50 net.

Deals with the revolt of the Greeks in 1821 against Turkish oppression. Mr. Beveridge and his son Horace fit out a privateer, load it with military stores, and set sail for Greece. They rescue the Christians, relieve the captive Greeks, and fight the Turkish war vessels.

BY G. A. HENTY

"Mr. Henty might with entire propriety be called the boys' Sir Walter Scott."—*Philadelphia Press.*

IN THE IRISH BRIGADE

A Tale of War in Flanders and Spain. With 12 Illustrations by CHARLES M. SHELDON. 12mo, $1.50 net.

Desmond Kennedy is a young Irish lad who left Ireland to join the Irish Brigade in the service of Louis XIV. of France. In Paris he incurred the deadly hatred of a powerful courtier from whom he had rescued a young girl who had been kidnapped, and his perils are of absorbing interest. Captured in an attempted Jacobite invasion of Scotland, he escaped in a most extraordinary manner. As aid-de-camp to the Duke of Berwick he experienced thrilling adventures in Flanders. Transferred to the Army in Spain, he was nearly assassinated, but escaped to return, when peace was declared, to his native land, having received pardon and having recovered his estates. The story is filled with adventure, and the interest never abates.

OUT WITH GARIBALDI

A Story of the Liberation of Italy. By G. A. HENTY. With 8 Illustrations by W. RAINEY, R.I. 12mo, $1.50 net.

Garibaldi himself is the central figure of this brilliant story, and the little-known history of the struggle for Italian freedom is told here in the most thrilling way. From the time the hero, a young lad, son of an English father and an Italian mother, joins Garibaldi's band of 1,000 men in the first descent upon Sicily, which was garrisoned by one of the large Neapolitan armies, until the end, when all those armies are beaten, and the two Sicilys are conquered, we follow with the keenest interest the exciting adventures of the lad in scouting, in battle, and in freeing those in prison for liberty's sake.

WITH BULLER IN NATAL

Or, A Born Leader. By G. A. HENTY. With 10 Illustrations by W. RAINEY. 12mo, $1.50 net.

The breaking out of the Boer War compelled Chris King, the hero of the story, to flee with his mother from Johannesburg to the sea coast. They were with many other Uitlanders, and all suffered much from the Boers. Reaching a place of safety for their families, Chris and twenty of his friends formed an independent company of scouts. In this service they were with Gen. Yule at Glencoe, then in Ladysmith, then with Buller. In each place they had many thrilling adventures. They were in great battles and in lonely fights on the Veldt; were taken prisoners and escaped; and they rendered most valuable service to the English forces. The story is a most interesting picture of the War in South Africa.

BY G. A. HENTY

"Among writers of stories of adventures for boys Mr. Henty stands in the very first rank."—*Academy* (London).

THE TREASURE OF THE INCAS

A Tale of Adventure in Peru. With 8 full-page Illustrations by WAL PAGET, and Map. $1.50 net.

Peru and the hidden treasures of her ancient kings offer Mr. Henty a most fertile field for a stirring story of adventure in his most engaging style. In an effort to win the girl of his heart, the hero penetrates into the wilds of the land of the Incas. Boys who have learned to look for Mr. Henty's books will follow his new hero in his adventurous and romantic expedition with absorbing interest. It is one of the most captivating tales Mr. Henty has yet written,

WITH KITCHENER IN THE SOUDAN

A Story of Atbara and Omdurman. With 10 full-page Illustrations. $1.50 net.

Mr. Henty has never combined history and thrilling adventure more skillfully than in this extremely interesting story It is not in boy nature to lay it aside unfinished, once begun; and finished, the reader finds himself in possession, not only of the facts and the true atmosphere of Kitchener's famous Soudan campaign, but of the Gordon tragedy which preceded it by so many years and of which it was the outcome.

WITH THE BRITISH LEGION

A Story of the Carlist Uprising of 1836. Illustrated. $1.50 net.

Arthur Hallet, a young English boy, finds himself in difficulty at home, through certain harmless school escapades, and enlists in the famous "British Legion," which was then embarking for Spain to take part in the campaign to repress the Carlist uprising of 1836. Arthur shows his mettle in the first fight, distinguishes himself by daring work in carrying an important despatch to Madrid, makes a dashing and thrilling rescue of the sister of his patron, and is rapidly promoted to the rank of captain. In following the adventures of the hero the reader obtains, as is usual with Mr. Henty's stories, a most accurate and interesting history of a picturesque campaign.

BY G. A. HENTY

"No country nor epoch of history is there which Mr. Henty does not know, and what is really remarkable is that he always writes well and interestingly."—*New York Times.*

WITH MOORE AT CORUNNA

A Story of the Peninsular War. With 12 full-page Illustrations by WAL PAGET. 12mo, $1.50 net.

Terence O'Connor is living with his widowed father, Captain O'Connor of the Mayo Fusiliers, with the regiment at the time when the Peninsular war began. Upon the regiment being ordered to Spain. Terence gets appointed as aid to one of the generals of a division. By his bravery and great usefulness throughout the war, he is rewarded by a commission as colonel in the Portuguese army and there rendered great service.

AT AGINCOURT

A Tale of the White Hoods of Paris. With 12 full-page Illustrations by WALTER PAGET. Crown 8vo, olivine edges, $1.50 net.

The story begins in a grim feudal castle in Normandie. The times were troublous, and soon the king compelled Lady Margaret de Villeroy with her children to go to Paris as hostages. Guy Aylmer went with her. Paris was turbulent. Soon the guild of the butchers, adopting white hoods as their uniform, seized the city, and besieged the house where our hero and his charges lived. After desperate fighting, the white hoods were beaten and our hero and his charges escaped from the city, and from France.

WITH COCHRANE THE DAUNTLESS

A Tale of the Exploits of Lord Cochrane in South American Waters. With 12 full-page Illustrations by W. H. MARGETSON. Crown 8vo, olivine edges, $1.50 net.

The hero of this story accompanies Cochrane as midshipman, and serves in the war between Chili and Peru. He has many exciting adventures in battles by sea and land, is taken prisoner and condemned to death by the Inquisition, but escapes by a long and thrilling flight across South America and down the Amazon.

ON THE IRRAWADDY

A Story of the First Burmese War. With 8 full-page Illustrations by W. H. OVEREND. Crown 8vo, olivine edges, $1.50 net.

The hero, having an uncle, a trader on the Indian and Burmese rivers, goes out to join him. Soon after, war is declared by Burmah against England and he is drawn into it. He has many experiences and narrow escapes in battles and in scouting. With half-a-dozen men he rescues his cousin who had been taken prisoner, and in the flight they are besieged in an old, ruined temple.

BY G. A. HENTY

"Boys like stirring adventures, and Mr. Henty is a master of this method of composition."—*New York Times*.

THROUGH RUSSIAN SNOWS

A Story of Napoleon's Retreat from Moscow. With 8 full-page Illustrations by W. H. OVEREND and 3 Maps. Crown 8vo, olivine edges, 75 cents net.

The hero, Julian Wyatt, after several adventures with smugglers, by whom he is handed over a prisoner to the French, regains his freedom and joins Napoleon's army in the Russian campaign. When the terrible retreat begins, Julian finds himself in the rear guard of the French army, fighting desperately. Ultimately he escapes out of the general disaster, and returns to England.

A KNIGHT OF THE WHITE CROSS

A Tale of the Siege of Rhodes. With 12 full-page Illustrations by RALPH PEACOCK, and a Plan. Crown 8vo, olivine edges, $1.50 net.

Gervaise Tresham, the hero of this story, joins the Order of the Knights of St. John, and proceeds to the stronghold of Rhodes. Subsequently he is appointed commander of a war-galley, and in his first voyage destroys a fleet of Moorish corsairs. During one of his cruises the young knight is attacked on shore, captured after a desperate struggle, and sold into slavery in Tripoli. He succeeds in escaping, and returns to Rhodes in time to take part in the defense of that fortress.

THE TIGER OF MYSORE

A Story of the War with Tippoo Saib. With 12 full-page Illustrations by W. H. MARGETSON, and a Map. Crown 8vo, olivine edges, $1.50 net.

Dick Holland, whose father is supposed to be a captive of Tippoo Saib, goes to India to help him to escape. He joins the army under Lord Cornwallis, and takes part in the campaign against Tippoo. Afterwards he assumes a disguise, enters Seringapatam, and at last he discovers his father in the great stronghold of Savandroog. The hazardous rescue is at length accomplished, and the young fellow's dangerous mission is done.

IN THE HEART OF THE ROCKIES

A Story of Adventure in Colorado. By G. A. HENTY. With 8 full-page Illustrations by G. C. HINDLEY. Crown 8vo, olivine edges, 75 cents net.

The hero, Tom Wade, goes to seek his uncle in Colorado, who is a hunter and gold-digger, and he is discovered, after many dangers, out on the Plains with some comrades. Going in quest of a gold mine, the little band is spied by Indians, chased across the Bad Lands, and overwhelmed by a snowstorm in the mountains.

BY G. A. HENTY

" No living writer of books for boys writes to better purpose than
Mr. G. A. Henty."—*Philadelphia Press.*

THE DASH FOR KHARTOUM

A Tale of the Nile Expedition. By G. A. HENTY. With 10
full-page Illustrations by JOHN SCHÖNBERG and J. NASH.
Crown 8vo, olivine edges, $1.50 net.

In the record of recent British history there is no more captivating
page for boys than the story of the Nile campaign, and the attempt to
rescue General Gordon. For, in the difficulties which the expedition
encountered, in the perils which it overpassed, and in its final tragic
disappointments, are found all the excitements of romance, as well as
the fascination which belongs to real events.

REDSKIN AND COW-BOY

A Tale of the Western Plains. By G. A. HENTY. With 4
color Illustrations by ALFRED PEARSE. Crown 8vo, olivine
edges, 60 cents net.

The central interest of this story is found in the many adventures of
an English lad, who seeks employment as a cow-boy on a cattle ranch.
His experiences during a " round-up " present in picturesque form the
toilsome, exciting, adventurous life of a cow-boy ; while the perils of a
frontier settlement are vividly set forth in an Indian raid.

HELD FAST FOR ENGLAND

A Tale of the Siege of Gibraltar. By G. A. HENTY. With
8 full-page Illustrations by GORDON BROWNE. Crown 8vo,
olivine edges, $1.50 net.

This story deals with one of the most memorable sieges in history—
the siege of Gibraltar in 1779-83 by the united forces of France and
Spain. With land forces, fleets, and floating batteries, the combined
resources of two great nations, this grim fortress was vainly besieged
and bombarded. The hero of the tale, an English lad resident in
Gibraltar, takes a brave and worthy part in the long defence, and it is
through his varied experiences that we learn with what bravery, resource, and tenacity the Rock was held for England.

STORIES BY G. A. HENTY

"His books have at once the solidity of history and the charm of romance."—*Journal of Education.*

TO HERAT AND CABUL

A Story of the First Afghan War. By G. A. HENTY. With Illustrations. 12mo, $1.50 net.

The greatest defeat ever experienced by the British Army was that in the Mountain Passes of Afghanistan. Angus Cameron, the hero of this book, having been captured by the friendly Afghans, was compelled to be a witness of the calamity. His whole story is an intensely interesting one, from his boyhood in Persia; his employment under the Government at Herat; through the defense of that town against the Persians; to Cabul, where he shared in all the events which ended in the awful march through the Passes from which but one man escaped. Angus is always at the point of danger, and whether in battle or in hazardous expeditions shows how much a brave youth, full of resources, can do, even with so treacherous a foe. His dangers and adventures are thrilling, and his escapes marvellous.

WITH ROBERTS TO PRETORIA

A Tale of the South African War. By G. A HENTY. With 12 Illustrations. $1.50 net.

The Boer War gives Mr. Henty an unexcelled opportunity for a thrilling story of present-day interest which the author could not fail to take advantage of. Every boy reader will find this account of the adventures of the young hero most exciting, and, at the same time a wonderfully accurate description of Lord Roberts's campaign to Pretoria. Boys have found history in the dress Mr. Henty gives it anything but dull, and the present book is no exception to the rule.

AT THE POINT OF THE BAYONET

A Tale of the Mahratta War. By G. A. HENTY. Illustrated. 12mo, $1.50 net.

One hundred years ago the rule of the British in India was only partly established. The powerful Mahrattas were unsubdued, and with their skill in intrigue, and great military power, they were exceedingly dangerous. The story of "At the Point of the Bayonet" begins with the attempt to conquer this powerful people. Harry Lindsay, an infant when his father and mother were killed, was saved by his Mahratta ayah, who carried him to her own people and brought him up as a native. She taught him as best she could, and, having told him his parentage, sent him to Bombay to be educated. At sixteen he obtained a commission in the English Army, and his knowledge of the Mahratta tongue combined with his ability and bravery enabled him to render great service in the Mahratta War, and carried him, through many frightful perils by land and sea, to high rank.